GET BENT!

THE HYBRID OF HIGH MOON - 1

RICK GUALTIERI

DEDICATION & ACKNOWLEDGEMENTS

For my wife and kids, the very last people in the world I would tell to GET BENT!

Special thanks to my awesome beta crew: Jason, Korionna, Amy, Noah, Ebony, Jana, Chris, Danae, Mike, Pamela, Simon, Martin, Katie, and Jill. You guys put the icing on this bloody mayhem cake of a story.

PROLOGUE
BEFORE

All things are possible beneath a blood moon.

Lissa MacGillis, the future Queen of the Monarchs, considered this as she stepped into the sacred glade. Her magic was the equal or better of any in her coven, and tonight, she intended to prove it.

While the others celebrated the rare lunar event with a barbecue, of all things, she'd slipped away. The walls between worlds were thinner on a night such as this. If she could make contact with an *outsider*, she could conceivably conscript it to her service, increasing her already formidable power. Elder spirits could be notoriously short-tempered, but it was worth the risk, partially thanks to increasing tensions between her people and the lycanthropes.

Those mongrels had been growing bolder in recent months. She'd heard it was all due to a young male vying for the position of alpha. He was seemingly intent on testing the limits of her people's patience – seeing how far he could stretch his leash before someone rapped him on the nose.

In a sense, it was ironic that, in scrying to find a suitable location for her ritual, she'd discovered this clearing deep in the lycanthropes' territory. It was a place of power, not unlike Stonehenge in centuries past. Unlike that old ruin, however, the energy here was fresh, untapped.

Tying her auburn hair into a tight bun, the young witch unpacked her supplies, then carved a circle into the dirt with a garden trowel. She filled the shallow trough with melted wax from a blessed candle, lit three more, and placed them all to match the four corners of the compass.

Perfect. Let's do this.

Lissa tentatively sat down inside the circle, immediately sensing a hum of power through her lithe frame as she opened the weathered tome she'd borrowed from her mother's personal library.

She cut both her palms with a ceremonial dagger, allowing the blood to slowly dribble out between her fingers and onto the ground – a tempting sacrifice for any spirit.

Almost as if in response, the plants, the ground – the very glade itself – began to glow a dull bluish green. It would seem something from *outside* had already noticed her presence.

Lissa smiled, noting the welcome side effect of now having more than enough light to read the incantation she'd opened up to.

The future queen chanted in an ancient tongue, and the glow of energy began to pulse in tune to her voice. She could sense the barriers between worlds beginning to peel away like an onion. It was starting to work.

Lissa raised her bleeding palms to the sky and the glade flashed a brilliant crimson, matching that of the moon high in the sky above.

Soon, very soon, the spirits of this place would answer her and then she would...

"*You know, you might want to put something on those cuts.*"

The witch spun toward the gravelly voice but saw nothing except the brush at the edge of the clearing. "Who's there?"

"*All I'm saying is that isn't very sanitary. You could get an infection, contract a flesh-eating virus, get your head bitten off. Stuff like that.*"

A pair of yellow eyes appeared between a gap in the trees. Lissa sensed a powerful body beneath them, barely hidden by the shadows. One of *them* had found her. "Come out now and I might let you live."

The eyes blinked once then changed, becoming smaller, *more human*. A young man in his twenties stepped out from the tree line. He was shirtless and shoeless, wearing nothing but a pair of ripped jeans beneath the washboard abs of his stomach. One side of his mouth was raised in a half-grin. "Such generosity humbles me, especially coming from the mouth of a silly little girl trespassing where she clearly does not belong."

He wasn't half-bad looking, for a filthy beast anyway, but the witch quickly pushed that thought away. After all, one did not consort with *pets*. One either assumed dominance over them or had them put down. It was up to him which of those two it would be. "This is a place of power. My people are attuned to them, as you well know."

"A pathetic excuse, nothing more." He crossed his muscular arms. "As *you* well know, these woods have already been claimed."

"Perhaps I know no such thing."

"Then you're either playing dumb or really stupid, but I'm going to give you the benefit of the doubt and assume the former."

"And why is that?" The witch forced her voice to

remain calm, but she began gathering her energy, sensing how this was likely to play out.

"I've seen stupid. Lord knows I have plenty of family who fall into that bucket. Believe me, I know the look. You don't have it."

"Too bad I can't say the same."

He put a hand over his chest and gave her a pained grimace. "Oh, you wound me so with your words, princess." At her surprised look, he smiled. "Yes, I know who you are. I've heard all about you. The Princess of Peaches or something dopey like that, isn't it?"

"Monarchs," she snapped.

"Oh yeah, that other is from a video game. I always get the two confused."

"Maybe I should educate you as to the difference." A wave of energy surged through the young witch, unraveling her hair and letting it fall loose where it began to glow as if aflame. She held up a hand, and a ball of fire appeared above it.

If the shirtless man was alarmed, he gave no indication. "And here I was hoping it would be a mushroom."

"Pretend it is," she replied. "Just like you're pretending to lead your people to a new future when all you're marching them toward is their destruction."

"I see my reputation precedes me." The man bowed before her, the impish grin never leaving his face.

It infuriated the witch, partly because she could imagine all the girls who'd probably fallen for his charm. Weak-minded fools. Not her, though. "It's a reputation that could easily get you killed."

"Then it's a good thing I don't have any plans for tomorrow." He looked up longingly at the full moon, bathed as he was in the glow still emanating from the glade. "Tonight, however, I'm all booked up."

"Oh? Am I keeping you from humping someone's leg?"

"Close. I have to teach a spoiled little brat a lesson she'll never forget, assuming I actually let her walk away."

"I'll do more than walk, wolf." The ball of flame above Lissa's fingers grew in intensity, changing color from orange to blue. "Maybe I'll find a nice spot in my bedroom for your pelt. I could use a new throw rug."

"First humping and now your bedroom?" he replied with a wink. "Who would have thought the princess of buttercups would be such a flirt?"

She gritted her teeth. "*Monarchs.*"

"As you wish." He smiled at her and his teeth became noticeably longer. "Pity for you I'm more Dread Pirate Roberts than Westley."

"Who?"

A look akin to horror appeared on his face. "You're kidding, right?"

"About what?" she asked.

"You mean you've never seen...?" He trailed off, glanced at the moon again, then turned back toward her. "What? Were you raised in a closet under the stairs? No. On second thought, don't answer that."

"Are you finished?"

"Sorry, but that's a serious mind-blower to me. I mean, I was just going to kill you, but now I'm wondering if I should take you to a movie first so you don't die culturally bereft. Seems the least I can do."

The witch made a derisive sound. "Nice try, but the only date you're getting is with your destiny."

"Ooh, more clever than I gave you credit for, princess." He blinked and his eyes turned yellow. "Still, I think you're right. An evening like this *is* made for destiny. What do you say? Shall we see whose ends here tonight?"

For a moment, the two stared at each other, neither

moving a muscle in the reddish glow of the enchanted glade.

"So be it." The witch unleashed the stored energy of her spell in his direction, but in her haste, she telegraphed the attack.

At the last second, her would-be target dodged out of the way, his muscles already rippling with the change, growing larger with each step.

He leapt at her, claws at the ready, but in the blink of an eye she brought up a defensive shield to ward off his strike. The werewolf hit it, bounced off, then skidded to a halt facing her.

The first blows struck and rebuffed, the future queen and alpha circled each other in the center of the clearing, power from the interrupted ritual surging around them.

With magic crackling off her fingertips and a snarl on his lips, they came at each other again – both intent on finishing their respective foe there and then.

What they didn't realize was that they were only partially correct. Destiny *was* about to change, but it wouldn't be for just one of them. It would be for *both*, and in a way neither would have ever guessed.

All things were possible beneath a blood moon, and that was especially true when it came to the extraordinary.

1

PRESENT DAY

I lay staring at the ceiling, listening with dread to the horrific ruckus which drifted through the walls, wishing it would stop.

Cries for mercy which were ignored; the slap of flesh striking flesh; a low, desperate grunting which gradually gave way to something akin to a snarl – as if a wild animal had been let loose into the fray.

After a while, I tore my gaze away from the ceiling, its white exterior – the color of innocence – a mockery of what I knew to be happening just down the hall. I turned toward Riva, my oldest friend. Her brown eyes were open wide like mine, as if refusing to believe this was happening.

But it was.

Again I prayed for it to end, for blissful silence to return, so that I could fool myself into thinking that I was just hearing things – that none of this was real.

Yet still the torment continued, ceaseless in its fury.

How much of this punishment could they take?

It was a question I didn't want answered. Not now. Not ever.

Sadly, it seemed fate was not in a merciful mood this evening. No reprieve was offered. In fact, it was quite the opposite. The snarling became louder, more pronounced. There came a crash from somewhere close by, and it was as if the whole structure shook.

Something tumbled off the shelf next to my head and clattered to the floor. It was the trophy I'd won a year earlier – second place in the Pennsylvania state wrestling finals. So close to grabbing the top prize, yet forever out of my reach.

It landed on the carpet with a heavy thud, and I looked down to find that one of the metallic laurel wreaths adorning it had snapped off.

Son of a...

"Oh, for Christ's sake!" I jumped to my feet and began pounding on the wall, making almost as much of a racket as was already going on. "There are kids trying to sleep in here, you know!" I turned again to Riva, the grin on her face making me want to pop her one. "My parents are so freaking twisted."

"Are you kidding? This is great." She sat up and muted the TV, upon which *The Howling* played unwatched. "I only hope my S.O. has this much stamina when I'm their age."

"Ugh! It's bad enough that those two are going at it like rabbits. I don't need for you to be their cheering section, too."

"Aww, what's the matter?" Her voice took on a childish tone. "Does widdle Tam-Tam need to have a talk about the birds and the bees?"

I glared daggers at her. To everyone else I was Tamara Bentley – Bent to a few close friends. Riva had been the one to pin that particular nickname on me, back in third grade before either of us realized it had a somewhat salacious undertone. Regardless, my father was the *only* one allowed to call me Tam-Tam, a holdover from my toddler days. At least, he was the only one who called me that and still kept their teeth.

Riva, however, simply smiled back with the smug look of one certain of their immunity from the righteous beating they deserved by virtue of their status as best friend.

I flopped back down onto my bed and covered my face with a pillow, wishing to smother myself just enough for sweet unconsciousness to take hold. A small part of me couldn't wait to get back to college ... and the somewhat more sympathetic friends I had waiting for me there.

Riva pulled the pillow off and tossed it to the foot of the bed. "Stop being such a prude, Bent. I seem to recall a certain someone who went camping last summer with a boy named Kevin, where they proceeded to..."

"Kevin aka *the minute man,* you mean? Pretty sure there's no comparison to whatever's going on in there." I hooked a thumb toward the wall. My parents' bedroom was actually two doors down, which made it even more insane. Thank goodness for my dad's office in between because I couldn't even imagine how crazy it would sound if we were right next door.

"Guess that's why rat boy moved down into the basement," she said, referring to Chris, my obnoxious elevenyear old brother.

Truth be told, I was beginning to think the little prick had the right idea. Hell must've frozen over. Who'd have thought I'd ever consider him the smart one? "I'm pretty sure it was so he could jerk off to his comic books without interruption."

That got Riva laughing.

"Seriously, you couldn't pay me to go down there without a bucket of hand sanitizer."

The pounding against the walls was replaced by the squeak of a bedframe being pushed to its limits.

"Guess it runs in the family," she replied with a chuckle.

"Who knows? There is that whole nature vs. nurture argument."

Chris was adopted, brought over as a baby from Vietnam. Normally, that might make for a beautiful Hallmark moment, but the little skeeve was spoiled rotten and usually in desperate need of an ass-kicking.

Even so, I couldn't deny he'd been wise in wanting to escape from our parents turning their bedroom into the Bang Bus at least once a week. Still, if there was any justice in this vast universe of ours, the sound was carrying down to him via the heating ducts. If one of us had to suffer, then all of us did.

Riva chuckled as the sounds became faster, more urgent. She'd slept over many a night in years past, and this wasn't the first time my parents had mistakenly assumed the upstairs was even remotely soundproof.

Don't get me wrong, I would never begrudge them a healthy sex life, gross as that might be, but there were times when their antics got a bit out of hand.

The snarling coming from my parents' room became higher-pitched, until suddenly it became almost a howl. "What the fuck?"

"Hot damn!" Riva was definitely enjoying this way too much. "Your folks are seriously kinky."

The howl rose until it almost sounded as if it were in the same room as us. Then, just as abruptly, it cut off, along with everything else going on down the hall.

"And the show's over." Riva looked down at her phone. "I really should have timed them. That was, what, half an hour, maybe forty-five minutes? I'm surprised your mom can still walk."

"Seriously," I replied, still in shock. "What the fuck?"

She let out a bark of laughter. "Beats me. Maybe it's a full moon or something."

Riva was awake and presumably already downstairs when I cracked my eyes open to the sound of my mother shouting from the bottom of the stairs.

"Tamara! Let's go. I made eggs. Get down here before your brother eats them all."

She sounded way too chipper for my personal edification. But hey, I guess there'd been nobody to interrupt her sleep. Me, it took a while after the *festivities* died down before I was able to drift off. The horror of what I'd heard kept replaying in my head.

This summer couldn't end fast enough.

I loved my parents, but back at school I at least had the option of finding whoever was performing midnight acrobatics on my floor and threatening to feed them my fist if they didn't quiet down.

I hopped out of bed, tossed on a pair of sweatpants, then grudgingly made my way downstairs. As much as I wanted to snap at the first person I saw, I had to admit the smell wafting up from the kitchen perked me up a bit. Go figure. Mom was a freak in bed *and* a damned good cook. I guess I could see why Dad had married her.

I entered the kitchen just as my brother was stepping up to the stove, where the last three eggs waited in the frying pan. "Touch them and die."

"It's not like you need the extra pounds," he replied, a shit-eating grin on his face where the first signs of acne were starting to show. Between that and his ridiculous haircut – somewhere between goth and skater-wannabe – he was practically begging to be decked.

I made a fist and he quickly backed up.

"If you're still hungry, champ, grab a bowl of cereal," Dad said from his spot at the table. He was finishing off some toast while reading the news on his phone.

That seemed to mollify my brother, but he made as if to spit on my eggs before I chased him off. For about the millionth time, I swore that when he finally turned eighteen my present to him was going to come in the form of a punch to his face. But it was a fantasy that could wait for now.

I scooped my eggs – over easy, just how I liked them – onto a plate, grabbed the hot sauce from the cabinet above the stove, and joined my family and Riva at the table. All of them appeared to be finishing up, which meant they'd been awake for a while. That fact did nothing to improve my mood.

"Morning, Tam Tam."

"Seriously, Dad?" I glared at him sidelong.

"My house," he replied with a grin, his eyes still on his phone, "my rules. That means I can call you whatever I want ... unless, that is, you'd prefer to discuss paying rent."

"Tam Tam it is, then," I replied, digging in.

Riva chuckled, so I tossed a crumpled napkin at her.

"A little decorum at the table, please," Mom chided.

Where I knew my father had a sense of humor about these things, she did not. Mom was a stickler for us doing things a certain way and was always quick to point out when we fell short of her expectations.

Still, she could cook a hell of a fried egg when she wanted to.

"You sleep okay, dear?" Mom asked my friend.

Riva glanced at me with a smile and I narrowed my eyes, trying to mentally project all the horrid things I'd do if she said the wrong thing. "Just fine, Mrs. Bentley."

"I'm happy to hear it. It's always nice to have you over.

We don't see you nearly as often now that you two are off at college."

That went double for me. Riva had been my best friend since ... well, forever. That she now went to a local school whereas I was a couple states away kinda sucked. On the upside, it made summer reunions like this all the more sweet, even if I knew that eventually life would take us in different directions.

But that was a concern for another day. We had plans for this one.

"So what are you two eligible bachelorettes up to?" Dad asked casually, glancing up long enough to make sure we hadn't left the room yet. He was an easygoing guy most of the time. Wouldn't hurt a fly, but he could be a little spacey. According to Mom, he'd been a bit of a dreamer ever since the day they'd met at a college mixer, way back when the dinosaurs roamed the Earth.

Riva turned to face me and a silent battle of wills ensued. She finally gave me a look that said it all. If we were going to lie to my parents, I might as well be the one to do it. She was right, but it still sucked.

Kinda sad that I even had to. I mean, we were both nineteen – adults, for Christ's sake. Mind you, chill as my dad was, he was always quick to remind me of his favorite catchphrase regarding his house, his rules.

And one of those rules was that me and my brother were to stay well clear of the hollows, the woods just east of town.

It was a subject they'd been adamant on ever since I was a mere toddler – something to do with a cougar attacking some hikers way back when. It was weird. The entire town of High Moon was pretty much surrounded by state forest on all sides, just three roads leading in and out. Yet, it was the hollows which freaked out my parents for some reason.

True, the hollows were rumored to be haunted, but that mainly seemed to be perpetuated by guys hoping to get into their girlfriends' pants. We're talking everything from ghosts to unwary hikers who went missing, only to be found later – their bodies partially eaten. Because what fun is an urban legend if it has a happy ending?

Mind you, the favorite time to share these stories was typically right around when you and your date parked and climbed into the back seat.

Somehow, I didn't think my parents were the type to be worried about ghouls and goblins. And their concern never seemed to be about whatever guy I might or might not be dating. No. Something about the hollows just freaked them out. Who knows? Maybe they tripped out on some bad acid there once. Hah! As if they were ever that cool.

Needless to say, the hollows was exactly where Riva and I were headed this fine evening. I just couldn't tell them that.

Before I could reply with my rehearsed fib, my brother chimed in with his idiotic two cents. "They're probably gonna rent a couple of chick flicks and bemoan the fact they're destined to die as dried-up old maids."

Though I outwardly scowled at the little dork, I was thankful for the distraction, however unintentional it might have been.

"That's not nice, Christopher," Dad chided. "Apologize to your sister."

His nose was still buried in his phone, so it went unnoticed when Chris's apology was accompanied by flipping me the finger. Whatever. I could wait until tomorrow to get back at the little shit. Such was the way of the *sibling love* between us.

For now, I simply said, "I'm staying at Riva's tonight. Her parents are in Connecticut for the week."

"Throwing a big party?" Dad asked with a chuckle. He was well aware that, adults or not, Riva's parents would string us both up if we trashed their house.

"Oh, yeah," Riva replied deadpan. "I'm bringing the bath salts. Bent's supplying the meth."

I shot her a look, then turned back to Dad. "We're probably gonna head out after breakfast, hang out by the lake for a while." That part at least wasn't a lie. It was looking to be a scorcher out there. No point in us suffering all day.

Speaking of suffering, though, Mom was quick to remind me to take my pills before I left.

Like there was any chance of me forgetting.

Screw the hollows, I had a curse all my own to worry about – a rare and exceptionally acute form of Gastroparesis. It's hereditary, a faulty gene from each of my parents. I was only three when I was first diagnosed. I'd been out shopping with my mom at Target when I fell ill and had to be rushed to the ER. I was too young to really remember it, but my parents say they almost lost me.

Ever since then, I've been on my meds. My condition might be incurable, but fortunately, that doesn't mean it's untreatable. Four pills a day, two every twelve hours like clockwork. Missing them is *not* an option. The symptoms are both quick to strike and unforgiving in their brutality. Enough so that, according to my doctor, it's unlikely I'd survive another attack like when I was a toddler. That's a risk I'm not willing to take.

I have too much to live for. My life might not be perfect, but I like it.

2

"**D**o you need a ride, Tam?"

"No thanks, Dad. Riva's got her car. We'll pop by later to grab my stuff for tonight."

"Okay," he replied. "Then I'll see you when I get back. Don't do anything I wouldn't."

I let out a laugh. My dad never struck me as much of a risk taker. He was about as milquetoast as they came. If I lived life the same way, I'd have never taken a gamble and joined the wrestling team in elementary school, never discovered I had a knack for it, and never would have gotten my scholarship.

That didn't mean Dad was a homebody, though. Both he and Mom frequently traveled for work. In actuality, this morning's breakfast, with both of them home, had been relatively uncommon growing up. But now it was back to business, since my dad had to go out of town for the next day or so.

Sad as I was to see him leave, I was more thrilled that only one of my parents would be home tonight. Chris was a handful, so Mom would be that much less likely to check on us and realize we actually weren't at Riva's house.

The weather was forecast to be gorgeous and there was supposed to be a full moon tonight. It was a perfect opportunity to be out under the stars, sitting around a campfire with my best friend in the world, and maybe passing a bottle of Fireball back and forth while we gossiped about shit.

It had been ages since we'd gone camping together, not since we'd been in the Girl Scouts. And this time we didn't have my mom along to continually yell at us. It was also the first time we'd be going alone, something we'd planned to do all through high school but had never gotten the chance to.

I grabbed my meds off the counter, shook two pills out into my hand, then stuffed the rest into my backpack. I'd already snuck my sleeping bag and a few other supplies into Riva's trunk the night before. My pack just contained clothes and a few toiletries, i.e. stuff that I'd take to a simple sleepover as opposed to, say, a jaunt in the woods.

I was about to close it up and head out when I spied Chris's portable Nintendo system lying unattended on the couch. Hmm. Riva did have a nasty tendency to fall asleep earlier than me.

"You snooze you lose, punk." I smiled and tossed it in with the rest of my stuff.

I left the bag lying in the foyer for when I came back, then stepped into the kitchen for a glass of water to wash my pills down.

Mom was in there loading up the dishwasher as Dad filled a travel mug with coffee. She glanced my way. "Heading out, dear?"

"In a sec."

She turned to my father. "Curtis, would you mind dropping them off on the way?"

"It's cool, Mom," I said. "He already asked. We're

fine." Gotta love parents. Once a child to them, forever more a child ye shall always be.

"Good," she replied. "I'd offer, but I'm heading in the opposite direction. Your brother has baseball at the 4H this morning."

"Have fun watching him strike out."

Dad stifled a chuckle, but Mom pursed her lips in disapproval ... for a moment, anyway. Then she smiled, too. "Your brother is getting better. Kind of."

Seems I'd gotten all the athletic genes in the family, which actually made sense since Chris was adopted. That didn't keep my parents from trying, though. So far, soccer and track had been a bust. Now, it looked like the Pirates wouldn't be beating down our door to recruit him anytime soon. Oh, well. The world needed dorks, too.

I swallowed my pills along with some water.

"Oh, I almost forgot. I'm taking Chris out tonight. If you need me, call my cell. Leave a message if I don't answer."

Yes! Even better! That meant the chances of her checking on us were pretty close to nil. Sometimes fate actually could be kind. However, I was sure to mask my glee by casually asking, "Oh? Anywhere good?"

"You know your brother. Some movie he wants to see. Nothing you'd be interested in."

"No doubt." Handing the glass to Mom, I turned to leave.

"If I don't see you later, stay safe tonight."

I let out a quick laugh. "Let me guess. It's the middle of summer, so all the weirdos will be out."

"Full moon, actually." She turned to my father and gave him a significant glance, which he returned. Considering what they'd been up to the night before, I could only guess what they were not-so-subtly signaling to each other.

Probably phone sex or, worse ... Skype. *Gross!* I so didn't need that imagery in my head.

She must've noticed me staring because Mom quickly added, "That means even more weirdos than usual."

Though her tone was meant to be light, something about it registered as a bit off in the back of my mind, but I didn't really have time to fully digest it. Besides, my digestive tract was going to be busy enough in a few minutes.

I shouted my goodbyes, grabbed my towel, then stepped out the front door and past the small army of garden gnomes my mother insisted on littering her rose bushes with. Their creepy concrete eyes seemed to follow me as I walked down the driveway.

Riva was already waiting behind the wheel of her ten-year-old Subaru Outback. It was a bit beaten up but ran well, and its all-wheel drive was pretty much a necessity in this part of the state.

Sadly, automotive issues weren't my primary concern at the moment. No, sitting down and buckling myself in was, especially since I could feel my meds starting to take hold.

For roughly eleven and three-quarter hours of their duration, I felt as normal as normal can be on my medication, but first I had to get through the first several minutes. We're talking nausea, vertigo and, worst of all, a feeling of fatigue as if I were weak as a kitten. All of that and more hit me as Riva started the car.

"You okay for me to drive?"

I closed my eyes and nodded. Moving or sitting still didn't make any difference. The side effects of my meds always hit me the same. I seldom, if ever, ended up puking, but that didn't mean I didn't want to. It was like being seasick on dry land. But, like I said, that was only half of it. I lifted my arms, suddenly very heavy, and managed to snap my seatbelt into place. I won't lie. I like to think I'm in pretty kick-ass shape for a girl. Heck, you didn't take second place in state's by being a pushover. Sadly, right then, that seemed like an eternity ago. The belt felt like it weighed a hundred pounds, and I'd have been hard-pressed to adjust the seat even if I wanted to.

Fortunately, this wasn't anything new. I didn't let it bother me as Riva pulled out. I knew damn well that the side effects would clear up as quickly as they hit. After that, I'd be right as rain.

In the meantime, I cracked my eyes open and tried to enjoy the drive to Swallowtail Lake. It was on the opposite side of town from our destination this evening, but it wasn't like High Moon was the size of Pittsburgh or anything.

We'd be there before you knew it, but hopefully not before I was feeling strong enough to actually get out of the car and stand up again.

"Yeah, that's right. Walk away, you ugly bitch," the man called after Riva, displaying rotten teeth that probably hadn't seen the inside of a dentist's office since before I was born. "Walk right back to whatever camel-humping country you came from, so long as it's not ... *Ooph!*"

I'd had enough, so as Mr. Dipshit Redneck continued to lay into my friend, I stepped in and cracked him one in the jaw. Fortunately, though wrestling was mostly about holds, grapples, and leverage, being a girl in a guy's sport had meant learning how to occasionally *dissuade* my detractors, preferably without breaking my hand.

Turned out I was pretty good at it. Maybe I should have given boxing a go instead.

Regardless, this jackass had been warned to back off. It

had been a nice day down at the lake, at least until Joe Sixpack here decided my friend's skin color wasn't to his liking. She tried her best to ignore him, making her practically a saint in my book, but even saints occasionally needed guardian angels.

Mind you, though I acted the part, I was still worried about biting off more than I could chew. At the end of the day, this guy probably had close to two hundred pounds on me. However, most of that was around his gut. His jaw, on the other hand, was mostly glass.

He stumbled back, blood pouring from his lips, and fell right onto his well-cushioned ass.

"Got anything else to say, Jethro?" I asked, sensing a small crowd of onlookers beginning to gather around us.

An insistent hand fell on my shoulder before I could step forward. "He might not, little lady, but me ... I'd like to have a few words with you both."

"Mom! Chris! I'm just grabbing my stuff!"

Nobody answered from inside the quiet house, leading me to believe they were already out. There was no way Chris's game had gone this long, so that meant they'd probably left for whatever activities she had planned with him. That, or maybe Mom decided to take him to the mall, hoping he'd pick up a new video game and stay out of her hair once they got home. Couldn't really blame her.

No skin off my teeth either way.

Riva and I ran upstairs to get changed. She took the bathroom, while I stepped into my room, peeling off my shorts, shirt, and the two piece underneath before throwing on clothes more suited to a night in the woods.

"Much better," Riva said after she was dressed.

"Don't feel that way. You looked great today."

The confrontation with that asshole earlier had made her feel seriously self-conscious afterwards, but it had nothing to do with her appearance – thin and with glossy brown hair I would have killed for. The guy had simply been a racist prick, nothing more.

Thankfully, the chief of police, Ralph Johnson, had been there with his family and stepped in. He'd been close enough to suss out what happened. End result was us walking away with a minor warning about keeping my temper in check, while the dickhead in question got himself a nice, new asshole chewed. Sometimes small-town justice did work.

"Thanks. So did you," she said.

"I don't know. I think my good side was obscured by that jerk's split lip," I replied, causing us both to laugh.

The truth was, I'd been hoping for some cute guys to scope out down at the lake, like maybe Gary from the Quick Lube downtown. Considering what happened, though, it was probably for the best that he hadn't been there. Say what you will about us living in modern times, but it was tough to find a man in this neck of the woods who wasn't easily intimidated by a strong woman, in the most literal sense.

At five-three, I was only an inch or so taller than Riva, but our bodies were in stark contrast. Where she had a slight build, I had biceps that put most boys my age to shame. It was a combination of my natural build and having been a wrestler for the past ten years. Where your average Cosmo cover girl was tall and paper-thin, I was short, with a physique closer to a brunette Beth Phoenix than a runway model. Don't get me wrong, I was pretty sure I rocked my swimsuit, but a lot of guys tended to get weird around a girl who could beat them at arm wrestling.

Such was life in rural Pennsylvania where men were

men and they expected their women to shut up, do the dishes, and raise the kids.

I glanced toward Riva and smiled. It was silly of me to think that way, especially since my friend had it far worse than I ever did. If I was a bit of an outsider here, she was practically from another planet.

Her parents were Hindi, albeit not overly strict about it. They moved to High Moon right around the time I was born. Both worked, although after all these years, I still wasn't sure exactly what they did. As for Riva, it wasn't easy being a girl of Indian descent in a town where any complexion darker than copier paper gave the local bullies ammunition. To top it off, she'd outed herself as bi, which was fine for a big city, but yet another strike in a county where buying Bud in a bottle was considered high class. The citizens of High Moon were mostly okay, don't get me wrong, but anywhere you'll find people, you'll find assholes. Our sleepy little town was no exception to that rule.

That's probably why we'd bonded so well as kids. Two black sheep who didn't conform, stuck in a small town where it was hard to go unnoticed.

Speaking of being noticed, I checked myself out in the mirror one last time. Not too shabby. Pity there was little chance of showing it off to anyone, not unless... "I don't suppose you'd be up for getting an oil change before we head out."

"Why?" Riva asked with a wry grin.

"I just figured maybe I could give Gary a personal tour of your back seat."

"And what am I supposed to do?"

"Wait in the lobby, I guess?"

"Nice try. But nobody's greasing their monkey in my car except me."

I let out a laugh. "You're no fun."

Dismissing any plans for a late day lube job, we walked back downstairs. Now, where was my ... ah, over there. I found my backpack lying on the couch. Someone had moved it after I'd left this morning, probably Chris. God forbid he saw something of mine and resisted the urge to press his sticky little fingers all over it. Oh well, no harm done.

I zipped it shut and we headed out to Riva's car, but not before stopping to grab a few bottles from my parents' liquor cabinet.

It was time to get this show on the road.

3

"**G**ary, Kevin, or Deke?"

"Deke?" I asked.

"The fat kid with the bad acne who sat behind you in physics. He was always staring at your ass while pretending to read his textbook."

"He did?" I replied. "Gonna have to take your word on that. No eyes in the back of my head."

"Probably a good thing for him," Riva said with a laugh. "So c'mon, what do you choose?"

I swallowed a mouthful of vodka, pausing to cough as it burned on the way down.

"Lightweight."

"Doesn't your religion forbid drinking?" I shot back.

"Probably. I really should look that up one of these days."

I passed her the bottle, the light from the fire glinting off the glass. "Fine. I'd marry Gary. I guess I'd fuck Deke. And then I'd definitely kill Kevin."

"I hear Deke got a scholarship to Clemson."

"So?"

"So, in a few years he's going to be making a couple

hundred grand. And where does that leave you? Married to Gary the grease monkey."

"I'll have my degree by then."

Riva laughed. "Because environmental science is where the big bucks are, right?"

"Yeah, well, Deke will probably still be gross. Money isn't everything, especially if I have to feel his Cheetos-stained fingers groping my tits every night. And, hey, Gary might get promoted to assistant manager one of these days."

"Ooh, big dreamer."

"Hey, here in High Moon that's practically royalty. We'll just get a second double-wide once I spit out our six kids."

"You slut!"

I pretended to look shocked. "What? I married the guy. You can't be a slut with your own husband."

"Debatable, but I'll let you have that one for now. How about this, then? What if you found out that Gary was hung like a mouse while hundred-grand Deke had a horse dick?"

I waved her off. "It doesn't work that way. You're changing the rules."

She glared at me. "Fine. Be happy with micro-dick Gary. Your turn."

"Emma Stone, Jake Gyllenhaal ... and me."

"Really?"

"Sorry, sister. I'm not lobbing any softballs tonight."

She took a sip, swallowing with no adverse effects, probably just to spite me. "That's easy. I marry Jake, because, damn, our kids would be good looking. But I fuck the socks off of Emma."

"And you'd kill me?"

"Sorry."

"I'm your best friend!"

"I know, but they're really hot."

"Okay, you want to play it that way." I grabbed the bottle from her and took another drink, pausing as a small wave of dizziness hit me. "Here's one for you. Emma again, me, and Darla McIntyre."

Darla was Riva's personal nemesis from high school. She was tall, blonde, and oh-so-white, three of her favorite things to constantly give my friend shit about.

"You can't go twice."

"Fuck that," I said. "You already cheated."

"Fine. I marry Emma and I fuck Darla."

"What?!"

"Oh yeah. I'd fuck her so hard that she'd never forget my face ... especially on those cold nights when she's lying awake all alone, longing for my touch." After a beat, she added, "I still kill you."

"Bitch!" I grabbed a clod of dirt from the ground and threw it at her. Riva just barely dodged, laughing as she did. Her balance was thrown off, though, and she ended up falling backwards off the camp chair.

After a moment when she didn't get up, I asked, "Are you okay?"

"I'm fine. Just checking out the sky. What a view."

I looked up. She was right.

"And the moon, it's so big and bright."

She had a point. One could practically hike through the woods without a flashlight on a night like this, albeit that wasn't something I really cared to try.

Riva folded her arms behind her head and continued to stare up. "Makes you feel so small and alone."

"Yeah, but you're not alone."

"I know that," she shot back. "I mean the two of us. It's so peaceful out here. So quiet."

She was right. Aside from the dying crackle of the campfire, there was nothing to hear save our voices. Even though we were both talking at a normal conversation level, we sounded very loud.

A thought hit me and I stood up while looking around.

"What's up, Bent? That vodka working its way through you already?"

"No. It's just that ... listen."

"To what?"

"Exactly. There's nothing. No bugs, no birds."

"So?"

"Weren't you the one complaining earlier that you weren't going to get any sleep unless the goddamned crickets shut up?"

"Maybe they were listening."

"I sincerely doubt ... whoa." All at once, I felt dizzy again. I blinked, thinking maybe I'd stood up too fast, but rather than help things, my vision instead doubled.

"You sure you're not feeling the..."

A branch snapped somewhere outside the small clearing we'd set up in, causing Riva's question to dissolve into a shriek.

Had the world not been spinning, I'd have screamed, too. It had sounded very loud in the quiet forest. Probably just a deer. I opened my mouth to laugh at my friend's skittishness, but then abruptly doubled over as my stomach clenched up. I fell to my knees retching.

All at once that wave of dizziness exploded into full-blown nausea.

What the hell?

Moments later, a wave of intense pain ripped through my innards. It had been a long time since I'd felt anything like that, but I knew instinctively what it meant.

Riva had climbed back to her feet by then and was standing over me. "I was right, you *are* a lightweight."

"Not ... that," I sputtered. "What time is it?"

There was a pause, then she replied, "About quarter to ten."

Fuck!

She apparently realized it, too. "Oh shit! You're late."

That was an understatement. My meds would have worn off almost two hours ago. I'd completely forgotten, like I was no more than a stupid child. I had a reminder set on my phone, but of course I'd left that in the tent.

"Get ... my ... bag," I whispered, struggling to not puke, although I had a feeling that was a fight I wasn't going to win.

"On it!" Riva stood, then hesitated. "What the...?"

I vaguely heard what I thought to be another branch snapping, but it was getting hard to concentrate. Once I took my pills, we could go back to debating whether Jason Voorhees or Michael Myers was stalking us out there in the woods, but that would have to wait. "Any ... year ... now."

"Sorry!" Riva bolted into the tent, appearing a few seconds later with my backpack. Seeing that I wasn't in much condition to do anything except retch, she unzipped it and began looking through the contents. "Where is it?"

"The ... top pouch."

She kept digging. "I can't find them."

"Next to ... the game system."

"I don't see a game system!"

That's when a horrible realization crossed my mind. I hadn't found the bag where I'd originally left it. It had been lying open on the couch. I knew my brother and, despite every nasty snipe we took at each other, was certain he would never misplace my pills on purpose. But what if he'd been looking for his 3DS? What if he'd been rooting through my bag and accidentally knocked my pill bottle out in the process? It wasn't entirely unlikely. We occasionally swiped each other's stuff to annoy the other.

I hadn't seen my pills on the floor or couch, but then, I hadn't actually looked for them either.

After another minute of searching, Riva upended the backpack and dumped out the contents. By then, my whole body was beginning to tremble.

"They're not here!"

She was right. No Nintendo 3DS and no pills. God, how stupid was I? I always double-checked that I had my meds whenever I went anywhere. Hell, my freshman year roommate at college had once inadvertently moved them and I'd almost lost my shit on her. Yet here I was, out in the woods, probably a good quarter mile from where we'd parked the car, and I'd stupidly left the damn things at home.

Riva obviously came to the same conclusion. She bent down and lifted my arm over her shoulder so as to help me up. "Come on. The car's not far. Let's get you home."

"Good id..." My acknowledgement of her rightness would have to wait as my stomach picked that moment to protest. I spewed its contents all over the ground, my belongings, and myself.

If I wasn't already feeling so sick, I'd have been seriously grossed out.

Despite the mess, Riva hauled me to my feet. "Let's go. You don't have time to be lying around."

That's my best friend, always a barrel of laughs. She was right, though. Shitty as I felt, this was only the beginning. It was either get to my pills or it would be all downhill from there. I didn't remember much of what happened when I was three, but I'd been told it was bad, *really* bad. My condition was normally kept in a state of equilibrium by my meds, but without them the onset of symptoms would be fast, brutal, and ultimately lethal.

Showing weakness to anyone wasn't my style, but right

then, I leaned on Riva as much as I could. It was either that or crawl back to the car.

She stopped long enough to grab a flashlight, then dragged me toward the trail we'd used to get here.

"Fifteen minutes, maybe twenty," she told me. "You can do this."

I was debating whether my stomach was settled enough for me to answer without barfing all over her when that decision became a moot point.

There came sounds from ahead of us. More branches breaking. Before I could reassure my friend that it was just a harmless woodland animal, the most godawful snarl rose up from the tree line before us.

I once knew a kid who had a pet Rottweiler. The thing was the size of a small bear, yet whatever was out there made it sound like a puppy in comparison.

We froze in our tracks. Well, Riva did anyway. By that point I was mostly coming along for the ride. "What the hell is that?" she whispered.

A plethora of semi-witty answers raced through my mind: a cougar, a bear, maybe some asshole with a bullhorn playing a prank on us.

Sadly, that last one didn't seem likely as Riva's flashlight briefly lit upon something. It was still mostly hidden by the trees, and there was likewise a good chance that I'd already started hallucinating, but I could have sworn I caught sight of dark brown fur, the white flash of teeth, and the shine of a predator's eyes. Worst of all, they'd been looking down upon us. Whatever was out there, it was big.

Apparently hungry, too. A howling roar rose up that caused the hair on the back of my neck to stand on end.

There came the crash of wood splintering and, disoriented as I was, there was one thing I was certain of.

It was coming for us.

"C'mon, Bent! We've got to keep moving!"

Moving? Was she crazy? I was lucky to still be breathing. It had been years since I'd missed taking my meds. So stupid of me. Got caught up in the fun and hadn't been thinking.

Now, with that thing after us I ... I...

I fell to my knees and puked my guts out all over the forest floor as yet another cramp wracked my midsection. The pain caused me to curl up into a fetal position while the stench from my sick left me dry heaving. Lucky me. Two for the price of one.

Even in the throes of my misery, I heard the sound of branches snapping underfoot. Whatever was after us wasn't even trying to be stealthy anymore. It had probably sensed my weakness, knew I was easy prey.

"Oh shit! It's getting closer." Panic colored the edge of Riva's voice. She was trying to keep it together but only doing a so-so job at best.

"Run." The words were barely audible as pain continued to eat away at my gut.

"I need to get you to a hospital."

"No ... hospital ... if we're both ... dead ... only morgue." Yep, that's me. A ray of sunshine in the middle of a shit storm.

I needed to convince Riva she had to leave me and find help. I was done for. Even if we weren't being chased by a goddamned grizzly bear, I began to suspect it had been too long. I'd been taking my medication religiously ever since I was barely out of training pants. I'd been late with my dosage before and paid the price, but it had never been this bad.

My body began to convulse and I cried out in agony. It was a challenge to not bite my own tongue in half as I tried to hold it together long enough to tell my oldest friend, "Go ... please."

Even if it was too late for me, she could still make it – get to the police. They could find my remains, hunt down whatever was stalking us. At least that way my family could have some closure.

With any luck, they'd throw me a beautiful funeral. Yeah, with tulips. I always liked those.

There came a snarl, terrifyingly close from the sound of it. That was no bear. Not a dog either, unless it was the size of a moose. *What the hell?* I cracked my eyes open and tried to force them to focus.

Still unable to do much more than grip my stomach as my innards churned, I saw Riva. Her eyes were wide as saucers and she was staring at something past where I lay. When she spoke, her voice was barely a whisper. "You need to get up, *now*."

What a joke. The only way I was moving was if that thing dragged me back to its lair. Right then, that actually didn't seem so horrible. The pain lancing through every inch of my body was enough to make me relish death's embrace – especially if it would save my friend.

I was easy prey. No challenge. Surely it would choose me over a foe who could fight back ... in theory anyway. Riva was a great friend, but I'd once watched a squirrel chase her out of her own backyard. "Please!" I begged, using every ounce of willpower to speak.

She backed up a step, then another, her eyes never wavering.

There came a crackle of leaves and the soft thud of a heavy foot setting down. Whatever it was, it was standing right behind me.

"Remarkable." For one odd moment, Riva's voice sounded disturbingly calm, but then she let loose an ear-splitting scream.

She was answered by an animalistic roar like nothing I'd ever heard before. Then, whatever had been chasing us stepped over me toward her.

The fuck?

Coarse brown fur, claws three inches long, legs seemingly made of pure muscle, and ... bipedal?

Surely I must've been hallucinating. Hadn't my doctor said something about that? Yeah. He'd been talking about worst-case scenarios for my illness. This was one of them, the last stages before my body began to shut down. After that, I'd slip into an irreversible coma. Death would follow shortly after.

Funny. If I had to hallucinate, I would've thought it would be of something a bit more friendly. Certainly, I could have imagined better – Gary, for example. Instead, I was serving myself up something straight from Chiller Theater, a nightmare to follow me down into the darkness as my organs seized and I went into cardiac arrest.

Riva continued to back up and the creature followed, affording me a better look. It moved with a disturbing sort of grace, a surety of step. It was almost as if it knew it were an apex predator stalking prey that would offer little in the way of resistance.

I couldn't see its front from my angle, curled in a fetal ball as I was, but it towered over my friend. At least six feet tall with broad shoulders. I could see the ridges of its spine, almost as if they were trying to tear their way out of the creature's hairy skin.

Atop a short, thick neck rested a massive head. Two ears poked out at the top, over its fur. It wasn't hard to imagine the rest – the cold eyes of a predator, a snout filled with rows of sharp teeth.

No way.

This was what my brain conjured up in the last few moments before oxygen deprivation set in – a freaking werewolf? I knew we shouldn't have watched that stupid movie last night. So lame, and not even in a Team Jacob sort of way.

The creature lunged at Riva. She squealed in terror and dove out of the way. It missed and gouged the tree she'd been standing in front of, scoring it deeply with its claws. My friend threw her flashlight at it, but the beast knocked the cheap plastic projectile away and attacked again, a lumbering strike which my friend just barely managed to avoid.

Or had she?

I knew a feint when I saw one. The attack had been sloppy, belying the grace with which the monster carried itself. It was almost as if it had purposely missed. That spoke of intelligence. It was trying to scare her first, drive her into a frenzy before it tore her to shreds.

Riva backed up, tripped, and then scooted away on her butt until her back was against another tree. "Please run, Tamara," she whispered in hitched breaths, her voice devoid of all hope.

In the final moments of her life, she was thinking of me.

Tears blurred my vision and with them came resolve.

No! I couldn't let that happen. Not like this.

It was too late for me – there was little chance of getting to a hospital in time, even if this thing didn't stand between us and escape. But not for her. She still had a chance and, by God, I was going to give it to her.

I bit down on my tongue, forcing my head to clear for a moment. Summoning everything I had, I pushed myself up with my arms. The movement almost caused me to empty my guts again, but I clenched my teeth until the feeling passed.

It was approaching her, slowly, seeming to savor her terror. The scent of urine caught in my nose and I realized

Riva's bladder had probably loosed itself. Either that or mine had. It was hard to tell in the state I was in.

Grabbing hold of the sapling nearest me, I pulled myself up, forced my legs beneath me, and willed them to hold. They didn't have to do their job for long, just enough for her to get away.

I took a shaky step away from the tree, then another, my legs supporting my weight. The creature either didn't notice or didn't consider me a threat because it continued to face my friend, despite my lack of anything remotely resembling stealth.

The truth was I should have been terrified, but all I could feel inside of me was a cold anger welling up.

"What are you doing?!" Riva screamed, seeing me approach. "Run!"

In response, the beast let out a grumbling sound that could have almost passed as laughter.

Yeah, well, fuck that.

"Go. Get out of here." My voice was barely a whisper as I sized up the creature. What I was thinking was absolute madness, the craziest form of suicide. At the same time, it definitely beat lying there waiting to die. At least this way my family would get a good story to share.

My family.

I mentally said farewell to my mother, father, and even Chris as I tensed up, gathering all the strength I had left. They deserved better, but I didn't have the time. So, rather than get hung up on long goodbyes that would go unheard, I flung myself at the creature.

Dizzy as I was, my aim held true. I leapt upon its back, wrapped my legs around its mid-section, and grabbed its massive right arm in a half-nelson.

Hah! Second place in state's, my ass. I'd like to see the guy who'd taken gold try this shit.

The werewolf snarled in anger and began to spin

around, no doubt hoping to shake me loose. The movement caught me by surprise and I subsequently puked all over its fur, but still somehow managed to maintain my grip.

"Get the hell out of here!" I screamed once my throat was clear.

It was an impossible fight against an even less possible monster. I was certain the creature would throw me off with ease – that my last memory in this world would be of my skull splattering against a tree trunk, but I held on.

"Bent!" Riva cried, but I was a bit too busy to acknowledge her.

Any second now this thing was going to peel me off like a tick and gut me on the forest floor. Why on Earth wasn't she running?!

No matter. I wasn't going to make it easy for this thing. I grabbed its free arm with mine and wrenched with everything I had – a feeble move, but one that would probably guarantee this beast would be pissed off enough to vent its anger on me, allowing my friend a fighting chance.

The creature abruptly stopped spinning and launched itself backward. Unable to shake me, it was going to crush me instead. This was it.

I screamed out in defiance, determined to make this thing's victory a costly one.

The *crack* of bone breaking rent the air and suddenly the wolf dropped to one knee, letting out a squeal that was unmistakable in its meaning – pain.

It was only then that I realized the massive limb I'd locked in an armbar now swung limply. I'd somehow shattered the creature's arm at the elbow.

"No fucking way," I whispered to myself.

If this was indeed the last hallucination of a dying mind, it was finally getting good.

4

I had to admit, I had no idea what to do next. The whole situation was so surreal. Me, covered in puke, breathing hard but somehow still alive while in front of me, down on its knees and squealing like a puppy who'd gotten its tail stepped on, was an honest to goodness werewolf.

Fine, maybe goodness had nothing to do with it. The thing had tried to gut my friend. Then I'd ... well, I had no idea what I did. Maybe it was one of those crazy adrenaline feats that people were supposed to be able to do when a loved one was in danger.

Whatever it was, I didn't think it wise to stick around and hope that lightning struck twice. I stepped past the creature toward where Riva was still sitting on the ground, watching us wide-eyed.

"Are you okay?" I asked. She nodded numbly, seemingly in too much shock to speak. "Good, then let's get out of..."

"Bent, behind you!"

Okay, so maybe not in as much shock as I thought.

Of course, that paled in comparison to what an idiot I

was. I'd just met a supernatural monster of the not-friendly-variety and what's the first thing I did? I turned my back on it. A Rhodes Scholar I was not.

Riva's warning had barely finished leaving her lips when I spun around, far faster than I thought myself capable.

The creature was back on its feet. One arm hung useless by its side, but it still had another tipped with wicked claws. The area around its eyes was damp, as if it had been crying from the pain, but that was probably too human of a concept to apply to this thing. It was breathing in hitched gasps, but a snarl managed to escape its lips as it lunged toward me.

With no time to think, much less plan, I simply balled my fist and swung before I even realized I was doing so.

I fully expected to break my hand against its jaw, assuming it didn't simply bite my arm in half at the wrist. Much to my surprise, though, bone did shatter, but once again it wasn't mine. Teeth flew and the creature's head snapped to the side. It stopped dead in its tracks and stood there for a moment longer, as if confused. Then, its eyes rolled into the back of its head and it crumpled to the ground.

All I could do was stare at it for several seconds. At last, I managed to pull my eyes away and look down at my hand, expecting to find a mangled lump of meat. The brightness of the moon, however, was enough to see that it looked good as new. Hell, I hadn't even broken a nail.

"Did ... you just p-punch out a ... w-werewolf?" Riva asked from behind me, her voice so shaky I could barely understand what she was saying.

I half-turned toward her, not caring to make the same mistake twice. She was back on her feet, leaning against a tree, but to say she was all right was probably a bit of an exaggeration. From the wild look in her eyes, I guessed she was maybe seconds from bolting blindly through the woods, regardless of who was still standing from the fight. "Are you okay?" I repeated.

Rather than answer me, she asked, "Is it dead?"

That ... was actually a really good question. I'd seen enough slasher films to know it was the height of stupidity to assume the killer was vanquished without double-checking.

I glanced at the downed monster, a massive lump of fur on the forest floor. It didn't seem to be ...

Wait. It took a chuffing breath, then another. "It's still breathing." Then, in a louder voice I added, "But maybe I should fix that."

This wasn't my usual way of dealing with things. I'd never shied away from a fight, but I didn't go looking for them either. I wasn't some icy-blooded psycho. But then I reminded myself that this thing had been hunting us, toying with us in preparation for the kill. If I hadn't ... done whatever I'd done, Riva and I would surely be dead by now.

And if this thing managed to get back up again, it would almost certainly try to finish the job. That was enough to make up my mind.

I started scanning the floor of the forest, looking for something – a stone or a sturdy branch maybe – that I could use to put this thing out of our misery.

"What are you doing?" Riva asked. I told her and she replied, "But what if it's a ... person?"

"I don't know what the hell this thing is," I snapped. "All I know is it tried to kill us. I, for one, don't want to give it another chance. Do you?"

The naked terror in her eyes was all the answer I needed.

It seemed my parents had been right to fear the hollows. Who'd have guessed it? In all fairness, though, I had a feeling neither of them had werewolves in mind when dishing out their vague warnings.

Riva grabbed hold of my arm, staying me for a moment. *What now?* "Hold on a sec. How are you feeling?"

"Huh?" I barely gave the question a second thought as I continued looking for a weapon.

She stepped around and faced me, concern etched on her face. "I'm serious. Are you all right?"

"I'm fine, Riva. Now, let me..." The words died in my throat as realization sank in. I *was* fine. My stomach was still churning a bit, but the horrible sickness I'd felt eating away at my guts seemed to be mostly gone. Make no mistake, I hadn't imagined that. Even if I hadn't outright been at death's door just a few minutes ago, I'd certainly been on its front porch. Yet, somehow I was okay now.

Hell, maybe even better than okay. It felt as if a great weight had been lifted from my shoulders, quite literally – like I'd been doing deadlifts but suddenly the barbell was gone.

It had to be the adrenaline from the fight. No doubt about it. Somehow it had amped me up and given me enough to deck this thing into next week. I was probably still high as a kite on brain chemicals. Once they wore off, it would be like coming down from the mother of all caffeine rushes. Worse, the clock was still ticking. Without my meds, I could keel over at any...

And yet I didn't *feel* like I was about to keel over. Not even close. What the hell was going on?

Unfortunately, introspection would have to wait.

Before I could say anything further, the woods seemingly came to life around us as vicious snarls filled the air, shattering the silence of the forest.

Riva jumped into my arms, and I'm not ashamed to admit I hugged her back. Just one of these things had been terrifying enough. If I hadn't been otherwise preoccupied with dying when it ambushed us, I'm pretty sure I'd have run for the hills and not looked back.

Now, all at once, it was like we'd stepped into Hell's dog pound. Snarls, yips, and – yep – howls pierced the night from seemingly all directions. Not to overdo the dog analogy, but it sounded like there was an entire pack around us. This was insane. We were only a couple of miles from home, but it was as if we'd stepped into a portal to...

"Ta ... mara."

"I know," I replied, trying to look in every direction at once. "If this is it, I'm glad you're here with..."

"You're ... crushing ... me."

What?! "Oh, crap! Sorry." I released my friend and she dropped to one knee, gasping for breath."

Guess that stew of brain chemicals hadn't worn off yet.

I was about to check on her when I spied movement in my periphery. "Uh oh."

Riva stood back up. She was still wheezing but joined me in looking around wide-eyed. Right on time, too, as massive shapes could be seen moving amidst the trees around us. I was still having trouble wrapping my mind around the concept of a single, real-life werewolf, and now it appeared we had a good dozen or more barely a stone's throw away.

This was bad. If they charged us, it wouldn't matter if I was hopped up on a gallon of adrenaline mixed with PCP. There would be little either of us could do except hope for a swift death.

The weird thing was, the more I thought about it, the less terrified I became.

I felt wary and definitely cautious, but the fear was

ebbing along with the last of my queasiness. If anything, I was becoming far more focused than afraid, which probably meant that Chris had been right all along and I actually was an idiot.

Riva, for her part, seemed frightened enough for both of us. If her eyes got any larger, I was certain they'd pop out of her skull. I was about to ask if she was okay again, but she seemed to be terrified beyond the capacity for rational thought, much less casual speech.

That wasn't good. There was no telling what she might do like this. That settled it right there. I had to take control of this situation, and fast.

How? No flipping idea, but it didn't appear I had a lot of time to strategize.

As the first of the creatures approached us, a massive snarling shape in the darkness, I whispered in my friend's ear, "Whatever you do, don't run until I tell you."

I wasn't sure whether that was a sound plan or not, but I was certain if she took off in a panic at least some of those things would chase her. I needed them focused on me. Only then did she have a shot of getting out of here. I didn't care to guess what her odds would be at that point, but they'd have to be better than staying with me. It was the best I could do in this messed-up situation.

More werewolves – amazing how quickly that stopped sounding crazy – began to approach, but I focused on the one that was closer than its ... err ... pack mates, I guess.

It moved forward, growling and sniffing the air. A shaft of moonlight hit it, giving me a much better look than I really wanted. Big as the first one had been, this one was much larger. Seven feet tall if it was an inch, its blood-shot yellow eyes darted between me and the wolf still on the ground.

I didn't know how smart these things were, but the look in its eyes seemed far more contemplative than any dog I'd ever met. I wasn't sure what would be worse: these things being feral monsters or thinking animals.

Speaking of canines, my parents had never let me own a dog, but Riva's mom had a Chihuahua for a while. I seemed to recall her telling us as kids that dogs were all about dominance. That if you wanted to show a dog who was in charge, you stared it down until it looked away.

Mind you, that was much easier to do when the dog in question weighed ten pounds soaking wet.

Screw it. I stepped away from Riva and approached the creature.

"Bent?"

"Stay put," I hissed at her.

The wolf walked toward me with a disturbingly human gait. Had the light of the moon been any less, I wouldn't have been at all surprised had it pulled off its head and turned out to be a person in a costume. Sadly, I had a feeling there were no big-budget horror movies being filmed in the area.

I kept my eyes locked on it as it approached, unsure of what I was going to do until I did it. Call me crazy or suicidal, maybe both, but whatever this monster was thinking, it obviously hadn't been expecting me to suddenly launch myself forward and wrap my arms around its waist.

Before it could do much more than chuff questioningly, I leaned back and put everything I had into it.

Something that size had to weigh at least three hundred pounds. I was in good shape, but realistically, all that should have happened was me getting a hernia and then hoping I died of embarrassment before this thing could gut me.

Reality, however, seemed to have a different plan.

I suplexed the wolf over my body like it was in the

flyweight division. As I said, crazy, but sometimes you gotta go with what you know.

It went flying past Riva and into one of its friends, taking them both down in a tangle of fur and claws.

Oh yeah. If I didn't have the pack's attention before, I sure as hell did now.

5

"How did you do that?"

It seemed that Riva wasn't too terrified to pick perhaps the stupidest time of all to start asking questions.

"I have a confession to make," I said as the circle of werewolves closed in on us. "I'm actually descended from a long line of monster hunters."

"Really?"

I stopped and glanced at her sidelong, giving her my best condescending glare. "No."

The werewolf I'd thrown untangled itself from the one I'd helpfully tossed it into and got back to its feet. Fine by me. That wasn't the only move I had. Too bad it wasn't alone. Pity that wrestling, outside of the stuff they showed on TV, was a one-on-one sport. Contrary to what some might think, I hadn't spent much time training for battles royale ... or fighting monsters, for that matter.

Where the others seemed to be approaching us more cautiously now, the one I'd tossed looked pissed. It lowered its head and appeared ready to charge.

"Get ready," I whispered out of the corner of my mouth. "When I say to..."

Another of those things, somewhere near the rear of the pack, let out a godawful roar – loud enough to rattle my bones. I expected the entire bunch to converge on us because if that wasn't a battle cry, then I didn't know what was.

However, the one getting ready to kick my ass stood down instead. It relaxed its body stance and backed up. *The hell?* Several more of the monsters stepped to the side revealing two massive werewolves, even larger than the one I'd thrown.

Holy shit! It was like these things came in large, extra-large, and fucking enormous.

"I think you pissed them off," Riva whispered, her voice sounding close to breaking.

"Ya think?"

Both beasts approached us, each well over seven feet tall. Their fur was jet black in color, mixed with hints of salt and pepper grey. Everything about them was even more exaggerated than the rest – bigger teeth, longer claws, far more terrifying, that sort of stuff. We'd just learned these monsters existed and already were meeting their jacked-up cousins.

Could this night get any weirder?

Yeah, I had to ask.

One of the uber-wolves stepped forward and growled at the one I'd tossed. They made chuffing sounds back and forth at each other. Mind-blowing as it was, it seemed like they were actually conversing. That told me these things were probably intelligent, but I couldn't help but feel that still didn't bode well for us. Somehow I doubted we'd be able to talk our way out of this.

After a few seconds, the smaller beast stepped away and approached the downed werewolf. It bent low and began to sniff it, occasionally prodding it with its nose, all while the bigger wolf looked on.

It wasn't just the big guy either. All of them were intently staring at the one still lying unconscious on the ground.

It was now or never, while they were all otherwise occupied. This was the only chance Riva was going to get to...

A low whimpering began to come from the one with a broken arm. It was finally waking up. Great. As if we didn't have enough of these things to worry about.

"Riva," I whispered again. "On my mark, get ready to..."

The words died in my mouth as one of the wolves turned toward the big one – the pack leader perhaps – and made a sound that was actually understandable, if just barely.

"*Alive.*"

"Bent," Riva said, "did that werewolf just..."

"Talk? I'm ... not sure."

That was the truth. Its voice had been low and guttural, uttered by a mouth that didn't appear designed for human speech. For all I knew, it could have just come out sounding familiar, like how some dogs could be taught to bark Christmas carols.

Either way, an answer didn't seem to be forthcoming. Several of the wolves converged on the beaten one and began gently helping it up. It appeared they were showing actual concern. If so, then maybe there was a shot they'd be too worried about their friend to notice us slipping away.

Unfortunately, we were very much still on their radar, though. My friend's sharp intake of breath from behind alerted me to the fact that the second of the two mega-wolves was approaching us.

There was an air of authority in its gait that the rest didn't seem to have. The other big werewolf appeared to be giving the orders, but the way this one carried itself told me it must have had some substantial rank within the wolf hierarchy – High Lord Ass Sniffer, at the very least.

I lifted my head, hoping to maybe stare the creature down, but then saw its eyes widen almost as if in surprise. It was by far the least aggressive thing I'd seen any of these monsters do so far. I hate to admit it, but if it had tilted its head to the side like a dumb dog, I probably would have laughed.

The massive beast continued to approach until it stood directly before me, casting me in shadow by virtue of its size alone.

"Tamara," Riva whispered.

"I've got this," I said without breaking my gaze.

The wolf glared down at me and gave a sniff. Then it looked back, toward where the others were still helping the one I'd beaten the snot out of.

It did this a few times, looking back and forth between us, as if contemplating what had happened. It was a very human-looking gesture for something so utterly alien.

As curious as I was to where this might be going, I also realized there likely wouldn't be a better time to make a move.

The wolf glanced back toward the others one last time and I picked that moment to act. I wasn't sure what sex this thing was, having not properly studied its wolf crotch, but I'd watched enough Animal Planet to know that packs were generally led by males. That was good enough for me.

I brought my foot up with everything I had and its eyes opened comically wide at the moment of impact. It let out a whimper that was unmistakably that of a male whose testicles had been flattened by a size six.

The werewolf fell over onto its back, its hands, or paws, grasping at its groin.

I opened my mouth to scream for Riva to run when the other big wolf let out a roar.

This time, there was no mistaking the meaning. It was aimed squarely at us, and it sounded angry.

"Run!"

"I'm not leaving you!"

Oh, I could have gladly pummeled her right at that moment ... or given her a big hug. Scared out of her wits as she was, she still refused to leave me behind.

Sadly, that was all the thought I had to spare. The lead wolf stalked toward us, looking far less friendly than its buddy had a few moments earlier. There was no mistaking its gait. It was readying to attack.

My years of training took over and I lowered myself into a defensive crouch. This was by far the most lopsided sparring match I'd ever found myself in, but if this thing thought I was going down like some screaming damsel in distress, it was sorely mistaken.

Or at least it would have been.

Just as the massive werewolf was almost within striking range, something big hit it from the side. It was hard to tell one of these things from the other without nametags, but it looked like it was the other big wolf, the one whose balls probably still had my boot imprint on them.

What the frig? Was it so pissed off that it was willing to fight for the right to kill me?

Either way, the two massive wolves ended up sprawled on the ground, snarling and clawing at each other.

I expected the rest of the pack to dogpile us, and not in a good way. But to my surprise, they gathered around the two battling werewolves until the combatants were hidden from my sight.

A hand fell on my shoulder and I spun, fist raised, causing Riva to jump back with a shriek.

"Don't do that!" I snapped.

She nodded, wide-eyed, then looked past me. "What are they doing?"

I glanced back, realizing this was exactly what I'd been hoping for. "Providing us the break we need."

There was no way of knowing if it would be enough for us to get out of these accursed woods, but I was willing to give it a try.

I grabbed Riva by the hand and dragged her with me away from the circle of werewolves.

Their snarls and cries followed us as we ran.

I could only pray the rest of them didn't as well.

6

"What is wrong with you?" I whisper-yelled at my friend. Probably a pointless effort since dogs possessed hearing that was far superior to any human's. No idea if werewolves did too, but it seemed a safe bet.

"What's wrong with *me*?"

"Yeah. I told you to run."

"So you could get yourself killed?"

"Trust me, that wasn't my ideal outcome. But better for one of us to make it out of there than neither of us."

"Oh?" she snapped. "So it's fine for you to sacrifice yourself, but you don't like it when I do the same for you?"

I didn't know whether she thought the danger was over, or if shock was setting in, but either way, Riva appeared to be much more her old self now that it was just the two of us fleeing through the woods.

"It's not that," I said. "It's just..." I trailed off as I realized I had no idea where I was going with that thought. We'd just escaped from a pack of monsters, but only now was it starting to sink in. Surreal didn't begin to describe it. Whatever words had been on the tip of my tongue dissolved into laughter.

"Are you ... okay?"

"It's just..." I stopped and leaned against a tree. "We just survived an attack by freaking werewolves. Not how I expected this night to go."

She stood there staring at me for several moments. Then, finally, she joined me in laughing. It was music to my ears. "We did, didn't we?"

I stepped forward and hugged her long and hard, although not as hard as before. I had no idea what was happening to me or whether it would last, but breaking my best friend's ribs seemed a poor way to top the night off.

Riva stepped back after we'd both gotten it out of our systems. She took several deep breaths, no doubt to steady herself, then dug into her pocket and pulled out her phone.

"Pretty sure the service out here sucks," I said.

"It does, but the compass app should still work fine."

"Good idea."

"You're the brawn. I guess that leaves me to be the brains." I laughed again as she pulled up the app. After another moment, she turned and pointed. "Says that way is north, so if we head in the opposite direction, we should eventually hit Crossed Pine Road."

Smart. There was little chance of finding our campsite again by wandering blindly. We'd gotten too turned around, but Crossed Pine Road bisected the entire area. If we made it there, it would be a minor issue to orient ourselves and then find Riva's car. Even if we couldn't, Chief Johnson sent regular patrols to cruise that stretch. I was pretty sure it was more to catch parked kids than to battle werewolves, but I would've been happy to see the boys in blue nevertheless.

Once the snarls of the werewolf pack finally faded away in the distance, the normal sounds of the forest returned. Soon, it was as if there were nothing out of the ordinary in these woods. It was almost as if we'd accidentally strayed into the Twilight Zone before stepping back over some invisible boundary to our own world again. It all felt so ... unreal.

"How did you do all of that stuff?" Riva asked after a while. By then, we were moving briskly but conserving our strength in case we needed to run again.

"I wish I knew. I'm still surprised I did anything other than keel over and die. The last thing I expected was..." I made a fist and slapped it into my palm.

"Do you think we somehow, I don't know, dreamt it all?"

"Like a shared hallucination?"

"Yeah. That, or maybe your parents have been buying the cheap stuff."

I chuckled. "Wouldn't that be something? To find out Dad has been spiking the booze with LSD. It's always the quiet ones."

The humor dropped out of her voice. "Seriously, though. Do you think maybe we imagined it?"

I stopped walking and curled my hand into a fist. "Guess there's only one way to find out."

"Are you sure you want to?"

"Not really. Just spare me the 'I told you so' until they reset the bones."

Bracing myself for the hurt if I was wrong, I hauled off and backhanded the nearest tree. The impact was like a shotgun blast in the woods. Bark and splintered wood flew from the gouge I somehow carved in the trunk. I pulled

48

my hand back and together we examined it under the light of her phone. Dirty, but otherwise undamaged.

"This is crazy," she said in awe.

"You're telling me."

"I mean, how does that even work? One minute you're dying, the next you're a superhero."

"Not sure I'd go that far."

"I'm open to suggestions."

I shrugged and continued walking. "No idea. Maybe I died and this is some sort of afterlife hallucination."

"Then how does that explain me?"

"A figment of my imagination, maybe. You're probably still back at camp performing CPR on me. Or maybe you're here, too, meaning you died from grief over losing such an awesome friend."

"Humility, thy name is Bent."

"Hey, I punched out a werewolf tonight. Not exactly a grounding experience."

Finally! I spotted the road up ahead through the trees and was damned glad to see it. All jokes aside, the rush of what happened eventually faded as we walked and, soon enough, I was feeling spooked to high heaven again. It was probably little more than paranoia on my part, but I couldn't help shake the feeling of being watched.

People told stories about the hollows being haunted, but who'd have ever thought that would be so true – and by things far worse than ghosts?

Regardless, I'd learned my lesson. Adult or not, it would be a cold day in hell before I came back here after dark again. Heck, I wasn't sure I even wanted to be here in the daylight.

Riva and I stepped tentatively onto the asphalt. I think

we were both afraid it would turn out to be some illusion, and that we were both still lost in the woods.

It was real enough, though, and a sigh of relief passed through her lips as surely as it did mine. We started looking for a mile marker, something that would give us an idea of where we were in relation to Riva's car. By unspoken consent, we walked in the middle of the road. Screw it. I'd sooner risk being hit by a car than have a hairy claw suddenly reach out of the bushes and grab hold of me.

"Over there!" Riva pointed to a sign on the side of the road warning drivers to slow down for curves ahead. We'd passed it shortly before finding our turnoff and parking. "We're less than a quarter mile away."

"Let's do this, then." My tone belied the fact that we were potentially walking back into the monsters' territory. Unfortunately, there wasn't much we could do about it. It was either ten minutes to the car, or over an hour hoofing it back to High Moon and Riva's house – longer if we went to mine.

We didn't spot any cop cars, but eight minutes of increasingly fast walking later did bring us to the turnoff leading to the little clearing where Riva's car still sat.

"Please tell me you have your keys," I said, staring at the vehicle, as if half-expecting it to stand up, sprout fangs, and start chasing us.

She let out a nervous laugh and pulled them from her pocket. "Don't hate me for saying this, but thank goodness you forgot your meds. I only grabbed them from the tent because you were sick."

"Three cheers for terminal illness."

Riva unlocked the doors and made for the driver's side.

"Wait!" I made a circuit of the vehicle first, peering in all the windows. "Okay, now."

"What was that about?"

"If I didn't check, you just know one of those things would've been waiting in the back seat."

"Good point."

To normally call Riva a cautious driver would be an understatement. Most days, she drove like an old lady, not helped by her parents' constant reminders that she was still on their insurance policy. That all went out the window in that moment. It was fortunate that Crossed Pine wasn't a big trucking route, because at the speed we hit the road, anything coming at us from either side would have killed us several times over.

It was only when we were accelerating away that she said, "You know we're gonna have to go back to get our stuff. That's my dad's tent."

"We?" She turned to glare at me. "Kidding! We can discuss it tomorrow, when it's light out."

"That works."

"Oh, and Riva?"

"Yes?"

"I know it's horrible of me to say this but, just for tonight, if anything steps out into the road in front of the car, especially if it's large and furry..."

"Run it the fuck over?"

"You read my mind."

7

It was decided, after we'd made it back to High Moon, that we'd head back to my house. Riva's dad owned a gun, which he kept in his office safe. Tempting as it was to retrieve it, I had a feeling that would have ended with us getting spooked and shooting out a window, if not ourselves.

She also brought up a good point. My meds were back at my place. I felt fine, the barest notion of nausea having long since faded away to nothing, but that didn't mean my symptoms wouldn't come back with a vengeance. At even the slightest hint of discomfort, I wanted them at hand.

Years of habit told me I should take two the second we walked through the door but, dumb as it might have been, I decided to hold off to see how things went. Who knows? It had been a while since my last medical exam. Maybe I'd gone into remission.

We reached my house shortly thereafter. There were no cars in the driveway but a light was on inside, although that didn't mean much. Mom usually left one on when she went out.

Unlike Riva, I hadn't had the foresight to grab my keys

when I was sure I'd been dying. They were still back in the tent. Fortunately, we kept a spare hidden on the porch.

It was a breakneck pace to run from the car, find the keys, unlock the door, then turn on every light on the main floor as if a couple hundred watts of LED bulbs would be enough to scare off any monsters. The only snag in the plan was me forgetting about Mom's goddamned garden gnomes and letting out a scream when I saw their freaky little eyes staring back from the bushes.

I made a mental note to smash the stupid things to dust ... when it was light out again.

My parents didn't own a gun, at least so far as I knew, but we had plenty of sports equipment in the garage, courtesy of Chris's ongoing quest to find something he didn't suck at. After finding and pocketing my pills, we closed the shades, armed ourselves with baseball bats and field hockey sticks, and held vigil on my living room couch – cranking up the volume on the TV so as to make it feel like we weren't alone.

"What time is your mom getting home?"

"No idea," I'd been wondering that myself. Glancing at the time on the DVR, I saw it was late. Surely she wouldn't have taken my brother to see a midnight matinee.

"Do you want to call her?"

"And say what? That we came back home because we were at the hollows against their wishes but then got chased off by monsters? My folks don't mark the liquor bottles, but I'm pretty sure they'll start if I tell them that." Realizing that what I'd said wasn't even remotely comforting, I added, "Don't worry. I'm sure she'll be home soon."

I only hoped it would be soon enough.

Aside from a quick shower on my part, after realizing I smelled of dried puke – during which Riva insisted I leave the bathroom door open – we continued our wide-eyed wait on the couch.

Hours passed and eventually we both must have fallen asleep, because the next thing I knew, the front door was being unlocked. I cracked my eyes open in time to see both Mom and Chris walk in the door. That couldn't have been right. I could see the yard beyond them, faint but visible, as if it were morning already.

"What time is it?" I croaked.

Mom stopped right inside the door, her eyes widening as if surprised to see us. Chris, normally one to blurt out something mean, stupid, or both, simply stood by her side, a glazed expression on his face. Not too surprising, I guess. If she'd kept him out all night, then he was probably dead tired.

"Almost six," she replied warily, before turning to my brother. "Christopher, dear, you've had a long night. Why don't you go to bed?"

Without saying a word, my brother walked past her toward the basement stairs.

"Night, bro," I called to him sleepily. He didn't acknowledge me back. *Fine, be rude, you little asshole.*

Before I could ask Mom why she was getting in so late, or early, she said, "I thought you were spending the night at Riva's."

Upon hearing her name, my friend stirred. She bolted upright, as if from a bad dream, but then looked around, noticed my mom, and quickly tried to compose herself. "Oh, h-hey, Mrs. Bentley."

Mom continued to stare at us strangely. I was starting to feel paranoid, like maybe we actually had crossed over into another dimension, but then I realized it might have to do with the fact that Riva and I were surrounded by sports equipment.

"There's a good explanation for all of this," I said after a beat.

"I'm sure there is," she replied, raising an eyebrow. "I can't wait to hear why you two felt the need to turn my living room into the field of dreams."

I instantly felt relieved. This was the Mom I knew.

Of course, the big question now was what to tell her. I'll be the first to admit, coming up with a believable story had been the furthest thing from my mind a few hours earlier. Heck, I wasn't even sure I should try.

I mean, werewolves were real, for Christ's sake. Not only that, but we'd encountered them only a few miles from where we lived. Crazy as it was to tell my parents that, who was to say someone wouldn't be hurt if I didn't? Could I live with myself if Chris or one of his loser friends went missing near those same woods, all because I was too worried about looking like a nut?

Riva, apparently sensing the conflict in me, said, "We need to tell her."

"Tell me what?"

"It's ... a bit of a story, Mom."

My mother put her purse down and walked past us. "Let's go."

"Where?"

"To the kitchen. I can see there's something you want to say. I'm going to put on some coffee, and you two are going to talk."

"But..."

"You're an adult, Tamara," Mom shot back. "There's no need to pretend like you're twelve and have a secret crush. I think we're a little past that."

Blunt as always, but she had a point. Heck, in another two years I wouldn't even need to swipe my parents'

55

liquor. I could just go out and buy my own. Mind you, acting like an adult and telling another older adult an insane story about your fight with supernatural monsters were two completely different things.

As we found ourselves seated around the kitchen table, I still wasn't quite sure what to say that wouldn't make it sound as if we'd both gone looney tunes.

Mom, no idiot, obviously sensed our hesitation. "Let me be blunt and to the point," she stated, worry in her eyes. "Did someone try to hurt you girls?"

"Well..."

"Not exactly *someone*," Riva said, glancing my way.

Mom waited impatiently, staring at us as she stirred creamer into her coffee – the spoon making *ding* noises as it hit the sides of her cup. "Do we need to involve the police? Because I have Chief Johnson's home number and I'm not afraid to use it."

It took me a moment to see where her line of questioning was going, but then it sunk in. There we were, two young women, who'd been out unsupervised for the night. No doubt her next question was going to involve whether someone had slipped something in our drinks.

I let out a sigh and decided to just rip the Band-Aid off. Riva, probably sensing the determination on my face, took a step back. Once again, my house, my parents, so my job to do the telling. Of course, that also meant I was going to catch the bulk of any shit thrown back at us. Hoo-freaking-rah. "We weren't at Riva's house last night."

"Call me psychic," Mom replied, "but I kind of figured that. So what was it? A party? One of those rave things? Were there drugs?"

"We went camping."

"Okay, and?"

"It was over in the hollows."

There came a beat of silence, followed by, "*What?* Are you insane?"

"It was just the two of us. No boys. No drugs." I stopped short of mentioning alcohol. No point in throwing more fuel onto that bonfire.

Mom didn't look even remotely happy. Maybe I should've said we went to a drug-fueled rave after all. "We told you not to go there."

Probably stupid of me to mouth off, but I threw her own words back in her face. "True, but like you said, we're adults now. So we made an adult decision."

"That's not an adult decision, young lady. That's pure stupidity."

"It was a nice night. We just went camping. That's all. It's not like we knocked over a 7-11 first."

"But why the hollows?" She stood, turned away from us, and slapped her hands onto the counter. "You could have gone to Foreman Woods instead. You'd have been safe there. It's neutral ground."

What? "Back up for a second. What do you mean by..."

Mom wasn't about to be distracted, though. "Never mind that. The hollows are a bad place, Tamara. Do you think we've been telling you that for our own amusement?"

Something clicked in my head. No. They wouldn't have tried to scare me for kicks. That wasn't Mom's style. Never had been. But they'd always been vague about it. Suddenly, I got the impression there was more here than meets the eye. "What do you know?"

She stopped talking, our eyes locked, and then she echoed what I asked her just a moment earlier. "What do you mean by that?"

"Exactly what I said. What did you think was going to happen to us there? All these years you've been saying what a bad place it is and how I'm forbidden to go there, but I'm just now realizing there's never been a reason as to why."

"I don't think I appreciate your tone, young lady."

Riva got up. "Maybe I should go home."

Mom pointed a finger at her. "You're not getting out of this that easily. Not unless you want me phoning your parents."

My friend couldn't have sat down faster if someone had tied an anchor to her butt. Adults we might be, but not so old that we'd shaken off the conditioning we'd grown up with.

Mom continued to glare at us for several seconds, the only sound in the kitchen the *clack-clack* of her fingernails on the countertop. "When your father gets home, we're going to have a long talk about what it means to be a responsible adult."

I couldn't believe what I was hearing. She'd come home to find me and my best friend obviously scared out of our wits and her biggest concern was that we'd gone camping?! My Twilight Zone theory was beginning to look more and more plausible.

"You are never to go near the hollows again," she continued. "Do I make myself clear?"

Now it was my turn to get angry. Mom was always the disciplinarian among my parents. Despite the typical threats of "wait until your father gets home," I always knew who ruled the roost when it came to punishment. As a result, she was the one I was least likely to cross. Don't get me wrong. Dad had a lot of bark when he got riled up, but there was seldom much bite behind it.

But damn it all, I'd cleaned a freaking werewolf's clock a few hours earlier. Mom had all the power in the world to ground me until I was finished with college, but I'd be damned if she was going to blow me off without hearing me out first. "Don't you even want to know what happened to us last night? What we saw?" I gave my best impersonation of her voice, which wasn't all that bad. "Oh, my dearest Tamara. I see that you're terrified for some reason. Why, whatever happened to you and your friend?"

The look on her face said she was less than impressed by my powers of mimicry. Rather than chew me out, though, she said, "You didn't see anything."

"What?"

"You heard me." Her tone was deceivingly calm, but I didn't buy it. "There was nothing out there in those woods. Whatever you think you saw, I'm sure it was just your imagination."

I turned toward Riva, flabbergasted at what I was hearing. Her face echoed mine, but she wasn't about to speak up. Her parents were old school and had, more than once, told mine that they were free to discipline her as they saw fit. No doubt she figured that rule still applied. Guess I had to be the one to grow a backbone.

"Under normal circumstances I'd say you were right, Mom. That maybe I was hallucinating."

"Tamara, don't," she warned, but I ignored her.

"After all, I left my meds here. Didn't realize until it was too late and I was certain I was dying."

My mother's eyes opened wide in surprise and something else ... *fear*. "You left your medication home? Of all the stupid things to do. You know better than that."

"It was an accident. I thought I had them with me." I considered throwing my brother under the bus but, tempting as it was, dragging him into this probably wouldn't help much. Besides, I'd started it by swiping his stupid game system. "They must have fallen out of my bag."

Mom's lips pursed, as if she was thinking. After a

moment, her expression softened. "Let me see if I have this straight. You forgot your pills, got sick, and then got spooked on your way back here because..."

"No."

"What do you mean, no?"

"I mean, yes, that was the plan. Riva was trying to help me back to the car so we could come back here and get my meds, but something happened first. We saw..."

"Tamara," Mom interrupted, "when was the last time you took your pills?"

For some reason I briefly felt the urge to lie. There was something in her eyes that told me she didn't want to know the truth. She wanted to hear that I'd come back home and swallowed my pills, just as I'd done every day for most of my life.

Things had gone too far, gotten way too weird for that. She was hiding something, and I had a feeling only the truth was going to set it free. "Yesterday morning."

She gasped. "No! That's almost twenty-four hours."

"Well aware, Mom. Trust me on that."

"Where are they?"

"In my pocket."

A look of relief crossed her face. "Good. It's not too late. I want you to take them now and..."

I stood and approached her. "What do you mean 'not too late?' Isn't that what I've been told my entire life? Take them or else. Hell, I felt the *or else* part. Puked my guts out all over the forest. Thought I was going to die right then and there."

"We can discuss this after you've taken your meds. I'll make an appointment with the doctor and we can..."

"You're not listening to me. I don't need the damned meds!" My frustration boiled over and I slammed my fist down with an audible *CRACK*. The countertop shattered beneath the force of the blow and Riva let out a screech of surprise.

Oh, yeah. Forgot I could do that.

Silence descended in the kitchen for several seconds.

"Um ... sorry?"

"Bent 1, Formica zero," my friend muttered under her breath.

"It's Italian marble," Mom corrected, her tone expressing annoyance more than anything else.

My mouth dropped open as realization hit. "You're not surprised, not even in the slightest, are you?"

Her eyes locked with mine and she replied in a voice that was as calm as a lake on a cloudless day. "Of course not, you stupid, stupid girl."

8

"Do you have any idea what you've done? How much danger you've put yourself in?"

"Would any of that danger happen to be from werewolves?" Riva asked in a small voice. I had to give her credit for speaking up. Good thing, too, because Mom and I would have probably bickered for the rest of the day about stupid things like the countertop.

My mother slowly turned toward her. "I'm sorry, dear, but you look tired."

Riva nodded. "I am, but I'm pretty sure I'm not getting any sleep anytime..."

"No. You're not listening." Mom's gaze locked onto my friend's and the strangest thing happened. I could have sworn they lit up for just a moment. Probably my imagination running wild again with... *Go into the other room and take a nap.*

Though I saw her lips move and heard the words leave her mouth, it was as if multiple voices had spoken at once. Some seriously weird reverb there. Maybe I was more fatigued than I thought. "She doesn't need a..."

Riva stood without a word, turned, and marched back into the living room.

"Um, where are you going? She wasn't being literal."

My mother, for her part, turned and poured herself another cup of coffee. "There. That should give us some privacy to discuss matters. She's seen far more than she should have, but I can take care of that."

Earlier, when Mom had first walked in the door, I'd been weirded out for some reason. I'd dismissed it as nothing more than nerves, but now that feeling was back again, and a lot stronger.

I walked to the kitchen exit. Interestingly enough, though she'd stepped away only seconds earlier, Riva was sacked out on the couch, snoring as if she'd been that way for hours. *The hell?!*

Last night had been weirder than anything I'd ever experienced in my life, but today was trying to give it a run for its money, and doing a heck of a job at it so far. I glanced back toward my mother.

Before I could speak – not that I knew what I was going to say – the growl of a car engine outside caught my attention. It was followed by the sound of a door slamming shut.

Mom stepped up beside me. "Your father always did have impeccable timing."

Sure enough, he stepped through the front door a few seconds later.

His eyes fell upon me and the first thing he said was, "Thank goodness you're all right!"

Pity for him, the first words out of my mouth were less cheerful. "What happened to your face?"

Dad was a mess – a black eye, dried blood beneath his nose, and numerous scratches covering his face and neck. He looked like someone had used him as a punching bag.

Mom pushed past me – not surprising, considering

the condition of her husband. But when she spoke, her tone was only partially sympathetic. "Are you okay? Who was it this time?"

"I'm fine." Dad averted his eyes. "Craig, but there's a good reason, Lissa..."

"I thought we talked about this."

This was crazy. They were acting like Dad, a guy who I couldn't recall ever even spanking me, had just come home from Fight Club. Weirder, Mom was acting like this wasn't the first time either. Truth be told, I was beginning to wonder whether I'd actually fallen into a coma after all. Surely this wasn't the same boring family I'd said goodbye to yesterday.

"I know, but you have to understand, I *had* to." He stopped and turned toward me. "Isn't that right, Tam Tam?"

Dad stepped past my mother and stood looking down at me expectantly.

"I have no idea what you're talking about, but I was just telling Mom that some seriously weird shit happened..."

"Language, young lady!"

"I think we can overlook it this time, dear," Dad said, turning back to me. "After all, I understand our daughter had a somewhat stressful night, out camping where she wasn't supposed to be."

What?! How did he know that?

"You're lucky I was there," he continued. "Although, next time, I'd appreciate it if you didn't kick me in the crotch."

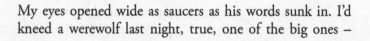

My eyes opened wide as saucers as his words sunk in. I'd kneed a werewolf last night, true, one of the big ones –

taking the fight out of it. Was Dad trying to tell me he was...?

No!

I shoved him away, sending him stumbling back across the living room. Then I stepped between him and my mother, fists raised. "Get back, Mom. He's not who we think he is."

"Really, Tamara?" Her tone wasn't exactly full of alarm like I was expecting. "Must we do this?"

I glanced back toward her just as movement registered in my periphery.

Dad had recovered his footing. "You need to calm down, honey ... whoa!"

I spun and threw a punch, intent on knocking him into next week but, much to my amazement, he dodged, moving faster than I'd ever seen him.

My blow, a sloppy haymaker thrown in panic, missed by a mile. The momentum sent me staggering past him. Before I could recover, Dad locked his arms – far hairier than I remembered them being – around me and held me in place. "That's enough!"

I tried to power my way out, but his strength was incredible. As strong as I guessed I was, he managed to maintain his grip. Pity for him, I wasn't out of tricks.

"Can you please calm..."

I shifted my weight, dropped low, and twisted. Dad was pulled off-balance, letting go enough for me to launch him over my shoulder.

He smashed through our coffee table, landing on his back with a satisfying crunch of glass and wood.

The commotion was enough to rouse Riva, who'd continued to slumber on the couch up until then. She woke with a start, her mouth opening and closing mutely at the sight before her.

"Mom," I called over my shoulder, "take Riva and get

out of here. I've got this." In reality, I didn't have a clue as to whether I had anything, but it seemed a reassuring thing to say.

"Oh, enough is enough!" Mom shot back. "I will not have you ruining my furniture because of some misguided temper tantrum."

I was about to ask what the hell was wrong with her, but the only thing that came out of my mouth was a surprised cry as something knocked me off my feet from behind.

One of the easy chairs had somehow slid across the living room floor, seemingly of its own accord, dropping me butt-first into it.

Before I could stand, Mom shouted something. "*Dhó Slabhrai!*" Whatever that meant, it again came out sounding as if she had three invisible backup singers screaming it out along with her.

But if I thought that was odd, it was nothing compared to the whips of bright orange light that appeared from out of nowhere and tangled themselves around me. No, that wasn't quite right. Light was intangible. Whatever this crap was, it felt solid. They wrapped around my arms and legs, holding me fast to the chair.

"Bent!"

"Don't make me tie you down, too," Mom scolded my friend before turning back to me. "I said that's enough."

I struggled against the ... bonds, I guess, but whatever they were they had me caught like a rat in a trap. Sadly, I didn't have a great deal of leverage, otherwise I'd have...

"Stop fooling around, Curtis, and help me here."

My father pushed himself to a sitting position and glanced sidelong at my mother. "You know, that actually did kinda hurt."

"Now is not the time for melodrama."

They looked at each other for a moment, then both

turned to me. I braced myself, uncertain what was going on or what would come next. Whatever they had planned for me, though, I'd fight them tooth and nail. I'd...

Dad got to his feet and leaned down over me. "Are you calm now, honey?"

Huh?!

I wasn't sure what to expect, but it hadn't been that.

9

M om folded her arms in front of her and pursed her lips. "Don't baby her like that, Curtis. She's not a toddler anymore."

"I'm just trying to reassure her that everything is okay."

I quickly glanced over at Riva. There was a look of total confusion on her face. Yep, no help there.

After a moment, as my parents continued to bicker, I began to get the sense that maybe Dad wasn't going to gut me after all. As for my mother, well, I wasn't sure what to think there.

Finally, I got a hold of myself enough to speak up. "Could you guys maybe talk to me like I'm actually here?"

"Sorry, Tam Tam," Dad said. "You're probably a bit confused at the moment."

"A bit?" I raised an eyebrow. "I'm tied to a chair with laser beams and you think I'm *a bit* confused?"

"Oh, yeah, that. We'll let you go if you promise not to overreact."

"That means no destroying the furniture," Mom added. "You know the rule about fighting in the house."

Strange didn't begin to describe this day so far. The fact that, after everything that had just occurred, my parents were talking to me like ... parents ... wasn't doing much to alleviate that.

"Maybe, I should go."

Mom froze Riva in place with a glare. "Sit down, young lady."

"A-are you going to knock me out again?"

Dad looked at Mom with something akin to minor disapproval on his face. "You didn't."

"It was just a minor sleep compulsion."

"Really, Lissa?" he asked, his tone stern but not surprised.

"What was I supposed to do?"

"You could have tried talking to her."

"Yeah," I replied, still stuck fast. "Talking's good. Much better than ... frying her brain, or whatever you did."

"Frying my brain?" Riva echoed in a small voice.

Mom's eyes narrowed as she surveyed the three of us. "Very well. She can remain conscious. But I'm warning you both, what is said in this house does not leave this house. Am I crystal clear?"

Riva lifted a hand and tentatively crossed her heart.

"I'd ask you to swear on Ernmas's good graces, but you probably don't know who that is. So I guess that will have to be good enough for now..."

"Would it help if *I* swore on her good graces?" I asked. "Because I'm still kinda stuck here."

"Oh, sorry about that." Mom waved her hand dismissively and the strands of light around me immediately dissipated.

I moved my arms and found myself once again free, so I stood up before she could change her mind.

"Now behave," she said in a scolding manner, "or it's back in the chair."

All at once, I felt like I was five again and being told to go stand in the corner. Yeah, she was Mom, all right. Or at least she was playing the part convincingly.

I figured it was best to breach that subject right away before anything else odd happened. "Who are you?"

My mother raised an eyebrow. "Please tell me you did not just ask that. Who do you think we are, young lady?"

Dad stepped behind her and began massaging her shoulders. "Be nice, dear. I'm sure this is kind of strange for her, too."

"Strange is one word for it," I replied, facing them both. "Especially since I don't recall you being a werewolf or you being a ... wait. Are you one, too?"

One corner of Mom's mouth raised in a half grin. "Of course not. I'm a witch."

"Oh, of course. I guess that makes Chris, what? A gremlin? Or maybe an imp?"

"Your brother is perfectly normal," she replied. "In his own unique way, at least. He doesn't know. And I'd prefer we keep it that way."

"Are you sure he's not?"

"Positive."

It figured. The one person in the house I was certain had been conjured from the netherworld was the only non-freak. It's like nothing made sense anymore. "Okay, fine. So how long have you two been..."

"Always," Dad said, looking somewhat embarrassed. "We've just been good at hiding it, up until last night anyway."

Mom pulled away from him to glare at me. "It would still be a secret if *someone* had stayed away from the hollows and taken their meds like they were supposed to."

My meds...

I studied Dad's eyes as she said this, a sense of dread beginning to form in my gut. He'd always been easier to read than Mom. I saw concern in them, but no hint of surprise either.

The werewolf and witch thing was going to seriously freak me out once it had a chance to sink in, but this? If what I feared was true, then freaked out was gonna need to take a back seat to royally pissed off. "I'm not sick, am I?"

My parents both looked at each other – a meaningful glance as if they knew this day would come, like this was a conversation about the birds and the bees or something mundane like that.

Finally, Dad shook his head. "No. You're not."

I won't mince words. I kind of lost my shit. In the wake of all the other questions I had, about how my life had apparently been one giant game of monster charades, this was the thing that really set me off. Betrayal didn't even begin to cover it. This wasn't just about their secrets, whether it was howling at the moon or casting laser rope spells. This was about me, their daughter. For nearly my entire life, I'd lived with a death sentence hanging over my head. Do you know what that does to someone? I'd been certain I was going to die out in those woods and not because of some stupid wolfman either.

"Was I ever sick?"

The silence from them was all the answer I needed.

"I can't believe this! All of that crap about the pills, about me being sick. All of it was bullshit? How could you do that to your own daughter?"

If Riva had been frightened by my parents, she absolutely shrank into the couch cushions as I laid into them. I felt bad about that, but reassuring her that she wasn't the target of my ire would have taken the edge off. Right then, I wanted that anger.

I *deserved* that anger.

"Listen, you're upset right now, not thinking clearly..."

"Do not!" I pointed a finger at Mom. "Upset is you renting my room to a hobo or buying Chris a car before me. This ... this is not upset. Do you know what it's like to be terrified of leaving the house without your medication? To have to search through your purse in a panic because you can't find it right away? Do you have any idea what it's like to be that afraid every *fucking day* of your life?"

"Actually, we do," Dad said in a small voice.

I ignored him, not even remotely in the mood to share the misery. This was my pity party and I was the only guest of honor. "What are they?"

"What?"

"The pills! Are they a placebo? Was it all in my head?"

"No," Mom said. "A placebo wouldn't have done the trick. It needed to be real. You were too powerful otherwise."

I turned to her expectantly. Whereas Dad looked guilty as hell, as if he wanted to crawl under the porch and hide, Mom seemed to be holding it together. If the truth was going to come out, I sensed it would be from her. "Go on."

"Mind your tone. I'm still your mother."

It was all I could do to not grab the nearest heavy object and throw it at her.

Before I could lay into her again, that thought gave me pause, the anger momentarily abating. It was something I'd need to keep in mind. If what was happening to me was permanent, then I had the potential to really hurt someone if I wasn't careful.

I remembered the creep I'd slugged the day before. It had been a moment of anger and I'd lashed out, putting him on his ass. But if I tried that right now, I'd probably knock his head clean off ... an overreaction if ever there was one.

Mind you, that still didn't mean I was in the mood to be brow-beaten by my parents. I simply folded my arms and waited.

"I won't lie to you, Tamara." She held up a hand when she saw the look on my face. "Anymore, that is. The pills were my idea."

"At first, we were just looking for a way to mask your scent," Dad said.

"Why would you need to..."

"Yes, and at first I agreed," Mom interrupted. "But then things changed."

"Things changed?" I asked. "How?"

She smiled, but it didn't reach her eyes. "Do you remember what happened in Target when you were young?"

I nodded. "Yeah. I had some sort of seizure. I started puking and then passed out. You said I almost died."

Mom let out a sigh. "Yes, that's what we *told* you. But do you actually remember what happened?"

I opened my mouth, closed it, then opened it again. "I guess I sort of remember the hospital afterwards. But otherwise no, not really."

"Of course you wouldn't. You were only three."

"So you're saying I didn't have an episode?"

My father chuckled uncomfortably. "Oh, you had an episode, all right."

That drew a glare from Mom. "The truth is, you had a bit of a tantrum over some toy I wouldn't buy for you. I forget which one, but it was something stupid that you had to have right at that moment."

"How did I end up in the hospital from a tantrum?"

She looked me in the eye and held my gaze. "You didn't. I did."

10

"**W**hat?"

"Yes. I was admitted with a shattered arm ... broken in three places, actually."

"What happened? How did you..." I trailed off as stark realization hit. "I did it."

"Up until that moment," Mom continued, "we'd only begun to suspect you possessed somewhat ... inordinate strength for your age. A broken toddler bed here, a crushed playset there. But that, that incident cemented it."

"Oh my God. I..."

"Calm down. That was almost seventeen years ago and I wasn't about to blame you for it. You didn't know what you were doing. As far as you were concerned, you were just stamping your feet and throwing a minor snit." Her tone lightened a bit. "Besides, you punished yourself pretty good afterward. Cried for almost a full day."

Dad nodded. "Trust me. I remember that. With your Mom in the hospital, it was up to me to try to cheer you up."

"So how did you come up with the pills?" Riva asked, looking more engrossed than scared by this point. Guess I couldn't blame her. This was some trippy-ass stuff right here.

Mom leaned against the kitchen door frame. "That took a bit longer. There was considerable trial and error, if you will. That's probably what you mistake as remembering what happened in Target. Some of our early attempts left you sick as a dog for the duration of the effect."

"Wait," I said. "That doesn't sound like something a doctor would agree to – using a healthy child as a guinea pig."

"Of course not," Mom replied with a sigh. "Modern medicine is wonderful, don't get me wrong, but it is woefully unprepared for toddlers who can crush cinder blocks with their bare hands."

This was getting deep and a wee bit scary, too. I kind of felt like Neo right before entering the Matrix. He was warned the rabbit hole went pretty deep, but took that damned pill anyway. This was my Morpheus moment right here, right now, but I had a feeling I'd already swallowed the wrong pill. We'd come too far to turn back. "But what about Doctor Byrne? Don't tell me you ... hexed him or something."

Dad let out a snort of laughter. "Sorry to break it to you, honey, but he isn't a doctor, he's your mom's uncle."

"Don't be insulting, Curtis." Mom turned back toward me. "True, he's family, but he does have a doctorate from Stanford."

"Okay, then..."

"But he's also a highly skilled alchemist, not to mention the only member of my coven who's aware of your special circumstances. That's a status quo we cannot afford to..."

"Whoa, hold on. Back up. Alchemy?"

"Of course, it's a tried and true science despite what

your textbooks might tell you. In fact, it was his idea to mix arcane knowledge with modern medicine. The old with the new, if you will."

"I'm not following."

"Your pills, dear. They're a mix of alchemical agents meant to suppress your power and render your scent more human, but they're combined with modern muscle relaxants designed to help keep your strength to more ... manageable levels."

"My scent? Why do I need..."

"Tell her the rest," Dad said.

"I don't think that's a good idea, dear."

"Tell her," he repeated. "She's already heard enough, she should know the rest. We owe it to her." Dad looked at me and I saw something I didn't often see in his eyes: shame. "I'm truly sorry, sweetie. You have to believe that. When you were born, we swore we'd do everything in our power to protect you..."

"Aww, that's sweet," Riva said.

I shut her up with a glare. Now was really not the time. "What do you mean?"

Mom let out a deep breath. Through all of this, she'd kept her cool, but now her face held something else – an expression much closer to my Dad's. "That's not all. The pills were designed to be ... addictive."

What ... the ... fuck? "What do you mean addictive? Like I'm some kind of heroin junkie?"

"Nothing so crass. But when they wear off, they trigger withdrawal-like symptoms in your brain – nausea, vomiting, dizziness."

I let her statement hang in the air for several seconds. "So, in other words, they're supposed to make me feel like I'm dying."

"I need to get out of here."

"Excuse me?" Lissa asked. I was having a real hard time thinking of her as my mother right at that moment.

"I need some fresh air, time to think."

"Tamara..."

"Don't." I held up a hand, one that I really wanted to curl into a fist and punch something with. "You made me a fucking addict!"

Dad stepped forward, his hands out in a placating manner. "Honey, it's not like that. You don't understand."

"Understand what? That every time I've been late, every time I've puked my guts up until I got my next fix, every time I've thought I was going *to die* ... it was just a sick joke? When all along I've been perfectly fine."

"Are you?" Mom asked.

"What kind of question is that? No, really. I'm a lot of things right now, but fine isn't one of them."

"I meant physically."

"Huh? Yeah. I mean, I'm kind of sick to my stomach by what I just heard, but I don't think that's too hard to believe." I stared at her. "Why are you asking? And don't give me any bullshit about really being ill."

"It's just that ... the symptoms were designed to last for days if necessary. And here you are, less than twelve hours later, apparently weaned off."

"Guess Doctor Byrne isn't as good of a witch doctor as you thought."

"It's Melissa," my father said. "I think she did it."

"What?" Mom and I asked simultaneously.

He turned to her first. "We don't know a lot about how Tamara's metabolism works, but I think it has something to do with adrenaline. When Melissa stumbled across the girls, they probably thought she meant to hurt them. It's possible the resulting adrenaline surge flushed things out of her system faster than expected."

They were doing it again, discussing this like I wasn't even in the damned room. "What are you talking about?"

"Melissa Haynes."

I shrugged, still not sure what he meant. "You mean little Melissa, who I used to babysit?"

He nodded. "The same one you put in the hospital last night."

I did what?! "Wait, that werewolf. That was her?"

He nodded. "She's a bit busted up, but she'll be all right." Before I could say anything else, he continued. "Don't blame yourself. You didn't realize it was her. And ... well, the young ones tend to lose it a bit during a full moon like last night's. Believe me, though, she wasn't actually trying to consciously hurt you."

I tried to wrap my brain around this. That snarling monster was little thirteen-year-old Melissa – the same bubbly girl who wouldn't stop talking about her crush, Bobby Shevlocky from the seventh grade?

And I nearly beat her to a pulp.

This was too much to take in all at once.

I walked to the door and grabbed my jacket even though it was probably too warm for one.

"Tamara!" Dad cried.

"I need to get out of here."

"You can't leave."

"Watch me," I called back.

"Hold up, Bent. I'm coming with you."

"Riva..."

"I'm sorry, Mr. Bentley, but what she said."

"I understand you're both upset," Dad called out as we stepped from the door. "Just promise me you won't leave the city limits. If you believe anything I've ever told you, please believe me when I say it's not safe."

11

I was storming down the driveway when Riva caught up to me and grabbed hold of my arm.

"What?" I snapped, causing her to flinch. "Don't try telling me that wasn't total bullshit back there."

"My car," she replied, hooking a thumb over her shoulder.

"Oh. Yeah, that'll probably work better than walking."

A few minutes later, we cruised aimlessly down the still quiet streets. As we passed house after house, I couldn't help but wonder what other secrets this town held – a place that until now I'd assumed was the epitome of dull and mundane.

I pointed at a yellow Colonial. "Creature from the Black Lagoon."

"Huh?"

"Mummy. Maybe a horde of zombies. Hmm, that's Mrs. Jalob's place. Definitely bride of Frankenstein."

Riva looked at me from the driver's seat. "What are you doing?"

"Oh, nothing. Just trying to guess which undying

horror lives in which house. Ooh, look at that beige Tudor. That's gotta be a ghost, or maybe a vampire."

"Why would a vampire live in a Tudor?"

"Why not?"

After letting me ramble about monsters for a few more minutes, she tried to change the subject. "Well, today definitely started off a bit different than I expected."

I glanced over at her. "That, my friend, is the understatement of a lifetime."

"So, let me get this straight ... just so I know I wasn't hallucinating due to lack of sleep. Your dad is one of those things, right?"

"Yep."

"And your mom is ... a witch?"

"I might substitute a B in there, but pretty much same ballpark."

"So what's that make you? A were-witch? Or maybe a witch-wolf?"

I laughed. It was either that or cry. "You tell me. Last I checked, I couldn't do so much as a card trick. And you were there last night. Pretty sure I didn't burst out of my clothes and start snarling."

"Yeah, but that's only because we didn't invite Gary along."

My pseudo laugh turned into a real one. I hadn't been expecting that. Riva was a good friend and obviously made of some pretty stern stuff if she was out here trying to cheer me up instead of home hiding under her bed. If our positions were reversed, I'm not so sure I could say the same thing.

"Maybe we should stop by the Quick Lube," she offered. "You could arm wrestle him. Winner gets to be on top."

I rolled my eyes. "And yet people call me Bent."

"My sweet, unassuming face hides great evil."

"I can see that." After a beat, I added. "Thanks, by the way."

"For what?"

"For not completely freaking out."

"I wouldn't go that far," she said. "Even I'm surprised I'm not lying in the back seat crying my eyes out. I probably will later on, after all this catches up to me."

"I might join you. That is, if you haven't wised up by then and run off screaming."

"Oh, stop. You're my best friend, and you also saved my ass last night."

"From a teenaged werewolf," I added.

"I don't care how old it was. That thing was a monster. I was certain we were gonna die."

"Certain or not, you didn't run, and believe me, you should have. I wouldn't have blamed you."

"Like I said, good friends are hard to come by." She turned to me and grinned. "Besides, do you know how long it's taken me to train you? You get eaten and *poof*, all that hard work goes down the drain."

I smiled as I turned to look out the window. "So glad to know I'm a worthy investment."

We drove in silence for a few more minutes, Riva taking seemingly random turns to keep us moving, with no real destination in sight. "You know, you're going to have to talk to them."

"I know."

"I hate to play devil's advocate, but there's got to be a reason they did what they did. I mean, I've known your folks for almost as long as you have, and they just don't seem the type to turn their only daughter into a junkie."

I considered this. "Yeah, but if I asked you yesterday, would you have guessed my dad was the type to strip naked, grow fur, and chase Bambi under the light of the full moon?"

"Touché."

"I don't know. Maybe they have a good reason and maybe they don't. But I couldn't listen to them anymore, at least not right now. I swear, if I didn't know better, I'd almost think I was dreaming and my brain was making this shit up on the fly."

In response, she reached over and punched me in the arm, or at least I think it was supposed to be a punch. More of a light swat, actually.

"You're supposed to say 'ow,'" she said after a moment.

"Fine. Ow."

"You're not very convincing."

"Hence why I'm not in the drama club. Any reason why you're using me as a punching bag?"

"Just trying to convince you that you're awake."

"You need to do better."

She took one hand off the steering wheel, held it up, and said in a toneless voice, "Oh, you mean I should turn my nails into wicked sabers and use them to gut you like a fish, now that you finally know this town's secret?"

My head spun toward her so fast I was surprised I didn't get whiplash.

After a moment, she laughed. "Jeez, you really are tense."

"Holy shit, Riva. Don't pull that crap. After last night, I'm liable to knock you into next week."

"Noted." She focused on the road again, then said, "I don't know about you, but all this crazy has left me starving. You up for breakfast?"

"Just like that?"

"Yeah, just like that. I mean, I'm awake, I'm hungry, and we didn't stick around for your mom to cook us up any dragon's eggs."

"Not funny."

"Maybe served with eye of newt."

"You really ought to drop out of school and become a comedian."

"Nah. My parents would kill me and, unlike yours, they'd have to do it the old-fashioned way."

Once the conversation turned to breakfast, I insisted on the diner over in Morganberg, the town just east of High Moon. Their hash browns were to die for and right then I wanted to lose myself in a pile of delicious carbs.

Riva instead suggested Gib's, a small coffee shop less than a mile from my home.

"They can barely toast a bagel."

"I know, but your dad told us not to leave town. He said it was dangerous."

"He's also been saying it was dangerous to not take my meds, and you see how that turned out."

"I know, Bent, but..."

"You're thinking like a kid. Trust me, I understand. If your dad handed me a lawnmower and told me to get to it, my first instinct would be to gas that sucker up and get mowing. It's all part of our parental conditioning."

"I don't know. He sounded worried."

I had to admit, she had a point. Something in Dad's voice had almost caused me to stop and turn around. Growing up, he was always the *cool* parent, willing to look the other way whenever I did something that would've caused Mom to have an aneurysm. He didn't put on his parent voice too often, so when he did, I listened. Or at least, I used to.

The thing was, I hated to be angry at him, but I *needed* to be. If I'd stuck around and let them talk me down, the next thing you know, I'd be popping my fake alchemy pills again and resigning myself to being a slave to meds I didn't need.

This was one instance where I felt justified in sticking to my guns. "Fuck them," I finally said, my mind made up. "They've had almost twenty years to tell me whatever they needed to say, so it can't be that important."

After some more minor bickering back and forth, I managed to browbeat Riva into going with my suggestion. That I offered to pay for her breakfast probably didn't really hurt my odds either.

"OH MY GOD!" I cried out a few minutes later.

"What? What is it?"

"Look at that," I said pointing to the street sign. "We left High Moon and we're still alive."

"Don't do that while I'm driving!"

"Oh, lighten up. The road is empty."

"Yes, but I'm still seriously high-strung."

"Then it's decaf for you today."

We arrived at the diner about ten minutes later.

As we were walking in, I held the door for some folks who were on their way out, not thinking much of anything.

"Tamara Bentley?"

My eyes opened wide and I instantly thought back to my father's warning, before realizing the face looking up at me was a familiar one. Although, in this case, recognition did little to ease my mood.

Emilia Carnesworth, the assistant vice principal of High Moon High School, was one of the few people I could claim to look down upon. She was a tiny thing, barely four foot nine. But, sitting across from her in her office, a far more common occurrence than I care to admit, she always seemed so much larger. "Is that you, Mrs. C?"

"In the flesh. You're looking well."

"Thanks," I replied dumbly, not really sure what to say. Gah, this was stupid. She was just another person now. Her days of being an authority figure to me were over and done with. There was no reason to act like I was about to be handed a week's worth of detention. "Um ... you, too."

She continued to stare at me like I was a bug beneath a microscope. "So tell me, how is school going?"

Okay, small talk. I could handle that. "It's going great. In fact, I can't wait for the new season to..."

"I meant your grades, dear."

I heard Riva snicker softly from behind me.

"Mostly B's. All passing."

"Are you sure?"

"Positive," I quickly answered.

She smiled at me from behind her glasses. "I'm very happy to hear that."

Oh, boy. First werewolves, now this. What was next? "Um ... is everything good at High Moon High?"

"Oh yes, all's well. In fact, things are a wee bit sedate now that you've graduated. Almost dull, actually. I'm forced to admit I kind of miss the challenge you presented."

"That's me. Always keeping people on their toes. Um ... you have a great day." *Please get the hint!*

She smiled again then started walking, but not before repeating an oft-heard mantra from my high school days: "Keep your nose clean, Ms. Bentley. You too, Ms. Kale."

I replied with the same answer I had throughout four years of high school: "I'll do my best." As she walked away, I couldn't help but note she was one of those people for whom one's best always seemed inadequate. Weird. Even without my newfound strength, I could've snapped her in half like a wet noodle, yet somehow she always seemed like the six hundred pound gorilla in the room.

Riva stepped up to me and I offered her a pained smile. "Maybe Dad was right about leaving High Moon after all."

We walked in, before we could be accosted by any more people from my past, and were shown to a booth. While perusing the menu, I noticed Riva looking around like she was expecting the sky to fall.

"What is up with you?" I finally asked once I'd told the waitress what I wanted, adding a side order of bacon and an English muffin to my order. I was never much of a stress eater, but I figured I'd earned it this morning. "Last I checked, Carnivoreworth was up my ass a lot more than yours back in the day."

"It's not her. It's..."

"What?" I prodded. "Please tell me you're not still worrying about what my parents said. It's broad daylight out. We've been here a hundred times and not once..." I lowered my voice to a whisper. "...were we attacked by monsters. I doubt they're going to start right now in the middle of the breakfast rush."

"It's not that. Well, it is. It's ... just ... your mom."

"What about her?"

"She's a witch. They ... know things."

"What does that even mean?"

"We're talking secret societies here. A supernatural underworld right beneath our noses."

"Yes, and lessons at Hogwarts," I replied with a chuckle. "Aside from knocking you out and tying me up with a magical light show, we have no idea what she can or can't do. It's all in your mind."

"I don't know. I just have a weird feeling..."

Riva jumped as her phone picked that moment to start ringing.

"Ooh, maybe the witches have co-opted Verizon." The laugh I was about to let out was cut short, though, as I looked down at the screen and saw my mom's number on the caller ID.

"Looks like it's for you," she said.

I was tempted to mute it, but I knew her. If she thought I was ignoring her, she'd start pestering Riva, who would almost certainly cave and start relaying questions back and forth between us.

"What, Mom?" I asked brusquely as I answered it. Riva stared at me wide-eyed, but I gave her a look to let her know I thought she was being silly.

"*Why aren't you answering your phone?*"

"It's still out in the woods, probably being digested by one of Dad's friends."

There was a pause as she probably contemplated scolding me for having an attitude. "*Where are you?*"

"We're at Riva's. I told you I need some..."

"*You're lying. You're at the Morganberg diner.*"

"Huh?" I quickly checked Riva's settings to see if she'd maybe turned on the Find Friends feature. "How did you know that?"

"*I've been scrying you.*"

"What?"

"*Magical viewing through an enchanted mirror.*"

I waited for the punchline, like maybe she'd followed us, but none came. "You're serious?"

"*Of course. It's child's play, especially considering how you don't seem to believe in ever cleaning out your hairbrush.*"

I made a mental note to hop on Netflix and catch up on old episodes of *Charmed* so I could have half a clue what she was talking about. "Fine. What am I doing now?" Riva raised an eyebrow as I made a face at her.

"*Stick your tongue back in your mouth. It's not ladylike.*"

Okay, this was definitely starting to get creepy.

"*Leave now and come straight back home. Your father told you it's not safe.*"

"I'm really not in the mood to discuss this at the moment." I lifted my hand high, middle finger raised.

"*How dare you make that gesture at your mother?!*"

"The same way I dare to do this." I hung up and set the phone to mute. "If she calls again, don't answer."

"But..."

"Or I swear I will crush your phone like a paper cup."

"Can you do that?"

"Care to find out?"

Riva turned her phone off rather than risk it. That was the beauty of the modern age. In the past, you'd need to hold someone's family hostage to get leverage over them. These days, it was as simple as threatening to cut them off from Facebook.

"Think she's still watching us?" Riva asked after a few moments of silence.

I deigned not to grace that with an answer. Problem was, it was a lot harder to stop thinking about. If Mom was spying on me now, then had she done it before and how often? I mean, how much did she know about my life, especially the bits I didn't want her to know about?

Paranoia began to set in and a lifetime of misdeeds – some minor, others a bit less so – began to play out behind my eyes: Riva and I burning down her swing set because we'd been playing with firecrackers, beating up Grant Higgins in the eighth grade and pantsing him in front of the entire class, losing my virginity to Jeff Schlesinger after the junior prom.

I tried to force those thoughts from my head. For all I

knew, Mom was purposely trying to weird me out. Hell, maybe she had a friend who was here and surreptitiously Skyping our actions back to her.

"I think you freaked out some of the other patrons by flipping off the thin air," Riva said after a few minutes.

"Huh?" I looked around and, sure enough, several customers were putting money on the table and getting up to leave. "Maybe they, y'know, actually finished eating. Speaking of which, I hope they don't take forever with our food. I kind of want to drown my sorrows in some potatoes right now."

She pointed toward the exit. "I'm pretty sure that couple came in after us."

"Okay, so they dropped by for a cup of coffee. Or they decided to hook up and are heading back to his place."

She glanced again and then made a face. "Eww. I hope I'm never that desperate for sex."

"The woman or the man?"

"Both."

"Love is blind."

"Yeah, it definitely can be..." Riva's voice trailed off and her eyes opened wide.

"They bringing our food?"

Movement registered in my periphery and I turned to find two large men approaching our table. If I had to guess, they were either truckers or farmers. They had that sort of look about them.

They stopped in front of our table and glared down at us ... or, more specifically, at me. I'd love to say my father's warning wasn't blaring out in my mind, but that would be an outright lie. What the fuck was up with this day?

"Can we help you fellows?" I asked in what I hoped sounded like an unconcerned voice. I was trying really hard to think of a reason for these guys to be here. Maybe they were lost. Maybe they were selling something. Heck, maybe they were random serial killers and it was just a coincidence they'd picked us.

Okay, that last one didn't really make me feel better.

The taller of the two was easily six-three. A day's worth of stubble sat on his broad face. He had on a red t-shirt, and was wearing a Phillies cap. His attire, however, was far less weird than the fact that he leaned over and ... started sniffing the air around me.

The fuck?

Suddenly, that serial killer theory didn't sound so farfetched.

He stood back up, looked to his buddy, and nodded once. The friend, wearing a stained wife beater and grimy, unadorned cap, turned back toward the counter – where our waitress stood with the cook – and gave them both a nod.

"Um, that's Dove ladies deodorant," I said, trying to remain calm. "Never leave home without it."

"Show us your real face, freak," Phillies Cap said, his breath reeking of bacon, coffee, and gingivitis.

"Bent?" Riva asked timidly.

"Stay calm," I told her, my eyes never leaving the two hicks. "I have a suspicious feeling they're not here for you."

"You gonna show us or not?" Wife Beater asked. "We know you're impersonating that Bentley girl, so there ain't no talking your way out of this. Your kind aren't welcome here."

They knew my name? Or sorta, anyway. And what was with that accusation? "You guys might want to cut back on the whiskey before ten a.m."

I glanced past them and saw the waitress locking the front door. That couldn't be a good sign. As for the cook, he was now approaching us, too, meat cleaver in hand. It was definitely turning into one of those days.

Fear began to well up inside of me, a reasonable

response for any young, moderately attractive woman being accosted by two Neanderthals. That the diner staff seemed to be joining in, too, was making this feel like something out of a bad movie. It was as if Riva and I had come in for breakfast and accidentally walked in on a meeting of the Stepford Rednecks.

I swallowed the fear back down, as much as possible anyway. It was going to take some time to get used to the fact that I could punch out a werewolf, much less the Buford brothers here.

That thought lingered in the back of my head. What had happened to me was real, or so I'd hoped. Sadly, it wasn't quite so easy to shake the feeling that I was about to have my ass handed to me. In the light of day, things like monsters and super strength sounded downright silly, almost unbelievable, even to someone who'd experienced them.

"Let my friend go." The words left my mouth before I was even sure I wanted to admit to myself that something was going to happen.

Wife Beater looked down at Riva, as if just noticing she was there. He took a sniff, then turned to his friend and gave a single shake of his head.

"We'll figure out what to do with her later," Phillies Cap replied. "For now, let's deal with this one."

"Listen, fellas," I said, making one last desperate plea. "I don't know who you are but..."

Sadly for us, he didn't need words to answer me.

He simply smiled, revealing teeth that were far too long and sharp to be human.

12

Rough hands reached out to grab hold of me, changing into ragged claws in the time it took Phillies Cap to close the distance between us.

For a moment, I was too stunned to react, but then he blinked and the dull brown of his eyes was replaced with bloodshot yellow – the same eyes I'd seen staring back at me from multiple hairy heads the night before.

No flipping way!

How? The full moon was last night. It was over, it wouldn't happen again for...

The questions would have to wait. Whether or not I believed what I was seeing, my reality was about to become seriously hairy.

The man's ... err, wolf's claws tore painfully through my shirt and started to drag me from my seat. I instinctively grabbed hold of the table to stop myself from being pulled out and felt its moorings groan in protest.

That gave me an idea.

"Lean back," I said to Riva.

There wasn't time to say more. I just had to hope she trusted me. I gave a yank, adding my own strength to my attacker's, and the table tore free from the wall. I flipped it up and slammed it into the waiting faces of both our would-be assailants, sending them staggering back.

Impossible as it had seemed only moments ago, apparently whatever I had in me functioned just fine in the light of day, too – a handy thing to know.

Pity that the same could also be said about our *gracious hosts*.

I turned to find the waitress and cook both *changing*. And I don't mean their clothes.

Both of them were growing taller, more muscular, and a lot furrier.

"I told you we should have gone to Gib's!" Riva screeched, huddled in her seat.

"Fair enough. Next time, you can choose where we eat. Stay behind me!"

Both Phillies Cap and Wife Beater recovered quickly and likewise continued to change. Hands became claws, ears became longer and pointier, and clothes ripped to shreds, affording me a far better view of them than I really wanted.

While I'd seen my fair share of horror movies, I didn't really consider myself a connoisseur. Still, one of the more obvious mistakes in them is that people always stand around gaping when they should be moving. It's like that old Michael Jackson video *Thriller*. The girl stands there for like five minutes as he turns into a monster, when she could have been halfway to the next county.

It was a lesson I took to heart.

The two truck stop werewolves were still busy snarling, snapping, and growing extra hair when I charged. I plowed into Phillies Cap, the larger of the two, shoulder-first. I half expected to rebound off the much bigger man – my mind still insisting we were playing by the normal rules. Instead, I took him off his feet, carried him across the room, and plowed into the mirrored wall of the diner hard enough to make the building shudder.

Glass shattered all around us and he let out a great big belch of air. Not satisfied that he was properly dissuaded, I drove a fist into his gut, the oddly undulating flesh giving way as I pushed the contents of his stomach up against his spine.

I backed up a step and he fell to his knees retching, just in time for me to sense movement from behind.

Wife Beater had double-timed his change, seeing that I wasn't going to stand there and scream like a good victim. *Eww,* a werewolf with a beer belly – not a good look.

He raced forward and I half turned so that my profile was facing him. At the last moment, I bent low, letting his momentum carry him into me.

Oof! Damn, these things were strong.

I lifted him up in a fireman's carry, meaning to dump his ass on the floor and put him in the danger position. But I underestimated my own strength and sent him flying instead. Oops.

"Um, I meant to do that." Oh yeah, some practice was definitely in my future ... if I lived through this.

Fortunately, if there was only one upside to fighting monsters, as opposed to wrestling, there was no such thing as being called for an illegal move. So I, in a rare display of unsportsmanlike conduct, hurried across the room before Wife Beater could get up and planted my foot into his face with a satisfying crunch.

Two down – for now anyway. That left two more asses to kick.

"Bent! Look out!"

Or not.

Yeah, that's what I'd been afraid of. Seeing that I was no pushover, it was only a matter of time before the other side threw the Marquess of Queensberry Rules out the window and rushed me all at once.

The others weren't stupid either, not like their hick cousins. There was no grandstanding, no attempt to intimidate me. They simply slammed into me as I turned their way, one high and one low.

It was like being hit by a fur-covered truck.

The wind was driven out of my lungs and I landed atop of the one I'd just given the boot to, the meat in a werewolf sandwich. I didn't consider myself a prude, but this was one kink I really didn't see myself getting into. A little hair on a man's chest was one thing, but even I had my limits.

Mind you, that was the least of my problems right then.

Fire raced up my leg as one of the wolves, the waitress I think, bit into my thigh, her teeth shredding my jeans and probably not doing wonders to the flesh beneath.

Before I could cry out, the one atop me – the cook most likely – slashed my face. There came a spray of blood, almost certainly my own, and my cheek instantly felt like it was on fire.

See if I leave you assholes a tip now.

I had no way of knowing how bad the damage was. For all I knew, half my face could have been gone. Unfortunately, stopping to check would only result in them taking the rest of it off. Vanity be damned. As much as I didn't fancy looking like I'd French-kissed a weed whacker, I much preferred staying alive.

Angry as I'd been this morning, I liked my life and wasn't quite ready to give up on it yet.

The wolf atop me reared back as the other continued to savage my legs. I tried to push myself up using what leverage I could, so as to dislodge him and...

Fuck!

Muscular arms encircled me from below. Wife Beater wasn't quite as out of the fight as I'd hoped.

This was bad. I was outnumbered and pinned, with little room to maneuver. Wrestling had taught me a lot, but not how to win a three-on-one handicap match. That shit was only for the pay-per-view events. Far as I could tell, my odds were getting worse by the moment, especially grappled as I was.

From somewhere outside my line of sight – which currently consisted of angry werewolves and the ceiling – Riva screamed my name. Unfortunately, unless she was secretly the queen of the harpies, there was little she could do to help.

Problem was, I had no way of knowing what these bastards would do to her once they'd finished me off.

"Run!" I shouted, hoping that this time she heeded my warning.

Above me, the cook-wolf snarled and raised both its fists into the air, no doubt preparing to ruin my day once and for all.

I braced for it as well as I could.

Bright light filled the room just as the beast's arms began to descend – a strange flash of multihued luminescence that left spots before my eyes.

I apparently wasn't the only one caught by surprise, as the wolf's attention turned toward the other end of the room. It let out a confused chuff that was almost doglike in its uncertainty.

And then it was silenced as something bright red lanced through its midsection, punching a fist-sized hole through its chest.

What the hell?!

The wolf at my legs looked up in surprise and its face shrunk in on itself – its muzzle retracting until it was at some halfway point between werewolf and human. "*You're not welcome here.*"

At my current angle, I couldn't see who or what she was speaking to, but I really didn't care. Shifting her position freed my good leg enough for me to bring a knee up into her face, sending her tumbling away.

That left Wife Beater, who was busy trying to scramble his way out from beneath me. I gave him an elbow to the throat for his trouble, then rolled off and prepared to engage the nearest...

"Mrs. Bentley?"

I looked up at the sound of Riva's voice and froze. "Mom?!"

At least I thought it was her. The face was the same, but the rest...

Her hair fluttered as if there was a heavy breeze – despite us being indoors – her normal auburn color looking like it was sheened in bronze. As for the rest, it looked like she was wearing a dress made of pure flame.

It was a good look for her – scary as fuck, but highly effective.

As I stood there gaping, the first wolf, Phillies Cap, recovered and charged my mother from the side ... or at least it tried to.

She lifted her hand and the next thing I knew, its head and half its chest were gone, a red-hot mess of cauterized flesh from its midsection up the only indication of what had happened.

It took one more step then fell to the ground, so dead that they'd probably have to bury it twice.

Daaamn!

A small voice in my head reminded me this was the same woman I'd flipped off and hung up on just minutes earlier. If this was indeed my mother, then I really had to make it a point to not do that again.

"Both of you, come here now," Mom ordered, sounding like she was both near and far. There was an odd chiming echo to her voice, as if someone was breaking glass in the distance. Either way, color me pretty darned impressed.

While I limped over, she continued to hand out brutal judgment. I glanced back just in time to see her utterly vaporize Wife Beater, leaving nothing but a faint outline of ashes where he'd been.

That left only the waitress. She held up her hands and backed away – fully resuming her human guise – until she was huddled against the far wall, naked and obviously terrified. "Please. I won't tell anyone."

"I know you won't," Mom replied, pointing a hand toward her, palm out. She closed it into a fist while muttering, "*A 'briseadh làmhan.*"

The result was swift and so extraordinarily brutal even I wanted to look away. It was as if someone had stuffed the waitress into a transparent car crusher, or maybe a black hole. She had time for one whimper and then her body folded in on itself – a cacophony of breaking bones and ruptured organs, until there was nothing left except a quivering pile of bloody meat on the floor.

Holy fuck!

All the while, Riva and I stood there watching as my mother committed what could only be called wholesale slaughter.

At last, when it was over and silence again reigned in the small diner, Mom blinked several times, staggered, and had to grab a nearby booth to keep from falling over. She began to cough as if catching her breath, and the glow around her faded away to nothing. Her hair dropped limp and the gown of flames snuffed out, revealing a simple summer dress.

Within seconds, she was just my mother again.

I exchanged a wide-eyed glance with Riva. The whole thing had been beyond surreal, and this coming from someone who'd spent the last few minutes trading punches with monsters. So I could only imagine how strange it was to my friend.

After a few minutes, Mom caught her breath. She stood up, straightened her dress, and said, "Let's go, both of you. There's no time to dawdle."

All thoughts of arguing instantly fled my mind at the sight of what she'd just done. Yeah, throwing shade at a one-woman wrecking crew did not sound smart. It made me wonder how I, at three years old, could have even remotely threatened, much less hurt, someone like her. Hell, forget being a toddler, it seemed impossible for me even as an adult.

So, for one of the few times in my adult life, I zipped it and stepped in line like a good little girl. Riva, too.

"Both of you, put one hand each on my shoulder. Don't let go."

We did as told without protest.

Mom lowered her head and let out a long breath, far longer than her lung capacity should have allowed. Her body began to glow again in an odd shimmering fairy light, for lack of a better phrase. Before my very eyes she began to fade, becoming translucent. I still felt her shoulder beneath my hand, though. Weird, but obviously part of the magic.

I looked over and Riva, too, had taken on that same ethereal quality. I wasn't sure what was going to happen or where we were going to end up, but I had a feeling it was going to be interesting at the very least.

Or utterly anticlimactic.

The glow faded from Mom as she and Riva simultaneously solidified. However, nothing had changed. We were still standing in a diner surrounded by a bunch of massacred werewolves.

"Um, so are we invisible or something?"

Mom glanced at me and narrowed her eyes.

"The astral plane?" I offered.

She turned to Riva. "Is your car outside?"

"Y-yes, Mrs. Bentley," my friend replied as if this were the Army and a general had just told her to drop and give him twenty.

"Good. Hand me the keys. I'm driving."

13

I made to hop in the shotgun seat, but then remembered Riva wasn't driving.

Also, the glare Mom gave me kinda hinted that I might be more *comfortable* riding in the back.

"I should have known that would happen." She put the car in drive and peeled out onto the road, not bothering to stop and check to see if we were about to be creamed by any passing eighteen-wheelers.

"Known what?" I ventured.

"I'm not particularly happy with you right now, young lady," she said rather than answer me.

"I kind of figured," I replied, remembering that I wasn't too happy with her either. Yeah, she had just annihilated a group of fairy tale monsters, something I could attest to by the freaked-out stare Riva was still giving her. At the same time, she'd needlessly drugged me for, like, nine-tenths of my life. "Join the club."

"You always did have a smart mouth. You get it from your father."

"Really? What else did I get? A tail and a tendency to scoot my butt over the kitchen floor maybe?" I meant what I said, but at the same time, it was really hard to push away years of parental love on a whim. "Sorry. That was mean," I added almost before I realized the words were out of my mouth. *Gah!* I so wanted to slap myself.

"The important thing is you're both safe."

"About that. What happened back there? How did you get in? The door was locked. And what was with you glowing? Was that just for show? And when did you learn Latin?"

"This is really not the time, Tamara."

"Really? Because I think it's a fine time. Don't you, Riva?"

She held up her hands and backed up against the passenger side door. "I'm staying out of this one."

"Smart girl," Mom replied. "Good to see at least one of you has some sense."

"You do realize I can simply kick this door right off its hinges and jump out, right?"

Riva turned toward me, her eyes wide.

"Oh relax. I know it's your car. I'm just trying to make a point."

"Fine." Mom locked eyes with me in the rearview mirror, but I refused to drop my gaze. "For starters, that wasn't Latin. It's Gaelic."

"Gaelic? But I thought wizards were supposed to speak..."

"You've been reading too much bad fiction, I see."

I couldn't help but notice we were accelerating, going at least fifteen miles over the speed limit and still increasing. Mom seemed awfully eager to get us back to High Moon, although I kind of understood. It was the first time I'd ever ordered a breakfast special that came with a side of murderous wolf men.

Regardless, she seemed to be in control, speedy or not,

so I persisted. "Works for me. Gaelic it is. Top o' the morning to ye."

"Don't be a snot."

"Okay, I've been trying to be quiet," Riva suddenly said, "but am I the only one who noticed that you..." She paused as if trying to find the right words, perhaps afraid she was going to set one of us off. "...kind of murdered those people back there?"

Tact never really was one of Riva's virtues.

"And I'm sure you noticed that those creatures weren't exactly playing catch with you two," Mom replied in an even tone as if this was a normal occurrence for her. "But I guess that's little more than mincing words. The truth of the matter is, there wasn't much choice. It had to be done."

"But why?"

"You really have no idea what's going on here, do you?"

I raised my hand from the back seat. "Make that two of us."

Mom gritted her teeth and, for a moment, I was sure she was going to keep driving and ignore us. However, we passed a sign informing us we'd entered the High Moon city limits and her demeanor visibly relaxed. She applied the brakes and brought us down to a speed that wasn't likely to get us pulled over.

"Lycanthropes and the Draíodóir. We've been enemies for centuries."

I blinked a few times. "Lycanthropes I've heard of. But the ... Dreidelor? Did you and Dad convert to Judaism and not tell me?"

Mom let out a sigh and pronounced it again. "Witches, wizards, magic users if you wish to be banal about it. My people."

"So you're at war with each other?"

"Not quite. More of a cold war. Things heat up every now and then, but we've managed to keep it from spilling over into full-blown bloodshed."

"Like blasting the shit out of four werewolves in broad daylight?"

"That was an ... *unfortunate* situation, brought upon by your stubborn refusal to heed your father's warning."

From the tone of Mom's voice, she didn't sound like she'd be losing much sleep over what she'd done, which kinda freaked me out more than her magic. I mean, this was the same woman who'd once scolded me for running outside with a fly swatter to kill a few bees buzzing around our deck, telling me they had as much right to be there as I did. More than once, she'd caught an errant lizard or mouse that had gotten into our house only to release it unharmed outside.

She wasn't quite what I'd call a hemp-soaked hippie, but I'd always gotten a sense that she respected nature. Apparently that respect had its boundaries, though, ones which were currently soaked in werewolf blood.

What the hell had my life turned into?

"It'll be fine," she continued, as if that made it better. "Your father will take care of that mess."

"Take care of it? Those people are dead! And for that matter, why did it even happen? I've eaten there before, been waited on by that same woman. She's never tried to kill me, even when I was a little short on the tip."

"That's because you never smelled like you do now."

Riva took a sniff of the air. "I don't smell anything." She turned to me. "It's not like you smell like wet dog. I would've told you."

"Thanks."

"Of course *you* don't smell it," Mom replied as if we were stupid five-year-olds again. "Do you know how sensitive a dog's nose is? Lycanthropes possess similar senses.

Even in their human forms, their sense of smell is on the order of ten times that of a normal person's."

"Would explain why Dad doesn't go down to Chris's room much," I quipped before turning serious again. "I still don't get it. Those things attacked me. They changed and it's not even a full moon out. And how are you and Dad married if you're at war? Not to mention..."

"Enough, Tamara."

"No. Not enough. I want answers."

Mom became quiet and I could tell from the look of her face in the rearview mirror she wanted to say something snippy back at me, like I was a little kid who'd just mouthed off, but after a few more seconds she said, "Very well. I can't promise you'll like what you hear, but the cat's out of the bag, so to speak. But it must wait until we get home, and you have to promise me no more storming out in a snit."

I held my tongue. It was a promise I couldn't make, at least not until I heard what other bombshells they had to drop.

Much to Riva's displeasure, Mom insisted on dropping her off at home.

Can't necessarily say I was happy with the decision either. "She already knows."

"I'm well aware of that," Mom replied. "Believe me." She turned to my friend. "This isn't personal, dear, but it's a family matter. Afterward, if Tamara wants to tell you..." She glanced back at me as she said this. "That's entirely up to her."

"But what if..."

"You'll be safe, trust me on this. You are not a player in this grand chess match. Neither of our factions has any quarrel with you, nor is there a need for them to know you are aware of their existence."

Ignoring our arguments to the contrary, she pulled out her phone and called Dad. He'd gone to retrieve the stuff we'd left in the woods, to save us from having to go back to that hellish place ... and apparently also to erase any traces that we'd been there. He agreed to pick us up on the way home.

Once she hung up, we both protested some more, but Mom held fast. It basically came down to this: if I wanted answers, it was going to be between me, her, and Dad. If not, then tough noogies.

Much as I didn't want to be separated from the one person I felt was truly in my corner, I was forced to agree.

Riva finally did, too ... or she did after we agreed to walk through her house first and make sure there was nothing lurking about. I could tell Mom was humoring her, but I felt better doing so. There were few clichés as annoying as the old "You'll be safe here" routine. Pretty sure every thriller ever made has used that one to bump off, kidnap, or otherwise terrorize a secondary character.

In this case, it was fortunately all for naught. Riva's place was clean, and I do mean *clean*. Her parents definitely had some OCD issues when it came to clutter.

As we were leaving, she pulled me aside. "If anything happens, call me."

"Same," I replied before running out to where Dad was waiting for us in his van.

Just as I was about to get in, it hit me. Holy shit! My mother was a witch, my dad a werewolf, and we owned a fucking minivan. Tell me that's not just a bit strange.

Dad greeted us like this was a normal pick-up, but then he looked at me and his eyes opened wide. "Are you okay, sweetie?"

It was only then that I remembered I'd been mauled.

In the excitement of our escape and subsequent bickering in the car, I'd almost managed to forget about it. Shit! I was seriously going to owe Riva a full detailing for her car when this was over.

"It looks worse than it is," Mom replied.

I was about to retort with something less than polite when I saw my reflection in the van's window. There was a lot of blood on my face, but it was dried by now. As for the scratches, they had become long, thin lines that had completely scabbed over. I then checked my leg – pants torn and soaked in dried blood, but the teeth marks themselves looked to be several days old.

I let this sink in as I climbed into the van and we drove home.

Once back at our house, I took some time to clean myself up, again noting that my injuries appeared to be days old instead of an hour or so. My face didn't even hurt. With any luck, there wouldn't be much scarring once the scabs fell off, which would be nice because I sure as hell wasn't going to be making time with Gary if I looked like the loser in a fight with a grizzly bear.

It wasn't until we were situated back in the living room that I noticed things weren't quite as I'd left them. "Everything is fixed."

"Of course it is," Mom replied.

"You guys had time to buy a new coffee table?"

She cocked an eyebrow at me.

"Magic?"

"Domestic trolls." She noticed my wide-eyed stare and grinned. "They normally come to tidy up at night when everyone is asleep, but I asked them to pay a special visit. Don't worry. Your brother slept right through it."

"Trolls?"

"Oh, relax. They're not like their larger bridge-dwelling cousins. They're small, but they can really put their backs into it."

"Great. So we have garden gnomes cleaning the place. If I'd known that, I'd have been far less careful where I dropped my laundry."

"Don't call them that," Mom chided. "They don't like that name."

"Of course not." I stopped short of asking her whether they were actually one and the same with the creepy little stone freaks in the garden out front. The truth was, I really didn't want to know. "Speaking of trolls, where's Chris? I thought we were going to do this as a family."

Dad shrugged uncomfortably. "*Mostly* as a family. I sent him to a friend's house for the afternoon. He doesn't know about this and I don't think there's a reason for him to ... yet anyway." His pause wasn't lost on me, but I decided to let it slide for now.

I wasn't in the mood to argue. Besides, he was probably right. "So how are we going to do this?" I asked, plopping down in the loveseat.

My dad made as if to sit next to me but then, no doubt realizing things were still a wee bit tense, thought better of it and sat on the couch instead. Mom joined him. There we were, three freaks sitting around the living room as if we were about to do nothing more extraordinary than watch TV.

Dad leaned forward and placed his elbows on his knees. I couldn't help but notice the cuts and bruises on his face were noticeably less prominent than they had been. I unconsciously reached up to touch my own cheek.

"I heal fast," he said, as if sensing my thoughts. "By dinner time, this will all be gone. Judging by what your mother told me, I'm going to guess that's something else you got from my side."

It was the first thing they'd said to me all day that I didn't want to argue against. I simply nodded, grateful that I wouldn't be needing a bag over my head when I went out.

"We talked it over and came to the conclusion that we owe you the truth." He held up a hand before I could say anything. "And yes, it's long overdue. Ask anything you want and we'll answer it." His eyes met mine, and I saw in them a glimmer of sorrow. "But I want you to know first how sorry we both are. Everything we've done, it's been to keep you safe. The pills, living here, all of it. I hope you can believe that and forgive us one day."

Mom, for her part, looked a bit less broken up, but then she'd always been the more pragmatic of the two. While Dad had been the type to give hugs and kisses whenever I fell down and scraped my knee, she was more likely to simply say, "I think you'll live."

I decided to take a page from her book and keep my cool. This morning I'd acted out of emotion, a sense of betrayal, and it had landed me in a diner full of werewolves. Not sure there was any real causality there, but it was best to not tempt fate. Besides, it had already been a long day and I really wasn't feeling the need to get my dander up again.

"Okay," I said. "Let's start with the obvious stuff. You're a Drei ... witch. And, Dad, you're a Lycanthrope, right?"

He nodded.

"So what does that make me?"

"Well..." He let the word draw out to an uncomfortable length.

"You're a hybrid," Mom said matter-of-factly. "A mix of the two races."

"Great. So I'm a mutt."

"Not quite the term I'd use," Dad replied.

I leaned back and sighed. "I don't even know what that tells me. You just said I'm a hybrid, like I'm not human or something."

"Of course you're human, dear," Mom said in that tone parents use to let their kids know they think they're special. "At least mostly."

"Mostly?"

She nodded and sat back. "Our legends say that the Draíodóir were once devout worshippers of the great court of the fae. In return for our devotion, Queen Brigid touched us and bestowed upon my ancestors a minute portion of her power, power which has been passed down from generation to generation. Those legends also say that whereas we were born of the Spring, the Lycanthropes came from the court of Winter as a check against the spread of our divine influence."

"If you believe that sort of thing," Dad interrupted, "but my grandfather told it a bit different. According to him, the first lycanthropes came about because of Valdemar. He's the master of the Wild Hunt. In Germanic lore, anyway."

"The Wild Hunt?" I asked.

"Yes. Back in the olden days it was kind of a big deal. So the story goes, Valdemar got bored with the usual game he and his hounds hunted: boars, stag, bears, that kind of stuff. None of them presented him with any challenge. He wanted prey that were strong, but also smart, creatures worthy of a god of the hunt." Dad leaned forward in his seat. "So Valdemar reached into the souls of the fiercest creatures and pulled out their essence, which he then placed into the hearts of warriors who had impressed him on the battlefield. They became the first shape shifters. And of them all, the wolves proved to be his favorites."

"Are there other kinds?"

"Not as many as there once were. But yes. Werewolves are the dominant shifters on this continent, but there's some small pockets of bear-kind in the northwest. Tiger shifters are more prominent in Asia, as well as..."

"Werebears," I repeated. "Guess that novel I downloaded last week wasn't total crap after all."

Mom reached over and patted Dad on the knee. "It's a ... cute story, dear."

"And yours is better?" he countered.

"At least the creation tale of the Draíodóir takes into account Lycanthropes. Your story pretends that we just met randomly out in the fields one day."

Mom and Dad continued to argue about whose gods were real and whose were figments of their imagination for a few more minutes until I held up a hand. "This is all fascinating and, if I take an ancient mythology elective back at school, I'm sure I'll want to hear all about it. What I'm more interested in, however, is the here and now ... mostly, why four werewolves tried to gut me over breakfast."

At this, both of my parents stopped their quibbling. They looked at each other for a moment, and I sensed that Mom was giving Dad the go-ahead to tell me something.

"Those werewolves last night," he said. "You know some of them."

"Yeah, you mentioned Melissa." I stopped short, not really wanting to think of how she was in a hospital bed because of me. How was I supposed to know?

"She's not the only one."

"Okay, so is this a revenge thing?"

Dad shook his head. "Not quite. After things calmed down, I explained to the pack that I thought you were ... a doppelganger."

"Hold on. You told them I wasn't me. I was just someone who looked like me?"

"Not someone," he explained. "Doppelgangers are rare. They're shape shifters, too, but not like the rest of us. They're demonic in nature – powerful, evil, and capable of taking on the form of pretty much any human they care to. Their true selves are, well, somewhat less pleasant."

I tried to make sense of this, but couldn't. "Okay, so you told them I was a demon instead?"

"In a nutshell."

"And that's why they tried to kill me?"

"Yeah. We normally attack them on sight. You have to understand, I panicked a bit. I also didn't expect you to leave High Moon this morning."

I stood up. "Hold on. One thing at a time. Why the hell did you tell them I was a demon?"

He and my mother turned to each other for several seconds. Finally, it was Mom who answered me.

"It's because you're not supposed to exist."

14

"Not supposed to exist?"

"Forbidden, actually."

"Technically, not even possible," Dad added.

I was hoping this little Q&A session would shed some light onto the weirdness of the day. It had, but not in a way that I was hoping for. Instead, it was like I had fallen into a rabbit hole, only to discover it was a bottomless mineshaft. And I was still falling.

Regardless, there would be plenty of time to feel sorry for myself later. For now, my parents had promised me answers, and by God, I was going to get those answers. I swallowed the bitter pill of my dad telling his puppy pals that I was a demon rather than his daughter. "Explain, because so far, none of this is making any fucking sense."

"Language," Mom warned.

That did it. "You know, I'm thinking right now you have a choice: bad language or I start punching holes in walls. I'll let you decide which you'd prefer."

"Calm down, both of you," Dad ordered. He turned to me. "I can understand why you're upset, but at the time, it was the best I had to go on. Heck, it was the *only* thing I had to go on. You see, doppelgangers can emulate a person's scent as well as their appearance, but only to a degree. It was the most believable thing I could come up with, the only thing keeping the entire pack from kicking down our door."

"Because I'm forbidden?"

"Precisely."

"Even though Melissa, and I'm assuming other were-wolves, know damn well I'm your daughter?"

"It's..." Dad trailed off. The look in his eyes told me that whatever he had to say was yet another bombshell. The way this day was going, I was beginning to feel more like a World War II bunker than a person.

"What?"

Mom glanced sidelong at my father then turned to me. "It's because they think you're adopted."

"Why would they think I was adopted?"

"Because that's what we told them."

What?! All at once I was glad Chris wasn't home. He'd have a field day with this one. Obviously he knew he was adopted. My parents had never tried to hide that fact. But I knew the little snot. This would have set him to cackling in that stupid way he had that made me want to punch his punk-ass lights out. "So ... am I?"

"Of course not," Mom replied, "but we had to say you were."

After I was silent for several moments, trying to comprehend the bizarre maze of words I was somehow expected to navigate, Dad finally found his tongue again.

"It's like this, Tam Tam. Lycanthropes and mages ... don't really get along. In fact, you could kind of say that we're sworn enemies."

"So I've heard. I'm assuming that's why your side of the family doesn't like Mom."

"Amongst other reasons."

She narrowed her eyes at him, and he quickly continued. "You have to understand, our two races have a deep-seated dislike of each other that goes back centuries, maybe longer. And with a rivalry that old, there's a bit of arrogance on both sides."

"Speak for yourself," Mom said.

"Oh really?" he asked with a wry smile. "Is that a fact, oh Queen of the Monarchs?"

"Must we do this now, Curtis?"

"Hold on," I said. "Queen of the Monarchs?"

"That's your mother's official title within her coven."

"The queen of kings? How does that even make sense?"

Mom sighed. "Monarchs as in butterflies. It's a hereditary title meant to signify my standing as a high priestess of our order, a supreme protector of nature and all of its secrets."

I blinked back at her for a moment or two. "That's ... a really stupid title."

Dad let out a chuckle. "I've been telling her the same thing for twenty years."

"Wait. You said it was hereditary. Does that make me the Swallowtail Princess?"

That set my dad to laughing, which really wasn't my intent. I mean, I was still mad at him for telling his friends that I was an adopted demon. Nevertheless, I allowed myself a small grin. It helped cut the tension by a smidgeon or two.

Mom, for her part, didn't seem overly amused. Her scowl served to remind me that I was letting myself get sidetracked from what sounded like a pretty big revelation.

"All right, enough of that. If you two are the great enemies you're telling me you are, then how did ... *this* happen?" I indicated the two of them. "Did you guys find out this stuff after you met at college?"

My parents shared a glance before turning back toward me.

"About that," Dad said. "That story of how we met is kind of ... not true."

"What?" They'd been pummeling Chris and me with that sickeningly sweet story for years, ever since I could remember. I could practically recite every vomit-soaked moment. It was a mixer at my Mom's sorority. Dad wasn't going to go, but one of his friends was dating a member and pretty much dragged him there. She saw him standing off in a corner, thought he looked cute in a shy sort of way, and they hit it off from there. I mean, I always assumed that when they said mixer they meant kegger, but from the look on my parents' faces, I got the impression the difference between that and the truth was a wee bit more than I expected.

"Yeah. We met under slightly different circumstances."

"What your father means is that he was trying to kill me."

"I was trying to scare you off. You were trespassing on our land. As alpha in training, it was my job to protect our territory."

"I was conducting a complex ritual, and that glade happened to be perfect for it. Forgive me for saying so, but I got the sense that its significance was lost upon you ... except maybe for marking the trees."

"Wait just a second. You were trying to kill each other?" I stared at both of them, but particularly at my father. Mom ... well, I could sort of see it, but the thought of Dad trying to purposely hurt anything was blowing my mind.

"Yes," Mom replied. "Your father interrupted me in the middle of a ceremony."

"You mean this father? The guy right here?"

"Of course."

Dad apparently took the hint from my look of disbelief. "Back then, I was ... a different person."

Mom nodded. "This all happened before I domesticated him."

"In your dreams," he said with a laugh.

"Anyway, I warned him off. He wouldn't leave. So I decided to teach him a lesson."

"Teach me a lesson? You were the one who was losing."

"Whatever helps you sleep at night, dear." Mom turned to me again. "Your father put up a good fight, dodging and weaving past my constructs, but it was only a matter of time."

"I'm not following. How did you get from trying to kill each other to *this*?"

Dad looked away, a blush rising on his cheeks. Mom, however, kept talking as if none of this was a big deal. "I mistimed a spell as your father was charging my position. I missed, he plowed into me, and we both landed on the ground. We started rolling around. Both of us had our dander up from the battle and..."

"And?"

"And you were born nine months later."

I sat there in stunned silence for several seconds, contemplating what had been said. I'd grown up hearing a sweet, if somewhat mundane, tale of how they'd met, only to learn the truth was more like some sick paranormal sex fantasy. "That's ... horrible."

"Quite far from it, actually," Mom said, throwing a wink Dad's way.

"Gross! I so didn't need to know that."

"Don't pretend to be such a prude, Tamara," she chided. "You and I both know you're not so innocent, or need I remind you of Kevin last summer. Or that boy Jeff from..."

"How do you know about them?"

"Oh please." She waved her hand dismissively. "Did you really think today was the first time I've ever scryed you?"

Dad leaned forward. "Hold on. Kevin? How come I didn't know about..."

Mom patted his arm. "Ignorance is bliss, dear."

I ran my hands through my hair, totally skeeved out. It was like discovering a hidden camera in my bedroom, except one that could – and probably had – spy on me anywhere.

While I sat there, debating the best way to express my distress at all of this, the doorbell rang. At that point I'd have welcomed even the pushiest of Jehovah's Witnesses, so I quickly stood up. "I'll get it."

I stepped into the foyer and pulled open the door before they could say anything else. I'd been expecting to see my brother, or maybe the mailman, but instead a different face greeted me, one no less familiar.

"Oh, hey, Uncle Craig," I said, glad for the distraction.

It was the space of a split second for me to make two connections. One, he was my uncle on my father's side and, two, while I'd seen him often growing up, it had always been at his place. I couldn't recall him ever showing up at our home.

In that one small moment, barely a heartbeat of time, I saw his nose twitch and then I was sent flying back as he tackled me head-on, his teeth bared in a snarl.

15

Oh yeah, he must be a werewolf, too.

The fact that I wasn't screaming in terror told me that I was rapidly acclimating to the fact that my life had become akin to an episode of *The Munsters*. I couldn't pretend to be happy with that, but for the moment, I had more pressing concerns.

Uncle Craig had never been an overly warm fellow. He wasn't the type to shower me with hugs and kisses when I was a kid – something I always attributed to his man's man persona – but he'd never been mean to me. And he'd certainly never wrapped his hands around my throat like he was doing now in our foyer.

Behind him, I saw he'd come with two companions: Dad's cousin Mitch and someone else, a younger man I didn't immediately recognize – some pudgy guy covered in, eww, warts. They stepped through the door and closed it behind them. I guess it wouldn't do for the neighbors to watch as they murdered me.

My air was cut off as I vaguely registered that Uncle Craig's arms were a lot furrier than I remembered. I realized, in a detached sort of way, that this was probably something I should seek to remedy lest my body begin to balk at the lack of oxygen flowing into it.

"Jesus, Craig! Get off of her!"

My uncle turned his head toward the family room. "Curtis? Thank goodness you're all right." After a beat, he added, "You too, Lissa."

I saw my dad step in, but Mitch and Wart Boy cut him off.

"Stop it!"

"Has your nose gone soft?" Craig asked, his voice coming out more like a growl. "She's the doppelganger."

I used the distraction to slide my hands up between Craig's and pry him off of me – no small feat. Damn, he was stronger than I was expecting, which wasn't saying much since I hadn't expected him to strangle me in the first place.

Before he could compensate and try squeezing my head off again, I let fly with a punch to his solar plexus. The resulting *whoosh* of air from his lungs gave me just the distraction I needed to refill mine. I shifted beneath him, preparing to throw him off before the rest of our uninvited company could join the party, but I was a moment too slow.

"*Mhéara ar tintreach!*"

All at once, the foyer lit up as sparks of electricity began to dance about, striking everything in reach. Several hit our uninvited guests, knocking them down and leaving them twitching.

I tried sitting up just as three of the miniature lightning bolts slammed into my chest. I expected to be thrown back, but instead felt nothing more painful than a minor static shock.

"That is enough!" Mom's voice rang out, this time in English. "You are in my home, violating neutral territory, I might add. Talk fast before I incinerate the whole lot of you!"

"I'm fine, by the way," I croaked, pulling myself to my feet.

Dad grabbed me and dragged me into the living room away from the others. "Are you okay, sweetie?"

"Peachy."

"Get away from that thing, Curtis," Craig snapped, shaking off the effects of whatever ... spell, I guess, Mom had just hit him with.

"It's ... not what you think," Dad replied, shuffling me behind him as if we were watching a movie and a sex scene had just come on.

"I said to get away from her," my uncle repeated, stepping forward. "Or do you need a repeat of last night's lesson?"

In a flash, Mom was in front of him. Though he loomed over her, she possessed the stance of one who wasn't going to be so easily dismissed. "I will warn you once, and only once, that you are in grave danger of violating our treaty. The very fact that you stepped foot into High Moon..."

My uncle held out a hand behind him to stay his two companions, but at the same time didn't appear ready to back down either. "Oh, really? I got word that four of my pack were killed earlier today at the Morganberg Diner. My people said the place reeked of gald. Care to explain?"

"Gald?" I asked.

"Magic," Dad replied quietly.

"I wouldn't know anything about that," Mom explained smoothly, the lie flowing effortlessly from her lips. "Unlike some, I respect our boundaries. Oh, and speaking of which, I told you to explain yourself. Your presence here is in violation of our treaty and I would be more than within my rights to summarily execute you, alpha dog or not."

Mom and my uncle, Dad's younger brother, stared at each other for several seconds. Now that I thought back on things, it was rare that they'd ever been in the same room together and it was never at my uncle's house in ... Morganberg, of course. It had always been at special events and only in public places – like birthday parties at Chuck E. Cheese's. And the few times they'd been face to face, I'd gotten the distinct impression neither particularly cared for the other. Watching them now, it all began to add up.

Finally, Craig backed up a step and adopted a formal tone, albeit with a generous dollop of sarcasm thrown in. "Very well. As alpha of my pack, I beg your pardon, oh esteemed mistress of butterflies, for this intrusion. I call upon the contingencies laid forth in our treaty which allows such transgressions to be made in times of emergency."

Mom glared at him for a moment, but then nodded and stepped aside.

"This is pack business," he added.

"So long as it's in my home, it's my business too."

Uncle Craig looked as if he was about to say something to that, but then he caught sight of me again. "Step away from it, Curt." He turned to my mom. "That isn't Tamara. It's a doppelganger." Then, back to my father. "I'm surprised you can't smell it. That's not like you."

I waited impatiently behind my dad, swearing silently to God that if they didn't drop the act and fess up, fists were going to start flying and I wouldn't be overly concerned with whom they hit.

Mom turned and locked eyes with Dad, and it was as if an unspoken conversation passed between them. Heck, I had no idea what my mother could or couldn't do. For all I knew there *was* a conversation going on. If they didn't completely sell me out, I'd have to make it a point to ask her about that.

At last, Dad looked at my uncle and the two others he'd brought with him. He took a step to the side, revealing me, and my heart leapt into my throat.

No, Dad!

But then he put his hands on my shoulders and said, "I can smell just fine, Craig. There is no doppelganger. This is Tamara, the same girl you've seen at her baptism, birthdays, and holidays."

Craig's eyes narrowed. "That's impossible. Take a good whiff of her."

"Like I said, my nose is working fine."

"But last night you told us..."

"I lied. She caught me by ... surprise, and it was the only thing I could think of to keep the pack from hunting her down. That's why I took a swing at you."

What happened the night before suddenly made sense. I'd thought my kick to the balls had driven him nuts or something. If what I was hearing was correct, then Uncle Craig was the pack leader and Dad had attacked him as a distraction so I could get away.

It also explained why he always seemed willing to take shit from his brother, despite being three years older. Craig was in charge. But hadn't Dad just told me he'd been alpha in training?

Uncle Craig looked confused, a sentiment I could very much agree with. "That doesn't make any sense," he said, echoing several of my thoughts.

"You're telling me," I commented beneath my breath, drawing a glare from Dad.

My uncle, either not hearing or choosing to ignore me, continued. "Are you trying to tell me you willfully adopted a demonic shifter?"

"She's not a doppelganger," Mom said.

"Nor is she adopted," my father replied a scant second after.

Uncle Craig's jaw dropped open. It was a confession apparently almost twenty years in the making, but I felt a small ping of love in my heart at hearing them say it nevertheless.

It was Mom who finally broke the impasse as she turned and walked toward the kitchen.

She stopped at the doorway. "I can see this is going to take a while, so I'm going to make some coffee. You take yours with bourbon right, Craig?"

He nodded.

"Think I'll join you. In the meantime, try not to do anything that even remotely provokes me."

If I was hoping that Mom's decree would lessen the tension in the room, I was mistaken. Uncle Craig, Mitch, and Warty, who I learned was actually named Jerry – possibly the least threatening werewolf name I could imagine – stayed where they were in the foyer right outside our living room.

For my part, I wasn't quite ready to relax either, despite being exhausted enough to close my eyes for a good week. Problem was, I couldn't be certain they'd ever open again if I dropped my guard around current company.

Craig opened his mouth several times, looking like he wanted to say something, but each time he glanced toward the kitchen and then shut it again. After a couple minutes of awkward silence, my mother returned with a tray full of steaming coffee mugs. To my annoyance, I only counted five of them. Pity, because if there was anyone in the room who could've used an Irish coffee at that moment, it was me.

She handed them out. Then, when our three visitors warily sniffed theirs, she said, "Oh please. Don't insult me by insinuating I would need to put something in them."

"Of course not, Lissa." Craig gave her a forced grin. "Just making sure it wasn't decaf."

"As if."

Right about when it looked like the conversation was about to pick up again, we heard a car door slam outside. I glanced out the window and saw a familiar figure running for the door. "You have got to be kidding me."

A moment later, my gremlin of a brother stepped in as if he didn't have a care in the world. He paused when he saw we had company, but then his stupid face widened in a big grin. "Hey, Uncle Craig! What's up?"

"Hey, champ," he replied in a friendly manner, reaching out to offer him a handshake. "Look how big you're getting." I couldn't help but notice his nose working overtime as he spoke.

Pity the only thing he was going to get a noseful of was unwashed preteen.

"What are you doing home, Chris?" Dad asked in a neutral tone. "I thought you were hanging out with your friend."

"Burt's parents were going out and he's not allowed to have anyone over unsupervised."

"Can't imagine why," I muttered under my breath.

He again turned to our uncle. "What are you doing here? Sticking around for dinner? Want to come down to my room and play some video games? I have a new copy of..."

"I can't stay long, big guy. Just popped in to have a quick word with your sister."

Chris grinned my way. "Let me guess. You finally figured out she was a troll in human skin?"

If there was a less funny joke that could have been told at that moment, I couldn't think of one. It was like the air went out of the room for a beat, and I could see the three men around my brother tense up ... right before he started laughing like he thought he was the funniest little prick in the world.

Oh, how I could have pummeled him. With my newfound strength, I could have given him a three hundred and sixty degree atomic wedgie, one his unborn grandkids would have felt.

I was still waiting to see how this would play out, and whether we were going to do this in front of him, when Mom said, "I'm glad you're home, Christopher, but don't get comfortable."

"Why not?"

"Because I'm running to the mall and I remembered that you need a new pair of sneakers."

"Really? But I want to hang with Uncle Craig."

"Yes, really." At the sulking face he made, she added, "If you're good, we can stop at Johnny Rockets before we leave."

That perked him up. My brother was nothing if not easily bribed by chili cheese fries.

"Go wait in the car. I'll be out in a second after I grab my keys."

"Okay." He paused and then turned to Craig.

Our uncle gave him a friendly slap on the shoulder. "It's okay, buddy. Me and the boys are heading out in a few minutes anyway."

It was kind of surreal, watching everyone pretend things were normal, just itching for him to leave so that the fireworks could begin again.

Honestly, I was sorely tempted to join my mother,

even if it meant an afternoon at the mall with Chris, but I had a feeling I wasn't going to escape that easily.

Chris gave our uncle a big high five then walked out the door, as blissfully unaware as when he'd entered. A part of me envied his ignorance.

A little bit anyway.

Mom turned back toward the kitchen, but I held out a hand. "If you're not going to drink that?"

She gave me a sardonic grin in return. "Talk to me when you're twenty-one."

Son of a bitch! Talk about adding insult to my probable injury.

16

After Mom poured out her drink and grabbed her keys, she stopped in front of Uncle Craig. "Let us be crystal clear. If there is even one hair harmed on her head when I return, there is no treaty in the world that will stop me from raining hellfire upon everyone you hold dear."

Whoa. Up until now, Mom had been acting pretty detached, but this ... it was nice to see her being, well, a mother. Despite myself, I felt my anger toward her ratchet down a notch or two.

Uncle Craig, for his part, replied deadpan, "I appreciate your hospitality and tolerance of our transgression in this time of *uncertainty*. You have my word. All I want are answers ... for now."

Mom stared hard at him for a moment. I could tell she didn't want to leave, but otherwise it was either spill the beans to Chris that his adopted family were a bunch of monsters, or hex him again like she'd done earlier. It seemed easier to simply remove him from the situation. The look she gave my father next said the rest – she was trusting him to take care of this.

All of this served to make me wonder if perhaps I wasn't being too hard on them, but then I remembered the whole adopted demon thing. Yeah, they still had plenty of strikes against them, but maybe I'd wait and see how the rest of this standoff progressed first.

She left and, a minute later, we heard the car start out in the driveway. It was only after she'd pulled away that our *guests* dared to speak.

Mitch glanced out the window, probably to make sure she was gone, then said, "God, what a bitch."

When nobody said anything to that, Craig stepped into the living room. "Since it looks like we're in agreement that talking is all that's on the table, mind if we grab a seat?"

Dad waved them in.

Finally, after everyone was sitting, Craig leaned forward. "So what the fuck is going on, bro? That witch messing with your head?"

"Of course not. You know that's against the..."

"Screw the treaty," Ugly Jerry said. He tried to sound tough but was sweating too copiously to pull it off. Eww. "Her kind doesn't give a crap about it. I don't know why we..."

Craig held up a hand. "Relax. We're not here to level accusations at the opposing team, especially since you never know when the walls might have ears."

"Or the people who live here," I added.

Cousin Mitch leaned forward and growled, his canines elongating into fangs. A day earlier that would have intimidated the hell out of me. Today, a bit less so.

"Just because we're family doesn't mean I won't make you eat your own teeth."

"You're no family to me," he spat.

"Enough," Craig snapped at his two backup puppies. "You two, pipe down for the moment." He turned to my father. "I guess that's the sixty-four thousand dollar question, isn't it? What is she? Because she sure as hell doesn't smell like my niece. And what was that shit earlier about her not being adopted?"

"Yeah, Dad," I replied. "What *was* that about?"

Craig pointed a finger at me. "What I said to them goes double for you."

"And what I said about beating the hell out of..."

"That's enough, Tamara." If Dad was using my full name, he meant business. Nearly twenty years of childhood survival instincts shot to the surface and I did as told. He turned to his brother. "I was lying back then. I'm not lying now. She's mine, which makes her your niece by blood."

"Then who the hell is her mother?" Mitch asked. Freaking idiot. I always did consider him from the shallower end of Dad's gene pool.

Uncle Craig looked at me, closed his eyes, and took a deep breath through his nostrils. He frowned and then his face started to change.

My first instinct was to leap to my feet as his facial features contorted, his jawline extending and his nose seeming to melt into the muzzle that formed.

Dad, however, was there to hold a hand out toward me. "It's okay, Tam Tam. Relax."

Relaxing wasn't quite what I had in mind as my uncle's features melted away and were replaced by something far more canine. I expected him to burst out of his clothes, a monstrous bipedal wolf intent on tearing me to pieces, but the change seemed to stop at his neck. His body remained human while his face was stuck in some sort of halfway point. It was seriously freaky-looking.

He took several more breaths, these more a wet snuffle than mere sniffs. Then, abruptly, his features retracted, melting back into my uncle's face again.

His eyes popped open, yellow and sinister for a moment, before he blinked and they were replaced with their normal pale blue coloration. Dismissing my look of shock, he faced my father again. "She's not a lycanthrope."

"I know that."

"Her human scent is in there, too, buried."

"Also aware."

"But there's something else. Not a witch either. I..." He trailed off, almost sounding embarrassed. "I've never smelled anything like her before."

Dad leaned forward and clasped his hands. "I think that might be because there's never been anything like her before."

"Anything?" I asked.

"Sorry, hon. I meant anyone."

"But ... how could something ... like *this* happen?" Mitch asked.

"Oh, c'mon," Dad said to his cousin. "Put two and two together already. When Lissa and I first suggested the new treaty all those years ago, put forth the idea that our people be joined by marriage to keep the peace, that the two of us should settle in the neutral territory as a check against each other..."

"Yeah?" Craig replied, his eyes narrowing.

"She was already pregnant at that point."

"I don't understand," Jerry said, his doughy face a mask of confusion.

"Do I really need to explain *how* it happened?"

Craig let out a sigh. "Not that. He means how is it even possible? One, you knew it was forbidden. And two, so far as I'm aware, we're not even biologically compatible, at least when it comes to reproducing."

Dad turned to me. "You might want to cover your ears for this." When I did nothing but glare, he shrugged and turned back to his pack mates. "I don't think I need to point out that the forbidden fruit is often the sweetest..."

"Gross!" I exclaimed.

"I did tell you to cover your ears, sweetheart, did I not? As for the rest..." He shook his head. "It happened during a blood moon."

17

C raig bolted to his feet, appearing like he wanted to kick over the coffee table or punch something. But then he seemingly thought better of it.

He still wasn't a happy camper, though. "A blood moon?! Are you fucking insane? You know better, man. You're lucky Pop's not still with us because he would lose his ever-living shit."

"You think I don't know that?" Dad replied, raising his voice – something he didn't do often.

"Then why? Was it to screw us over? Did she get in your head?"

"It's because I love her!"

Silence descended on the room as everyone appeared to take this in, as if it were a new revelation which – based on what I was hearing – it actually was.

I decided to take advantage of the lull to ask, "What's the big deal about a blood moon?"

Craig rounded on me, but Dad quickly answered, "They're ... special, magical. During a blood moon, our powers are stronger than they normally are, but so are the mages. If you believe the stories, the walls between our world and what lies beyond are thinner on nights like that."

"All things are possible beneath a blood moon," Craig said, repeating it like it was less an answer and more a mantra.

"What?"

"It's something our father used to say," Dad told me. "He said the cycle of the wolf was at its strongest during such a lunar event. That the impossible no longer was."

Craig let out a breath which sounded more like a snarl and ran his hands through his mullet. "And you just happened to pick that night to screw a witch. This is fucking crazy." He stepped up to my dad and pointed a finger at his chest. "And you. You said this was all for the pack. To keep us safe. You stepped down, left us, and we all thought you were a hero for making the sacrifice, when all along this was some Romeo and Juliet bullshit. That's what hurts the most, Curt. The lies. How the hell are any of us ever supposed to trust you again, knowing ... *this* exists because of you?"

Dad stood up and looked him directly in the eye. "That's my daughter you're talking about. Your niece."

"She's an abomination, man. But you're too busy playing house to see that. I don't know what the hell that witch has done to you, but you're not thinking straight. We have rules, a covenant! That's how we've survived this long. And you'd just throw that all away." He hooked a thumb at me. "You saw what she did last night and you know what's coming next month. You can't tell me this is a coincidence, her ... *this* happening now."

I could see the other two getting agitated. My mother's warning or not, I had a feeling that violence was still on the table. If that happened, though, whose side would Dad fall on? I hoped it would be mine, but the way Uncle Craig kept brow-beating him had me worried.

Glancing toward the window, I began to consider contingencies. I sincerely doubted Craig and his friends would turn into werewolves in the middle of the day on our front lawn. Of course, I didn't know that for certain, but sometimes one has to hedge their bets. If so, maybe I could...

"Do *they* know?" Craig asked. "And don't play dumb. You know damn well who I'm talking about."

Dad shook his head. "They're in the same boat ... mostly."

"*Mostly?*"

"Lissa's uncle. He helped concoct the formula that kept her powers submerged. That's it, I swear, and he's sworn to secrecy."

"Like the word of a witch..."

"You know how they are."

Craig glared hard at him, but then nodded. "Yeah, that stupid nobility shit they all adhere to. Fine. Okay, I'll buy that for now."

"It was only by accident that Tamara even found out. She missed a dose of her *medication*."

I was sorely tempted to remind Dad that those meds were akin to making me a methhead, but I held my tongue. No point in pouring more gasoline onto this dumpster fire.

Craig was silent for several seconds. Finally, he said, "Maybe it's not too late. Put her back on that stuff. Keep her on it and maybe we can..."

"You can't be serious," Jerry cried. Wart-covered dickhead.

Craig glared at him and good ole' Jer sat his butt right back down. "Shut the fuck up. Nobody asked your opinion."

"Not going to happen," I said.

"Tam Tam..."

"No, Dad. No way am I taking that shit again. Ever."

"Maybe we can find a new formulation, one that doesn't have…"

"I said no!"

Craig stepped up to me. "I don't think you understand, little lady. We aren't asking. The only reason I'm giving you this chance is because we're related." He glared daggers at my Dad. "And, despite his stupidity, I love my brother. I love my niece Tamara, too, but you ain't her right now. If you go back, though, this can all be forgotten." I opened my mouth, but he wasn't finished. "Before you say anything, know that there isn't another option on the table. Our ancestors were very clear on this. No diluting our bloodline with those magic-flinging freaks. It's a covenant I intend to uphold."

I held his gaze, feeling my own temper begin to fray. Much more of this crap – being talked of as if I was a thing and not a person – and I'd gladly throw the first punch. Hell, Mom's warning had been for them. She hadn't said anything about me rearranging their faces. Sometimes the devil is in the details.

So tempting, but before things devolved to that level, I decided to take the high road one last time. "You said it yourself. We're blood, family. You've known me all my life, Uncle Craig. I'm still the same person. Are you trying to tell me that some edict passed down by long-dead assholes means more than that?"

A hand fell on my shoulder – Dad's. I didn't look his way, though. Instead, I kept my focus on Craig.

Finally, he said, "You're family, true, but you're not a member of the pack. Those ties run even deeper than blood."

"So, what? You're like supernatural Scientologists now? If I'm not a dues-paying cult member, then I don't count as a person?"

Before Craig could say something that would give me a reason to split his lip, Dad asked, "What if she was in the pack?"

"What?" the three wolves and me replied simultaneously.

"You said it yourself," he continued. "She's not one of us. But why not? She's blood-related and I think she's proven she can keep up with us. She could be inducted. We've brought in outsiders before."

"Those were special circumstances and you know it. People we needed help from, folks who married into..." Craig's voice trailed off again and a different expression, almost thoughtful, crossed his face.

"What is it?"

"Married. That might be it."

"What might be it?"

But he ignored me, continuing to speak to my Dad. "The witches, they couldn't know. And she'd need to be loyal. She'd have to follow my lead and do as she's told. That's the only way I can convince the others, especially if they ever learn what she is."

"Convince?" Dad asked dubiously. "Aren't you the alpha?"

Craig raised the sides of his mouth in a snarl. "Yeah, I'm the alpha, and I'd prefer not to be torn limb from limb by my own pack for making a stupid decision."

Dad shrugged. "Okay, I'm listening."

"What she really is, her true parentage, doesn't leave this room. The pack will go ape-shit if they find out."

"But the others saw what she could do..."

"You think I don't know that? I'll make up something. Demonic possession maybe, from living with your pet witch. It's happened before. That'll buy her some sympathy, but she'll have to keep her antics in check."

Antics?

Dad nodded. "Okay. So who then?"

Craig smiled and turned toward the other two. "Easy as pie, bro. Congratulations, Jerry. You're now engaged."

What the ever-living fuck?!

"Huh?" Jerry asked, apparently as dumbfounded as me.

"You're about the same age," Craig said. "And you're single, right?"

"Yeah ... I guess."

"Well, not anymore. You and Tamara here are going to get married so we can properly indoctrinate her into the pack."

Jerry turned my way and sized me up, undressing me with his beady eyes while running a wart-covered hand over the stubble on his chin. "She's not really my type, but I guess she ain't too bad."

Ain't too bad? Oh, I was so going to feed him his own bottom jaw. "I wouldn't count on..."

Dad stepped in front of me. "And she'd be safe?"

Craig nodded. "Like I said, she has to behave herself. But as a member of the pack, anyone messes with her and they deal with me."

"And what if I say no?"

Dad turned to me. "That's enough, Tamara."

"But..."

"I said that's *enough*."

It wasn't so much what he said as how he said it. He put on his dad voice, which caused my mouth to shut so fast that I was barely aware it had closed.

"The Draíodóir can't know about this," Craig said to my dad, ignoring me like I was property.

"Lissa will find out."

"Lie to her."

"I won't do that."

"How the hell do you live with yourself, knowing how badly you've shamed your own people?"

"That's my wife you're talking about."

"Whatever," Craig said, disgust practically dripping from his lips. "But you'd better explain to her that this is the *only* way Tamara gets to live."

"She's not going to take that well."

"You're her husband," Craig replied mockingly. "You'll figure out some way to break it to her. And if she has a problem with it, you can also explain that you're the one who agreed to it. Sound fair?"

Dad glanced back at me, but then quickly looked away as if not wanting to meet my eyes. Finally, he nodded.

"So be it," my uncle said after a beat, his tone suggesting he considered this discussion finished. "The ceremony will take place next month. Fitting in a way. Almost like going full circle."

"Why's that?" I asked, finding my voice.

"Check your lunar calendar, girl. A month from now, you'll be taking your vows beneath another blood moon."

18

Every time I tried to speak, Dad would ignore me as he agreed to Uncle Craig's terms, basically offering my hand in marriage to warty Jerry.

It was a good thing that my uncle kept his visit short, because otherwise it would have almost certainly gotten violent. Once the door shut behind Craig, Mitch, and my new *fiancé*, Dad turned to find me waiting with clenched fists. "Okay, I'm waiting for it."

"Waiting for what?" he asked wearily.

"The plan of action. The big reveal. The con we're playing."

"There is no con."

"What do you mean?"

"Don't you understand? Craig means it. He wants this to happen. He's decreed it."

"So just tell him to go pound sand."

"It's not that easy. He's the alpha."

"But I thought you said you were the..."

"I *was*," he explained. "But, in marrying your mother, in taking up the charade of pretending to honor our treaty, I had to step aside. That meant accepting him as pack

141

leader, adopting a beta mindset, anything to protect you. And, before you ask, I wouldn't change a damn thing about it."

Dad put a hand on my shoulder. "Craig wasn't lying. You're ... not supposed to be possible. But you are. You're my darling little girl, a once in maybe a thousand lifetimes miracle." He turned away, leaning his head against the wall. "But you have to realize this isn't a fairy tale. Miracles come with a price. Believe me, no matter what your mother says, her people wouldn't react any differently. You have to understand, I'm doing this to save you, Tam Tam."

"Don't call me that."

"Listen, honey, I'm not any happier about this than..."

I stepped up behind him, spun him to face me and then, before I barely even realized what I was doing, grabbed him by the shirt and slammed him into the wall hard enough to crack the drywall. "Let me be crystal clear: happy isn't a word I'd use right now."

His eyes opened wide, probably more in shock than pain. After a moment, I took a deep breath and dropped him. I started to apologize, but caught my tongue before the words could form.

Instead, I turned away. "I need to get some fresh air."

"You should stay here. Your mother will be back soon. Besides, it's not safe for you out there."

I glanced over my shoulder and fixed him with a glare. "You know what's not safe? Trying to get in my way right now."

I practically dared him to try to stop me. The truth was, I was spoiling for a fight and didn't particularly care much who with. Would I have felt bad about it later on? Probably, but Dad had already proven that he healed quickly.

Who better to take my frustrations out on than the guy who'd sold me like a piece of meat. Even better, any bruises I left wouldn't debilitate him for long.

But he didn't try. He let me go without another word. I made a show of grabbing the keys to the minivan from the hook near the door before I stepped out. Petty of me, yeah, but sometimes letting my bitch face out to play could do wonders for my mood.

A few moments later found me pulling out of my own driveway, still fuming. Had anyone dared try to cut me off before I turned from our block, I would have gladly put the airbags and my parents' insurance premiums to the test. Fortunately, that didn't happen.

As I sat at the stop sign waiting to turn, it all caught up to me and I let out a primal scream, letting my lungs release the pent-up rage that I really wanted to hand off to my fists instead. My anger spent, I lowered my head to the steering wheel and tried to get myself back under control.

After several minutes, a car beeped behind me, making me realize I was still sitting there. I wiped the tears from my eyes and drove toward the only place I could think of where I'd be met with a sympathetic ear.

"It's not funny, Riva, I mean it."

We were downstairs in her house. I'd arrived to find her napping on the couch, catching up on the lost sleep from the night before.

Though I doubted it had ever been used – considering her dad's somewhat doughy frame – they had a full-sized punching bag in their basement. I was using it to blow off a little steam.

I slammed a fist into the bag, almost knocking Riva from her feet as she tried to hold it from the other side.

"Ow, watch it!"

"Sorry, but you kind of had it coming."

"Oh, come on, Bent. You have to admit this is pretty wild. I mean, I was always afraid that one day my parents would up and announce that they'd arranged a marriage for me with some guy in Bangladesh. Yet instead it's your folks, two of the whitest people I've ever met – no offense, by the way – who've arranged for you to get hitched."

"None taken," I replied, drilling the bag with an uppercut that drew another complaint from my friend. "Still not funny. Did I tell you what this guy looks like?"

"Warts and all." She stepped away from the bag before I could slug it again.

"He's a total skeeve."

"I wonder if he has warts in other places."

"Ugh! That's nasty!"

"Ooh." She spun toward me with way too big of a grin on her face. "Do you think he'll only want to do it..."

"Don't say it," I warned.

"Doggy style?"

I drew back and hit the bag with a solid jab that tore the hook straight out of the rafters and sent it flying across the room. Even I stared wide-eyed at what I'd done. "Um, sorry."

Riva stepped up next to me. "Really glad I moved when I did. Remind me not to piss you off."

"You know I'd never do that to you."

"Yeah, but collateral damage is nothing to sneeze at."

She suggested we head upstairs and grab something to eat before I trashed the rest of her house. There was some leftover vindaloo in the fridge and, while I wouldn't have trusted Riva to crack an egg correctly, her mother was a hell of a cook.

A few bites later left me feeling marginally better. This week was supposed to be about fun, hanging out, and maybe recovering from a hangover or two. Instead I'd somehow ended up as the bride of Frankenstein, if Frankenstein's monster had even worse skin. Ugh! Just the thought of Jerry trying to consummate our sham of a union was enough to make me lose my appetite.

"What am I going to do? And I swear if you start laughing again, I'm going to throw my spoon at you."

"Did you tell your mom yet?"

"No, not yet."

"Well, then that's your first step."

I considered this. "Uncle Craig did seem pretty wary around her. I got the sense that he didn't want to piss her off."

"Neither would I. But that's good. Oh, by the way, you need to take him off your Christmas card list ASAP."

"Don't think I already haven't." I took another bite. "The only present my dear uncle is getting from me this year is a sack of coal, preferably upside the head."

"Okay, so let's see if your mom can maybe sort this out."

I shook my head. "There's one potential problem there. Mom acts all tough, but Dad's got her number. He could probably sweet talk..."

"Her pants off?"

"Thanks for going there. I was going to say talk her into going along with this stupid sham."

She appeared to mull this over. "Well, what if it's just that, a sham? Maybe all you need to do is show up, say 'I do,' and then it's all fine and good. They can claim their victory, while you tell Jerry to go stuff his warty prick into some other knothole."

"I was thinking about that, but I didn't get the impression they see it that way. Craig seemed pretty adamant that this meant I'd be a part of the pack. Call me paranoid, but I think he either wants me as a weapon or wants to neutralize me as one by ensuring I start popping out wart-covered puppies."

"Does PetSmart offer baby registries?"

I tossed a scoop of rice at her.

"You'd better clean that up or my mom is going to flip out."

I handed her a napkin. "Any idea when they're getting home?"

"No clue," Riva said, brushing rice off her shirt. "The day after tomorrow maybe. My Dad loves to give me crap about not wanting to leave me alone, but it's all BS. I guarantee he's lying next to a pool somewhere, trying to milk it for as long as he can. Looks like I'll be sleeping with the lights on for a few more days."

"You could always come by my place ... or I could stay here."

"True, but I'm not sure it's a good idea to ignore this for too long with your parents."

She had a point. If I wasn't there to say anything, they'd have a chance to talk it out without me adding my two cents. If so, my fate could be sealed. There would be nothing I could do except...

"I am such an idiot."

"Nah. You're just a moron."

"Bite me," I replied without any real rancor. "No. I mean, I was just thinking that I'd be screwed if my parents had too long to discuss this without me there. But then I remembered I have this little thing going for me called being an adult."

"Good point. But technically you're still living under their roof."

"Yes, but as an adult, perhaps it's time I made the adult decision of returning to college."

"Running away from your problems?" she asked with a

grin. "If there is a more mature way to handle this, I haven't heard of it."

I knew she was joking, but I wasn't. "It might actually be for the best if I leave, remove myself from this madhouse my life's become."

"What if your parents say 'no'?"

"They only pay for a small part of my tuition. My sports scholarship covers most of it. Worst they could do is cut me off. If so, I get a job."

"The world could always use another stripper working her way through college."

We both laughed. "I was thinking more a part-time job at the athletic center, or maybe waiting tables."

"Too bad," she said. "I'd have paid good money..."

"To see me swing on a pole?" I asked, one eyebrow raised.

"Maybe. But mostly to see what would happen if any of your clients tried to get fresh."

"Nah, probably not a great idea. I'd make all the bouncers jealous."

She got up to put her bowl into the dishwasher. "That, and you also dance like a white girl."

"Do not."

"I remember you at prom trying to do the Electric Slide. My eyes almost bled."

She kinda had a point. A future contestant on *Dancing With The Stars*, I was not. Still, I wasn't about to concede the argument so easily. "Nobody's going to care if I'm prancing around like a three-legged buffalo so long as I've got the goods on display."

"Challenge accepted," she said, turning around and facing me. "Strip."

"What?"

"Start shaking it. I think I've got a twenty around here somewhere."

"In your dreams."

"Pussy."

"I'm not stripping in your kitchen."

Riva laughed. "See? That's a problem. I'm your best friend. We've gotten changed in front of each other like a million times. And here you are wussing out. I hate to say it, but you're probably back to waiting tables."

"And I repeat, we're in your kitchen and the windows are open."

"Pity. Mr. McGreevy could probably use a thrill. I don't think the poor guy's been on a date since before we were born."

"Hence my refusal. I don't need to be burdened with thoughts of your geriatric neighbor jacking it to me."

"Chicken."

"Don't make me deck you."

19

Our banter served to put me in a slightly less murderous mood, although I'd made up my mind about returning to school early. I had plenty of friends who'd be happy to see me and there was little doubt my coaches would appreciate me being around for some extra training. And I knew someone in housing who could probably find me a spare bed in one of the open dorms.

Speaking of college and coaches, my thoughts turned toward the upcoming season as I got back in the van to head home. I sincerely doubted anyone, least of all myself, had expected me to return to school *a lot* stronger than I'd left it. Wrestling was all about leverage and skill, but it was stupid to dismiss raw power. It was hard to pin an opponent who could toss you around like you weighed next to nothing.

Hmm, now that I thought about it, would it even be fair for me to compete? I mean, technically it wasn't cheating. This was all me, who I was. If anything, I'd been doing the exact opposite of juicing for my entire career. There was also the little fact that coming clean to my coaches and admitting I was a werewolf / draío ... whatever mix would likely get me benched, less so for having supernatural strength and more for sounding like a complete and utter loon.

Not to mention there was likewise the itty bitty problem that if I dropped off the team, *poof*, there went my scholarship. My grades weren't bad, but there was no way I was getting a free ride on them alone. I'd have to get loans up to my eyeballs, something I wasn't keen on doing. I'd heard more than enough horror stories about people who were still paying them off two decades after the fact. No thank you.

I continued to muse on this as I drove. Maybe I could make it work. With my newfound power, I'd have to hold back, even against the super heavyweights – not that they'd ever pair me with them.

Much as I believed in fair play, I just didn't see me pretending to be Clark Kent on this one and staying off the team. I'd just have to be smart about it. Keep myself in check and not decimate everyone in the field, no matter how much fun that might be.

Well, okay, maybe Justin Helferman. He was going into his senior year, captain of the team, and was an arrogant prick. Him I might consider utterly destroying. Maybe just once or twice, though.

I considered things. It was a pity I was only finding out about my powers now. Had I known about this a couple of years ago, I could have taken the state championship, gotten a full ride and...

Hold on.

Memories of that day raced back to me. I'd come into that meet unbeaten for the season. News crews were all over the place, local ones anyway, all of them waiting to see if a girl would make history and go all the way.

But I hadn't. I'd been beaten, pinned. In fact, I'd been

off for the entire tournament, just barely squeaking by in matches against opponents I'd had relatively little trouble with prior to that day.

And that's when it hit me. Mom, supposedly worried that the excitement and exertion would have an adverse effect on my *condition*, had insisted I take a booster dose of my meds right before the meet began.

Son of a bitch!

I stormed back into my house, all thoughts of marriage gone from my head for the moment. It was immediately apparent that Mom was back, especially since Chris was in the living room eating a slice of pizza.

"What's the matter?" he asked, slurping down some cheese. "Forget to put on your skank-off today?"

"Don't start with me, you little twat," I growled, stalking past him to find the kitchen empty.

"They're upstairs in their room," Chris called from the living room.

"Thanks."

"Pretty sure they're both in a mood, too."

"Join the club," I replied under my breath.

I headed up and, without thinking, barged over to their bedroom and opened the door.

Thankfully, they hadn't been in the middle of a repeat performance from the other night. Not sure I could have handled that. They were both fully clothed and apparently in the middle of a discussion.

Three guesses who it was about, and the first two don't count.

"We knock in this house, Tamara," Mom said crossly.

Yeah, right. She's lucky I didn't knock the damn door off its hinges. "I have a question."

"We were just discussing..."

"Not that." I interrupted. "We can get back to that later." I turned to glare at my mother. "Did you purposely overdose me during state's my senior year?"

I had to give her credit. She was cool as a cucumber, didn't even miss a beat in answering. "Overdose is a strong word, don't you think? I merely ensured that you were well within the threshold of a normal girl your size and build."

"You purposely sabotaged me."

"I'm not the one who pinned you out there on the mat."

"You cost me a..."

"Don't pretend to play the victim here. You're still attending the same school you would have otherwise."

"I would have gotten a full ride!"

"Yes, so instead you have a *mostly* full ride and we're covering the rest. What's the difference?"

"I would have made the papers. They'd have plastered my face from here to the West Coast."

There came a crackle of energy from my mother's eyes, lighting them up for a moment and causing me to back up a step. If she was trying to intimidate me, she was doing a pretty good job. "That is precisely what we didn't want to happen. How many times must we explain it to you? This was for your own safety. We supported you from day one, but we also realized that going too far, knocking down too many barriers, was dangerous. That kind of attention could have turned questioning eyes your way. As you saw earlier, that's something we'd sought to avoid."

"For my own safety," I repeated without much fire.

She put her hands on my shoulders. "Exactly. Please try to understand that."

I nodded.

"Good," Dad said. "It's not much different with what I had to agree to with your uncle..."

"You don't get off that easily," I fired back, stepping past Mom to jab a finger into his chest. "State's is over and done with. Ancient history. Hard to get pissed off about something I can't go back and change. But this? Marrying Jerry the wart-dicked werewolf? Not happening."

Mom, rather than admonishing me for my language as was her usual wont, held up a hand and snickered into it, drawing a glare from my father.

"You don't have a choice. It's already agreed upon," he said.

I turned to Mom. "And you?"

"I don't like it. Not one bit. But, for the moment, your uncle sort of has us over a barrel."

"Not us, you," I said with finality. "In fact, that's why I came home. I decided I'm heading back to school early. High Moon has gotten a bit too crazy for my tastes. I think everyone needs to chill out a bit and move on to other items of importance, find new trees to sniff, that sort of thing."

I turned away, but Dad caught me by the arm. "You can't."

"Sure I can." I pulled free from his grasp. "I can get a job, work my way through school. If Jerry shows up, I'll call security on him. If that doesn't work, I'll beat his head against a car door for an hour or two."

"Your father's right," Mom said. "It's bigger than you now."

"Why? If that wart-covered dickhead wants a girl-friend, he can get a Tinder account, or maybe Petfinder. Who cares?"

"You're not understanding, sweetheart," my father said, his gaze intensifying. "Your uncle called me after you left."

"Yeah, and?"

"And, it seems he was thinking the same thing you are.

153

He let me know, in no uncertain terms, that if you tried to run, he'd kill everyone in High Moon."

I let that sink in for several seconds. "Excuse me? How did we go from an arranged marriage to threats of Armageddon? I mean, he looked ticked, but..."

Dad nodded grimly. "The revelation here, it caught your uncle by surprise. He had to think on his feet."

"Not one of his better virtues," Mom added.

Dad looked sidelong at her for a moment, but then said, "Your mother's not wrong. But after leaving, he had some time to mull it over and came to the conclusion that this is ... a bit more important to the pack than he initially thought."

"A bit more important?" I asked numbly. "Understating it much? We're talking hundreds of people here. What did they ever do to him?"

"It's not them, it's High Moon itself. This town, it exists as a buffer between our two races, mine and your mother's. We both have claims to territory close by, some of it dangerously close."

"So, it was decided, long ago," Mom continued, "that we had a choice. We could either go to war, decimate both sides along with anyone else who got in our way, or we could forge a truce, establish High Moon as a sort of demilitarized zone between us."

"Kind of like the Romulan Neutral Zone," Dad said.

"What?"

"Star Trek? No? Fine, go with your mother's example then."

"Still not following."

"Craig is threatening war. Well, not all-out war, but he's making the argument that your mother and I have ...

tainted the spirit of the treaty, and as a result, we've like-wise forfeited the lands the treaty encompasses."

I turned to Mom. "Won't your people step in and do something?"

She shrugged. "Unlikely. We can hem and haw about it, lodge official protests, that sort of thing, but if we actually make a move to stop them then..."

"War," I concluded.

"Yes. It would be the same on their end if the Draíodóir decided to act. Neither of the sides, outside of our immediate family, has a true claim within this town. If the other decided to cleanse it, for lack of a better term, we'd most likely let them so long as it didn't spill over into our territory."

"That's totally nuts!"

"Is it?" Mom asked. "You have no idea what a war would do. Yes, it would start out small, localized, but it wouldn't stay that way. Both races have family, clans, around the world. It would potentially escalate and, if that happened, then there's little chance we'd remain a secret. Mankind would join the fray and, at best, we'd be looking at the total annihilation of at least one of our races, if not both."

That ... didn't sound good. Mind you, the threat of mutual destruction was a classic standoff technique. I'd learned as much in my history classes. Once one side gained the advantage, though, there wasn't much to keep them from acting. Right now, Craig's side had that advantage by knowing more about me than the other side. Maybe we needed to change that, level the playing field again.

What that meant for me, I had no idea. But perhaps it was time to find out.

"Why don't we tell the Drai ... the witches? Your side, Mom."

"What?" her and Dad asked together.

"Exactly what I said," I replied, shelving any plans to start packing. No matter what happened, it seemed I was stuck here for the time being. "We even the playing field. Bring them up to speed on me. You said it yourself, Mom, your uncle is already in on it."

"Yes, and he's sworn to secrecy on pain of death."

"Pain of death?"

Dad shrugged. "Your mother doesn't fool around with these things."

"Not where my family is concerned."

I waved my hands dismissively. "Okay, fine. So why not bring in the rest?" I thought about it for a moment, then snapped my fingers. "How about Aunt Carly? She always liked me. Or are you going to tell me she's the only person I'm related to who isn't a part of this in any way?"

"Oh no, Carly is a skilled aerokineticist," Mom replied. "But you're not grasping the situation. My people won't react any better than your father's." She turned to him and sighed before addressing me again. "If anything, they might take it even worse."

"Why? I saw what you did to those wolves at the diner. No way am I messing with a whole family of that."

"It's not even remotely that simple," Mom said.

"Try me."

"Honey," Dad warned, but Mom was already stepping away from him.

"Sorry, but some things need to be shown, not told."

"What?" I asked. "Is this some..."

"*Dorn an bháis!*" she screamed in that weird triple echo voice of hers. A black tendril of energy shot from her outstretched hand and slammed into my chest.

The collision pushed me back into the wall, almost knocking the breath out of me. "What the hell was that for?!"

"Do you see?" she asked, breathing hard as if she'd just run a mile.

"Yeah, I get it. You can do far worse."

Mom threw up her hands in frustration. "No. You're not understanding. I *can't* do worse, not by much anyway. That spell I just hit you with would have sheared a truck in half. It would outright kill anyone, man or wolf."

I blinked stupidly as I took in what she was saying, then glanced over to my father who simply nodded.

"That was black magic, *killing* magic," Mom explained, "something my people are taught to never use against another living being unless they have no choice."

"But you just used it against me!"

"That's because I knew what would happen. Don't you get it, Tamara? You have a resistance to offensive magic that is ... unparalleled. Nothing, and I mean *nothing*, I have ever encountered, including some pretty powerful undines, has that kind of immunity."

"I d-don't get it," I sputtered. "Earlier, you tied me to that chair. And what about that magic potion crap you guys have been feeding me all this time?"

"That was defensive magic earlier," Mom said. "It couldn't have hurt you if I tried. It was just meant to calm you down. Believe me, I put a lot into it, and it just barely held you as long as it did."

"And my meds?"

"They bypass your external defenses, go straight into your digestive tract. And even then, it's potent stuff." She stepped forward and put a hand on my arm, actually looking embarrassed. "Why do you think I didn't immediately bring us back home from the diner? It wasn't because I wanted to drive out of there in a blaze of glory. It was because I couldn't."

I backed away from her, letting this sink in. "And if your family found out I can't be hurt by magic..."

She shook her head. "Your unique abilities are part of why Craig is so desperate to bring you into the fold. But the Draíodóir, when presented with the existence of someone against whom their magic is essentially useless, I fear they will react far worse. There will be no sham marriages, no offers of reconciliation."

She looked me deep in the eye and held my gaze. "They will demand your death and, as their queen, they'll expect me to lead the charge."

20

"Mmm, that's nice."

"You like that?"

"Oh yeah. Think I'll like this even more."

Slam!

"OW! FUCK!"

Shit! "Are you okay?" I stepped away from Gary, reluctantly disengaging as he doubled over holding his back. Guess I'd been a little too forceful shoving him against the wall of the closed Quick Lube station. I'd been trying to be playful, see where that led us, but had gotten a bit too into it, forgotten myself. The last thing I wanted to do was accidentally put him in the hospital with foreplay-related injuries.

"Y-yeah. Just kind of wrenched my back." He looked up at me and let out a pained chuckle. "Remind me not to get on your bad side."

I laughed with him, but there was little humor behind it. Though the Quick Lube wasn't exactly my idea of a romantic getaway, I'd been hoping that maybe tonight we could seal the deal, so to speak. The truth was, I'd have gladly jumped in the sack with him after our first date, about three weeks back but, much to my chagrin, he'd turned out to be a gentleman.

Just my luck – the one guy in rural Pennsylvania who wanted to get to know a girl before getting into her pants, and I had to choose him.

Under different circumstances, I might have found it cute, but with impending nuptials less than a week away and me more on edge every day, I really could have done with some stress relief that wasn't battery-operated.

"I have an idea," I said, trying to salvage things. "Why don't we go back to your place. I could rub your back ... maybe you could rub mine."

He tried to straighten up, then winced again. "Think I'm gonna call it a night, Tammy. I have the early shift tomorrow and I'm pretty sure I'm going to need to ice this for a while."

I smiled despite inwardly cringing at his nickname for me. Oh, he was so lucky he was cute, otherwise I'd have wrapped a tire iron around his neck and showed him the true meaning of pain.

No! That wasn't nice. I stepped back and pushed those thoughts from my head. Aside from Riva, Gary had been the best thing about this summer.

After learning that it was either get married or watch my town be wiped out by monsters, I tried to lose myself in various distractions, but it wasn't easy. Going to the gym was pointless, as maxing out the weight machines did nothing except turn curious eyeballs my way. Hanging out at the lake was made more difficult since some of our old high school foes, including Darla McIntyre – former queen bitch of the cheer squad – had been spending their days loitering there. I also reached out to a few of my college friends via Skype, but the conversations fizzled quickly once I realized that I had to dance around the truth or sound like a nutcase.

Ironically enough, it was all that crap and more which had finally given me the push to go for broke and ask Gary out – taking the minivan in for an oil change and then subtly suggesting we grab coffee afterward. Then bringing it back a few days later after my first attempt went right over his head.

Cute and oh so sweet, but perhaps not the sharpest tool in the Quick Lube garage. He was my tool, though, and I wasn't about to let him go so easily.

We stepped outside, he locked the doors, and then we headed toward his pickup. It was time to put all my cards on the table. Damn it all, but I had some wild oats to sow before my wedding and I planned on sowing them good and hard. "Look, I like you, Gary."

"And I like you, Tamm..."

"I know. And I want to get to know you *better*."

He smiled at me, so cute I could feel my panties growing moist. "I want to get to know you better, too. Hey, I have an idea. Why don't you pop by during my lunch hour tomorrow and we can hang out?"

Argh! Guess I needed to spell it out in big neon letters. "Let me just put this out there. If we go back to your place, you can do whatever you want to me. Whatever sick fantasies you have in that head of yours, I'll make them all come true."

Before he could reply, I threw my arms around his neck, pulled him down, and shoved my tongue as far back into his throat as I could. Hopefully that was enough of a hint, because, if not, my next step was probably sending an engraved invitation asking him to shut up and fuck me already.

He returned the kiss, and damn he could kiss, too. It was all I could do to keep from shredding our clothes right there and taking him on the hood of his truck. He tried to pull back, but he wasn't getting away from me that easily. I held him tight, and there was no way he was breaking out of my...

Headlights illuminated us as another vehicle pulled into the otherwise empty lot. My first thought was a cop coming to check on things. Annoying, but easy enough to deal with, unless they were in a mood to give us shit. But then I noticed the shape – too big to be a car and definitely not an SUV.

A minivan.

You have got to be kidding me!

The van parked alongside us and the window rolled down, revealing my mother.

"Tamara," she said cheerfully, "I thought I saw you standing out here. Figured I'd check to see if you needed a ride home. Hello, Gary."

"Hi, Mrs. Bentley," he replied in that clueless tone of his.

"You *saw* me here?" I asked. "Behind the building, from out on the street that's in front of the building?"

"What can I say? A mother knows her own. Hop in, we can grab some ice cream on the way home."

"Ice cream? That's okay, Gary and me were just..."

"It's fine, Tammy," Gary said, causing my left eye to twitch. "Like I said, I have the early shift tomorrow. I'd better go home and get to bed."

Exactly what I was trying to do!

Before I could say anything else, he bent down and gave me a polite kiss on the cheek, like I was his grandma or something.

I turned toward my mom and debated toppling the minivan over onto its side. Wasn't entirely sure I could, but in my current mood, I wouldn't have bet against me either.

"Goodnight!" Gary called from behind me.

I numbly waved to him over my shoulder, then walked around and got into the passenger side of the van.

Mom gave Gary a wave and pulled out of the parking lot.

"I can't believe you just did that," I said after we'd driven a block or so.

"He seems like a … nice boy."

"I didn't want him to be a nice boy," I pointed out, forgetting for one moment that I was talking to my own mother. "I was purposely trying to get him to *not* be a nice boy."

"As I'm well aware. You do realize how unbecoming that is for a young lady, don't you?"

"This coming from the woman who got it on with the werewolf that was trying to kill her."

"It was a different time."

"You've been scrying me, haven't you? Scrying *and* cockblocking me?"

"Such a vulgar term," she replied, giving me side-eye. "But in essence, yes."

"*Why*? It's not bad enough I have to marry Jerry Wartdick next week? You can't even let me have one last good memory before I start spitting out blemish-covered puppies?"

"Sandwich," she said.

"What?"

"That's his name, dear. Jerry Sandwich, not Wartdick."

"You're kidding me, right?" She shook her head. "Can you maybe run us off the road then, because I'd sooner die in a head-on collision than become Tammy Sandwich."

"It is a bit of an unfortunate name."

"Just a wee bit, but it still doesn't explain why you…"

"Do you honestly think the lycanthropes haven't been watching you, too?"

I turned toward her. "I thought they stayed out of High Moon. That it was neutral ground."

"Yes, well, extenuating circumstances allow them to cross the border. And in the space of a month, you have become quite the extenuating circumstance. Don't think for one second Craig doesn't have eyes on you. He won't dare come near our house, he knows better, but the second you step out, it's wise to assume you're being watched – especially after dark. Hard for me to tell for certain without a hair sample to track, but believe me, I can feel them here."

"Feel them? Are you sure you're not being paranoid?"

"If your uncle hadn't called last week to specifically remind me to make sure you were on your best behavior, I would probably agree."

"He did *what*?"

"Called me up, something he's never done before, and told me that I needed to step in before your little romance went too far, lest he and the pack be ... displeased."

"And you didn't tell him to sit on your wand and spin?"

She looked over at me from the driver's seat and actually laughed. "I might have to remember that one. Sadly, no. Don't think for one second I'm afraid of your uncle. He's lucky I didn't roast him in his fur the moment he put his hands on you in our living room."

"So what then?"

"He now knows your father and I are married for real. Before, when he thought it was political, a marriage of convenience only, the advantage was mine. Now, that dynamic has shifted."

"Did he threaten Dad?"

"Craig knows better. The relationship between an alpha and his beta is a tenuous one. If he wanted to punish

Curtis, he'd need to do it personally, otherwise it would make him look weak to the rest."

"And he wouldn't because they're brothers?"

"Partly. Call me biased, but I doubt he wants to tangle with your father for real. No. The problem is on my end. He threatened to tell *my* family."

"But they already know you and Dad are married."

"Married, yes. In love? That's a different matter entirely. I sincerely doubt this will shock you to hear, but the Draíodóir can be a somewhat conceited people."

"You don't say," I replied with a grin.

"When your birthright involves control over the very elements of nature, tell me that wouldn't go to your head eventually."

"Touché."

"There is an assumption among my kind that I'm a martyr, living my life in squalor for the sake of my people."

"Squalor?"

"Metaphorically speaking, of course. That I'm *forced* to share a domicile with a lycanthrope is cause for both respect and pity amongst my family and followers. But there is also the assumption that I do not lower myself to engage in..."

"In?" I prompted.

"*Relations* with your father."

I couldn't help it. I tried to keep in the snort of laughter, but just couldn't do it.

"I expect that sort of behavior from your brother, but you?"

"Sorry, but, well, you guys are about as subtle as..."

"You and that young man were back in the parking lot of that garage?"

"I don't suppose there's anyway for me to block you from spying on me."

She smiled. "I'm the Queen of Monarchs. My powers are vast and nearly all seeing, but if you were to surround yourself with salt at all times, that might help dampen my ability to scry you."

"That would probably do the same to dampen my love life."

Mom turned toward me and shrugged in a way that said such a thing wouldn't bother her in the least.

"I guess I could always start dating goths."

"Or someone possessing a college degree and not working as a grease monkey."

I turned toward her, my mouth agape. "Seriously? The full moon is less than a week away, which means I either have to marry a wart-covered werewolf or risk kick-starting a supernatural war, and you're going to give me shit because my boyfriend changes oil filters for a living?"

"Sorry, can't be helped. I am your mother, after all."

Yeah. She was a mother, all right.

21

"**H**ey."
I ignored my brother as I tried to concentrate on the episode of *Game of Thrones* playing on the TV. I didn't have cable back at college, so I figured I'd catch up on my shows while I had the chance. Mind you, that was proving to be difficult with my dipshit brother trying to crawl up my ass.

"Yo, wham, bam, thank you, Tam, I'm talking to you."

I hit pause on the remote and turned toward Chris. "Did you come up with that all by yourself, or was it a group effort between you and your forever virgin friends?"

It was rare for him to not take the bait, but he ignored my snark. "I know you haven't been around much the last few weeks, but have you noticed that Mom and Dad have been ... kind of tense?"

He was right on both fronts. I'd been doing my damnedest to stay out of the house, either hanging out with Riva, Gary, or wandering the town on my own. "They're not the only ones."

"What, are you and Mom both on the rag or something?"

I narrowed my eyes, the show forgotten for the moment. "You're lucky we're out of hand sanitizer, otherwise I'd punch your stupid lights out."

"I'm serious. You haven't noticed it?"

My little brother wasn't a part of all the shit going on, but he probably deserved to be. It was funny in a way. My parents had been upfront with him about being adopted, but not with the fact that he was the only normal human in the house. Tell me that wasn't going to put the poor kid into therapy at some point. I was tempted to spill my guts, but I knew our parents wanted to keep him in the dark, let him live a relatively normal childhood with his boring dipshit friends.

I let out an involuntary laugh. There I was, being sold down the river, a mail-order bride at best, and yet I was still worried about respecting their wishes.

Fuck that noise.

I clicked off the TV and gave Chris my full attention. "Okay, here's the deal. Dad's a werewolf and Mom's a witch. In two days, I'm being forced to marry another werewolf from Dad's pack, one named Jerry Sandwich. If I don't, there'll be a huge supernatural war that'll kill us all."

Chris blinked at me several times. "Remind me not to do drugs when I go off to college."

"You asked, turd muncher."

"I wanted to know if they were getting a divorce, not if you've been eating mushrooms from the backyard again."

That's what he thought the problem was? If only I could get that lucky. Not that I wanted to see my parents split, but it would be a shitload easier than the reality of the situation. Splitting the holidays I could handle. Becoming Mrs. Jerry Sandwich not so much.

I was tempted to tell my brother to take a flying leap onto a greased flagpole, but when I looked back at him again, I saw real worry in his eyes, so I put a hand on his shoulder instead. "Relax, kid. Mom and Dad aren't getting a divorce."

"Are you sure?"

"Positive. They are ridiculously in love with each other, even beyond the realm of what is natural."

"You aren't shitting me?"

"If I was, I'd go see a doctor immediately." I could see that he still wasn't quite buying it, so I added, "It's not them. They're worried about me. I have some ... issues going on that I'm working through."

He pulled back, looking somewhat relieved. "It's drugs, isn't it?"

"No, it's not drugs."

"Your illness isn't getting worse, is it? I mean, you're not dying, right?"

"Hopefully not anytime soon." Albeit I couldn't quite promise him that, knowing what I did. "It's relationship issues, nothing you need to worry about."

"Oh? I see."

"Good."

"I'll tell my friends to keep their dogs inside, just to be safe."

I balled a fist at the little dickhead, causing him to flinch.

The front door opened and Dad walked in. Chris was right – he did look off, although that wasn't a surprise. The fact that I was able to wake up every morning, knowing what was ahead of me, without puking my guts up was a near miracle. I had to assume some of that stress was wearing off on my folks, too.

"Hey, champ!" Dad greeted, ruffling my brother's hair despite knowing how much he hated it. He turned to me. "You're home."

"Yep." Riva was a great friend and all, but we didn't

like the same shows. Call me crazy for being besties with someone who didn't want to lick the screen whenever Jon Snow came on, but sometimes opposites attract.

He turned to Chris. "Why don't you go play video games for a while, then get packed. I want to talk with your sister."

My brother gave Dad a knowing grin and nodded. Before leaving the room, though, he mimed cracking an egg into a frying pan. "This is your brain on drugs."

"Get out of here before I scramble yours, feeb."

He left the room, which prompted Dad to turn to me. "What was that about?"

"Oh, he thinks the reason I've been on edge is that I'm shooting heroin or something. If only I could get so lucky. Why are you making him pack, by the way? I thought he was past the return date."

"Your mom thought it best to let him stay with relatives for a few days."

"Whose relatives?"

He smiled sadly. "Not mine. Speaking of which, I just had a word with your uncle."

"And the wedding is off?" I asked hopefully.

"No." Before I could comment further, he continued. "It's the Draíodóir, your mother's family. They're not blind. They've noticed his people have been skulking around High Moon. It's making them nervous."

"So?"

"So, nervous sorcerers in close proximity to nervous lycanthropes do not make for a particularly stable situation. We're basically at DEFCON 2 right now. Go to the west end of town and you can practically feel the gald in the air, and not in a good way. It's rapidly turning into a powder keg. I gotta be honest, It hasn't been this bad since ... well, right before your mother and I met."

It wasn't particularly pertinent to my fate three days

from now, but I found myself curious nevertheless. The real version of how they'd met was definitely creepier than the one I'd been spoon-fed growing up, but it was a hell of a lot more interesting, too. "Really?"

"Your mother and I were both young, stupid, and held growing influence within our ranks. At the time, the concept of eradicating our age-old enemies was ... cool. Even with High Moon between us, both sides were taking potshots at the other, hoping to start something. People got hurt, threats were made, that sort of thing. It didn't get better until ... well, until your mother learned you were on the way and we both realized there were more important things than being at each other's throats."

That part of the story was kinda nice, and at a different time I might even find it heartwarming, but it was the past. This was the present, and I didn't see myself magically falling in love with a werewolf with bad skin and an even worse name. And even if I did, that still only accounted for one side of this mess.

"Can Mom fix it? I mean, she's the daffodil queen or something. Don't they have to listen to her?"

Dad chuckled and sat down. "Your mom's family loves their titles and ceremony, but it's not as cut and dry as that. For starters, there are lots of kings, queens, lords of summer, grand poohbahs, whatever. It's just a regional thing. Each family of covens has their own leader, their own title, and their own ability to tell the other groups to take a flying leap."

I leaned forward. Much as I wanted my Westeros fix, what I was hearing now was of potential use. What use? I had no idea, but there was that old saying about knowledge equating to power. Also, after almost twenty years of lies, it was like the dam had burst and my parents were finally coming clean with everything. Didn't make me less angry at them, but they were still family.

"Your mom is technically considered the high priestess, if you will, of her group of covens." He paused and shrugged. "Or whatever they call them in Gaelic. Don't know, don't care. But anyway, when there's a big gathering, she's the one who leads them in their rituals, that sort of stuff. But it's not much different than, say, the monarchy over in England. She has a nice title, but her word isn't exactly absolute. She's strong, your mom, like really strong, and the Draíodóir have a lot of rules along the lines of might makes right, but there's only so much she can do. And the truth of the matter is, I'm not sure she wants to."

"You think she's looking to fuck over your pack?" He raised his eyebrow, to which I replied, "Really? That's what we're going to get hung up on? I'm an adult. Adults say fuck. Can we get past that already?"

He leaned back and smiled. "You'll always be my little girl. But fine, your mom's not home, so we can talk like real people. To answer your question, no. Lissa doesn't like my pack any more than I like her family. It's just how it is. But we're not actively working to get the other side killed ... at least I'm not. And I don't think your mother is either. But, at the same time, she can only push so much before it looks suspicious. There are factions on her side that are seriously old school. They were against the truce our marriage is supposed to represent. If she's too vocal about wanting them to back off against my people, they're going to get emboldened. They already tried once to prove that your mom was going soft, back when we first got together. Believe me, we had to throw some pretty convincing fake fights to make it seem like we hated each other."

"So what you're saying is she's between a rock and a hard place?"

"Pretty much, Tam Tam. The safest course of action for her is to ignore it all, act like it's no big deal. "

"Even if it ultimately causes a war that you'll have to be on opposite sides of?"

He reached over and patted me on the knee. "Better to work toward a solution from the inside than to be quite literally thrown to the wolves. And trust me, we are."

I thought about it and kinda understood what he was saying, but it still didn't make me feel any better. "All of this talk about keeping the peace, maintaining the status quo, and yet I still get to play the sacrificial lamb."

"You're not a sacrifice, Tamara. Forget for one second all the other lives that could be saved. The hell with them. *You* get to live. That's what matters to us."

I stood up. "It doesn't feel like living if I don't get to choose my own life."

"We're not a normal family. We don't have that luxury. We have to make compromises if we're going to keep surviving."

"Everyone keeps talking about compromises." I turned away from him. "But I can't help but notice I'm the one who's expected to live with it all. Maybe it's time I changed that."

Before my dad could say another word, I walked out of the room.

I had some thinking to do. There was no way I was about to willingly sacrifice the lives of so many people but, at the same time, blindly accepting my fate just didn't sit right with me.

22

"**T**his is crazy, Bent. They're going to kill you."

"Oh ye of little faith," I replied into the Bluetooth microphone positioned over the driver's seat.

"*You're not supposed to go into Morganberg,*" Riva replied over the speaker. "*They made that pretty clear the last time we were there.*"

I could hear the annoyed edge to her voice. Danger or not, she was more ticked off that I was doing this without her. But it had to be this way. It's why I decided to call her *after* I'd already crossed the town line. Otherwise, I had little doubt she'd have talked me into letting her tag along. No thanks. Things were bound to be hairy enough without worrying about her, too.

I let out a tiny chuckle at my silent pun.

"*Something funny? Because I'm not laughing.*"

"Inside joke," I replied, stopping at a light. "But anyway, the wolves decided to drop their decree for the blood moon. I'm allowed in, otherwise they can't have their happy nuptials, can they?"

"*So that's your plan? You're heading over to what, get your hair done, maybe see if they'll give you a bouquet of dead rodents to throw?"*

"Nope. See, I'm pretty sure that Uncle Craig meant I was allowed in tonight, when the moon was up. But he was kind of sloppy with his words. He didn't expressly forbid me from popping by during the day, so that's what I'm doing."

"Why?"

"I asked around. Found out where my blushing groom-to-be works. I wanted to have a word with him, get to know him a bit."

"You're going to kick his ass, aren't you?"

I gave the receiver a shocked look, as if Riva could see me. "No. I'm going to talk to him. Explain that we're doing this to prevent all-out war. That it's going to be nothing more than another marriage of convenience, like Mom and Dad are supposed to have."

"Your mom and dad go at it all the time."

"Trust me, I'm well aware. I could hear them last night. Good thing I wasn't getting any sleep anyway. Guess werewolves get a bit randy around the full moon."

"So what makes you think that your new husband won't want to show you the meat in a Jerry and Tamara sandwich?"

Ugh. "Thanks for making me almost throw up in my mouth."

"Fine. Bad joke. But seriously."

"I'm going to tell him that's the way it's going to be, and that if he wants to see other people, it'll be fine by me. I have to go through with this because otherwise Craig is going to freak the fuck out." I left out the part where he'd descend upon the town and tear everyone in it limb from limb. That was one tidbit I hadn't shared with anyone outside of my family. "But that's it. There's no love here, and there's definitely no physical attraction. That means we hold hands and look like a nice werewolf couple on paper, nothing more."

"*Think it'll work?*"

"It has to work, because that's the way it's going to be."

"*What if he tries to go all...*"

I knew where she was going, so I cut her off at the pass. "Let me guess, decides to go all doggie style on me?"

"*You said it, I didn't.*"

"Bite me. Fortunately, I'm not exactly a damsel in distress. If Jerry decides to get grabby, then he and my fists are going to have a long discussion about it."

Riva was silent for several seconds before speaking again. "*Gotta say, this isn't much of a plan.*"

"I know, but it's the only one I've got."

"*What if it doesn't work?*"

That was the big question right there, wasn't it? Sadly, I didn't have any answer other than false confidence. "It will. I have an ace up my sleeve." Now if I could only figure out what that ace was...

"*All right, but If you need me, I'm there for you.*"

Despite knowing she couldn't see me, I smiled. God, she was a good friend. If there was one person I needed in this world right now, it was her. But tonight was something I had to do on my own. I couldn't risk it otherwise. "Thanks, I mean it. But I need to do this and you need to stay inside tonight. It's not only a full moon, it's a blood moon. According to my parents those are rare and ... weird."

"*Define weird.*"

"I don't know. They wouldn't say much, just that it's sacred for both sides and ... again, weird. Not sure what that means, but I have a feeling the wolves are going to be a bit more wild tonight than usual."

That was only a guess on my part, but it seemed logical, more so because I could kind of feel it myself. I couldn't explain it, but somehow I was certain I felt the pull of the moon. It was like a low hum reverberating in my bones. Maybe it was just nerves, but I didn't think so. And it made sense in a way. I was half-werewolf, after all, so it should stand to reason that at least some of their rules applied to me.

But that was probably the least of my worries.

For now, I was on my own. Dad would be at the "ceremony" later, but he'd almost certainly be wolfed out. In fact, I hadn't seen him since early this morning. For all I knew, he was already here in Morganberg, out in the woods somewhere.

As for Mom, she'd mentioned something about heading west to Crescentwood, pretty much the witch equivalent to Morganberg – its sister town, if those sisters hated each other. Chances were she had her own stuff to do with her people tonight. But witches and warlocks were a concern for another time. For now, I had a small army of werewolves to keep from descending upon High Moon and tearing it to shreds.

"*The wolves are going to be even crazier than last month?*" Riva asked with an audible shudder to her voice, no doubt remembering our harrowing encounter in the hollows. "*And yet you're driving there to marry one of them?*"

"Not my first choice."

"*Let me guess, your only choice?*"

"Something like that. Anyway, I'm almost there, Riva. Let me get going."

"*Be careful, Bent.*"

"I will."

"*Oh, and try to look beautiful.*"

"Why?"

"*It is your wedding, after all.*"

I let out a laugh. "I'll take pictures. I'm sure you and the *Weekly World News* will both get a kick out of them."

Riva and I said our goodbyes and then I reluctantly hung up. I didn't want to, but I needed to get my head in the game, steel myself for whatever was to come. Besides, I had also just pulled into the parking lot of my husband-to-be's place of employment: Shop Haven. There, Jerry Sandwich — werewolf, Compound W aficionado, and aspiring bridegroom — held the awe-inspiring title of stock boy.

And yet Mom dared to berate me for dating a grease monkey.

It felt like all eyes were on me as I stepped into the supermarket. It's quite possible they were. For all I knew, the entire town was populated by fucking werewolves. It was probably something I should have asked Dad when I had the chance but, at the time, demographics didn't seem like an important detail.

I walked down the produce aisle, glancing at people as I went and feeling like an unwanted outsider, as if shopping for celery was punishable by death. One sour-faced old lady in particular made eye contact and gave me a look that was full of daggers.

Rather than back down, a sign of weakness in any dog pack — or so I had heard — I approached her and stepped up to the challenge.

"Chill, grandma. It's okay for me to be here. Craig gave me permission."

She stared back at me, her scowl growing. "Who the hell is Craig?"

Huh? "You know — Craig. Alpha werewolf. Leader of the pack?"

She blinked several times, then patted me on the arm.

"Dear, take the advice of someone who's been there. Don't do drugs. They'll just screw up your life."

With that, she stepped past me and proceeded to scowl at the price of Brussels sprouts.

Okay, so much for the entire town howling at the moon tonight. I made a mental note to not make a complete ass of myself and continued on.

I passed aisle after aisle, most of them full of shoppers or bored-looking employees, but so far, no wart-riddled fiancés to be seen. I was just starting to wonder if he'd maybe taken the afternoon off when I turned a corner and saw Jerry down on one knee, as if he were proposing ... to the rack of potato chips in front of him. And they say romance is dead.

Oh well, nothing was going to get accomplished watching him debate whether Lays or Wise got prominent placement on the shelf. I strolled up to him as casually as I could and stood there for several seconds before finally saying, "Hey."

"I'll be with you in a moment, miss. I'm..." Jerry turned toward me and the color drained from his face.

Jeez, the lipstick I was wearing wasn't my favorite shade, but it wasn't *that* bad.

"You?" he said, backing up a step on his knees. "What are you doing here? You're not supposed to..."

Hmm, quite the nervous Nelly when he didn't have his friends around. Something to remember. "Relax, Jer. I'm not here for a rumble in the snack lane. I just came to talk. I figured maybe with, you know, us getting married tonight, it might not be a bad idea."

"You shouldn't..." He lowered his voice to a whisper. "You're not supposed to be in Morganberg. You know this."

"Craig gave me permission."

"That was for tonight."

179

"He should have been more specific then. But who cares? I'm here now and so are you."

"I'm working."

"Duh."

"I'm not supposed to fraternize with the customers."

Fraternize with the...

I decided to ignore that and concentrate on what I'd come here to say. If anything, it seemed like the ideal time. For starters, Jerry came across much different than last time I'd met him, which had been the only time I'd met him. Second, for a guy who could turn into a murderous wolf beast at will, he sure seemed to be overly nervous about being docked a few minutes on his paystub. "Not even with your bride-to-be?" Ugh, I could have gagged on those words. "Like I said, I'm just here to talk."

Seeing that I wasn't leaving and his chips weren't getting sorted so long as I was there, he finally nodded. "Fine, but not now. I get off in an hour."

I debated continuing to talk to him regardless of how much work he had, but then realized that would make me an asshole for asshole's sake. I wanted this conversation to go smoothly, and that wasn't going to happen if I was purposely needling him. Besides, there was still time. It was already afternoon, and we'd be pushing toward late afternoon by then, but there was plenty of daylight left for us to hash out the details of what wouldn't be happening during our wedding night.

"I'll be waiting out front," I said at last. "Don't make me come looking for you again."

I really hadn't meant that as a threat, but it came out sounding like one and I didn't bother to correct myself. I simply patted him on the shoulder and walked past. It wasn't my plan to lead off with violence, but so long as Jerry remembered that was an option, then maybe it wasn't a bad thing.

Fortunately, it was a nice day - cool for late summer, but with a clear sky. I'd brought a jacket for later but, for now, it sat on my lap. Had it been warmer, it wouldn't have been a bad day to get some sunbathing in, but I was kind of glad it wasn't. Working on my tan wasn't really at the top of my priority list anyway.

I spent the time checking Facebook and people watching, catching enough angry stares to tell me that either Morganberg was home to some pretty cranky people or that not all of the clientele of Shop Haven were fully human.

Finally, I looked up and spotted Jerry stepping out of the store. He looked in the opposite direction first, didn't see me, and his body visibly relaxed. *Nuh uh, Mr. Sandwich. It's not going to be that easy.*

He turned in my direction and I made it a point to wave at him, enjoying the way his face fell. Mind you, if this was how he was going to act during our years of *marital bliss*, then maybe I didn't have much to worry about. Safe to say, Jerry wasn't anywhere close to being an alpha dog.

I walked up to him with a friendly grin on my face. No point in starting this off on the wrong foot. "How was your shift?"

"So ... what do you want?" he asked, his head scanning the parking lot as if he was afraid of us being seen together.

Fine, right to the point it is then. "What do I want? We're getting married in a few hours. Your boss's idea, not mine." No, it was wrong to start off by pointing fingers. "Anyway, I was hoping maybe we could find a quiet spot to talk."

"About what?"

Dear God, this guy couldn't be this dense, could he? Hell, so far he made Gary look like a PhD candidate by comparison. "About us, genius. Call me crazy, but I kind of want to ... know what I'm getting into. I mean, you do realize that once we're married we're going to have to talk, right?"

He shrugged uncomfortably. "I guess. But afterwards ... it'll be different."

That was an understatement. I'd be Mrs. Tamara Sandwich. No way was I living that down once I got back to school. I had already resigned myself to the fact that there would be lots of sandwich jokes thrown about, followed by lots of fat lips. "Is there somewhere we could talk? A park, your place?" *Ugh!* "I mean, I drove over so..."

"You have a car? Neat!"

Really? That's what excited him? I glanced toward Shop Haven, noting the attached liquor store next to it. Just a few more years and I'd be legally able to walk in, buy whatever the hell I wanted, and drink until conversations like this were nothing more than a blurry memory. But for now... "Yeah, I do. So how about..."

"We can't go back to my place."

"Okay, that's..."

"My mom doesn't like the idea of me getting married. She heard what you did and she's kinda mad at Craig. Thinks you're possessed by demons."

Wonderful. A mother-in-law who didn't think I was good enough for her little shelf stocker. The holidays were bound to be a blast. "Fine. Then where?"

He thought for a moment, his face going blank as if he didn't have enough horsepower upstairs to think and chew gum. After several seconds, he lifted a finger and pointed.

"Okay, north. Good. What's there?"

"The hollows. Craig wants us all in the woods early tonight. Big ceremony and all that."

"Our wedding?"

"The blood moon."

"Oh, of course."

"Maybe we can talk on the way. There's this clearing along the path. That would be a good place to chat. Also, it's like halfway there, in case we go long."

I couldn't help but notice that when he started talking about the woods, he suddenly became a lot more loquacious. Maybe that was somewhere he felt safe, in control. Or maybe it was the wolf inside of him talking, being that in a few short hours there'd be a lunar event that was the supernatural equivalent of Christmas, if a bit rarer. That might have been it. Heck, the later it got, the more I felt that strange buzzing in my bones, an anxiousness as if I'd just guzzled a quart of Mountain Dew.

Regardless, for the first time since I'd found him, he seemed somewhat at ease. At the very least, it would make for a better conversation if he was able to give me more than one word answers.

It wasn't lost upon me that the hollows were wolf territory, his pack's backyard so to speak. He was essentially granting me an audience, but only if I gave him home field advantage.

And he'd have it, too. Just the thought of the hollows sent a small shiver down my spine. Despite everything, the events from last month had still scared the crap out of me. More than once I'd woken up in a cold sweat, unable to get it out of my head.

Fuck! It wasn't like I could avoid the woods later anyway. At least this way I wouldn't get lost trying to find where I was supposed to be going. It's not like Craig or even my own dad had given me precise directions.

"All right. Let's do this."

Perhaps a poor choice of words, but it was time to put this puppy to bed – before the puppy I was walking with tried to get me into his.

23

To my surprise, a few of the leaves were already changing colors. Looked like it was going to be an early fall. Mind you, not that it mattered to me since school would be in by then.

Still, the walk wasn't a bad one. The scenery itself was gorgeous. Had I been on an actual date, with someone I actually wanted to be with, this would have had some serious romantic potential ... if we'd been anywhere but the hollows.

Ah, but romance, or the lack thereof, was precisely what I'd come here to discuss with Jerry.

Pity that sentiment appeared to be one-sided.

He abruptly steered me off the trail, one of his warty mitts grabbing my bare arm. Eww! My pulse raced, but it had less to do with him and more to do with the growing shadows of the forest.

We walked for a bit through overgrown scrub grass, climbed over roots, and ducked below branches. Finally, just about when I was sure we were hopelessly lost, we stepped past some bushes into a clearing and my breath immediately caught in my throat.

I didn't know what it was, but that humming in my bones seemed to increase tenfold. It was ... it's hard to describe, but it was like this place had a voice all its own. Strange, because while it looked pleasant enough, there wasn't anything that seemed to make it otherwise stand out. I mean, it was just a clearing in the woods, maybe thirty feet across. It was circular, almost close to being a perfect circle from my vantage point, but that wasn't anything to write home about. As for the view ... you guessed it, trees.

Regardless, for a moment it made me completely forget that we were in the hollows.

"You like this place?" Jerry walked to the middle of the glade. There, he closed his eyes and began to turn in a slow circle as if in ecstasy. Weird, but whatever. I couldn't lie and say I didn't feel *something*, some energy or force from this place. But I was there to talk, not bask in the glow of nature or some other hippy shit. If he was hoping to win me over by sheer virtue of a nice picnic spot, he had another thing coming.

I walked toward him, then stopped and spun back around, certain that I'd heard someone whispering. The hairs on my arm stood up, but then I realized it was nothing more than the breeze blowing through this place. Or at least, that's what I told myself. I'd only been in this clearing for about two minutes and already my opinion of it was rapidly changing from enchanted to creepy as fuck all.

"Magical, isn't it?" Jerry said. "My mom used to call spots like this Groves of the Valkyries. She said they were sacred places where the walls between us and the old gods were thinnest."

"Sacred, eh?" I couldn't help but notice Jerry's tone had changed. He wasn't quite back to being the prick he'd appeared to be at my home, but he was a long way from answering in monosyllable. It was hard to tell if it was really this grove or the added confidence of being in the woods and knowing his pack mates were near. Still, this was what I had hoped for, a back and forth conversation, not a one-sided debate with someone who was semi-comatose. "So ... is this where it's going to happen?"

"Where what's going to happen?"

"You know ... us."

He opened his eyes, revealing the tiniest bit of yellow at the edge of his irises, then shook his head. "No. Not here. My mom also used to say that places like this were for quiet contemplation only. You didn't do anything of importance here – ceremonies, any of that – without expecting conse-quences." He blinked and his eyes were back to being dull-old Jerry eyes again. "Craig doesn't really believe any of that, but there's a spot deeper in the woods he likes better anyway, kind of our pack's meeting place. There's a lot of deer, no humans within spitting distance, and it's far from the road."

"Sounds dreamy," I replied deadpan.

"Once you've been there enough times, it's easy to find. You'll get used to it. After all, it's going to be your new home."

That last part had come out of his mouth easily and naturally, as if it were law. But that was the first I'd heard of it. "Hold on. New home? I thought you lived..."

"With my mom? Yeah, but she's not going to let you move in with us."

"So I'm supposed to change my name to Sheena and live in the woods instead?"

Jerry's eyes opened wide for a moment, but then he laughed. "It's not that bad. There's some cabins there. Craig had them built a few years back. He's going to give one to us."

"Oh, so it's Daniel Boone instead."

"Who?"

"Basic American history?"

He let out a nervous laugh. "I wasn't really a good student."

Color me surprised, but I held my tongue. This conversation wouldn't go well if I immediately laid into him about being a fucking idiot. "Okay, so about why I wanted to talk to you..."

"I thought we *were* talking about that."

"No." I stepped forward, toward the middle of the clearing, and that buzzing in my bones intensified again. The hell? Was there a powerline buried here? "*You* were talking about me moving into a cabin in the middle of werewolf woods, something I hadn't agreed to. What I wanted to talk about was our mutual ... *expectations*, if you will, for our married life."

"Expectations? Like what time you should have dinner ready?"

Had he put even the slightest amount of attitude into that, I'd have knocked him clean across this clearing, but it seemed we were back to clueless Jerry again. So be it. If one of us was going to hold up this conversation, it might as well be me. "That's one expectation. Not one I have, mind you." There was no point beating around the bush, literal or otherwise. Besides, the sooner we finished and left creepy hollow here, the better. "What I mostly mean is our marriage and our ... *relations* after. As in, there won't be any."

"Relations? Like talking to each other?"

"Like sex!"

"How are we supposed to have pups then?"

"Pups?"

"You know, babies, or whatever they'll be like with you?"

Whatever they'll be like ... no. I wasn't going to take the bait. "Simple. We don't."

"But Craig said..."

"I don't care what Craig said. I haven't been privy to those conversations. It seems this past month everyone has been talking at me or about me, but nobody's bothering to talk *to* me."

A worried look crossed Jerry's face. "He told me we had to do it. Consummate the marriage, that is." Big word for such a dimwit, but this wasn't a spelling bee, so I let him finish. "That we'd eventually need to raise a family in the tradition of the pack, so long as they came out ... normal. But he also said I'd need to show him proof."

"Wait up, hold on a second." I wasn't sure where to start, because Jerry had just dropped two brand-new bombshells on me, neither of which were going to make this bride blush with anything but anger. "Proof? Meaning what?"

"That we did it. I don't know exactly what he meant. Video maybe, I guess."

My left eye twitched and again the wind sounded like disembodied whispers. I imagined they were telling me to do some very not nice things to Jerry. It did nothing to improve my mood. "And that thing about normal puppies ... err, babies?"

"Oh, that," he replied, his tone conversational as if we were back at the store, discussing potato chips. "He was pretty specific that they had to be like me. Normal werewolves. No more half-breeds or weird stuff like that. That's why he wanted you to mate with one of us, make sure we neutralized the unsavory elements of your genes."

Once again, Jerry seemed to spontaneously jump about fifty IQ points. As he spoke, I once more detected the slightest hint of yellow in his eyes. It was like his wolf half was the smarter of the two, and it was gradually growing more dominant the later it got.

I glanced at the lengthening shadows. The sun was starting to set, the gloom threatening to overcome this place. Up in the sky, the full moon was just barely visible. It wasn't in all its bloody glory yet, but it was definitely a sign that the day was transitioning to night and my time was growing short. Worse, it would soon be dark and I'd still be in the hollows.

A shudder passed through me, but then I realized Jerry was still talking – with no sense of irony whatsoever – about us raising litters of normal werewolves. I forced myself to focus on that and my growing annoyance with it.

"Okay, stop right there. For starters, you can forget about taping me for Wolfhub or whatever it is you guys jack it to. Ditto on your werewolf eugenics program. I'm stating it here for the record: there will be no sex. Our marriage is one of convenience only. I'll join your pack, follow your rules, do what I have to so we can keep the peace between you guys and Hogwarts on the other side of town. But you and me, it's not happening. Sorry, but you're not my type – my type being guys I'm not forced into an arranged marriage with. You can take that fifteenth century shit and stick it where the sun don't shine."

Oddly enough, that should have been this clearing, as the sun had slipped down far enough for us to be cloaked in shadows. Yet we weren't. Despite the very edge of the sunlight barely touching the eastern tip of the glade, it was almost as if this place glowed with a light all its own. Some weird trick of refraction maybe. No idea. Physics wasn't my top subject.

"None of that matters." Maybe it was another trick of the weird light, but I could have sworn I saw more yellow in Jerry's eyes. The more important question, though, was whether he was seeing the proverbial red in mine. "Craig told me what we have to do."

"I don't report to Craig."

"You will. He's our alpha."

"And you seem to be forgetting there's a difference between being a good pound puppy and being a slave. Craig can tell me where I need to live, how to act in public, all of that. I don't like it, but I'll go along with it. But he can't tell me what to do with my own body."

"But I'll be your husband. You're supposed to obey me."

I turned and threw my hands up in frustration. Only in the middle of fucking Pennsylvania would you find a group of werewolves worshipping some ancient Germanic god, yet perfectly willing to also go along with backwards Bible bullshit. I swear, some preacher somewhere would have a field day with this bunch. "I think we should have a little discussion about our vows tonight."

"And even if you don't," Jerry continued, ignoring me, "you still have to do what Craig says. *Everything* he says. You know what will happen if you don't."

I spun and stalked toward where he now stood, near the western edge of the clearing. He should have been draped in shadows, but instead, stood in sharp contrast to the rapidly darkening woods behind him. What the fuck was it with this place?

It didn't matter. I had bigger fish to fry. "Can you honestly tell me you're okay with that? There's a whole town full of people minding their own damned business and you're fine with dropping a death sentence on them?"

Jerry looked uncomfortable, but it only lasted for a moment. Then he merely shrugged. "Craig's the alpha."

All at once, I saw why my uncle had picked this guy ... well, aside from the fact that he'd been at my place that day. Jerry was a follower, someone who'd happily munch down Tide pods if he thought everyone else was doing it. He was a foot soldier, one who did what he was told under the auspices that those who were doing the telling had the authority. Go back seventy or eighty years and he would've been a happy little Nazi leading Jews to the gas chamber all because he was told to.

Worse, I had little doubt he would be the first to look confused if someone tried holding him accountable for any crimes he committed following those orders.

As much as he physically repulsed me, this side of him – the unquestioning follower – made me despise him.

The whispers on the wind, the thrumming in my bones from this weird-ass clearing, being in the hollows after dark, all of it had put me on edge and this asshole was making it worse by the second.

But if I thought that everything he'd told me up until then had been playing with fire, what he said next really lit the fuse.

"Craig's the alpha," he repeated. "He said that if you don't do what you're told, then what happens next is on your head. And to make sure you know it, he's going to start with that friend of yours, Riva Kale."

"*What?!*"

24

Unable, and maybe unwilling, to stop myself, I grabbed Jerry by the lapels of his Shop Haven shirt, spun, and threw him toward the center of the glade.

He landed with a heavy thud, rolling head over heels, but I was on the move before he'd even slid to a halt. I pushed him down and straddled him – the closest he was going to get to cowgirl style. His eyes were dazed but when he opened his mouth, fangs began to sprout. It made me remember the last time I'd been in these woods, how weak and helpless I felt as a monster toyed with my friend's life. And now they were daring to threaten her again.

Barely aware I was doing it, I hauled off and slammed a fist into the side of his face, resulting in an audible *crack*. I let another punch fly free, then threw back my head and screamed in both fear and rage, the sound echoing across the clearing.

My own voice reverberating through the trees cleared a small bit of the blinding emotions swirling around in my head, enough for me to regain control. I climbed off of Jerry, stood, and pulled him up with me.

Balling his shirt in my hand, I lifted him off his feet. "Why did you say Riva's name?" His reply was a snarl, which did nothing except set me off again. I slapped him across the face, the impact like a shotgun blast in the clearing. "Focus, Jerry. Tell me how you know about my friend."

He reached up and tried to grab hold of my wrist. His strength was definitely no longer human, or at least not what one would expect from a guy who looked like he did, but it wasn't anything I couldn't handle either. If he was trying to make a fight of this, he was barking up the wrong tree.

I drove a fist into his stomach. "Tell me about Riva!"

He was desperately trying to change now, getting both heavier and hairier, but I guess some concentration was required because each time I hit him, he seemed to revert back. I didn't really care so much about keeping him human, though, as much as I did making sure he could still talk.

"Tell me!"

Finally, Jerry held up his hands in surrender. He was stuck mid-transformation. His body had enlarged to the point where his clothes were strained. Wicked claws had sprung from his fingers and coarse, thick hair covered most of his body. He sorta looked like how one might picture a Neanderthal ... assuming Neanderthals wore shirts proclaiming them to be proud members of the Shop Haven team.

His face had begun to elongate, but he was still able to speak. "*It ... was Craig.*"

"No shit, Sherlock."

"*H-he ... he ordered us to stay in High Moon after we confronted you at your home.*"

"Stay?"

Jerry nodded. "*We parked down the block, waited to see if anything would happen.*"

I definitely remembered that day – storming out, heading over to my friend's house to commiserate while she made bad jokes at my expense. "You followed me?"

He nodded again. "*We asked around town, staked out her place later that night. Learned what we could.*"

"Why?"

"*Leverage. Craig wasn't sure his threat was enough. Thought you might try to bolt or get that witch involved.*"

"You didn't think threatening to murder the entire town would be enough to sway me?!"

Jerry ignored my question and kept talking, his voice growing more gravelly with each word. "*Don't trust witches, or those connected to witches. Needed to ... make sure you understood.*"

"Understood what?"

"*Your family ... is protected by the treaty,*" he growled, "*but your friends aren't. Make sure you knew that disobedience would be met with blood ... those you loved most. If you ... didn't obey, he was going to send me ... to ... do ... irrrr!*"

The rest was lost in a snarl, but I understood enough. I never suspected my uncle could be such a cold-blooded bastard. And this monster had willingly gone along with it, had happily agreed to be Craig's hitman.

I barely noticed that his weight was no longer on my arm, that his feet were now planted firmly on the ground. As he finished confessing, Jerry also completed his transformation, adding a good foot to his height, not to mention fur and lots of sharp teeth. I'm sure it was an impressive sight, but all I saw at that moment was red.

The sons of bitches. It was bad enough they'd threatened my town, people who had nothing to do with this. If it had been a bluff, that would be one thing, but listening to Jerry, I was now convinced it wasn't. That wasn't good enough for them, though. They had to make it personal. My uncle and his buddies wanted me to hurt, and for what? Because I was different, something new, something they didn't understand?

I hadn't wanted to become their enemy, but they seemed dead set on making me one. Maybe it was time to accept that.

Jerry grabbed hold of my wrist and yanked it away, tearing what was left of his Shop Haven shirt.

Had the asshole tried to apologize, shown even the slightest hint of remorse, I might have cut him some slack. There was that old saying about not shooting the messenger. But he was in this too deep. Even if he didn't have the brainpan to grasp it, he was still a willing participant.

Worst of all for him, he was right there in front of me when I lost my fucking temper.

Completely transformed as he was, Jerry's strength increased by a considerable margin. Factor in his teeth, claws, and size advantage and nobody would have blamed me for being scared, especially out here in the hollows again.

Too bad for him, being the underdog was nothing new to me. I'd been one for my entire wrestling career, competing in a sport where I was often dismissed as a mere novelty. This was no different, save for one little detail – I wasn't actually the underdog in this fight.

Jerry bent down, lowering his head to no doubt try and bite my face off. That was awfully thoughtful, putting himself well within reach of my much shorter arms. I offered him my *thanks* by way of a roundhouse punch to the muzzle.

Then I followed up with another, just in case he didn't feel that first love tap.

Drool flew from his mouth with each blow. Gross. Bad

enough these things were man-eating beasts of legend, but they were slobber monsters, too. Ugh! It's one of the reasons I had never wanted a Saint Bernard.

Jerry took a wild swing at me, claws and all – telling me he meant business – but I ducked, sidestepped, then brought up a knee into his midsection.

He doubled over, wheezing, so I grabbed him by his stupid wolf ears and forced him to face me – noting that even as a werewolf, his skin was still wart-covered. "You tell Craig to stay away from my friends, away from my family, and the hell away from me!"

I shoved him back, hard enough so that he landed flat on his ass. My point hopefully made, I started to turn away. If this kept up, something bad was going to happen. I tried to tell myself I didn't want that, yet was more than aware that a part of me very much did. This wasn't the first time I'd rearranged someone's face for giving my best friend grief, but most of that had been nothing more than petty kid stuff. This ... this was different. They'd threatened her life. It was ... I could...

I could hear those strange whispers again – much louder this time. They were unintelligible, yet it somehow felt like they were egging me on. What the hell was up with this place? The sun was rapidly setting now, darkness taking over, yet the clearing still had a strange luminescence to it, almost as if it were glowing with its own power. Whatever was going on, I needed to get out of there, stop breathing the fungus spores or whatever the fuck was in the air.

That would have to wait, though. Footsteps registered in my ears, coming up fast. Freaking Jerry. Too brainwashed to say no to murder and too stupid to know when to stay down.

Enough was enough.

I spun and crouched at the same time. Jerry's

momentum carried him forward, and my arms did the rest, catapulting him over me and sending him flying.

There came a high-pitched yip from behind me. I turned to find Jerry had landed on the business end of a root sticking up at the very edge of the glade. He'd been impaled through the stomach and was now lying there with a jagged shard of wood sticking through his gut.

Crap!

It was ugly, and for a moment, my heart went out to him. I'd just meant to rough him up a bit, send a message, nothing more. But then I remembered what Dad had told me about werewolves healing quickly. Hell, I'd seen it with my own eyes.

While I didn't pretend to know the limits of their powers, it wasn't like I'd shot him in the face with a silver bullet, assuming that wasn't Hollywood bullshit. Still, I couldn't just leave him like that.

I stepped forward and he whimpered as I approached. "Oh, relax. Serves you right for being an asshole. Let's see if we can get you off of that."

He took a swipe at me the moment I was in reach, causing me to pull back just in the nick of time. "Knock it off, dickhead. I'm trying to help you. I'll get you back to the edge of town. After that, you can find your own way to the hospital ... or vet."

Jerry tried to claw at me again, but I caught his arm this time and forced it down. "I said, I'm trying to help."

In response, he threw back his head and howled – long and loud – a mournful sound that echoed across the clearing and probably far beyond.

At first, I thought it was because of the pain, but then it kept going and I realized he wasn't screaming in agony so much as calling for help.

Shit! "Hey, knock that off."

He snarled at me. Then he pulled back his lips in what

could only be called a gross mockery of a smile, lifted his head, and did it again.

"I said, stop that!"

Despite the howls, those whispers rose up inside my head again, almost like a swarm of mosquitoes in my skull. It was making it hard to form coherent thoughts. Fuck it. I could take some Advil later. For now, I needed to shut Jerry up.

I tried to cover his muzzle with my hands, force him to quiet down, but he fought me, drawing me closer until my face was within reach for him to...

Enough!

I grabbed Jerry on either side of his head and twisted his jaws away from me with everything I had, not realizing just how angry I was. There came the sickening *CRACK* of bone breaking and then his head fell limply to the side, his tongue rolling out of his mouth.

Oh no! "Jerry?"

There was no response.

"Um ... Jerry, are you okay?"

I felt like a complete idiot asking it. Of course he wasn't okay. Despite the shock of what I'd done, it was painfully obvious what had happened. I'd snapped his neck like a toothpick, killing him instantly.

"Oh, shit," I muttered backing away. The guy was an ass, but I hadn't meant to kill him. "Shit!"

This couldn't have ended in a worse way had I tried.

But then, a moment later, as I continued to watch Jerry in the hopes that maybe his werewolf DNA would pull a Lazarus, I realized how wrong I was.

The buzzing in my head became higher-pitched, sounding like a dentist's drill had been shoved into my brain. But then, just as it reached a level where I was sure it would drive me mad, it abruptly stopped. In that moment, the clearing, still slightly aglow despite the setting sun, put to rest the thought that I'd been imagining things. It was as if someone turned a blue spotlight on the place, illuminating it from the ground up.

What in the name of...?

The weirdness wasn't done yet, though. The strange, ghostly illumination began to change. It wasn't all at once, but gradual, like the blue aura of light was slowly being drowned out by a darker shade – the color of blood.

I looked up and saw the moon. It was full and beginning to take on the reddish tinge that gave it its name, the same color that was now beginning to suffuse the glade.

Certain I was losing my mind, I glanced back down at Jerry and saw something that made the revelation that monsters were real seem like a minor blip in comparison.

The blood that had pooled beneath his body had taken on a strange hue, almost as if someone had taken a picture, loaded it into Photoshop, and turned the contrast up to maximum. It stood out against the grass in bas relief then, as I watched, it was sucked into the ground.

I'm not talking about draining into the dirt or mixing with the soil. I mean sucked, as if the very Earth itself had gotten a taste and now wanted the rest, leaving nothing behind.

Within moments, even the grass, stained red by Jerry's impalement, was fresh and green again. It was only then that I realized the color of the light in the glade was changing in proportion to how much of Jerry's blood was being lapped up.

As the last drop was pulled into the ground, the clearing lit up in an angry shade of crimson and that humming began again, this time cranked up to eleven. It was like being right in front of the speaker array at a rock concert. Every bone in my body vibrated painfully until I was certain they'd shatter from within, leaving me a quivering heap of flesh on the forest floor.

That would have been a hell of a way to be found. Jerry dead – impaled but bloodless – and me next to him, my skeleton pulverized into powder. I didn't pretend to know the finer nuances of either werewolf or Draío ... witch culture, but I had to imagine that would be weird even by their standards.

But then, rising above the buzzing in my head, even if just barely, I heard the howls – low and distant at first, but rising in pitch as more and more *voices* joined in. The pack. Jerry had been calling to them in his final moments, and they'd heard him.

I shook my head, clearing whatever hold this freaky-ass grove had over me and began to back away – all while making myself a promise to listen the next time my parents told me to stay the hell out of the hollows.

The moment my foot stepped down outside the edge of the glade, it was as if someone turned off a circuit breaker. One second the entire place had been nearly ablaze with crimson light. The next, it was no different than the rest of the forest – just a small clearing bathed in shadow. It was the same with the strange whispers in my mind. They too fell instantly silent, as if they'd never been anything more than my imagination.

That was way too fucking weird.

I glanced once more toward where Jerry's body lay. I hadn't wanted this, felt sick to my stomach at what I'd been forced to do. But at the same time, I couldn't lie to myself and pretend it would've played out different had I been given a second chance. The threat against Riva was too much for me to take. My loved ones were my personal line in the sand, and he'd crossed it.

"I'm sorry."

A moment passed and I was about to turn away, but then movement caught my eye. Jerry... In the gloom, his body appeared to be shrinking in on himself. I blinked several times, but couldn't tell if it was a trick of the light, him reverting back to his human form, or if something else was happening.

Just before I stepped back into the clearing to check for certain, those howls began again – closer this time – and I forced myself to look away.

The pack was coming, and once they saw what I'd done, it would only get worse from there.

I needed to get out of these cursed woods, make it back home, and warn the people I loved before hell was unleashed upon them.

25

I considered heading back to the car. That would have been the most logical move, but perhaps not the smartest. Mind you, neither logic nor acting smart held much sway right then.

There was no telling how far away the howls I'd heard were. They definitely carried some distance. That said, it didn't strike me as the best course of action to step foot back into Morganberg now that the sun had set. Sure, not all of them were werewolves, but I had a feeling enough were. And, considering what had happened at the diner last month, I'd have to be an idiot to assume they'd have any qualms about changing into their monstrous forms within the city limits.

At the same time, I had no intention of staying in these woods a second longer than I needed to. Every shadow was a potential monster in hiding, every breaking branch a probable enemy in pursuit. Between these woods and knowing what I'd done to Jerry — that I'd crossed a line and become a killer — it took all of my effort to focus.

I couldn't afford either grief or panic, not when I needed to get back to High Moon and warn the people there. Okay, first I'd need to figure out a way to convince them I wasn't a fucking loon, but I had a feeling that would be less of an issue once a pack of bipedal wolves started rampaging through the streets.

My talk with Jerry had convinced me that's where they'd be headed, whether or not I was there. Uncle Craig was proving to be a spiteful son of a bitch, and if he had more willing foot soldiers, monsters ready to kill at his command, then it was going to be bad.

As for the innocent people who just happened to live there because it was a quiet place to raise a family, well, talk about accidentally building your home atop a minefield.

Rather than give in to the fear that threatened to consume me, I focused on all the lives that would be lost if I couldn't keep my shit together.

I raced through the darkening forest as quickly as my legs would carry me, trying to backtrack from that freaky glade, but it still wasn't fast enough. Damp leaves, roots, branches, all of it served as a veritable obstacle course, each one determined to dump me on my ass and slow me down.

Somehow, whether it was dumb luck or some guardian angel giving me a chance to fix the clusterfuck I'd set in motion, I managed to head in the right direction. I heard the sound of wheels on pavement and a rumbling engine from somewhere off to my left. Crossed Pine Road! I could have wept with joy at the sight of its bumpy, pothole-riddled surface, but there was no time to spare.

I'd never been much of a sprinter. My legs were muscular, the result of years of sports, but they weren't the long graceful limbs of a runner. Of course, up until recently I hadn't known that I was about as strong as the average bulldozer.

There were a lot of things I hadn't tested regarding my

newfound powers – speed and endurance being two of them. My warning to High Moon wouldn't be much use if I died of a heart attack before reaching the city limits, but it was pretty much a case of now or never.

More howls rose up from somewhere behind me. These were different in pitch. I didn't pretend to speak werewolf, but could have sworn I detected an undertone of anger.

Call me a pessimist, but if I had to make a guess, I'd have put my money that some of Jerry's pack buddies had found him.

More howls answered in response, these coming from different parts of the forest. They sounded equally as pissed. I had a feeling that Google Translate would have come back with something along the lines of "Get that bitch!"

Whatever head start I had given myself was about to run out. If ever there was a time to test out the true limits of my power, it was now.

The sign proclaiming I'd reached the border of High Moon came up sooner than expected. Thank Goodness!

While I couldn't pretend I had gotten there faster than by car, I'd been moving at a good clip, enough to make me think any speed traps in the area would have probably registered me as an offender.

Amazingly enough, I felt pretty good too – physically anyway – like I'd just warmed up for practice.

Sadly, a warm-up was just what I needed if Craig's wolves were hot on my trail. I hadn't heard anymore howling since that last angry volley, but that didn't mean anything. I sincerely doubted they were going home to have a nice quiet wake in Jerry's honor – especially tonight. I glanced up and, sure enough, saw a reddish glow shining down from high over the trees. The blood moon had risen.

I stopped at an intersection and considered my next move. Dad was over in... *Shit!* My dad! What would he think once he found out about Jerry? Craig was the alpha and he the second-in-command. Would he heed his brother's orders to ravage High Moon? If he refused, would they turn on him?

Despite how much shit I'd given him this summer, he was still my father. So far as I knew he'd never hurt a fly. But then again, according to what he'd told me, once upon a time he was considered something of a badass. What if that was his true nature – something he kept in check for the benefit of his family, but always lurking right below the surface?

Argh! If I continued with this train of thought, I'd end up standing in place all night while the werewolf brigade blew past me and tore my town to pieces. That wouldn't help anyone.

I had to trust Dad was okay and would do what he felt was the right thing. There wasn't much I could do about it otherwise.

As for the rest of my family, Mom had made certain Chris was out of town. He was safe, or as safe as a normal kid could be among a coven of ridiculously powerful witches. Hopefully she was with him, as opposed to zapping him into stasis and leaving him in a closet somewhere. Mind you, that option worked, too.

Either way, that made the choice a bit easier. Though a part of me wanted to run home, lock the doors, and turn on the TV loud enough so that I could pretend nothing was amiss, I instead turned right and headed toward Riva's house.

She wasn't a part of this and I needed to make sure it stayed that way.

My subconscious was *kind* enough to torture me with all sorts of unpleasant thoughts along the way ... most of them involving finding my friend and her family being eaten alive on their own front lawn.

Did werewolves actually eat people or just tear them limb from limb? At some point I really should've asked my dad if he was a cannibal. That was probably an important detail to know, but I filed it away for later as more images of slaughter invaded my mind.

By the time I reached Riva's cul-de-sac I was in such a panic that I nearly collapsed in tears upon seeing that everything looked normal. Garbage cans had been moved to the curb in anticipation of pickup tomorrow. Front porch lights were on. The street lights were aglow, and people could be seen through windows going about their evening.

That normalcy wouldn't last, however. My uncle had promised that much.

Rather than stand there and play voyeur, I headed straight to Riva's place. Everyone here needed to be warned, if possible, but call me selfish. I needed to make sure my best friend was safe first. Once that was out of the way, then I could do what was necessary for everyone else.

I walked up to their front door, rang the bell, and waited. A pack of angry monsters was probably on their way even now, yet some habits died harder than others.

"I got it!" a voice cried from inside, followed a moment later by Riva opening up, a look of surprise on her face. "Aren't you supposed to be getting married right now?"

"Change of plans."

"Don't tell me you left Wartboy standing at the altar."

I smiled sheepishly. "Something like that, except he wasn't exactly standing."

26

R iva stood there, a blank look on her face as she apparently tried to process what I had just told her. "Are you saying that you..."

"Yes."

"Wow. Holy shit. I mean, how did it happen?"

I shrugged. "Impaled him on a tree branch and then kinda snapped his neck."

"Whoa," she muttered. "So that was the ace up your sleeve? Kill him if he said...?"

"No!" I quickly lowered my voice. "I didn't plan on it ending that way. It was ... some of the things he said. Stuff which we *really* need to talk about."

"Who's at the door?" a slightly accented voice asked from further in the house – Riva's father.

I instinctively answered, "It's just me, Mr. Kale."

"Oh. Come in, Tamara," he called back. "Why are you standing out there like some stranger?"

I couldn't help but smile. While Riva's mom could be a bit standoffish at times, her father had always been nothing but welcoming to me. Pity this wasn't a social call.

Riva automatically led the way toward the stairs

heading up to her room, but I stopped as we passed the living room, where her parents were busy watching some reality show.

"C'mon, Bent," she said in a hushed voice. Her parents weren't overly fond of that nickname. "Sounds like we need to..."

"There's no time," I interrupted, realizing I was falling into our normal routine far too easily. And why not? Everything was as it should be. It required no effort to pretend that death wasn't even now racing toward us. Heck, I almost wished I could've fooled myself into thinking I'd imagined it all, but I couldn't. "I need you and your family to leave High Moon tonight ... *now*, as a matter of fact."

I'd purposely raised my voice so it would be heard by her parents. There was little time for beating around the bush. The sound of the TV muted in response.

Riva gave me a questioning look, but I simply nodded to her and stepped into the living room.

"Did you just say we needed to leave town?" her father asked, the expression on his face suggesting he was certain he'd heard wrong.

I slowly nodded, the two sides of my brain at war with one another. A part of me didn't want to sound like some maniac, but the rest realized that playing it safe could cost them their lives.

Screw it, I went for broke.

"My uncle is leading an army of werewolves here from Morganberg. I was supposed to marry one tonight, but I sort of accidentally ended up killing him instead, and now they're coming to murder everyone in town, starting with your family."

There came a beat of silence, long enough for me to register just how batshit crazy I sounded. Then Mrs. Kale stood up with a sigh. "I'll go make some tea."

"But..."

"It's okay, Tamara." Riva's dad stood, too. He was a short man with dark skin, a mustache, and rapidly thinning hair on top of his head. That was offset by bright eyes and a welcoming smile, a smile that didn't leave his face even as he spoke to what he surely thought was his daughter's best friend gone nuts.

"Dad, she's telling the..."

Mr. Kale held up a hand. "It's okay, Riva. I understand."

I glanced back at her then toward him. "You do?"

"Yes, I do. Have a seat, child."

"There isn't..."

"Please, I insist." He gestured toward the couch, and both I and Riva automatically planted our butts in it. "Now, you two may find this hard to believe, but I was young once."

Again, I and my friend shared a glance. Somehow, I had a feeling that what he was about to say didn't involve supernatural creatures, but stranger things had happened this summer.

"I went to college, I experimented," he continued. "Why, there was this one time, back at the University of Calcutta. I ate some mushrooms and then spent the entire afternoon having an enlightening conversation with Ganesh before realizing I'd been talking to nothing more than a lawn ornament."

The voice of Riva's mom floated back to us from the kitchen. "You're not telling that stupid Ganesh story again, are you, Arjun?"

"What do you know, woman?" he shouted back. "It's a great story." He turned back to us. "Now, where was I? Ah, yes. It's okay to be young and stupid, but you need to step back and let the hallucinations pass before you run off telling people that ... what was it again?"

"Werewolves," I replied deadpan.

"Yes, werewolves. You need to realize that some of those things you've been smoking or snorting can cause you to see..."

The somewhat surreal PSA we were listening to was interrupted by the sound of tires squealing outside, followed by the crunch of metal against metal.

"Oh, now what the hell?" Mr. Kale cried, stepping to the window. "I told Brentberg he needed to hide his car keys from that idiot child of his. I swear, if he's dented our mailbox again, I'm going to call the homeowners' association."

Riva and I joined him at the window. The mailbox wasn't just dented – it had been obliterated. A muscle car now sat atop it, halfway onto the front lawn, the rear wheels sitting on the sidewalk.

"What in the name of..."

The doors on both sides of the vehicle opened and two men stepped out, but they were only men in the vaguest sense of the word. Both were in the middle of transforming, their clothes ripping to shreds even as they planted their feet onto the well-manicured grass.

"My God, what are those?"

Unfortunately, I had a feeling neither God, Ganesh, nor any other compassionate deity had anything to do with what was coming for us.

"Maryam!" Riva's father shouted.

The tone in his voice must have sounded urgent because she returned from the kitchen at once.

"No questions," he said. "Take the girls and go upstairs. Dial 9-1-1." He paused to look out the window again, where the two wolf-men were growing hairier by the second. "Tell them there's a burglar. Anything to get them here."

"But..."

"NOW!"

Without any further hesitation, Mrs. Kale pushed past us. "Come with me, girls." Her tone was brave but with an undercurrent of worry beneath it as she waved us toward the stairs. She grabbed my arm and began steering me in that direction after I stood unmoving for a second too long.

"But, Mr. Kale..."

"He has a gun," Riva's mother replied, "in his office. Let him handle this."

"No."

"Tamara, get upstairs now." She put on her mom voice and I actually found myself lifting my foot before realizing what I was doing.

Fortunately, Riva was in the know. "Mom, trust me. She's got this."

That was perhaps an exaggeration. So far this night I'd accidentally murdered my fiancé, run from the scene of the crime, and managed to save exactly nobody before the bad guys showed up.

In all fairness on that last one, I hadn't expected them to drive here. Fucking twenty-first century werewolves, screwing with my expectations.

At least they were predictable in that, within the next few seconds, the front door was literally kicked off its hinges. Mrs. Kale screamed in surprise, but if she thought that was shocking, then she definitely wasn't ready for what was waiting in the now open doorway – two fully grown werewolves, each at least seven feet tall, the light from the porch illuminating them in a way that gave no doubt that they were the real thing.

Two sets of yellow eyes locked onto me and I pulled

free from Mrs. Kale's grasp. This was my fault, my mess. That meant it was my job to fix it.

Or it would have been had Riva's dad not picked that moment to reenter the room and open fire on the two monsters advancing upon us.

27

I had absolutely no idea if my powers offered any protection against bullets, so I made what I thought to be the safe assumption and backed up until my heels hit the stairs and I stumbled into Mrs. Kale's arms.

Riva's dad was thankfully one of those gun owners who believed in walking the walk when it came to home protection. He was in a shooter's stance, squeezing off carefully aimed shots, one after the other. In some ways, seeing his well-loved face – always so friendly and welcoming – dead set on protecting his home was a lot scarier than the creatures coming for us.

Or it was until I realized he'd hit the lead wolf with multiple rounds yet still wasn't doing much to slow it down.

Bloody bullet holes stood out on its chest, but you'd have thought they were little more than bee stings. As the gunfire ended, the wolf in front glanced from Mr. Kale back to me and actually chuckled through its massive teeth – a guttural sound that was anything but cheerful.

"Run!" her dad cried as he worked to slam a fresh

magazine into place. Sadly for him, I had a feeling more ammo wasn't the answer here. That meant it was my turn.

I pulled free from Mrs. Kale's grasp.

"Tamara, don't be stupid!"

Eh, I'd been called far worse.

Both of Riva's parents screamed at me to get back, but I did the opposite, marching forward to meet the beasts who'd come for my friend and her family.

The wolf continued to chuckle, as if it had been told a particularly funny joke in dog language. It actually waved me forward like it wanted to test my mettle. Craig had said that he didn't plan on letting my true nature become widely known among the pack. This idiot seemed to confirm that. If so, the advantage was mine and I wasn't about to waste the opportunity.

The cries of my best friend's parents reached a fever pitch, but I ignored them as I cocked back a fist. If this thing wanted to see if it could take my best shot, who was I to say no?

Remembering what these monsters were here to do, I let loose with everything I had. Turns out that was more than even I realized. I expected to double the beast over, maybe drop it to the ground retching, but instead my hand punched right through its gut – becoming intimately acquainted with its intestinal tract.

Eww!

The wolf's chuckle turned into a pained wheeze, and its eyes bugged out of its head as it gasped for air.

I should have been horrified at what I'd done, but there was no time to dwell on that. This monster had come here intent on murder and it wasn't alone.

Grabbing hold of the impaled wolf with my other hand, I spun and sent it flying. My arm pulled free of its stomach with a spray of blood and a disturbing *schlup* sound right before the monstrous beast crashed through the front window. It landed on the lawn, where it tumbled end over end before collapsing in a heap on the grass.

Seeing that I wasn't quite the easy target his buddy had assumed me to be, the other wolf hesitated for a moment. Then it tried to race past me to where Riva and her mom still cowered on the stairs.

Needless to say, I wasn't having any of that shit.

It was fast, but not quite fast enough. I plowed into its flank before it could get to them, slamming it into the wall and leaving a crater in the drywall. Hopefully Riva's family had very forgiving homeowners insurance.

The wolf grunted, the wind knocked out of it. Before it could recover, I dragged it away from them and threw it face-first onto the floor.

It was there I realized I had a hard choice to make – both now and as more of these monsters poured into my town. I could incapacitate this beast as best I could, but they healed fast. Knocking them down would be little more than spitting into the wind. As for expecting mercy, that was likely a fool's errand.

There was nothing to keep them from getting back up and resuming their slaughter.

No, that wasn't true. There was me.

Mr. Kale had reloaded by then, but before he could line up a shot, I jumped onto the wolf's back.

"Tamara, get out of the way!"

"Don't bother," I replied in a cold voice devoid of emotion.

Killing Jerry had been a terrible accident, but there was nothing accidental about what I was doing now.

I grabbed the wolf's upper and lower jaws in my hands and began to force them apart. The creature made a keening yip of pain as I put on the pressure, reminding myself that it had been sent specifically to kill my friend. Had Jerry not said anything, I might have gone home or to the police first, not realizing that Riva had been targeted. If so, these things would have walked in here unopposed and...

I gritted my teeth in anger and there came a rippling *crack* as the werewolf's head split in two along its jawline.

Its body went limp beneath me and I stood, staring down at it for several seconds, trying to come to terms with what I'd done and what still needed to be done. Maybe it took a monster to stop other monsters.

So be it.

As for this one, it certainly appeared dead. I nudged it once with my foot ... nothing. I then glanced out the front window and saw the first wolf lying unmoving where it had landed. It, too, looked down for the count.

Weird. Shooting it point blank seemed to have about as much effectiveness as slapping a grizzly bear with a fly swatter, yet where bullets failed my fists had gotten the job done.

It was only then that I realized the only reason I had time to think these thoughts was due to the stunned silence that had descended upon the Kale household.

Riva's dad stared wide-eyed at the dead werewolf on his living room floor. He looked up at me and his expression didn't change. If anything, I saw him glance once at the gun still in his hand, as if considering it. It hurt to see that thought pass through his eyes, but it was also hard to blame him.

"Are you okay, Bent?"

"Riva, stay back..."

"It's okay, Mom."

I turned to see my friend trying to push her way past her mother, who was doing her damnedest to hinder her daughter's progress, as if I was as big of a threat as the monsters I'd vanquished.

"That's enough, Maryam." Riva's father met my gaze

and I saw that he'd composed himself, apparently having decided that I was the lesser of two evils. "She saved us."

"She's..."

"We don't know what she is."

"Wow, nice way to call her a freak, Dad."

"I didn't call her a freak."

I couldn't help but chuckle as I said to Riva, "He's right. *You* did."

"Is ... is it dead?" Mr. Kale asked.

"I hope so."

"You killed it."

"Again, I hope so."

He stepped forward hesitantly and nudged its broken jaw with his foot. "What the fuck is it?"

"Arjun! Language."

He turned to his wife and gave her perhaps the most incredulous stare I had ever seen. "Are you kidding me? Do you see this thing? It came here to kill us and you're worried about my language?" His wife didn't have a quick answer to that. "Open your eyes and look at this ... monster! What is it? Why did it come here? Are there more? And why in hell was it driving a Mustang?"

I shared a glance with Riva and she nodded at my unspoken question. The cat was out of the bag, so to speak. While I wished this could be explained away as a bad drug trip, the dead bodies and damage to their house was hard to ignore.

Not to mention, this wasn't over, not by a long shot. I had a feeling these two were little more than the advance guard ... a couple of good ole boys who just happened to have a faster ride than everyone else.

I turned toward Mr. Kale, prepared to give the shortest barrage of answers I could that would both satiate their curiosity and allow us to get moving, but before I could say anything, his cell phone started ringing.

He held up a hand and fished it out of his pocket.

"Really, Arjun?" his wife asked. "Ignore it."

He threw a glare her way. "It might be important."

"We almost died!"

He ignored her protests and answered it with a disturbingly polite, "Hello, Kale residence." If I thought that was odd, though, what he said next definitely threw me for a loop. "Oh, hello, Lissa. I hope you're having a pleasant evening." *Lissa?!* "Why, yes. She's right here. Just one moment."

He turned to me and held out the phone. "It's your mother."

28

I took the offered device with a blank look on my face.
There was no way this was mere coincidence.
"Hello?"

"*Care to tell me what happened?*"

"How did you know to call... You were spying on me
again, weren't you?"

"*It's called scrying,*" Mom said.

"Whatever. Why didn't you just call me on my..."

"*I did. Check your pocket.*"

I went to pull out my phone and immediately realized
things were amiss. What was left was little more than a
crushed piece of broken plastic with a shattered screen.
Guess my scuffle with Jerry was a bit more physical than
I'd thought.

My sigh was apparently all Mom needed to continue.
"*I repeat, what happened? Why are you at Riva's house
instead of in Morganberg?*"

"I thought you said you were scrying me."

"*It's a busy night, lots of stuff going on. Much as I'm sure
it'll come as a surprise, the world doesn't revolve around you.
Besides...*"

I could sense she was hesitating for some reason. "Besides what?"

"*I ... was having trouble seeing you earlier. There are spots in Morganberg that make it ... difficult for me to... It doesn't matter. Bring me up to speed, Tamara. Now!*"

Difficult? Did she mean she couldn't lock on to me or that something was jamming her reception? I doubted she was talking about Shop Haven, but right at that moment, it seemed like the least of my problems.

Rather than argue, I begrudgingly stepped to the far corner of the room, while Riva and her family conversed among themselves, and gave my mother a very compacted retelling of events.

"*You just had to kill him,*" she replied with an annoyed huff. "*Do you have any idea what this means, Tamara?*"

"I didn't want to. It just happened. I didn't set out tonight to become a..." I lowered my voice to a bare whisper, "a murderer. I know you must think I'm a monster, but you have to understand what he said about Riva. I ... just lost it. I'm sorry, Mom."

"*Oh, honey, I don't care about that. Quite frankly, your uncle is lucky I let any of them live after that stunt he pulled showing up at our house.*"

I pulled the phone away from my ear for a moment and stared at it, not quite believing what she was saying. Whoever Mr. Kale's cell carrier was, I really hoped they weren't listening in right now.

"*I kind of wish I had just vaporized them all. Would have saved us a lot of trouble. But that's neither here nor there. What matters is that events have been set in motion, events that I'm not sure can be easily fixed.*"

"They're coming, aren't they? And there isn't anything I can do to stop it."

"*I'm afraid not,*" she replied in an eerily calm voice.

"What can I do?"

"*Run. Get out of High Moon.*"

"I can't do that. I can't leave these people here to die because of me."

"*I know, but I had to say it. You are my daughter, after all.*"

If she was trying to coax a smile out of me, it worked, although I had a feeling it was the last bit of mirth that would be crossing my mouth for some time. "I'm going to fight them."

Rather than explain to me what a monumentally stupid idea that was, she said, "*Then fight smart. Even you can't take on all of them at once.*"

"I kinda figured. Any chance of getting help from your end?"

There was a pause, as I knew there would be. Mom's hands were pretty much tied on this one. But I had to try anyway.

"*There are more eyes focused on High Moon tonight than you know, dear,*" she replied. "*Some of them quite nervous, too. I'm doing what I can. We're currently discussing ... a response.*"

"A response? Like what, a sternly worded letter?"

"*Something that's unlikely to provoke a war.*"

"Picket signs, then?"

"*Don't be a smart mouth, Tamara. If we move in force against the lycanthropes, the entire town will be smoldering ash by morning.*"

"Sorry. Yeah, I know. So I'm on my own, then."

"*Not necessarily. Help those who can't help themselves, but fight alongside those who are able to.*"

That wasn't particularly helpful. "How?"

"*Your father's people are strong, but they aren't unbeatable.*"

I again lowered my voice. "You sure about that? I just

watched Riva's dad unload a Glock into one and the thing laughed it off."

"Not surprising. They heal fast and their constitutions are off the chart. Not to mention I sincerely doubt Arjun keeps silver bullets in that little gun of his."

I blinked several times. "Wait, that's real? I mean, silver?"

"Of course. But it has nothing to do with the power of goodness or claptrap like that. Silver is a natural retardant for otherworldly energies. It's excellent for binding unnatural creatures, entrapping, injuring, or outright killing them."

"So we need a ton of silver to stop them all. Great. I'll start digging, see if I can find a mineshaft."

"Catastrophic injury works as well. Much as I'm sure your uncle would love for you to believe they're invincible, very few creatures can claim to be able to get back up after a beheading."

"Even better. Silver and swords, two things I just so happen to be fresh out of."

"In the garage, behind the cleaning supplies. Look for a loose board in the wall."

"What?"

"If you can make it there, you'll find things to help."

I let out a laugh. "If I can make it there. That's a confidence builder for when I'm being swarmed by..."

Wait a second. Something didn't add up.

"Tamara, are you still there?"

I was busy looking at the mutilated werewolf corpse on the living room floor. "Hold on. I took out Jerry and two of his friends. Last I checked, I'm neither made of silver nor karate chopping heads off."

Mom let out a long sigh, as if she was about to say something she preferred not to. *"That was you, dear."*

"I know it was me, I was there."

"*Not you specifically, but who and what you are. You see, otherworldly creatures are vulnerable to other such beings. We can kill each other. It's part of why your father's people and mine have been at each other's throats for centuries. It's not differing ideologies so much as it is the unique threat we present to one another. And both our blood runs through your veins.*"

"But you said your magic doesn't work right against me."

"*As I am aware. You're highly resistant to magic and you possess physical power that's a match or more against your father's kind, power that is at your beck and call at all times regardless of the phase of the moon or your physical appearance.*"

It was as if a lightbulb went on in my head. Before now, everything I'd heard seemed to point to the wolves hating me because of arrogance, thinking I was some sort of abomination of two ancient bloodlines being tainted and thus made impure. But now it all made sense.

Almost as if reading my mind – and let's be honest, it was entirely possible she was – my mother gave voice to those thoughts.

"*Your father's people sought to control you and now seek your death. And mine, if they learned of your existence, would no doubt try to do the same. All because of fear. For centuries, our two races have played a great game of chess, both sides gaining and losing ground over and over again. But only now, with your existence, does the possibility of a true checkmate exist, one that could be used against us both.*"

29

I numbly hung up the phone and passed it back to Mr. Kale.

"I hope your mother is well and you passed on my regards to her," he said.

Riva's mother threw up her hands. "Have you gone mad? That's what you're worried about?"

"Just because we've been attacked by monsters is no reason to be rude."

I had a feeling things were going to get somewhat *rude* regardless of our efforts this night. As it was – between gawking at the wolf bodies and my mother's phone call – too much time had already been wasted. "We need to go. More specifically, you and your family need to get somewhere safe."

"It's me, isn't it?" Riva asked. One of the benefits of being friends for so many years was that you often didn't need to explain these things.

"You?" her mother replied, immediately taking on the stern persona of a parent who'd just caught their child sneaking cash from her pocketbook. "And what do these beasts have to do with you?"

"It's not her, Mrs. Kale. They're after me. I can't explain it, we don't have time, and I'm not even sure I believe it myself, but it's true. I pissed them off and they know Riva and I are friends." I held up a hand before she could say anything. "Yes, sorry about the language." Jesus Fucking Christ, this night was getting weirder by the moment. "The problem is, they didn't trust me from the start, so they had me followed and learned where Riva and you all live. Their plan was to use your family as collateral against me."

"Collateral for what?" Mr. Kale asked.

"She was supposed to marry one of them," Riva replied, before turning toward my stunned expression. "Well, it's the truth. Easier to say it upfront than think up some bullshit excuse."

Her mother opened her mouth, again no doubt worried that our language was somehow more important than being torn limb from limb, but I was quicker on the draw. "Like I said, it's a long story."

Riva's father nodded. "We were talking about that while you were on the phone."

"Me getting married?"

"No. Finding somewhere safe."

"I don't know if they're watching the roads or not, but east is out. If you head west you'll..." I trailed off before saying they'd be heading into Witch Central. Hopefully that wouldn't be an issue, but the truth was, I had no way of knowing. Probably something I should've asked Mom before hanging up.

"No matter," he said. "I know of a place."

I was really hoping he wasn't going to explain that they'd be safe hiding upstairs or in the garage, because if so, I was going to have to put my fist through a wall to illustrate why that was a piss poor idea.

"The Crendels over on the southern tip of town."

"What about them?"

"They have a root cellar in their backyard."

"I don't think..."

"It's a converted bomb shelter. The previous owners built it in the 1950s."

A bomb shelter? That had potential.

"Isn't Edgar a little paranoid?" his wife asked.

"Exactly! It won't take too much convincing for him to agree to lock us down there all night." He turned to me. "Tamara, please tell your family they are welcome to join us."

I shook my head. "They're all ... out of town tonight. Something about a harvest festival." It was bullshit and the look on Riva's face told me it wasn't particularly convincing bullshit at that, but it was the best I had.

Fortunately, her parents didn't question it.

The good thing was my house was on the way. If so, we could stop there and I could see what Mom was talking about in the garage.

But first, as she had told me, we had to get there.

"You're sure that's real silverware, not plated?"

"They were a gift from my mother," Mrs. Kale said from the front seat, as if that was an answer.

"And you're certain it will work better than my gun?"

I glanced over at Riva's dad. "No offense, but your gun didn't work at all. So offhand, I'd say yeah."

It had been tempting to steal the Mustang those two assholes had driven, but — as it turned out — none of us could drive stick. We must've been the only foursome in rural Pennsylvania who'd been raised entirely on automatic transmissions.

Her parents' Toyota was first in the driveway, so we'd piled into that instead.

"We really should do a better job warning the neighbors," Mr. Kale said as we pulled out of the driveway. He wasn't wrong, but I had to prioritize.

Our marathon session of racing through the cul-de-sac, knocking on doors, and screaming at people to run because a tornado warning had just been issued – the best plausible threat any of us could come up with on short notice – had garnered far more confusion than fear, probably not helped by the fact that it was a clear, windless night.

"I promise you, I'll try. But we need to get you all someplace safe first. Believe me, they're going to be looking specifically for you."

"You need to hide with us, Bent," Riva said from my side.

"No chance. I started this, I need to try to stop it."

"But..."

"She's right." Mrs. Kale turned around in the front seat. "And this kills me to say as a parent, but I saw what you did in our house. I've never seen anything like that before. They tore through our front door like it was paper, but they barely touched you. Save who you can, but if it gets too much, please come and join us."

"I will," I lied as I rolled down the back window.

Riva raised an eyebrow. "What are you doing?"

"It's a nice night for some fresh air and for keeping my ears open."

"Listening for tornadoes?"

"Yep, big hairy ones."

Turns out that was a smart idea. We hadn't gone more than two blocks when the first howl drifted in. It was still distant, or so I hoped. Was kind of hard to tell in a moving vehicle.

"What are you doing?" Riva's mom asked her father.

"There's a stop sign ahead."

"Who cares? There's an army of monsters invading the town."

"Just because we're being hunted by werewolves is no reason to risk a speeding ticket."

Riva and I shared a glance as the surreal conversation happened up front, but we both realized it was best to keep our mouths shut. On the upside, I was impressed. A part of me hoped to one day be in a relationship so comfortable that not even an apocalyptic nightmare could derail the mundane realities of life.

Someday, perhaps. But first, I had to survive the night.

We were maybe a block away from my house when the howls rose up in earnest, much closer and far more numerous. Up until then, we hadn't seen anything other than typical evening traffic ... people heading home from work, maybe going out for dinner. But I had a feeling that was all about to change.

Turns out I was more right than I'd ever want to be. A van and a pickup truck both turned onto the street up ahead, driving at a pace far greater than the twenty-five mile per hour residential limit.

"Oh my goodness!"

Mr. Kale was right to cry out. Beneath the glare of a streetlight, I saw someone ... or more like *something* leap from the back of the pickup and go racing off into the darkness as the two vehicles continued heading toward us. I had a feeling it wasn't alone.

Shit! "Forget my house," I said. "Turn here and floor it to the Crendel place."

"But what about...?"

"Just do it!"

Though I was barely old enough to qualify as an adult, something about the tone of my voice seemed to get through to Riva's dad. He made a sharp left down a side street and immediately sped up, all fear of speeding tickets seemingly forgotten.

My family wasn't friends with the Crendels, but I knew who they were. They had a reputation as preppers, which was probably why they kept their *root cellar* in good repair. If so, then maybe they had guns, too. Doubtful on the silver, but something with higher caliber than what Mr. Kale owned couldn't hurt.

It was probably for the best that I planned to stay busy fighting werewolves. Their son had once asked me out back in high school. I said no because he was a bit of a dweeb but then, when I'd learned it had been on a dare, I'd ended up blackening both of his eyes. It was probably not the ideal background for me to hide in cramped quarters with his family.

The sound of sirens began to fill the night. While it was possible the cops were just responding to a fender bender, I doubted that was the case. We knew that at least some of the pack was already in High Moon. No doubt those unlucky enough to live at the eastern fringe of town were already well aware that strangeness was afoot this night.

A few moments later, as if to confirm this, houselights all over the block we were driving down abruptly went out. Fortunately, there had been a green agenda rolled out during the last town election which had resulted in an effort to upgrade the town's street lights to solar. Nevertheless, the effect was dramatic as all the homes – warmly aglow as families began their evening routine – became pitch black almost as one.

No way was this a coincidence, not with a pack of

paranormal predators about to descend upon us. If Uncle Craig wasn't a complete idiot, and it was probably wise to assume that was the case, the phone lines and cell towers would be next. As rural as High Moon felt, it wasn't like we were at the northern tip of Alaska. Isolation was merely a state of mind in this modern age, unless one took steps to ensure that outside help couldn't be reached.

Sadly, it looked like this assault had been thought through in advance.

So much for hoping the National Guard would come rolling into town to save our asses. For all intents and purposes, we were on our own.

30

I hid in the bushes and waited for the Kales and Crendels to head out back to the fortified vegetable cellar.

Though I didn't see the point in letting the Crendel family know I was even here, lest they try to stop me from running off into the night, I didn't want to leave until I was certain Riva was okay.

Fortunately, I didn't have to wait long for the back door to fly open and the two families to head on out. From the look of things, Edgar Crendel and his wife were well-armed as they led the way.

Howls, sirens, and now a blackout. Many would have dismissed it and stoically waited for the weirdness to pass, assuming it was nothing to worry about. But thank goodness for the truly paranoid. It didn't take a whole lot of convincing to get them to break out the survival gear. Gotta love folks who can't wait for the end times to get here.

I was tempted to throw out a few howls of my own to get them to move a bit faster, but that would've done little more than get me shot. So I waited as the two families filed toward what I hoped was safety. Riva stalled for a moment, looking around, perhaps sensing I was nearby. I sorely wanted to run out there and give her one last hug before seeing her locked away, but I held my ground.

Finally, she walked down the stairs and I saw the form of Mr. Crendel descend and close up the doors behind him.

As sure of their safety as I was going to get, I quickly turned away lest I sit there all night while the rest of High Moon became a slaughterhouse. They were okay – locked up tight, with food, provisions, and weapons, including all of Mrs. Kale's silverware if worst came to worst.

I had only myself, but – call me conceited – that was good enough for now ... assuming I didn't get swarmed by a dozen werewolves at once, something I needed to make sure didn't happen.

Apparently that would be easier said than done. No sooner had I broken cover and stepped out onto the side-walk when a minivan turned onto the block ahead of me and drove up onto the curb.

It stopped, the side door opened, and three monsters piled out and ran howling off into the night.

Had I not been aware of how dangerous these crea-tures were, I'd have probably laughed my head off at seeing this soccer mom mobile turned into a troop transport for a nightmare army.

The driver's side door opened and a much smaller figure stepped out. She actually beeped the van to make sure it was locked before tearing out of her clothes beneath one of the street lamps. It was almost too much for me to take. Fortunately – depending on one's definition of the term – the minivan wolf spotted me before I could completely dissolve into laughter.

The creature snarled, then broke into a loping run, dropping to all fours and picking up even more speed.

Being the accommodating type, I decided to meet it halfway.

I still wasn't sure if Craig had come clean with his pack about my true heritage. The muscle car wolves from earlier suggested that he hadn't, as they'd stepped right up for an ass-kicking.

The one in front of me, however, actually skidded to a halt. Its long, wicked nails scraped against the asphalt and its eyes opened wide in surprise as I closed the distance between us.

It was possible my uncle had finally wised up and clued the rest in. Of course, it was equally likely that werewolves were simply more used to people running away from them. Charge toward one in an aggressive manner and it might not know what to make of that.

Unfortunately for this creature, I knew exactly what to make of it ... short work.

Pummeling each and every one of these beasts into submission with my bare hands was an awesome idea on paper, but a bit less than practical. Case in point, the soccer mom wolf I had just beaten the shit out of, leaving her lying in a drainage ditch with her arms and legs broken in multiple places. I debated finishing her off, but the creature's pathetic whimpering was off-putting, making me feel like I was about to curb-stomp a helpless puppy instead of a monstrous beast. In truth, I felt relief at showing it mercy. Becoming desensitized to killing, even murderous monsters, was not something I wanted to do.

It was definitely down for the count, though. Fast healing or not, there was little chance of it getting back up before the sun rose. By then, hopefully some semblance of sanity could be restored to the town.

Besides, more were coming. I could hear them running about, wreaking havoc. Every second I wasted on a defeated foe was one that another werewolf could be using to tear someone apart.

"Stay down," I warned the she-wolf. "I see you again tonight and I'll be wearing your teeth as a necklace."

That was a crock of shit. As if I could tell the vast majority of these things apart from one another. But she didn't need to know that.

Without further ado, I took off again into the night, racing toward the center of the street so as to make myself an easily seen target. Rather than go chasing after shadows, I decided to adopt a different tactic – one designed to lure the monsters to me.

I began to scream bloody murder, as if Satan himself were hot on my tail. My goal was to get home, find Mom's stash, then hopefully hook up with whatever police were out and about ... assuming I could convince them to not shoot me. But, in the meantime, I might as well make myself a tempting target for any wolves on the prowl. Better me than someone who couldn't fight back.

As expected, I didn't have to wait long. The padding of heavy feet reached my ears before I could even make it to the end of the block – another solo wolf, probably one from the group that soccer mom had dropped off before getting her ass handed to her.

I began to wonder if perhaps there was little strategy to my uncle's assault against the town. The hodgepodge of cars and trucks racing to the far ends of High Moon. Werewolves hopping out and heading in whatever direction they pleased. It was chaotic, as if their orders had amounted to little more than "Go get them!"

Maybe it really was as simple as that. Why not? The advantage in raw power was entirely theirs. This wasn't a war so much as wolves descending upon a herd of sleeping sheep.

Problem was, it was also stupid. More importantly, it was something I could potentially use. As most athletes will tell you, half of any competition takes place in your mind. Knowing all the moves, the skills, making them second nature was key, but you needed to watch, observe, *think*. And the reason for that was you oftentimes needed to strategize on the fly.

Like now, for instance.

The wolf charging in from my flank was probably thinking they'd tackle me, knock me senseless against the asphalt – assuming their initial hit didn't outright kill me – and then finish me off, earning themselves a notch on their werewolf bedpost.

There was little doubt this one was going for the kill. That much was apparent in the split second before we collided, at least three hundred pounds of muscle looking to slam into me at greater than twenty miles per hour.

I leapt into its clutches as it reached me, the force of its inertia enough to almost knock the wind out of my lungs. But I was made of hardier stuff than most, and before it could bring its natural weapons to bear, I wrapped my arms around its thick neck and twisted my body, overbalancing the creature.

My grip was rock solid and, as it went down, I rolled, pulling its body over me and allowing me to land atop it as we skidded to a halt ... leaving me relatively unscathed.

That wouldn't last for long, though. I could already feel its claws reaching for purchase. Having it in a head-lock put me dangerously close to its jaws. Almost as if in response, it snarled furiously and snapped at me ... missing, but drenching me in drool. Yuck!

Damn these things were big. Strong or not, it was an effort to keep my comparatively short arms wrapped around its thick neck. But that was okay, because I only needed to hold on long enough to give it one good twist.

Crack!

I kept the pressure on for several more seconds until I was certain it was over, then let go and pulled myself back to my feet. That one wasn't quite as kind to me as my previous scuffles this night. I had a feeling come the morning I was going to have some nice new bruises.

That wouldn't do. I needed to be smarter. Damage tended to be cumulative. The more battles I fought, the more banged up I was going to get. And the more banged up I got, the better chance that each fight would be my last.

Much as I wanted to fool myself into thinking I was a one-woman army, I knew better. I was more than capable of taking care of myself, but it wasn't just my life at stake. Allies and weapons were needed if the tide was going to be turned and this town saved.

Riva and her family were safe for now. It was time to focus my attention toward the greater good.

31

"**G**od bless you, whoever you are!"

I didn't stop to acknowledge Mrs. Jalob's thanks as I stepped through the broken door back into the dark night. There was no time, and I had a feeling that saying too much was risky.

As much of a rush as I'd been in, a nagging bit of practicality had hit me once I'd finally reached my home. Adopting a bit of positivity and assuming at least some of the town survived the night, what then? There would no doubt be some people, outside of mine and Riva's family, pointing fingers my way. How was I to explain things without being labeled a freak or, worse, having enough publicity thrown my way that the threat to the west of town didn't nuke us from orbit?

Much as I knew that I'd be pushed to my limits fighting a small army of werewolves tonight, I didn't relish the thought of doing the same against a battalion of witches tomorrow.

The solution had been simplicity itself. I'd raced inside, pushing aside the desire to stay there and hide, and grabbed a leather jacket and an old black t-shirt – both from my short-lived Goth phase. Fortunately, the danger awaiting outside my walls left little time to rue my days as a fashion nightmare.

Luckily, I remembered a trick Chris had shown me. A couple of years back he'd been all into kung fu movies, during which time he'd shown me how to tie a shirt around my head in a manner that made it look like a cut-rate ninja mask. Never thought I'd say this, but thank goodness for dorky little brothers.

My *disguise* firmly in place, I'd headed out to the garage to see what surprise Mom had left behind.

Turns out it was a pretty nasty one.

There, stuffed into a duffle bag that had been shoved into a hidden alcove in our garage, had been a dozen or so spikes. With handles made of steel, the ends terminated in eight inches of sharpened silver. There was no mistaking what these were for. This was not something you put out on the table when company paid a visit. Nobody would be buttering any bread with these babies. No, there was only one practical use for weapons like these – hunting werewolves.

There was one brief moment where I wondered whether Dad knew about this cache, but I pushed it aside. No matter the case, I was happy to have them as I locked up and stepped out onto the front lawn, eyeing the garden gnomes standing in silent vigil near the bushes.

"Don't suppose you fellas want to help?" They continued to stare at me with their creepy dead eyes. "Didn't think so."

There wasn't much time to wonder whether my newly acquired weapons would actually work before I was forced to put them to the test. From down the block had come the sound of splintering wood, a snarl of anger, and a cry for help.

It hadn't been particularly sporting of me, but I'd raced

in and jabbed the bastard in the back with a spike, taking it out nearly instantly. The wolf barely had time to let out a yelp before it had fallen to the ground dead.

The cranky old woman who lived in the home, Mrs. Jalob, was unhurt, thank goodness. Unfortunately, I wasn't able to do much more than tell her to hide before the sounds of more destruction caught my ear, followed closely behind by gunfire.

The opening volleys were apparently done. The brunt of the war had descended upon High Moon.

My heart was heavy as I finally closed in on the main thoroughfare of my small town. I'd managed to take out two more werewolves since saving Mrs. Jalob, but now the grim reality of the situation was made clear to me.

Both of those wolves had already gotten their pound of flesh and more. Mauled bodies lay on front lawns and their fur was practically drenched in blood by the time I engaged them.

With silver in hand, it didn't take me long – one impaled through the skull with a spike, the other shanked through its ribcage. But in the short time it took to finish them off, it became abundantly clear that my uncle wasn't playing games.

Before that moment, I'd housed a secret hope that perhaps he'd been merely trying to scare me into acquiescing to his demands. But all of that was gone now, and with it went any last vestiges of mercy that I could show these monsters who masqueraded as men during the day.

The bastard wanted a war, but he was too chickenshit to start one with Mom's people, instead taking on what he thought to be an easily winnable skirmish.

It was time to teach him the error of his ways.

There was something big going down over on the rather unimaginatively named Main Street. It was the heart of the town – home of the police station, fire department, borough hall, and myriad shops that ran the length of it on both sides.

I had a feeling as I closed in that whatever happened there would most likely determine whether High Moon would live or die.

Snarls and howls filled the night from up ahead. They were answered in turn by gunfire, shouts, sirens, and the revving of engines.

As much as I wanted to leap into the fray, a silver spike in each hand, I forced myself to slow down.

Whoever was out there fighting, there was little doubt their dander was up. It wouldn't take much for someone to spot me, clad in a black ninja mask, and decide that the safer course of action was to shoot first and not bother with the questions.

That wouldn't do any of us much good. I instead crept along the side of a building, an old pawn shop that had been here since before I was born and would likely still be here long after I was dust. Reaching the edge, I peeked out and around. Through some bit of luck, I was behind the line of fire for the home team.

Cop cars, SUVs, and even the town's few firetrucks had been spread out as a barricade across the street, their flashers all on and lighting up the night. More vehicles – pickup trucks and cars – were parked behind them.

It seemed that not only had the town officials realized something was amiss, but several of the locals had as well. In addition to the police, I spied Jeb Peterson, who owned the local pharmacy, standing by their side with a shotgun in hand. Next to him was Mr. McGreevy. He was Riva's elderly neighbor, although apparently not too old to handle a rifle.

Further down, I was surprised to see Mrs. Carnesworth helping out, too. The assistant vice principal was holding a pistol that seemed far too big for her tiny frame and squeezing off shot after measured shot, looking like she was Dirty Harry's little sister. Having seen her over in Morganberg the month prior, I'd been wondering if maybe she was on team Craig. Good to know that wasn't the case.

I recognized more and more faces in the crowd, all doing what they could to defend their town.

A smile crossed my face as I realized my uncle's mistake. It was still early. Night had only fallen a short while ago. Many of the people of High Moon were still out and about, either working late or heading into town for dinner when the wolves had attacked. So incensed had the pack probably been at me skipping out on my wedding – oh, and leaving the groom dead – that they'd wasted no time heading here.

Had they waited, there would have doubtlessly been a smaller response as many more would have been home already. But they hadn't and, as a result, I now saw that there was cause to hope.

But I likewise saw that hope might quickly be quashed. I arrived just in time to spy a bulky figure on the opposite side of the street slipping through the shadowy spaces between buildings. The werewolves might look like oversized bipedal dogs, but they thought like people. And people were crafty when it came to war. While the towns-folk were focused on a frontal assault, some of the wolves were sneaking around to hit them at their flank.

That had to be Craig's plan. The howls and snarls rising up beyond the police barricade told me there was a decent amount of fur headed this way, but they were bait, a distraction, while a few slipped behind the lines and tore the resistance to shreds.

It was a good plan. Evil as fuck all, but good.

Pity I was there to throw a wrench into it.

Malevolent yellow eyes stared from the alleyway nearest the town's defenders. Two of the local police force were close by, but their attention was diverted elsewhere. Too bad for the wolf in question mine wasn't. Securing both my mask and bag of weapons, I took off running across the street with a spike in hand.

"Who the hell is that?"

"Hey! Come back here!"

So much for my ninja mask actually making me invisible to the untrained eye. Unfortunately, there wasn't time to stop for introductions. I had to hope that it was painfully obvious to those with guns that I wasn't a werewolf. Good thing I'd shaved my legs this morning.

The cops near the alleyway noticed me heading their way. They immediately scrambled for their sidearms.

Oh crap! This was going to be close.

I jumped up onto the hood of the police cruiser parked near them and launched myself over their heads.

They spun to follow, just in time to see me stab the werewolf that had been seconds away from turning them into human guacamole. I slammed the silver stake through its chest hard enough to pin it to the side of the nearest building.

The wolf let out a choked howl, then fell limp.

Sadly, there wasn't time to do a victory dance as another beast followed the first, charging out of the alleyway toward the person it no doubt perceived to be the biggest threat. One guess who that was.

As it closed the distance, I yanked the bag full of metal spikes off my shoulder and swung it like a club – its weight giving it some serious heft. It collided with the wolf's head, sending it staggering back several steps.

Good timing on my part, because it seemed as if everyone else picked that moment to open fire.

32

I hit the pavement, throwing my hands over my head and hoping that no stray shots managed to do Craig's job for him.

It was a near eternity later when the gunfire finally petered off. By then I was pretty certain my ears were bleeding. Mind you, I'd take that over the rest of me.

"It's down!" I heard someone shout.

I dared to lift my head, happy to see the vast majority of the defenders seemed more focused on the werewolf than the strange masked girl who'd appeared from out of nowhere.

The wolf in question looked like it had just taken a leisurely stroll through the North Korean demilitarized zone. Half its face was missing and one arm had been blown clean off. There was little doubt at least some of the weaponry on display was considerably more powerful than Mr. Kale's little handgun.

I remembered what Mom had told me about werewolves and catastrophic damage. If this thing – looking pretty goddamned dead as it was – managed to get back up and walk it off, then the town's only real hope was for its citizens to run as fast as their legs could carry them.

I continued to stare at it, waiting to see if it showed any signs of life, when hands grabbed me and pulled me to my feet.

"Who the hell are you supposed to be, Batgirl?"

"More like your friendly neighborhood dog catcher," I replied to the police officer giving me the once over. I'd seen him around town but didn't know his name, which meant he likely didn't recognize my voice. I hooked a thumb over my shoulder at the dead wolf hanging off the building and then reached for the bag I'd brought with me.

"Nice and slow there."

"If you really think I'm the worst threat here tonight, then by all means open fire." I bent down and unzipped the bag, realizing that was far from the most intelligent answer I could have given. Since no bullets perforated my brain pan, though, I guess it got my point across. Mind you, the irony was that I potentially *was* the biggest threat in town, but perhaps it was best to keep that to myself.

I showed him one of the spikes. "These are silver."

"You're shitting me."

My answer was to again point at the werewolf bodies behind me. "You realize those aren't Halloween decorations, right?"

Ralph Johnson, the chief of police, picked that moment to walk over. He was a fixture in town and had even been in attendance during my failed attempt to win the state championship. But hopefully my year away at college had dulled his remembrance of my former status as a local celebrity, especially since I'd had a run in with him a month prior. "What have you got there, Sullivan?"

The officer who'd been grilling me turned to him with a sheepish grin. "Um, silver stakes."

"Why the fuck not?" Chief Johnson replied with a shrug. "Makes as much fucking sense as anything else in this goddamned town tonight." He turned to me. "You, Ninja Girl, I saw what you did to that thing. So let's cut right through the bullshit. If you know something, you're gonna tell me. Are we clear?"

I appreciated him getting right to the point. It was one of the reasons he kept getting reelected. He had a reputation for a no-nonsense attitude, keeping a cool head, and having an open mind – a rarity in rural Pennsylvania, but just what this town needed on a night such as this.

Before I could say anything, he turned and barked some orders, making sure his men and the volunteers kept their guns loaded and their eyes open. Judging from the pitch of howls rising up from further down the street, things weren't about to let up for those holding the line.

Then, back to me, he cocked his head expectantly.

"The movies are right. Silver works," I said, trying to lower my voice an octave. "Hand these around. If any of those things get close enough or if they're still twitching after you've gunned them down, stake them."

"Through the heart?" the first cop asked.

Johnson snorted laughter. "That's vampires, genius."

I shook my head and shrugged. "I have no clue. All I know is that these monsters heal really fast and it takes a lot to keep them down. But if you use silver, it's a different story."

"And you know this how?" I glanced back over my shoulder again to which Chief Johnson replied, "Okay, I get the point. Fine. Either way, it's better than trying to fight these bastards hand to hand."

Staying calm and collected was one thing, but damn, this guy was stone cold. "If you don't mind me saying so, you're keeping an awfully level head considering that we're fighting werewolves here."

Johnson raised an eyebrow. "Same could be said of you, Mystery Lady. All I'll say is that anyone who's served on the force in High Moon long enough tends to develop a tolerance for the weird and unusual. And that's all you need to know. So what's your story? Any reason why you're running around out here after dark with a shirt wrapped around your head? You recently convert to Islam or something?"

I raised the corner of my mouth in a half smile, although he couldn't see it. Rather than waste time on words, I stepped to the police cruiser I'd vaulted over, grabbed hold of the rear door, and ripped it clean off its hinges with a screaming squeal of metal.

Officer Sullivan let out a quick *eep* of surprise, which he quickly tried to cover up as a cough. As for the chief, he merely frowned. "You do realize that's public property, right?"

"Sorry. Figured it was the quickest way to get my point across. Besides, I'm pretty sure we'll have bigger things to worry about by the time this night is over. "

When the wolves hit the blockade on Main Street, they hit it hard. But the people of High Moon weren't quite ready to give up so easily. More townsfolk came to bolster us as what sounded like World War III broke loose.

Chief Johnson did a hell of a job ordering the counter-attack, not hurt by the fact that a good chunk of the population were either part-time hunters, sportsmen, or skeet shooters. Go figure. It was one of the few times I wanted to cheer the good ole boy mentality.

I was tasked with picking off any wolves who tried to flank our location, of which there turned out to be more than a few.

We managed to hold our own for a time, as the makeshift militia of citizens and police hit the first wave of werewolves with enough firepower to topple a small nation. I ran back and forth like a chicken trying to keep its head from being cut off. Hitting hard, fast, and without mercy was key. I knew that if I stopped and thought about my actions, it could be disastrous. So I put my head down and made with the swift savage action, doing my damnedest to ensure the brave souls defending this town from my selfish stupidity didn't need to worry about their backsides, too.

It seemed we were making progress, or at least not giving ground, but then a trio of pickups pulled onto the far end of Main Street. Their beds were packed to the gills with werewolves. No surprise there. What none of us were expecting, though, was for some of them to be armed.

Whether it was ignorance or arrogance, we all assumed that the creatures attacking us would act like monsters from a movie – feral creatures attacking with fangs and claws. Up until that moment, it had seemed a safe assumption. But I should have remembered my father and the other wolves I'd seen up close. Though they took on the appearance of beasts, they retained their human minds ... as well as their opposable thumbs.

The trucks headed toward our makeshift barrier, picking up speed while the wolves in the back opened fire. It didn't matter if they had little chance of hitting anything. Moving at the speed they were, they effectively neutralized our defenses as the people holding the line either ducked or scattered.

I had just finished dispatching a werewolf who'd leapt down from the fire escape of Burt's Hardware Emporium when I turned and saw all of this happen. The wolves and drivers jumped from their vehicles at the very last second, sending their trucks slamming into the street-wide barrier at three different spots, leaving it a mass of burning and broken metal.

Most importantly, it upended what had been a semi-organized defense, leaving people dazed as a good dozen wolves cleared the blockade and tore into whoever they could get their hands on.

Cries, screams, snarls, and gunshots erased any semblance of what should have otherwise been a nice, quiet evening. All the while, the blood moon stood high in the sky, continuing to bathe us in its eerie crimson glow.

My back to the ground with snapping jaws only inches from my face might be someone's idea of fetish porn, but it wasn't really a kink I was into. My hands were bruised and bloodied as I held the wolf barely at bay, but bloodied was a lot better than instantly amputated if it managed to close its teeth on my fingers.

Sadly for me, it had two arms to go with the living chainsaw that was its mouth. I had my legs wrapped around it, adding to the strange fetish feel of it all, but that was more to keep it from gaining any additional lever-age. Unfortunately, my defensive strategy did nothing to keep it from sinking its claws into my back.

Sooner or later it was simply going to lacerate me to death if I didn't...

"Hold on!"

Darla McIntyre appeared behind the creature, silver spike held high. She'd been a cheerleader back in high school, not to mention a racist asshole who used to give Riva shit on a daily basis. Probably would have done the same to me, too, if I didn't have a reputation for letting my fists do my talking for me.

The irony of her being a backstabbing bitch wasn't lost upon me as she slammed the weapon into the werewolf – not that I was complaining about the save.

It wasn't exactly a lethal blow, but it was more than enough for the wolf's eyes to open wide in pain and for its jaw muscles to ease up on the pressure long enough for me to...

Crack!

I pulled and twisted, breaking its muzzle and ramming its broken jaw into the soft spot of its throat.

The result was immediate. It collapsed atop me, several hundred pounds of dead meat pinning me to the ground. Sadly, I was in no position to take what was soon going to become a much-needed rest.

I thanked Darla once I'd shoved the dead wolf off, making sure my blood and sweat soaked mask was still in place. It was, if barely. That was good, because now really wasn't the time for two high school rivals to learn an important lesson in bygones being bygones.

She tried to pull the spike from the wolf's heavily muscled back, but it was stuck fast – for her anyway. I yanked it free and handed it to her with a nod. I doubted we'd ever be friends, but seeing her here was a definite boost toward my faith in humanity.

The moment over, I turned away to see what else needed to be done.

What a joke! The entire street was chaos as far as the eye could see. Broken windows, warped metal, snapped or burning wood ... and that was the least of it. Gunshots continued to ring out – from both sides – the lull between them filled with snarls and howls. The worst of it, however, were the bodies littering the street – some dead or dying, but many more injured. And that wasn't even counting the wolves.

I'm not an inhuman monster. Though I was doing what needed to be done, that didn't mean I had no heart. How many of their kind were fated to die today all because of my uncle's stupid fear? I had to imagine at least some of them didn't want to be here. They couldn't all be bloodthirsty beasts. I at least knew my father wasn't. Yet here they were anyway. Fucking pack mentality. And people wondered why I hadn't joined a sorority back at school.

Sadly, compassion for our enemies was a luxury that wouldn't buy us much leeway in this fight. Sure, I'd seen a few werewolves do little more than knock down their human opponents before running off to attack someone else, but I'd seen just as many lay into their victims with all the glee of a rabid dog. Unfortunately, the wolves weren't wearing nametags to differentiate themselves.

Forcing any regrets I had to the side, I immediately dove back into the fray, tackling a wolf before it could do the same to Mrs. Carnesworth as she paused to reload her comically oversized handgun. It went down with me on top. I grabbed it by the scruff of its neck, pulled back, and rammed it face-first into the asphalt, resulting in a disturbing *crunc*h that was either its face or the street cracking. It was hard to tell which.

Regardless, it had the desired effect and the monster fell limp beneath me.

Mrs. Carnesworth threw me a thumbs up. "Thanks! Keep up the good work."

"I'll do my best." I stopped dead in my tracks as the words – my go-to excuse during high school – slipped automatically from my lips.

By then, she'd turned away to open fire on a pair of werewolves advancing on Chief Johnson's position. If she heard or recognized me, she gave no indication, instead focusing on the fight all around us.

Whew! Close one.

Terrifying as this all was, if there was one benefit, it was seeing so many people having the backs of their neighbors. But singing Kumbaya would have to wait.

No sooner had I stepped away, to see who else needed an ass-kicking, when I was blindsided. Something large, heavy, and furry plowed into me from the side and we both went tumbling end over end.

Luckily, it was one of the smaller wolves. Less lucky was that it still had at least two-hundred pounds in its favor, maybe more since I was sweating pretty hard by then. Say what you will about being attacked by a horde of monsters, but it made for damn good cardio. CrossFit had nothing on this shit.

We both regained our feet at the same time and launched ourselves at each other. I grappled the werewolf and spun, keeping our positions ever shifting. Friendly fire was definitely an issue, but of greater concern was the wolves that were still armed. They'd be less likely to care about firing into hand-to-hand combat, knowing their side healed from just about anything.

Fortunately, it seemed everyone and everything else in the area was currently occupied, leaving me to continue dancing with my furry friend.

"Mind if I lead?" I threw an uppercut that slammed its jaws shut with a click of teeth.

I lowered my shoulder and drove it into the beast's midsection, lifting it from the ground for a moment before slamming it back into the pavement, hard enough to knock the wind out of it.

"Time to say good night, asshole." I got back to my feet and prepared to plant the heel of my shoe into its windpipe.

That's when it began to change.

It was the first wolf I'd seen try to shift back into its human form this night. Everything else had stayed ugly and hairy, even as death took hold. I had actually begun to wonder if maybe they were incapable of changing back during the blood moon.

Apparently not, though. The creature's form shrank in on itself and the fur began to recede, revealing pink flesh beneath.

Why now? What was different about this one that caused it to...

"*Please.*" Its voice was guttural at first, but rapidly taking on a human intonation.

A moment later, the transformation completed itself and it all became clear to me as the scared young face of Melissa Haynes, the girl I used to babysit – and the same wolf I'd put in the hospital the month before – stared up into my eyes.

"Please don't hurt me."

33

"**W**hat the hell?!" I cried, my voice muffled by my frayed mask.

That bastard Craig. He'd sent them all on his mission of petty vengeance. Melissa was fucking thirteen years old, barely a teenager, and he'd sent her here to either kill or be killed.

"Please, no more," she begged again. "I don't want to be here."

"Then why..."

A low-pitched howl rose up in the night, increasing in volume until I could hear the few windows remaining on the street beginning to rattle. I could feel it reverberating in my bones and when I looked up, I saw the reason why.

A massive wolf stood atop the roof of Penneker's Bakery, looking down at the street and the chaos contained within. In the light of the blood moon, it appeared to have nearly crimson fur, but its size gave it away. It was Craig, the alpha of the pack.

Uncle Craig raised his muzzle to the sky and again let out a howl, one that echoed through the street.

It was as if a switch had been thrown. The wolves on

the ground disengaged from whoever they'd been attacking and went bounding away, all in the same direction.

Craig looked down and I was certain his eyes locked with mine. I heard a strange guttural chuffing coming from him and realized a moment later the bastard was laughing. What a fucking cock. He'd unleashed hell upon this town and had the gall to think it was funny.

All at once, I realized what he was doing, where he was sending the others. Here there was resistance. Though many lives had been lost in the fighting, there was no shortage of werewolf corpses littering the street either. Deeper in the town, though, lay the residential areas. I'd run into wolves there earlier, but I realized now they'd been mere scouts, forerunners sent to stir up chaos. Now he was sending the bulk of the pack.

Going door to door, neighborhood to neighborhood, it would be a slaughter.

I turned and looked around, finally spotting Chief Johnson. "They're going for the homes!" I screamed out. "They're..."

"No!"

I turned back toward Melissa. She had regained her feet and was standing nude in the middle of the street with her head turned skyward. *No?* "What are you...?"

"I don't want to."

I followed her gaze up to where Craig stood looking down at us. He let loose a snarl at the girl that faded into a low-pitched growl.

"I'm so sorry," she said.

"Sorry? About what?"

Goddamn, I could be so stupid when I wanted to be.

I should have seen it coming. Should have guessed it. But I was tired, having been running or fighting for what seemed like hours now. Melissa caught me off guard. She spun, her body morphing even as she moved.

The change wasn't an instantaneous thing. From what I'd seen, it took at least several seconds to complete. But sometimes a full transformation wasn't necessary. And it only took an instant to change a part of their bodies.

Melissa's claws, now far longer than her fingernails had ever been, raked across my stomach, cutting deep furrows through my shirt, skin, and muscle.

A choked gasp escaped my lips as fire seemed to erupt in my gut. Within the space of a second I could feel blood soaking my shirt and beginning to drip down into my pants.

"Please forgive me..."

Before the pain took over and sent me to my knees, I hauled off and backhanded Melissa, sending her flying. I didn't want to hurt her, but there was no time for restraint, and though I couldn't understand the growls coming from above, I was pretty certain that he was ordering her to finish the job.

Melissa and I both crumpled to the ground at the same time, but where she lay unmoving, unconscious at the very least, I pressed my hands to my stomach and rolled over onto my back, trying to keep from crying out.

Craig again let out that chuffing laugh. I fully expected him to leap off the building and use the opportunity to gut me good and proper, but the bastard instead turned and loped off into the night, following the rest of the pack.

Son of a bitch!

He had me dead to rights. Could have finished me off and ended this. But I saw now what a petty dick he was being. His meaning was more than clear. I wasn't enough. He'd promised to destroy the town and he meant to do just that. He'd make sure I suffered for the sin of being born different, and only then would he come back and finish me off.

I squeezed my eyes shut as a spasm of pain roiled through my stomach, and when I looked up again, he was back, standing atop of the bakery, his massive form staring down at me.

Had he changed his mind?

But he just stood there. No laughing, no howling, just looking at me.

After a moment, I realized my mistake. It wasn't Craig. "Dad?"

Unfortunately, before I could tell for certain, the pain became too much and I passed out.

"Hold her still. This is going to hurt."

I heard a brief clicking noise, followed by the pain of what I was sure was teeth biting down into my already agony-wracked gut.

My eyes flew open and I flailed out.

"I said to hold her!"

"She's as strong as a fucking ox! You hold her."

I tried to sit up, and a hand pushed down on my shoulder. My first instinct was to grab it and break the arm it was attached to into multiple pieces, but fortunately, a voice stayed me before I could do any harm.

"Relax! It's me. We're trying to help you."

I blinked several times to clear my vision and found myself surrounded by people – humans fortunately – including Chief Johnson, who was kneeling in front of me next to a guy with a big stapler in his hand. "Ugh, how long was I out?"

"Just a few minutes."

That was a relief. I turned to the guy with the stapler.

"Don't bother hanging up flyers. Pretty sure those things ate your lost dog."

Chief Johnson smiled. "Sorry, best we could do for now."

"Best for...?"

"To get you back on your feet. That thing got you good. We're trying to close up your wounds. You'll probably want a tetanus shot later, but at least you won't bleed out."

"Thanks," I replied weakly.

"Don't mention it."

I reached up to rub my eyes and realized my face was still covered. "You didn't unmask me?"

"Wasn't my top priority," he said. "Besides, didn't seem sporting considering all you've done for us. Oh, and don't worry, I'm not even going to try telling you to sit this one out."

"Yay for me."

I dared a glance down at my midsection. Part of my shirt had been torn away, although not enough to reveal anything that could cause me to start throwing punches. Two ugly gashes continued to ooze blood, while two more had been closed up in a manner best described as pretty fucking nasty. "Good thing bikini season is over."

"Sorry about that," Johnson said, inclining his head at the other guy. "And even more sorry because we're not done yet."

Oh shit. Still, it was better than bleeding to death, if just barely.

I laid back down and gritted my teeth. The sooner I was back in this fight, the better chance we had of ending this.

34

Lying there listening to them staple my guts back together gave me some time to think. It was far better than concentrating on what they were doing, or the biting pain that followed each click of the stapler.

Fortunately, I had a little secret. Werewolves healed fast, but so did I. Pity it wasn't fast enough to not make this hurt like a motherfucker. So instead, I tried to focus on how to stop this mess without leaving the town a lifeless ruin.

Thankfully, my uncle was *good* enough to provide the answer. He'd finally shown his face, no doubt to gloat in his wolfish way about how he planned to be an asshole to the very end. But Melissa had proven that at least one of the pack wasn't all that keen on what he was doing. If there was one, then there had to be others. He was somehow forcing them to do his bidding. I wasn't sure if it was instinctual pack mentality, some sort of psychic ... I dunno ... compulsion, or the others simply being afraid of him. Maybe it was a mix of all the above. It didn't really matter. What did was that he was the puppet-master here, whether or not his people liked it.

But what if he wasn't?

If someone else was calling the shots, then perhaps this entire thing could be stopped with little more than pointing a finger toward Morganberg and telling them all to go fetch. Would it work? No idea, but I had to try. Both Mom and Dad had given me enough clues to make me think I had a shot, such as Dad's bruises the night after I first discovered my abilities. He'd challenged his brother as cover for letting me get away. That told me the position of alpha was fluid. Might made right. Yeah, I wasn't a giant dog, so there was no telling if he'd accept my challenge, but I was pretty sure I had that one covered if he tried to weasel out.

As for me taking over the pack and ordering them the fuck out of town, well, Mom had provided that answer – fear. There were already going to be fewer wolves returning home than had come here, and I was responsible for a good chunk of them. If I added Craig to that number, I was willing to bet the rest would trip over themselves to get as far away from me as they could.

Either that or they'd all attack at once and rip me to shreds.

Considering how my stomach felt once I was back on my feet, I might not have minded that option too much.

Unfortunately, in the time it took me to get mobile again, a lot of the formerly organized resistance broke up as the townsfolk realized what was happening. Between that and those lost in the fight, there was maybe half a dozen people remaining. Bodies, human and otherwise, littered the street. A few brave souls were trying to cover them with blankets, sheets, flags, anything they could find.

It broke my heart to see so many cut down and for such stupid, selfish reasons. I was well aware that part of that selfishness was on me, but the pity party would have to wait. If I didn't act, soon every street in town would look like this.

"What's your plan?" I asked Chief Johnson once I was up and relatively certain my guts weren't going to spill out onto the ground with the first step I took.

"You mean besides early retirement if I live through this shit?" he asked with a sigh. "We can't fight these things all over the goddamned town. They'll pick us off like flies. Phone lines are down and so are cell towers, so the chances of getting help to come to us in time are pretty slim."

"What's that leave?"

"Going old school. We go door to door evacuating people, then bring as many as we can somewhere safe."

Again, I was surprised by how level-headed he was. However, rather than voice my concerns, I simply nodded in agreement.

"We need a defensible location, otherwise those bastards will have us for supper."

Again I nodded. "Any ideas? Town hall? The police station?"

"Too small. I'm thinking Saint Matthews over on Elm. It's big enough, the walls are made of brick, and there's only a few entrances. Doesn't hurt that Reverend Keller owes me a favor."

"That could work."

"Yeah, *could* being the operative word, if we can get everyone there."

"I think I can help with that. If what I have planned works, most of these things will have their eyes on me."

"Throwing yourself to the wolves?"

"Something like that."

"I'm not going to fight you on this, because I'd probably lose," he said. "All I'm going to say is good luck and try not to get yourself killed. Oh, and come tomorrow, if I were you, I'd lose the mask and play dumb as a brick to anyone asking what you were up to."

I couldn't help but laugh. The chief was way too calm, collected, and rational for what was going on. He had to know something, but since he seemed cool with keeping my secret, the least I could do was not push my luck.

When I was finished, I thanked the men who'd helped patch me up and turned away.

"Oh, and Ninja Girl?" Chief Johnson called after me.

"Yeah?"

"Thanks. A lot of people here owe their lives to you tonight."

I wished I could've accepted that praise, but being that I was the cause of this, it didn't feel right.

I wasn't sure it would ever feel completely right.

But I knew something that would help. And that was finding my dear uncle and kicking his ass from here to the far end of High Moon.

The blood moon continued to bathe the streets an eerie color, but it at least made traversing them much easier. This whole mess would have been a lot harder if I was tripping over things every five seconds. Super strength was awesome, but I sure as hell wouldn't have said no to night vision. Mind you, I wouldn't have said no to laser eyes, or the ability to kill enemies with my thoughts either. But we work with what we have.

Fortunately, I didn't need a good sense of smell or super tracking abilities to home in on my quarry. Seemed they couldn't go five minutes without one of them howling at the moon, and once one of them did, a bunch more joined in.

I tried to focus on the direction where the largest concentration of howls seemed to be coming from, because I had a feeling that's where Craig would be. No real reason, but if I were the one calling the shots, I'd want to make sure I was in the middle where everyone could hear me calling them.

Focused didn't mean heartless, though. I'd barely gone two blocks before the sound of wood splintering caught my ear, followed by a cry of terror.

It was close, too close for me to ignore.

Though I couldn't move quite as quickly as I had earlier, not without tearing my already aching stomach to shreds, I hoofed it as best I could.

I'd handed out most of those silver spikes but had kept one for myself. It definitely made me feel a bit better to have it. Besides, if there was anything that was going to help me even the odds, it was shoving one of those in a werewolf, preferably where the sun didn't shine.

My heart immediately leapt into my throat as I realized the source of the cries was coming from a familiar single-story ranch-style house, or at least one I'd hoped to make familiar.

No!

I hadn't seen Gary since our aborted date. His absence at the Main Street standoff had me hoping he'd chosen this night to be somewhere – *anywhere* – else.

The broken front door, however, told a different story.

I was split between caution and wanting to race in screaming his name, but I forced down my panic and instead focused on anger instead. Because if so much as a hair on his near-perfect head was harmed, then the werewolf responsible was going to wish it had turned itself in to the dog pound.

"Who's there? Stay back! I'm warning you!"

The sound of his voice from further in the house

almost caused me to whoop with joy, but then I remembered I was supposed to be incognito. I readjusted my mask, making sure it was on straight, then crept in.

The lights were out but the place was small. It didn't appear there were too many spots for a monster wolf to hide. A beam of light from a few rooms down caught my attention.

There, in a back room, I found Gary. He was standing with a baseball bat in one hand and a flashlight in the other, protectively guarding ... a woman and two small children?

What the?

I stood dumbfounded in the doorway for several seconds, trying to take this in. After a moment more, I noted the conspicuous lack of werewolves in the house, but it was as if it were a secondary concern – like that was the least interesting thing going on right at that moment.

"What happened?" I was seriously confused at the sight before me, but coherent enough to at least remember to lower my voice an octave or two. The kids looked absolutely terrified, which helped snap me out of my fugue. "It's okay, I'm not one of them. I'm wearing this because ... I'm sorta like a superhero." I quickly stuffed the silver spike into my belt to help ease the tension in the room a bit.

That seemed to calm the children down, even if the two adults continued to have wild-eyed looks about them.

"That thing ... I've never seen anything like it," Gary said at last.

I kept my hands out in what I hoped was a placating manner. "Believe me, I understand. Um ... where did it go? Did it hurt anyone? Are you and ... your sister okay?"

"Sister?" Gary shook his head after a second, as if incorrectly deciding that wasn't the important part of my question. "No. That thing broke in here, snarling like a wild animal. I was helping my girlfriend put the kids to bed when it happened. We grabbed them up quick as we could and I told them to get behind me. I thought that thing was going to tear us to pieces."

"Girlfriend ... as in someone else who's not here?"

"No, he means me," the woman replied in a rather snotty voice.

I did my best to throw her some shade through my mask. "Of course he did."

As the sense of unreality gave way to smoldering anger, a small part of me vaguely wondered how long it would take before I got tired of punching them both in the face. But then I glanced past them at the kids again. They were terrified but alive. Everyone here was. Sure, Gary deserved a kick to the balls when next I saw him, but at least he was intact to get them kicked. I tried damn hard to convince myself that was the important thing. "So, what happened ... err, I mean the werewolf. Did you beat it off or something?"

Oh yeah, real slick.

"It just stopped," Gary said, my obvious discomfort flying way over his head. "It looked at us, then let out a howl and ran back out the way it had come."

Hmm. More fuel to my theory that not all of them wanted to be here.

I turned around and prepared to get out of there before I said something that gave away my identity ... or he said something that would cause me to kick his cheating motherfucker ass. But then I stopped and looked back as I remembered Chief Johnson's plan. "The chief of police is rounding people up. They're going door to door to get everyone over to Saint Matthews. Keep an eye out for them."

"I have my truck."

"Stay here until they come get you. There's a lot of

those things out there and you don't want to run into one that's less discerning about who it eats." I paused for a moment. "Also, I passed your truck on the way in, and I think that monster got to it first."

I left without saying another word – just turned around, stepped out of the house, and walked away.

But first I kicked his front tire hard enough to shatter the axle.

I was glad to see that Gary was okay, but that didn't mean he was getting off the hook so easily.

35

Working to track down the bulk of the pack, I considered what I'd learned at Gary's place.

No, not that he was a cheating asshole with a whore girlfriend. That didn't require much thought. What I tried to focus on was the wolf attack or lack thereof. Though it was possible that the werewolf knew Gary, in his human guise anyway, I thought it equally likely that they'd seen the kids and had a change of heart.

It gave me hope that I was right and there were others here like Melissa, those who weren't entirely comfortable with their leader's orders to pillage and burn to their heart's content.

If so, then my plan to kick Craig's ass and order the rest of them to leave might have a chance in hell of working.

I put a bit more spring into my step as a chorus of howls rose up in the distance, wincing as my stomach protested. Fortunately, it wasn't as bad now. Perhaps my own enhanced healing had gotten a chance to kick in. Either that or my brain was so awash in adrenaline that I just didn't care.

Somewhere behind me the sound of sirens rose up again, telling me that the chief was hard at work putting his plan into motion.

That was good, especially if my part didn't pan out. The chief was smart, competent, and apparently as unfazed by this shit as a human being could get. He hadn't questioned a damned thing he'd seen. Had merely taken it in stride and worked it into his defense strategy. Don't get me wrong, it was a lot better than some skeptic thinking that maybe they were dealing with swamp gas or some other bullshit rational explanation. At the same time, perhaps I'd best be coy around him in the future lest he put two and two together and figure out I was his mysterious *Ninja Girl*.

Ugh! I also made a note to not let Chris ever hear me called that. The little shit burger would never let me live it down.

As I continued onward, walking down familiar streets toward what sounded like the center of werewolf activity, I noticed a lot of frightened people out on their front porches. Many were no doubt curious as to what was going on. Some were kind enough to call me over to offer sanctuary in their homes, while others warned me to stay away. A good many were armed. Though I didn't have time to start ringing doorbells like I was on a Halloween candy bender, I did try to tell everyone I saw of the chief's plan.

Curious enough, for a time I saw fewer and fewer werewolves the further I got from Main Street. Most were from a distance, running from homes they'd invaded or simply disappearing into the shadows before I could chase them.

It was strange. Had Craig called off the attack? Had he figured that he'd made his point, so enough was enough? Were we destined to play this whole thing out again next month ... with maybe a new fiancé picked out for me and the threat that this time was merely a warning? That didn't seem a wise strategy, but then, Craig hadn't exactly struck me as Mensa material.

No, that wasn't it because I never stopped hearing them. Even though I didn't see them, the pack's howls grew ever louder as I continued walking.

Then, all at once it seemed, I found them again. It was like I crossed the street and stepped into a nightmare. One moment I was getting curious glances from people looking out their doorways. The next, there were snarls, the sound of splintering wood, and large shapes looming in the shadows.

I glanced around and suddenly it made sense. Craig had pulled the bulk of his pack away from the main thoroughfare – and source of resistance – and had them converge on a different part of town, one that should have been obvious to me from the start. Whether subconsciously or not, I'd been heading in the direction of my home ever since setting out from Chief Johnson and his brave defenders, essentially retracing my steps.

And here now, only a few blocks away, did it finally sink in. What better place for my uncle to focus his wrath? Not only was the resistance here minimal, a few unlucky souls trying to defend what was theirs, but it allowed him to concentrate his spite on the place where the leader of his enemies lived.

I had a sinking feeling that there would be more than just some creepy garden gnomes waiting for me when I got home this time.

But first, I had to get there.

Luckily for me, it seemed that once the battle of Main Street was over, most of the wolves decided to ditch their firearms in favor of good old-fashioned monster carnage, otherwise my night would have probably ended far sooner than I hoped.

Conserving my strength, I tried to pick my battles as I fought my way toward my house. If a wolf ran from me, I let it go, especially since I wasn't in much condition to give chase anyway. If one came straight at me, though, I took it out with extreme prejudice.

Thankfully, the vast majority seemed to favor that first strategy. Even if they didn't know the truth of what I was, it seemed many understood what I could do. For any who didn't get the memo, dispatching them with a silver stake through the chest or skull ended up being a really good way of dissuading any others nearby.

Even so, the continued action was slowly taking its toll. I was pretty sure my stomach was preparing to call its lawyer and serve divorce papers to the rest of my body. Likewise, I could have started a collection with the number of bruises I'd managed to sustain. In short, I was injured and close to exhausted by the time I stepped onto my street.

Or at least I thought it was my block. It more resembled a small slice of Americana as pictured through the eyes of a post-apocalyptic wasteland. Doors were kicked in, fences knocked over, cars overturned – some burning. Hell, a few of the homes looked like they'd been outright bulldozed.

I didn't even want to think about what had happened to the people inside.

From what I could see, it appeared only one structure remained wholly intact – my house. It stood untouched in its lot near the middle of the street, even as the sounds of destruction filled the air from the homes around it.

Standing on the sidewalk and looking up at my home was Craig. He was easy to tell from the others ... larger and a lot scarier-looking. Even in silhouette from half a block away I could identify him.

What was he doing? Was he saving my home for last or...

I chuckled to myself. Or was this my mother's doing? Had she left some nasty surprises for him, knowing he'd eventually end up here? Knowing Mom, I wasn't about to discount that.

All night long, I'd been bemoaning what a spiteful asshole my uncle was but, to be fair, Mom hadn't struck me as an amateur in that arena either. She...

Fuck!

A wolf rushed me as I walked toward where Craig stood. I should have expected it. The entire place was crawling with monsters, but I'd been so focused on him that I let my guard down.

I managed to block with my shoulder in the moment before the beast hit, cushioning some of the blow, but it still took me off my feet.

The wolf carried me about ten yards, onto the front lawn of one of our neighbors – the Cavendaugh place judging by the look of things. Not the most friendly family to ever grace this Earth, but not so bad that they deserved to have their home invaded by monsters.

That was all the time I could spare to them, however, as I was sent sprawling onto the grass. I hit the ground hard and the silver spike went flying out of my hands, tumbling away into the darkness.

Fuck me!

The wolf fell atop me and my stomach screamed in agony. The creature must have noticed my grimace because it lifted its head and chuffed in that strange wolf laugh they seemed to like to do. Then it plunged forward with its teeth, no doubt looking to ease my pain permanently.

Pity that it underestimated me. Trying to grapple a grappler was a dicey proposition, especially for creatures who were mostly top-heavy like these things. However, being that there was no referee here to count it out, I didn't see much use in going for a pin ... or playing by the rules, for that matter.

I jabbed upward with an open palm, catching it by the throat just before it could clamp down on my face. But I wasn't trying to push it away. No, I was done playing that game. My fingers closed on its windpipe and I clenched them shut with everything I had.

The wolf let out a quick yip before its air was cut off. For a moment we struggled in silence, but then the impasse was broken by the sound of wet meat being ripped apart as I pulled back and tore its throat out.

A small geyser of blood sprayed from the wound and its body fell slack atop mine.

I shoved it off and stood up, realizing that the neighborhood had suddenly grown quiet as the proverbial grave.

All around, I could see yellow eyes peering at me from doorways, windows, and bushes. If they hadn't been aware of my presence before, they definitely were now, which was probably not a great thing as I counted nearly a dozen wolves from my vantage point alone. Most importantly, I turned back toward my house and saw the big cheese himself, Craig, standing and staring back at me.

I'd gotten his attention, albeit perhaps not in the manner I'd meant to.

Now to see if I could keep from getting killed long enough to take advantage of it.

36

C raig's massive form shimmered and then began to shrink in on itself. The shaggy hair covering his body receded. His ears became shorter and more rounded. The long snout on his face began to pull back, for a moment leaving the oversized teeth still sitting within in a strange semblance of an overly wide smile.

He lost probably a good two feet of height, and the rippling sound of his bones and muscles contracting could be heard even from where I stood. If the transformation hurt – and it certainly looked painful – he didn't show it, continuing to stare at me as his flesh contorted and rearranged itself. He was still a big man, don't get me wrong, but compared to his wolf form he was far less impressive.

I guess maybe that was supposed to be the point.

Well, that, and he could speak clearly again.

"You had to know this would happen, Tamara." His voice sounded almost rueful, but then he paused for a second. "It's okay. It's just us here. No need for Halloween masks."

He was right. I whipped my *disguise* off my head and

tossed it to the side. It was actually nice to breathe fresh air again. As well as the mask had served me, it had been starting to get mighty ripe. Unfortunately, the freshness of the night air was tainted with the smell of blood and other odors that I really didn't care to identify.

I began walking forward, intent on giving him a piece of my mind while I had a chance to do so, but stopped as he came more clearly into view. "Um, any chance you could maybe throw on a pair of pants first?"

He lifted his hands up as if stretching. "This night is ours, child. Why should we hide who we are, what we are?"

"So you're saying you're a dick?"

That actually caused him to chuckle, but then his mood quickly turned grim. "You could have avoided all of this, you know. Joined our pack, followed our rules, been our ally. But you turned on us. Took my offer and spat it back in my face."

"An ally?" I asked, moving toward him again, albeit making it a point to keep my eyes focused above his neck. "You didn't want an ally. You wanted me barefoot and pregnant near the woodstove. You wanted a slave. You wanted someone you didn't have to fear."

"You think I'm afraid of you?"

I locked eyes with him. "I know you are."

"Is that why Jerry is missing?"

Missing?

"Yeah. We heard him, calling for help right before his cries cut off. Don't know what you did with him, but we know it wasn't good." He raised his voice. "So I ask again, is that why you killed one of our own?!"

The fact that they hadn't found Jerry was odd. Or maybe not. Near the end, there'd been some freaky ass things happening in that glade. I guess that also accounted for the fact that I was able to make it to High Moon in time to warn Riva. Strange, but not nearly at the top of my priority list right then.

Snarls rose up from all around me. I could see what Craig was doing – riling up the troops before setting them loose on me. Even fresh, I wouldn't stand a chance against those odds. They'd tear me apart while he stood there with his dick swaying in the wind.

"You threatened my town," I shot back. "You had me followed and threatened to kill *my best friend*. And for what? I'm just one person, the only one of my kind. The only *hybrid* between the two races."

I let that sink in for several seconds. As expected, hushed murmurs rose up around us. I couldn't understand what they were saying, but there was definitely sentiment other than anger in the air ... confusion and maybe even some worry. Craig had given them a bullshit story so as to avoid a mass freak-out. Pity he hadn't counted on me to spill the beans.

"Let's face facts: you went to some extreme lengths to ensure I followed your lead like a good dog." I raised my voice as well. Two could play at this game. "If those aren't the actions of someone who's scared shitless, then I don't know what is."

"You watch your tone, girl," he warned, flashing teeth that had seemingly doubled in size in the time it took him to open his mouth.

"Sorry, but I've seen that trick before." I turned and addressed the wolves in the neighborhood, those I could see and those I knew to be hiding just out of sight. It was time to play that fear card against them. "And in case you're all wondering why several of your pack mates aren't here with you now, let me assure you that I'm the reason." I pointed a finger at Craig. "But he's the cause."

More snarls rose up, no doubt some whose dander I

managed to raise. But just as many chuffs and whispers could be heard out there in the crimson-stained night.

They were unsure. They'd never met a boogeyman, or woman, like me. And now here I was presenting myself out in the open. I knew they probably all wanted to kill me, a product of a union with their ancient enemies, but which of them would be brave enough to go first – especially with a seriously broken wolf lying just a couple of yards behind me?

"You're an aberration, nothing more," Craig said. "The result of an ill-conceived union after your whore mother bewitched one of our own."

Kudos to Craig for not outright mentioning my dad. They were brothers, after all, and if it became common knowledge that Dad was actually in love with a witch, there was bound to be some blowback. As for the slight about my mom, I wasn't so easily riled up. I mean, heck, I'd been in high school not too long ago. That was practically a softball.

"He should have cut her belly open and let you spill out onto the sidewalk the second he learned what she'd done to him."

Okay, that pitch was a bit faster.

"To think the Monarch Queen fooled me for so long about what you were. Had I known, I'd have slit your throat as a mere babe."

And there we were, the mistake I'd been hoping for. Oh, he wasn't getting to me at all. Fuck no. I'd lived with my trash-talking dweeb of a brother for over a decade. After a while, it all just became white noise. But his statement was a spark that I was happy to pour some gasoline on.

"So that's the brave alpha of the wolves, is it? First you threaten the innocents of this town. Then you threaten my friend. And now, here I finally am, and the best you can do is wish you'd killed me in my crib. You're real tough when it comes to everyone but the person you should be threatening."

"I'm not afraid of you, cunt."

Ooh. That was going to cost him. I had a very strict rule when it came to guys who pulled out the C-word. Good thing it already coincided with my plans for him.

"Prove it," I said. "I'm right in front of you. You can kill me outside of my own house, which is what I'm thinking you had planned all along. Unless, that is, you're just standing out here admiring Mom's flower beds."

We were close, I could feel it. I flexed my stomach muscles – still tender, but not as bad as before. My own healing was definitely starting to catch up. Hopefully enough so that I could wear a two piece again without my stomach looking like a jigsaw puzzle. But worrying about the beach was for later. For the moment, I'd be happy with my guts not spilling out all over the street.

Now to add the finishing touch. "Or are you going to order your underlings to do what you're afraid to do yourself? Let them take all the risk while you stand there, a pretender to the throne?"

Several of the yellow eyes that had been on me abruptly shifted over to Craig. This wasn't some crusty old monarchy where a spoiled rich kid was allowed to sit on the throne while the peasants went out and died in whatever war they felt like waging. In the wild, the strongest led, but only until such time as something else proved itself stronger. I wasn't exactly Jane Goodall, but I knew enough to understand that weakness was not a trait alphas showed if they wished to keep their lofty position.

"You think you're smart, do you, girl?" Craig asked, his voice growing deeper, more gravelly.

I knew what was coming next. Truth be told, a part of me dreaded it. I mean, I wasn't so stupid to think I was invincible. On the upside, at least he'd be hairy enough for me to forget he was naked. Glass half full and all that.

"*You are a mere genetic aberration. I am a descendant of Valdemar himself,*" he cried as his canines elongated into cruel spikes. "*His divine blood flows through my veins.*"

"Dude, you drive a tow truck. Let's not pretend either of us is being crowned King Shit anytime soon."

If Craig had anything to say about that, it was lost as he continued to change. Coarse hair sprouted from his body and his muscles began to enlarge. By the time they were done, he'd be nearly twice his original size.

That was, assuming I let him finish – something I wasn't particularly keen on doing.

37

I was on the move before the change was even half-finished. As my father had been good enough to show me, a werewolf's power began to increase at the very start of the strange transformation from man to beast, so there was no doubt that Craig was already well on his way to beefing up. But he wasn't fully there yet.

Pity for him, I wasn't above using that to my advantage. My gut didn't particularly appreciate the sudden burst of speed I put on, but since my intestines didn't immediately go splaying out across my front lawn, I figured they'd hold for now.

Craig adopted a defensive stance even as his body continued to ripple and morph. The upside for me was that the transformation wasn't entirely uniform. While his body had already expanded to the point where it was nearly a foot taller, his arms hadn't yet gained enough reach to bat me away like a gnat.

That still didn't mean he was helpless. He threw an ungainly punch which I blocked before stepping inside his defenses. Grabbing hold of his torso, I spun, noting how disturbing the feel of his rippling flesh was. Fortunately, I didn't have to hold on for long.

I let go and sent him flying toward our garage. Though I didn't care to imagine the blow-up Mom would have if I survived this night, I wanted to fight this battle with as much of an advantage as I could muster ... even if it meant I'd be waiting tables to pay for a new garage door.

Much to my surprise, though, rather than plow through the aluminum, there came a crackling flash of light and Craig rebounded off it. He rolled away, his hair smoking from whatever had just happened.

It was Mom's doing, had to be. Either that, or Dad had invested in a hell of a home security system recently. Regardless, that seemed to answer why Craig had been standing just outside our property line. He knew.

More importantly, now I did, too. Home field advantage was a good thing, but it was even better when the field was booby-trapped against the opposing team.

Sadly, Mom's spell seemed to be aimed at keeping people like Craig out, not instantly vaporizing them. Guess that was too much to hope for.

My uncle lay on the grass, the creepy lawn gnomes staring impassively as he finished his transformation. So much for them being an extra layer of security, too. Guess Mom really did just like the freaky little things.

My uncle rose from the ground, fully in his wolf form. The only indication that he was even slightly inconvenienced by Mom's wards was a slight bit of smoke rising from his fur. That wasn't good. I'd hoped to take the wind out of his sails with one shot, but I guess it wasn't going to be that easy.

The hair on the back of my neck prickled, and I dared a glance around to find the entire street seemingly full of werewolves – all of them watching us.

No, not just watching. I had a feeling they were also

there in case one of us lost our nerve and tried to make a run for it. They were our audience, but also our prison. Guess I was in for both a penny and a pound.

Speaking of which, I had a feeling that Uncle Craig was going to be looking for his pound of flesh. He threw back his head and let out a roar. This was no mere howl at the moon. It was full-on rage from a nightmare beast. He started heading toward me.

Wolf muzzles didn't appear too conducive to long soliloquies, but they were capable of blurting out the occasional understandable word.

"*Die!*"

And yes, the meaning was quite clear, despite his voice sounding like he had been gargling broken glass. Even if I hadn't understood, the sight of him picking up speed, a locomotive on legs, was more than enough to get the point across.

"Let's do this!"

And that was all the time for words I had before he was all over me like a new suit.

Craig swung a massive arm at me. It was like someone had grafted a tree trunk to his body. I tried to block it but was sent flying instead. My own strength might have been formidable, but he had physics on his side. His size and mass eclipsed mine by several times over. I might have had the advantage when it came to center of gravity, but that meant little when I was being batted aside like a Wiffle ball.

I flew across our driveway and slammed through the vinyl fence that separated our yard from the Havenstock's, our next door neighbors. Mind you, considering the current state of their house, I doubted they'd be too worried about it ... or the granite birdbath on their front lawn that eventually halted my momentum.

Ouch! That was definitely going to leave a bruise.

Of course, that assumed I'd be alive enough to enjoy a bruise, something Craig seemed intent on not allowing. Guess the posturing was over and done with, as he appeared – larger than life – in front of me before I'd fully recovered. He lifted his arms over his head, no doubt meaning to batter me into a greasy grass stain.

Unfortunately for him, something like this was more my speed when it came to fighting. Playing whack-a-mole with each other had been a poor strategy on my part. But now I had a chance to make up for it. Instinct, and several years of drills, took over. Where he went high, I went low.

I grabbed hold of Craig's legs before he could pummel me and pulled them out from beneath him. He went down on his back, and I rolled over him as if going for the pin. He was far too big for that, but his size was just right for me to bring the heel of my foot crashing down square onto his muzzle.

He let out a yip of pain and I quickly rolled off before he could retaliate. I didn't go far, though. We both got to our feet at the same time, but I ducked down low and again kicked his legs out from under him.

Dropping him to the ground wouldn't do much to hurt him, but it put him in prime position for me to end this fight the same way I'd ended a few others this night.

I threw myself on top of Craig and grabbed hold of him – one hand on his muzzle, the other on the side of his head. I simultaneously pulled and twisted, hoping to snap his neck like a twig.

Ugh! Come on!

Sadly, I underestimated him. He was a werewolf all right, but on steroids. It was like he had muscles on top of his muscles. I'd barely managed to turn his head to the side before he grabbed hold of me with his massive paws. "ARGH!"

His claws dug into my flesh, easily turning my leather jacket into confetti. God, I was stupid. I'd been so eager to end this with one move that I'd handed myself to him on a platter.

Searing pain flared up from my sides as he put on the pressure. I was in a bad spot of my own making. I might have been wrestling for years, but apparently I was a rank amateur when it came to life-or-death struggles. Taking my hands off his muzzle to pry his claws out of me would leave me wide open to his maw of massive teeth. Christ, it was as if a mad scientist had grafted arms to a great white shark.

Craig, not quite the idiot I'd made him out to be, chuffed in amusement, fully aware he had me where he wanted me. It was either let him continue to shred my body, or accept that the last thing I would see in this world was the back of his throat.

Thankfully, my coaches over the years had been up to snuff – not only drilling me on what was expected, but teaching me to think on my feet so as to escape when things went south.

Faced with a choice of being chomped or fileted, I chose option C. I let go of Craig's muzzle with one hand and jammed my thumb into his eye instead. I didn't have claws quite like his, but I'd been growing my nails this past month, trying to look a bit more feminine for Gary. I guess some good had come out of dating that cheating jackass after all.

I shoved good and hard, not caring if I got eyeball gunk all over my hand. The result was music to my ears.

Craig screamed and did his damnedest to push me away before I could properly finger-bang his brain. I was tossed off him like I weighed nothing, back toward my own yard, where I went tumbling head over heels until I skidded to a halt next to one of Mom's favorite rose bushes.

Oh well, at least I hadn't hit it. Not only would that have hurt like a bitch, but I'd have heard about it for a long time to come. She was kinda partial to them, after all.

Lying there bleeding as I was, I had to consider the upside. The way this fight was going, I probably wouldn't have to worry about the landscaping for much longer.

38

I stayed on the ground longer than I should have or wanted to. Couldn't be helped. Craig had done a job on me. At the very least, he'd perforated the skin and muscle on both sides of my body. I had no way of knowing if he'd popped anything of importance inside, but it sure as hell felt like it.

Maybe I'd get lucky and keel over dead the moment I stood up.

Thankfully, I'd given my dear uncle enough of an *eyeful* that he hadn't immediately fallen upon me and ended this. Double lucky that his pack believed in the honor system when it came to one-on-one battles.

I turned my head and saw one of Mom's goddamned garden gnomes staring judgmentally at me with its unblinking eyes.

"Fuck you," I whispered to it. Then, with far more effort than I cared to admit, I rolled onto my stomach and tried to push myself up.

"GAH!" I went down to one knee again as the pain of my half-shredded body set all of my nerve-endings aflame.

I glanced up and saw Craig had regained his feet, one

paw furiously rubbing at his face. He was making a strange snuffling whine, which I interpreted to mean he'd definitely felt it.

Good!

His remaining eye locked onto me as I again tried to get to my feet. I looked down at myself. Though the light cast off the blood moon probably wasn't helping matters, I was a mess. You'd have thought I'd been dragged five miles behind a car then dumped into a wood chipper.

"What the fuck are you staring at?" I asked, forcing a grin onto my face. "Don't you know that beauty is in the *eye* of the beholder?"

My joke didn't make him happy one little bit. He dropped his paw from his face, revealing his ruined eye socket. I had no idea if it would grow back. Hopefully not. If he managed to kill me, I'd rest a lot easier knowing I'd at least forced the fucker to wear an eyepatch for the rest of his days.

Fortunately, in addition to making sure I'd thoroughly fucked up his binocular vision, I'd apparently done enough to make him more cautious. Had he rushed me then and there, he could have ended this as I was still finding my footing, but he approached warily, taking his time.

My legs finally stable beneath me, I side-stepped into his blind spot, forcing him to correct course. Much as my sides burned, I wasn't about to make things easy on him.

Now that I was back on my feet, I felt a bit better, more steady. Maybe the damage hadn't been as bad as I'd originally thought. Either that or I was moments away from dropping dead. Whatever worked.

Wish I'd thought to borrow that stapler. As if my dear uncle would have let me take a time out to suture myself up.

Craig, for his part, decided to try a new tactic. Rather

than getting all close and personal for a love bite, he stayed at arm's length and took a swing at me. I leaned back at the last moment and felt the rush of air as his claws sliced the space my head had been occupying a moment earlier.

So that was his plan then, treat this like a boxing match and let his superior reach do the talking – a boxing match in which his gloves were tipped with broken glass. I seemed to recall Chris watching a movie like that once, but my brother's shitty taste in entertainment was going to do little to help me here. I needed to think fast.

Wrestling was all about getting close, establishing leverage and dominance. That was going to be tough with him swinging his elephant trunk arms at me. Another blow came my way that I just barely ducked, feeling as if my insides were on fire.

Craig pulled his lips back in a mockery of a smile. He knew he had the advantage and that it was only a matter of time before he connected. The asshole could take potshots at me all night if he wanted. Eventually he'd wear me down.

I needed to turn the tables before...

Damnit!

It wasn't just Craig's reach I had to worry about, but his stride, too. He took a big step forward, putting him well within range, and swung for the fences again. It was too close for me to duck this time.

I raised an arm to try to block him, but he caught me by the wrist, his massive paw practically swallowing my hand. Before I could pry him off, he stepped in again and grabbed hold of my other arm, too.

Fuck! I was caught like a rat in a trap and he knew it. He let out a chuckle and, before I could do anything, pulled my arms out wide and lifted me off my feet – effectively crucifying me, minus the cross.

That grin appeared on his stupid furry face again and

he began to exert pressure, pulling my arms further apart, no doubt trying to split me like a wishbone.

If I'd been normal, he could've torn my arms out at the socket with one good yank. But the idiot forgot I wasn't exactly chopped liver. If he wanted to play a game of werewolf mercy, then I'd give him a good run for his money.

My arms nearly strained to their limit, I tensed my muscles and began to pull. Butterflies had been a part of my workout routine for years, so my core was already pretty darn strong. Add some supernatural genetics to the mix and the game was on.

Uhhhh! Craig's strength was nothing to sneeze at, though, and he had my arms at maximum extension, meaning my leverage was shit. But still I continued to fight with everything I had left, making sure that if he wanted to tear me in two, he'd have to earn it first.

I managed to gain a little ground, my arms shaking from the effort, but that was the best I could do. How the hell could something be so strong?!

But then I looked to the side and realized I wasn't the only one straining in this test of strength. Craig was still grinning, but the tremors coming from his own limbs told a different story.

Nice try, fucker.

I'd competed long enough to know half the battle was psychological. My uncle was trying to win that war – intimidate me into giving up hope – but I saw through his façade.

Unfortunately, while his confidence might have been little more than a dog and pony show, his teeth weren't a bluff. They were more than enough to uneven the odds. It was one advantage I desperately needed to negate.

Being of modest height could sometimes be a real pain in the ass. You always had to ask for help for anything on the high shelf. Hell, in another year, Chris was going to be taller than me. But a smaller size also had its advantages, too.

One of them was being able to squeeze into tight spots others had trouble with, like a tiny sports car, or the small space between my body and Craig's drool-covered muzzle.

My legs were already hanging off the ground, so all I had to do was bring them up and plant my feet against his body, one foot on his muscular chest, and another right in his windpipe. It was a solid position to both keep his teeth at bay and be uncomfortable as fuck for him when I put on a little pressure.

I kicked out with everything I had, pushing away from him with my legs even as he tried to rip me in two. The added pressure, not hurt in the least by years of squats, was enough to force him to ease up on my arms. His bug-eyed look as my sneakered foot disappeared into the fur at the base of his throat was kinda cool, too.

Unfortunately, my sides were screaming from the exertion. I just had to hope that if one of us was going to pass out, he'd be good enough to do it first.

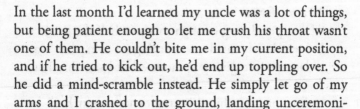

In the last month I'd learned my uncle was a lot of things, but being patient enough to let me crush his throat wasn't one of them. He couldn't bite me in my current position, and if he tried to kick out, he'd end up toppling over. So he did a mind-scramble instead. He simply let go of my arms and I crashed to the ground, landing unceremoniously on the back of my head.

Not exactly my most shining moment.

He wasn't finished, though. Craig grabbed hold of my ankle, swung, and sent me flying. Add another downside of being relatively short — I made for a good shotput.

Craig was no lightweight either. He launched me like a rocket, and I came slamming down onto the roof overhanging our front porch.

Thankfully, I didn't trigger whatever protections Mom had set on the house. Either that or my weird magic immunity buggered it up. Mind you, that didn't mean my situation was exactly wine and roses. I sent shingles flying in every direction and left a good-sized dent in our roof before sliding off and crashing face-first onto the ground below.

Hey, at least my newly smashed nose took my mind off the burning pain in my side for a few moments.

Dazed as I was, I had to do something. The longer this battle wore on, the more I seemed to be fighting Craig's fight. And the more points he accumulated on his scorecard, the bolder his pack would get. Yet, despite knowing all of that, there I was – lying face down on the grass while Mom's stupid garden gnomes gawked at me with their stupid unblinking eyes from just a few feet away.

Howls began to rise up from all around. Again, I didn't pretend to speak werewolf, but they sounded pretty darned triumphant. Though I couldn't hear them above the cries of the pack, the thud of heavy footsteps reverberated in the ground beneath me. Time was up. I needed to turn the tide in my favor now because I doubted there would be a later. Reckless action wouldn't help me, though. I needed to be smarter, think strategically.

I waited ... forcing myself to lie still while my uncle came for me. It went against every fiber in my being, but I held myself in check until...

There came a chuff of air – Craig exhaling as he leaned down. He was right behind me, reaching down to grab...

Now!

Hoping I timed it right, I gritted my teeth against the

pain and rolled – scissoring my legs so that one of my uncle's knees became sandwiched between them.

Power could be a defining trait in a fight, but everyone had weak spots and – large or small – most people had the same ones. For example, hit someone in the back of the knee hard enough and their leg will buckle beneath them, putting them on the ground. Fortunately for me, that rule held true for werewolves, too.

Craig landed next to me, but I was already in transit, ignoring my injuries as best as I was able to. Taking someone down in wrestling was one thing, but the follow through was what won the match. Resting on your laurels was a good way to get pinned ... or killed in this case.

I rolled to my feet before my uncle could get back to his, grabbed hold of the thick fur at the scruff of his neck, and dragged him forward.

"Eat vinyl siding, asshole!" Counting on Mom's magic, I plowed my uncle face-first into the front of my home.

There came a flash of energy and we were both pushed back by the discharge, although Craig definitely got the short end of that stick. He let out a high-pitched yelp as smoke rose from his charred face.

"Like that?" I asked. "How about seconds?"

I shoved him forward again, planting my feet this time so I could properly grill his noggin until it was well done.

Craig's muzzle slammed into the siding with a satisfying sizzle, as if he were a cockroach who'd just stepped into the world's biggest bug zapper.

Heh! That shut up the howls coming from his friends. Now it was just a matter of seeing how long it took until he was extra crispy.

He screamed out again and I put on even more pressure to hold him in place. *Good! I hope there's enough juice there for everyone you hurt tonight, you son of a...*

My hands suddenly closed on nothing and the pressure I'd used to brace against his massive body instead carried me forward.

What the?!

I rebounded off the house, my sides screaming in agony even though my nose took the brunt of the impact. There wasn't time to waste on pain, though. I quickly shook my head and spun around.

What the hell had just happened? There should have been no way for him to slip out of my grasp ... unless, that is, the fur I'd been holding onto was no longer there.

Craig, back in his human guise, was retreating away from me across the front lawn. *Goddamn it!* I really needed to remember the one fundamental aspect of shape shifters – they could shift their damned shapes!

Mind you, changing back to his smaller – and still disturbingly naked – human form wasn't necessarily a bad thing for me. No teeth, no claws, and him a couple hundred pounds lighter meant I could potentially end this quickly. A small part of me worried about the ethics of putting my fist through his now human face, but perhaps that was a moral quandary for tomorrow – after I'd finished scrubbing his spinal fluid off my knuckles.

The downside was I had to listen to him talk as he backpedaled across my front yard.

"You fucking bitch!" he screamed, pointing to his charred face and ruined eye, almost tripping over his own feet as he tried to get away. "Look what you did to me!"

"Don't worry. I'll give you a matching set." Ignoring my aches and pains, I pushed myself to my feet and set off in pursuit. Victory was within my grasp.

I realized my mistake about a second too late. He'd baited me, and I'd latched onto it hook, line, and sinker.

Even as I closed to within striking distance – mentally debating between snapping him in half and beating him with his own arms – I saw him change. It made his earlier transformation look like slow motion. I saw now, as his body became almost liquid in its fluidness, that he'd been toying with me earlier, making me think I was taking stock of his abilities when in reality he'd been holding back. The transformation took all of a second. It wasn't enough for him to fully change, but it was plenty of time for the bulk of his size, strength, and reach to return.

He lashed out with a fist, catching me full on in the gut before I could reach him, almost certainly popping every last staple still in my stomach. All of the air in my body was instantly knocked out of me. I didn't even have enough left to cry out.

The blow would have been more than enough to send me flying again, but Craig's reflexes were lightning fast. He grabbed me by the shirt and held me aloft, leaving my feet dangling at least a foot off the ground.

I was too busy trying not to puke my guts up to do much more than hang there, waiting to see whether he'd eviscerate me or twist my head off like a beer cap.

CRACK!

Neither apparently, as he hauled off and pimp-slapped me in the side of the face, hard enough to make me momentarily forget that my innards had just been rudely rearranged.

I should have been worrying about the people of High Moon and what the werewolves would do to them once I was gone. Yet, the only thing that seemed to pop into my dazed mind was all the money my parents had wasted getting me braces back in the sixth grade.

Kinda funny what we think about when the end rears its ugly head.

Craig did it again, making sure I had a matching set of

bruised cheeks and a ringing in my ears that wasn't likely
to end anytime soon.

Barely cognizant enough to realize what was happening, I felt myself lifted higher. Craig held me aloft with
one arm, then threw back his head and howled at the
blood moon above us.

The others quickly joined in, their voices drowning
out all other sounds. I knew what it meant. My uncle was
proclaiming victory and his pack was chiming in to
acknowledge him as their one true master.

I also knew what that meant for me. The end was....

"How disappointing."

Huh?!

Craig must've knocked more than a few screws loose
in my head, because what I'd heard wasn't possible. Not
only had I somehow clearly heard a voice above the
braying of the wolf pack around me, but it was one I knew
as well as my own.

"Riva?" I sputtered, spitting out blood.

I cracked open my eyes. Yeah, I'd definitely been hit
too hard. There, standing only a few feet behind Craig,
was my friend, looking just as I'd left her a few hours
earlier.

She was staring up at me with a curious look on her
face – whole, unmolested, and seemingly unconcerned
that she was about to be torn to shreds by werewolves.

39

"Are you dead or am I hallucinating?"

The question was lost to the continued howling of Craig and his pack, yet Riva inclined her head as if she'd heard me.

"Neither," she replied, her voice as clear as if we were chatting in a quiet room.

Somehow I didn't believe her.

"What you believe is irrelevant," she replied to my unspoken statement. Oh yeah, I was definitely going loopy in these last few minutes of life. "Or it will be if you continue along this path."

I looked down and saw Craig rearing back with his free hand, the claws splayed wide. Call me paranoid, but I had a feeling he was about to make a jump rope out of my intestines.

I'm open to suggestions.

"You were given life during a moon such as this," Riva replied in a tone more at home studying for a math test than surviving a monster apocalypse. "We saw an opportunity to bring you into existence. You, a rare thing that has only existed once before."

Oh yeah, that's real helpful.

"Little did we know then how you would honor our deed with a blood sacrifice." Riva smiled. "Almost as if some part of you instinctively knew where you came from. You empowered us, threw down the walls keeping us out. For this, we thank you."

Riva was talking gibberish now, leading me to believe that I probably had brain damage at this point. I guess it could have been worse. A hallucinatory Chris could have appeared and started discussing his collection of Pokémon cards, something that would have made my last few seconds feel like an eternity.

"We offer you this boon," Riva continued, choosing to ignore my thoughts. "The blood moon empowers your foes, as it does all those touched by the wyrd. That includes you, Tamara. Know that all things are possible beneath a blood moon. That included your birth and most certainly includes your continued survival."

Her words were interrupted by that chuffing laugh Craig seemed to be fond of.

I glanced toward him to find his eyes, or eye anyway, locked on me. I guess he finished howling at some point while I was having a discussion with...

The street behind him was empty once more. Riva was gone, as if she'd never been there, which was probably the case. Still, a small part of me felt sad that her hallucination hadn't even bothered to say goodbye.

Turning back to Craig, I saw his hand ready to gut me as my feet continued to dangle in mid-air a good four feet above the ground, putting them almost level with...

I remembered back to my original encounter with these werewolves – beating the first one, then running into a whole bunch of them. The big wolf who'd approached me, I'd been unaware at the time that he was my father because otherwise I wouldn't have kicked him in the...

Riva's words echoed in my mind. *"All things are possible beneath a blood moon."*

Perhaps that counted for repeat performances, too.

In the split second before Craig gutted me, I lashed out with my leg. There wasn't time to aim, or even pull back so as to get a little extra momentum going. That was fine, though. After all, Riva said the blood moon empowered me as much as it did the wolves.

So let's hope it empowers this enough to send his nuts into orbit!

My foot hit home, the soft fur on Craig's crotch easily giving way to the not so soft parts within.

Eww!

The sick fucker had been sporting a stiffie as he'd been about to rip me open. Well, with any luck, I'd just turned his wood into a pile of sawdust.

The world seemed to slow down for a split second as Craig's eye bulged out of his head and I suddenly found myself dropping to the ground.

Everything still hurt like hell, and my vision kept losing focus, but even a blind man would have had a hard time missing the wall of furry flesh in front of me.

Ignoring my pain and focusing instead on the blood moon, I imagined the red light raining down from it as some sort of power boost meant only for me – kind of like from the comic books my brother enjoyed. No way was I telling him that, though. The little asshole would never shut up about it.

I pushed aside thoughts of my baby brother and let my fist fly, giving the gander's gut a taste of what he'd given the goose a few moments earlier. Beaten as I was, I half-expected to break my hand against Craig's stomach, but I underestimated myself. A *whoosh* of air escaped from his lungs and he doubled over, again silencing the howls of the wolves around us. Ah, sweet silence. I, for one, had no intention of hearing them again this night.

I stepped in, planning on breaking Craig's jaw before he could recover, but was stopped in my tracks when he opened his mouth wide and projectile vomited all over me.

Fucking gross!

For a moment, I was terrified that this was some new previously unseen werewolf attack, but then, as the foul gorge of bile and meat chunks washed over me, I realized I'd just hit him harder than I thought.

It wasn't the first time I'd been puked on. Heck, I was a college student. Getting yakked on by drunken friends was practically a rite of passage. That said, nothing could have prepared me for a shower of werewolf barf. In that moment, I was certain that if I lived to be a hundred and took three baths a day for the rest of my life, I still would never be clean again.

On the upside, it's not like I had a boyfriend to worry about anymore, although I wouldn't have minded giving the cheating bastard a big hug at that moment.

Sadly, being drenched in Craig's last meal – *please don't let it be someone I know* – was more than enough distraction for him to recover.

He launched himself forward, a locomotive of muscle and fur. There was no way to dodge in time. Craig slammed into me and both of us went tumbling back onto my front lawn.

I hit the ground hard and saw stars, the grass doing little to soften the blow to the back of my head. Even dazed, however, I had enough years of training in me to know to get my knees up before he could pin me. This was no match, but if that happened, then it was over.

As it was, I just barely got them up in time as he fell upon me, and even then it did little to negate the massive size advantage that my uncle had. It was just enough to keep his snapping jaws from closing directly on my face.

Putrid bile was still dripping from his maw, causing my own stomach to churn. If I threw up now, I'd have to fight Craig while battling to not choke on my own puke.

My uncle, however, didn't seem interested in giving either of our innards time to settle. I think we'd finally reached the point where he didn't care how he won so long as I ended up dead.

As he pressed down upon me, I was stuck, unable to do much save fend off his grasping claws. It was a losing battle. He was on top and my legs were pinned between us, but I had no leverage with which to shove him off. Worse, I felt him trying to inch up my body, no doubt hoping to get far enough so as to negate my meager defenses and properly use his teeth on me.

Shit! Unfortunately, being covered in wolf bile left me a bit more slippery than usual. As I grasped hold of Craig's wrists in an attempt to keep from being shredded, he slid up further on me and I could only watch as his jaws came at my face.

I was certain that was it, but his teeth clicked shut on nothing, barely an inch away. One more push from him and that would be it. I did the only thing I could think of – threw my own head forward and head-butted him right in the snout.

His nose, as it turned out, was cold, wet, and pretty darned sensitive.

Craig lifted off me for a second and let out a choking cough as he raised his hands to cradle his injured muzzle.

Seeing an opening I wasn't likely to get again, I rolled over and pushed off, hoping to put some distance between us. Sadly, he wasn't that badly hurt. His massive hands grabbed hold of me before I could get more than a few feet.

For a moment, I feared it was game over, but being covered in puke worked both ways. I slipped out of his grasp before he could drag me back. Who'd have ever guessed being coated in bile could be a life saver?

Sadly, my balance was off, so I merely ended up stumbling a few more steps before falling on my face again, finally coming to a rest in front of my mother's rose bushes and the stupid gnomes staring mirthfully at me from around them.

"We have to stop meeting like this." Behind me, I could hear Craig scrambling my way. "If you guys have any advice, now would be a good time."

Heck, hallucinatory Riva had said that anything was possible under a blood moon. So maybe that included these stupid things lending me a hand.

Wait a second...

Maybe they already had.

Just barely managing to push myself up to my knees, I realized what a mess I was – cut, bleeding, pretty much one gigantic bruise, and drenched in puke. But, for all the checkmarks against me, I wasn't ready to die yet. After tonight, I was fairly certain the pack wouldn't forget me anytime soon, but I wanted that to go double for my fucking creep of an uncle.

I reached for the gnome closest to me and grabbed it by its conical hat just as I heard the snarl that told me Craig was right behind me. With no options left, I turned and swung with everything I had, feeling the surprisingly heavy weight of the little garden statue in my hands.

The gnome impacted against the side of Craig's head, shattering and sending teeth flying. I was left with nothing but the shaft of its pointed hat still in my hands as my uncle staggered back several steps, dazed by the blow.

His blind eye was to me, but it wouldn't be for long. I quickly shook off the surprise that my attack had actually worked. There wasn't a moment to spare.

Twirling the gnome hat in my hands so that the pointy end faced out, I leapt at my uncle just as he recovered. His jaws opened and a roar of pure rage came bellowing out, one that was instantly muffled as I rammed the business end of the stone hat into his mouth.

I wrapped my legs around his body and grabbed hold of the back of his head so as to steady myself and, more importantly, give my arms some leverage. With my other hand, I pushed as hard as I could, calling upon every last bit of strength my strange biology and the blood moon afforded me.

Craig tried to close his mouth as I shoved the hat into the back of his throat. A few more inches and he'd sever my arm unless...

With one final scream, I put everything I had left into it. My uncle gave one last choked growl and then the bloodied point of the hat erupted from the base of his skull.

For a moment, he stood there motionless, with me hanging off of him. Then his body began to spasm and we both toppled over onto the ground.

I didn't allow myself the luxury of a nice nap there on the grass, as much as I wanted to take one.

No. If I did that, everything I'd just endured would be in vain. Forcing a neutral expression onto my face, I sat up and turned toward Craig, relieved to see his remaining eye glazed over and staring sightlessly up at the night sky. He was dead as the proverbial doorknob. I felt bad that it had come to this, but he'd chosen his path.

Now to make sure I didn't follow him.

I couldn't show weakness to the wolf pack. So, I bit my tongue to contain the scream of pain that wanted to come flying out, and pushed myself to my feet.

What a surprise, I saw werewolves, lots of them. Even the ones that had been busy making a mess on my block had stopped to gawk. The looks on their faces said it all – wide eyes, open mouths, unblinking stares – disbelief. Who was I to let the harsh reality that I was beat to hell interfere with that?

"Who's next?" I cried out, putting an extra dollop of scorn into my voice. "Because I have more where that came from!"

No sound met my challenge, save for some snuffling and mumbling from the assembled masses – werewolf whispers, if you will. Worked for me, but I figured I should put some icing on this victory cake. I turned to the nearest wolf, a six and a half footer about thirty feet away, and locked eyes with it. "You want a piece, Fido?"

It quickly averted its gaze, finding something interesting on the sidewalk that needed studying.

Holy shit, this was actually going to work.

"Listen up!" I yelled, ignoring the burning in my lungs. "Craig is dead. That puts me in charge..."

A bloodcurdling roar rose up in the night, drowning me out completely. I spun back toward my uncle, fearing the worst, but he was still busy being dead.

So who then? Had one of his minions grown a set? Maybe some young pup with delusions of grandeur or...

Those thoughts and everything else running through my mind evaporated in an instant as a massive figure stepped from the backyard of the house across the street. All eyes turned that way as an enormous black wolf, possibly even larger than Craig, with salt and pepper streaks in its fur strode forward. Its teeth were bared and its yellow eyes were locked on me as it marched my way.

Dad?

The few werewolves standing in my father's way immediately scrambled to the side, moving as if a fire had been lit under their asses. As for me, I could only stand there, slack-jawed. I mean, I knew my father was in the pack, had even been fairly sure I'd seen him earlier, but the truth was, I simply hadn't expected him to make an appearance like this.

Now that he was here, though, what did it mean? He

crossed the street toward me with purpose, but at the same time wasn't rushing either.

The funny thing was – despite his hairy form, massive size, and overall monstrous appearance – his gait reminded me of the times he'd been forced to put on his dad hat and punish me for something I'd done as a kid. Was that his purpose? To come over here and give me a lecture on how dangerous this all was? Because if so, he was a bit late to the party.

Also, call me a prude, but any such lecture would be a *lot* more effective if he was wearing pants. I could only hope he didn't decide to turn back into a human, because that wasn't a sight I really wanted etched onto my retinas.

Or maybe this was all nothing more than show. After all, I didn't begin to understand how werewolf society functioned. Maybe this was some sort of passing the torch thing.

I decided to wait and follow his lead, anything that would help end this nightmare sooner.

He approached, still taking his time, and finally stopped in front of me. He reared up to his full height – yeah, definitely bigger than Craig – then looked from me to his brother's body.

Wait ... his brother! *Oh shit.* I was his daughter, true, but I'd just killed his younger brother in cold blood. How would that affect...

Before I could finish that thought, I was knocked off my feet by a sweeping blow that sent me rolling ass over teakettle onto the grass.

So much for the beta mindset.

It wasn't a particularly hard hit, but I'd been on the go for hours and had just gotten the crap kicked out of me by my big bad wolf of an uncle. All of that I could deal with, but it was my Dad handing out the beating this time.

I mean, yeah, I'd spent the majority of the last month

pissed at him, but I still loved the guy. He was a part of nearly every good memory I had growing up.

Unfortunately, this was not destined to be one of them. Right at that moment, he was bearing down upon me in the guise of a bloodthirsty monster hell-bent on revenge.

I wasn't sure if I could bear to tell Mom that I'd been forced to kill my father, her husband. But then, I had to actually make it that far. The pain racking my body told me that was easier said than done.

If it had been another of the minion wolves, then maybe. Even exhausted I could hopefully have held my own against one, but these elite wolves? Craig had been bigger and a hell of a lot badder than the rest, and I'd seen nothing to suggest my dad was anything but the same.

Still, I pushed myself back up. Lying down and dying wasn't what I did, especially not if my father still intended to follow through with his brother's plans for the town. I didn't want to believe that – had hoped, prayed even, that by taking Craig out of the equation the rest of the pack, Dad included, would happily turn tail and trot back to Morganberg where they belonged.

Wishful thinking.

My father remained standing in the place where he'd clocked me. He could have finished me off by now, but instead he simply waited, growling with bared teeth, his composure anything but relaxed. His meaning seemed clear enough: he was challenging me for the leadership I'd just stolen from his brother.

I was at a loss at what to do, but then he made the decision for both of us.

He charged me and I just barely dove out of the way

in time. It was either hit the driveway or land on Craig's body. I chose the less gross, but far more harsh, option, forgetting for a moment that my shirt and jacket were pretty much shredded, leaving me with very little cushion as I hit the asphalt.

My stomach lurched from the impact, reminding me that ab crunches were probably out for the immediate future. I tasted blood again in the back of my mouth and spat it out, just as I left the ground not of my own free will.

Dad had grabbed me by the back of my torn jacket. He held me up for a moment, then tossed me onto the grass like a sack of potatoes. I hit the dirt and rolled with it. That minimized the damage but still didn't leave me in great shape to pop back to my feet and take the fight directly to him.

I glanced over at Mom's garden. There were more of those gnomes and they were practically begging me to club someone senseless with them. Sadly, they were out of reach, not to mention I still wasn't sure I could do that to my father.

Mind you, that was a decision I needed to get serious about soon if I wanted to live to see the morning. And that was probably all the answer I needed. I loved my dad, but was I truly prepared to die for him?

If it was to save his life, that would be an easy answer. But dying to allow him to murder the innocent people of this town? No fucking way.

This entire summer, I'd been wrestling with that weird transition period between leaving my youth behind and embracing my adulthood.

Now it was finally time to make an adult decision.

Dad stalked toward me, his gait confident, almost arrogant. He thought he was going to win this easily. Well, he would probably win regardless, by virtue of me being a mess on the verge of passing out, but I'd be damned if I made it easy.

I stood up again, but slowly this time, playing possum – if just barely. But even a fraction less than I was capable of put a slight advantage in my corner. I doubled over, pretending to catch my breath as he approached.

He stood over me and chuffed once, in a manner I took to be disparaging. All the while, I tented my fists together, waiting for a chance.

Time must have sped up, because suddenly it felt like Christmas morning. Dad leaned down, his muzzle only inches from my face, and snarled. He was probably trying to intimidate me, throw some werewolf shade before he tore my head off. I don't know. I didn't wait to find out.

I swung for the fences before he could pull back, connecting with a solid blow that snapped his jaws shut and knocked him onto his ass dazed.

Damn his head was hard, but then, so were my fists. The only problem was I didn't know if I had another one like that in me. I could feel fresh blood dripping down my sides from where I'd reopened the cuts from earlier. This needed to end now.

Dad shook off the blow, his eyes still a little fuzzy, but they quickly opened wide when he realized I was approaching.

Faster than I would have expected, he pushed himself to his feet and charged, head down, moving at a speed that said he intended to barrel right over me.

Pity that I had other ideas. As I said before, I had no intention of becoming a professional wrestler, but that didn't mean I hadn't learned a few moves.

Dad slammed into me, making my stomach wish it

belonged to someone else, but I'd been ready for him, had braced myself for the impact. As he carried me off my feet, I grabbed him around the neck in a front headlock and latched on to a big clump of fur on his back with my other hand.

We were about halfway across my front yard when I swung my legs back, planted them on the ground, and lifted.

Dad's momentum sent him airborne over me as we skidded to a halt and then I dropped down, planting his face onto the ground via a DDT that would have made Vince McMahon proud.

I wasn't about to let go, either, as Dad tried to squirm out from under me. I held fast, putting on the pressure in an attempt to choke him out. Silver might have been their Achilles heel, but so far as I was aware, the need for oxygen was pretty much universal for all living things.

I briefly considered shifting my grip to try and snap his neck in one quick clean move, but hesitated. This was still my Dad and, despite everything, I just couldn't bring myself to do it.

My compassion was my undoing.

Dad managed to roll, dragging me along for the ride until he had his feet planted under him again. Much as I had the advantage in leverage, he was just too big. It was nearly impossible for me to maintain control when my arms just barely fit around his neck, much less the rest of him.

He managed to gain some purchase even as I squeezed harder – cutting off his air and the supply of blood to his brain. I only needed a few seconds more before he dropped, assuming the normal rules applied. If not, then I needed to...

I screamed as he planted his massive hands on either

side of my body, the pain from my earlier injuries flaring up and making me loosen my grip.

That was a mistake, potentially a fatal one, as Dad reared up to his full height, taking me with him. He shoved me away, breaking my grip, and I found myself airborne again. I watched as my front yard sailed past below me, almost in slow motion, and then I was falling, headed straight for our driveway. Strange how that part was anything but slow.

I landed face-first on the asphalt and lay there panting, the impact enough to have rattled every bone in my body. My gas tank was on empty. Whatever strength I had left seemed focused on keeping my insides from leaking to the outside. Pity that my opponent wasn't anywhere near close to quitting. I'd gotten a few good shots in, but I'd squandered my opportunities to win this. Much as I wanted to think I was a badass, deep down I was still daddy's little girl, no matter what skin he was wearing.

A massive hand grabbed hold of my shoulder and flipped me over onto my back. It would seem I was the only one in this fight burdened by love. I wasn't sure whether he was angry at what I'd done, or if his sense of pack hierarchy overruled all other instinct in his wolf form, but it really didn't matter.

The killing blow was his to take. All I could do was lie there and hope it didn't hurt much.

41

One of Dad's hands, or paws – I still wasn't really sure what to call them – wrapped itself around my neck as he bent down over me until his muzzle was mere inches from my face.

He opened his mouth and I watched with growing horror as I realized what he intended. But, rather than tear my face off in one bloody chunk of bone, muscle, and meat, he grumbled something unintelligible.

"*Yerld!*"

The hand around my neck had me pinned down but wasn't gripping hard enough to cut off my air. I allowed myself one last moment of defiance, something for the masses to remember me by. "Sorry, but I don't speak asshole."

Dad narrowed his eyes and snarled. He lifted me up a few inches and then slammed me back into the hard ground, doing a damn good job of silencing my snark. He coughed, almost sounding like he was clearing his throat, then leaned in again. "*Yield.*"

What?!

He must've seen the dazed lack of comprehension on

my face, because he lifted his other fist high, as if to pound my skull into a pancake, then repeated the word.

Was that even an option in a fight to the death?

Dad locked his eyes with mine and I realized the clock was ticking. This didn't appear to be one of those decisions I was allowed to sleep on, at least not if I wanted to wake up again.

My choices seemed fairly limited. I might have been able to mount a small bit of defense, but doubted it would be enough to keep him from cracking my skull like an egg. It was either tap out or die. I couldn't say either really appealed to me, but at least the former offered the possibility for a rematch.

It was the state championship all over again, and once more I was coming in second fucking place.

"I yield," I whispered. "You win."

Dad growled at me, to which I repeated myself, louder this time. "I said, I yield!"

With that, he let go of my neck, stood up straight, and threw his head back to howl at the blood moon shining down upon us both.

Another wolf joined in, then another. Soon, the entire pack was howling, a sound which almost certainly carried all the way across town, possibly further.

What now? Had I doomed High Moon with my weakness? Would the rest fall upon me in a feeding frenzy, leaving only a pile of bones for when the sun rose again?

After what seemed an eternity of howling, Dad leaned down again. I guess he was ready to dish out whatever death he thought I deserved. Fine. I balled my fists, having had a moment to catch my breath. I might have tapped out, but that didn't mean I was going down without at least one sucker punch. Sportsmanlike conduct be damned.

Before I could take a swing, Dad's face shimmered.

His muzzle retracted maybe about halfway, and his features became somewhat more human-like. I'd seen them do this before. It was easier to talk this way without sacrificing a lot of their power.

"Stay down," he growled, baring his teeth. "Don't move and don't look. I mean it."

I wasn't sure what he was talking about, but the part about not moving was at least easy to follow.

He disappeared from my line of sight and I heard him walking away, toward the street, his footfalls growing less heavy with every step.

I was tempted to incline my head to see what he was doing, but he'd warned me not to look. Rather than disobey – yet anyway – I decided to give him a moment, see what happened next.

"The hybrid is defeated!" he cried, his voice sounding like its normal self.

Howls and a few human cheers rose up into the night, but they didn't last long. Apparently Dad wasn't finished yet.

"Our leader is dead and I have vanquished his usurper. As is our right of combat, I claim the title of alpha."

More howls came, a few perhaps with questioning cadence, but they mostly seemed cool with his proclamation.

"As for the hybrid, she is no threat to us or our power ... *my power*. She has yielded to me and as such is now under my command."

A human-ish voice rose up. "But..."

"But nothing!" Dad shouted with an authority I'd never heard from him, not even when Chris and I were being total pains in the ass. "*I* declare this! The hybrid will follow our rules, be subservient to our pack. She will do this or she will die. Does anyone challenge my proclamation?"

I was tempted to raise my hand but managed to refrain. At least he hadn't promised my hand in marriage. At the same time, he also hadn't reversed Craig's decision to invade...

"Our war here is finished," he continued, and I could have sworn I heard a few chuffs of relief from the rest. "It's time to go home. We have no further quarrel with this place or its people. No harm shall come to any human who does not stand against us."

My head was still facing our house, but I heard what sounded like the padding of feet, lots of them, and they were heading away. It wasn't long before the sound of footsteps grew faint.

I attempted to push myself up so as to take a look around, but my body didn't seem to like that idea. Instead, I tried to roll over, and that's when something caught my eye. It was the goddamned gnomes in my mom's garden. Maybe it was a trick of the light, but I could have sworn I saw them turn as one to follow the sound of retreating footsteps, almost like they were watching to make sure the wolves were really leaving.

One of the freaky little things glanced back toward me, as if aware it had been seen, and actually winked.

Needless to say, of all the strange events I'd witnessed that night, that was by far the creepiest.

I was still staring at the gnomes, waiting to see if they'd do anything that might warrant smashing them into itty bitty pieces, when the entire lawn seemingly lit up.

What now?

For a moment, I wondered if maybe I'd triggered some new security lights, but then I realized it wasn't coming from the garage. Individual gouts of flame seemed to shoot up from the ground around me. Before I could properly pee my pants, they coalesced into more solid shapes ... albeit no less terrifying.

They were people, but at the same time more so. Their eyes were ablaze with power, and though the night was still, wind seemed to whip around their bodies and...

Hold on, I'd seen this before. Back when Mom...

"Look! There she is!"

"Oh, my darling baby girl!"

I turned my head and saw my mother racing toward me with Aunt Carly by her side. Energy crackled around both of them, but then Mom held out a hand to her sister.

"I've got this. You and the rest form a perimeter. Keep an eye open for any pedestrians who might see us."

"But she's..."

"I *said* I've got this."

There was something in Mom's voice that caused my aunt to cease her protests and go do as she was told. As she and the others fanned out, Mom dropped to her knees by my side.

I expected her to say something to echo her earlier concern but, rather than speak, she reached into her pocket, pulled out something small, then proceeded to shove it into my mouth. Before I could protest, she whispered, "Swallow it. Trust me, it'll make you feel better. Don't argue with me, Tamara."

That last order was a familiar one, ingrained into my head like a Pavlovian response. I dry swallowed almost before I was aware I was doing so.

"There," she said. "Just give it a few minutes."

"All clear," Aunt Carly said, walking ... or more like *gliding* back over to us. "Looks like the mutts high-tailed it out of here."

"They must have smelled us coming," Mom replied, confidence practically dripping from her voice.

My aunt dropped to her knees on the other side of me. "How is she?"

Mom smiled, then took hold of my hand. "She's a bit banged up, but she'll be okay."

"What the hell was that bastard Craig thinking?"

"Thinking was never his strong suit. And besides, I don't think this was him." She turned and pointed. I didn't need to incline my head to know it was in the direction of where a large furry corpse lay cooling on the front lawn.

"Is he...?" my aunt started to ask, but then her voice trailed off, probably because the answer was obvious. "Do you think Curtis did that?"

"Looks that way."

"Finally grew a set, did he?"

Mom shrugged as if she didn't care. "I'm less concerned with him and far more concerned with Tamara right now."

"Which one do you think did this to her?"

"Does it really matter? They're lycanthropes, Car. Once they change, they're capable of anything. You know this."

Aunt Carly made a sound of disgust. "We should wipe them out to the last pup. They're too dangerous to let live."

"Table it for another day. For now, I want you to gather the coven. Find any survivors. Save anyone you can. I have it on good authority there's a bunch over at Saint Matthews on Elm."

Saint Matthews? How does she know?

"Should we blank them?"

Mom nodded. "Every last one. Go door to door if you have to. Nobody can be allowed to remember what happened here."

"So not only do those mutts get to live, but we have to clean up after them, too?"

Mom locked eyes with her sister. "You know as well as I do it's not that simple."

After a moment, Carly nodded and glanced back down at me. "Her, too?"

"Yes, her too."

"Sorry, sweetie," Carly said as my stomach suddenly lurched, and not in a pleasant way. Then she turned toward my mom again. "Need any help?"

"I've got this. Get started with the others. Half the night is already gone. We don't have any time to lose."

Carly nodded and stood up, but before she walked away, she looked down at me. "Feel better, Tamara. You won't remember this in the morning, but know that your aunt loves you."

"Love you, too," I whispered just as my guts tied themselves up in knots again, causing me to curl into a fetal ball.

Once my aunt was out of earshot, I looked up at Mom. "What ... was that about?"

"We need to wipe everyone's mind. Make them forget this happened. Oh, don't look at me like that. It wouldn't work on you even if I tried."

"But all those people who died..."

"I know. We can't bring them back. The best we can do is conjure a memory, a different tragedy, one people can more easily accept."

"I can't believe..." I closed my eyes as another spasm hit my stomach. "...Uncle Craig did this."

"I can," she replied. "He was an asshole ... *was* being the operative word. Your doing?"

I nodded.

"Good. He had it coming."

"But Dad..." I almost had to choke back tears. Now that the fight was over and the adrenaline was wearing off, everything was starting to hit me. "He..."

"Shhh, darling. I know what your father did."

She did? "I'm sorry. I must have pushed him over the..."

"You did nothing of the sort. He played his part just as he was supposed to."

"What? As he was...?" The question fell off my tongue as my midsection clenched up, making me want to hurl.

"Your father and I aren't stupid, dear," Mom replied, putting a hand on top of my head. "We know our own daughter."

"But..." The nausea was getting worse. I knew this feeling. It was the same I'd felt whenever I'd taken my...

"That's enough for now, Tamara," Mom said. "Let your meds do their job and we can talk about this later, after this mess has been cleaned up. Trust me, it's for the best. You don't want my family finding out about you, especially not in your current condition."

I would have argued with her, but she was probably right. Besides, I was too busy lying there in the driveway of my home, being sick as a dog.

42

Sometime around mid-afternoon I woke up in my own bed, having apparently slept through the majority of the day. I was wearing pajamas and the lacerations I'd suffered the night before had all been cleaned and bandaged – albeit they still hurt like hell. Unfortunately, it seemed my so-called medicine robbed me of my enhanced healing as well as my strength. The worst was probably behind me, considering I was no longer bleeding out, but it was going to be some time before I'd be up for a night of clubbing.

Mom was waiting for me when I stepped out of my bedroom – a warning on her lips to play dumb in case anyone asked, and pills in her hand which she insisted I take.

She explained to me that Chris was staying at my aunt's for a few days while Dad was away at a "conference" working to consolidate his new "promotion." There was also the fact that High Moon was currently an unfriendly place for those with a penchant for howling at the moon, being that the town was still crawling with Mom's family.

My uncle had made quite the mess, and cleaning it all up was easier said than done.

Left unsaid was whether our fight the night before was part of the reason Dad was staying away. I couldn't help but think that was going to be one hell of an awkward reunion.

The phone and cell lines were still down and half the town was without power, making communication difficult. So I threw on some clothes with the intention of heading out and making sure Riva was okay.

Sadly, Mom was adamant about me making as few public appearances as possible for the time being. My freshly depowered, injury-racked body was in no position to argue. Heck, the sheer act of walking down the stairs seemed to take half an eternity.

I was left to worry myself silly until there came an insistent knock on the door a few hours later. Mom opened it to find the best sight in the world – the anxious face of my friend.

"Riva," she greeted. "I'm glad to see you're okay. We were so worried."

"You too, Mrs. Bentley. Can you believe what happened?"

Mom crossed her arms and looked hard at her. "Yes, it's terrible. Who could imagine such a thing?"

"I know!" Riva replied. "You think it's going to be a boring night and then a gang of bikers rides in and tries to burn the town down. It's like something out of a bad movie."

Bikers?

Before I could question that, Riva looked past her and saw me. "Oh my God! Are you okay? What happened? Those assholes didn't hurt you, did they?" She quickly turned back to my mother. "Sorry."

"I'll make an exception in this case," Mom replied,

before giving me a quick shake of her head once my friend's back was to her.

"Um, no," I said. "I was ... out of town with my family. I tripped and fell down my aunt's front steps."

"You are such a klutz, but better stairs than psychos, I guess." Riva plopped down next to me, as if my bullshit story was the most believable thing in the world. "It's crazy, but I heard all of downtown is wrecked."

"Oh?"

"Yeah." She lowered her voice. "Mom told me not everyone was lucky enough to make it."

I quickly raised an eyebrow. "Your mom's okay? What about your dad?"

She nodded. "We're all fine. It's the weirdest thing. We went over to the Crendels last night for dinner when we heard sirens going off. Their dad freaked and insisted we all head to their bomb shelter to wait it out."

"He didn't!"

"Yeah. Turns out he was right to be paranoid. We pretty much missed the entire thing. Lucky for us, too. We got home to find the house trashed. Looks like they rode up onto our lawn and kicked the front door down."

"You don't say." I narrowed my eyes, hoping she was putting on an act, but fearing my mother had made good on her promise to *blank* the town. "Anything else weird go on?"

"*Anything else?* Like that wasn't weird enough?"

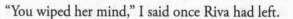

"You wiped her mind," I said once Riva had left.

Mom shrugged as if it were no big deal. "I should have done it a month ago."

"But she's..."

"Normal. That's what she is. And she's happier that

way. Trust me. Most people are. Very few can handle the truth for long, and even fewer can keep their mouths shut about it." She sat and put an arm around me. "Believe me, dear, I love Riva almost as if she were my own daughter, but this is for the best."

"So she doesn't remember *any* of it?"

"No. We can't afford it. Same with the rest of the town. Fortunately, Chief Johnson was good enough to collect as many people as he could down at Saint Matthews. That made things a great deal easier."

"Yeah, how exactly did you find out about that? And speaking of knowing the truth, the chief seemed…"

"It's not important," she interrupted. "We have our ways. And as for your friend, just know that I gave very specific instructions for her. All remembrance of were-wolves, witches, any of that, were to be replaced with happy memories. As far as she's concerned, you two had a great time chasing boys down at Swallowtail Lake this summer. Oh, and while we're on the subject…"

"What about it?"

"Sorry, sweetie, but we also blanked that boy Gary. He doesn't remember dating you."

I opened my mouth to protest, but then remembered the night before. "It's okay. He…"

"Already had a long-term girlfriend?" She must've seen the look on my face because she added, "Of course I knew. You thought I wouldn't scry him, too? Don't worry, honey. His new memories mostly involve a lot of itching and a nasty rash that just wouldn't go away."

I couldn't help but laugh which, of course, caused my stomach to clench in protest. *Ugh!* In the end, he'd been a cute fling, but the attraction had been mostly physical. I was still pretty peeved, but I'd get over it. "Guess it's better than me tearing off his car door and beating him senseless with it."

"True," Mom replied with a raised eyebrow. "But about that..."

"Yeah?" I had a feeling I knew what was coming.

"You do realize you need to start taking your meds again, right?"

I looked away.

"It's for your own good. This town is a powder keg. I hope the last month ... *last night* ... proved that much. It's bad enough the lycanthropes know about you now."

"Exactly. I need to protect myself."

"No. Your father is taking care of that."

"Like he took care of it last night?" I asked, a healthy dollop of bitterness flavoring my words.

"As I said, he simply acted his part."

"Yeah, what exactly did you mean by that?"

"Please, Tamara. You didn't think my arrival was a wee bit fortuitous?"

"I thought ... the gnomes told you."

Mom's face grew blank. "The gnomes?"

"Yeah, the garden gnomes. I figured with your magic they were ... um, alive or something."

She actually looked at me for a moment like I was crazy. "Are you being serious? They're just garden gnomes. I bought them off of Amazon."

What? "But I saw..."

"I arrived exactly when I was supposed to," she continued, ignoring my interruption. "As I said, we both realized you'd probably do something rash. I've raised you since you were born. I know how you think, Tamara. You don't take ultimatums well. We knew something would happen. We just didn't know what that would be."

"So you pretty much assumed I'd set Craig off, but didn't do anything to stop it?"

"It's not that simple," she explained. "I already told you my people couldn't get involved. That much is true.

We also weren't entirely certain that Craig was serious. Your father, bless his heart, thought your uncle was bluffing. I told him he wasn't, but Craig's his baby brother, and your father has always had a soft spot for family. He didn't want to challenge your uncle unless he had cause to, and by the time he realized what was happening, it was too late. The pack was riled up and all he could do was damage control to keep the casualties to a minimum."

"A lot of people still died, Mom."

She put a hand on my shoulder. "Believe me, I know. And we all have to live with that. But trust me when I say it wasn't nearly as many as it could have been. Your father purposely goaded your uncle to lead the pack to our house, and I made sure ahead of time that the block would be mostly empty."

"So Craig could try to kill me?"

"Yes, *try*," she replied. "And fail, as I knew he would."

"He almost..."

Mom waved me off. "Almost is a garbage concept, Tamara. Our entire lives are lived via a series of almosts. Every day people almost get hit by a car, almost board a plane that ends up crashing, almost eat shellfish despite being allergic to it. We are constantly in a state of *almost* dying. But you didn't. You won. And if you hadn't..."

"I'd be dead."

"No, your father would have stepped in sooner."

Again that bitterness reared its ugly head. "To try to kill me, too?"

Mom stood up and put her hands on her hips. "Don't act stupid. We raised you better than that. Think about it. Your father had to put on a good show for the pack. They wouldn't have accepted less and they definitely wouldn't have accepted you as their leader, no matter what you might have been thinking."

"But he..."

"No, he really didn't." When I didn't say anything, she continued. "I'll admit, I don't think either of us has the full picture of what you can truly do, but we're smart enough to have an idea of what you can handle. Your father didn't dish out anything you couldn't take. The truth of the matter is, he was the one in greater peril because he couldn't exactly communicate that to you without being overheard."

I took in what she was saying, replaying the fight in my mind. Yeah, Dad had knocked me around pretty good, but now that I thought about it, there had been a couple of opportunities for him to finish me off, yet he hadn't ... opting for glancing blows instead of claws and teeth. I hadn't seen it at the time but, looking back, her words sorta made sense. "So I was never in any real danger?"

Mom let out a sigh. "Of course you were. You were in loads of danger, just not from your father."

"Oh."

"And you still are, Tamara." She sat back down next to me. "The Draíodóir are suspicious. They know something set off the pack last night. They just don't know what. I'd prefer to keep it that way, because otherwise, we're going to find ourselves in an even worse situation because they won't waste time on threats. They will rain fire down upon you wherever you step and there will be little I can do to stop them, assuming they don't turn on me first."

"Would they?"

"For birthing you by our sworn enemy? For lying to them these past twenty years? For doing everything in my power to protect you if they found out? Don't think they wouldn't. I may be their queen, but queens can be deposed."

I thought about what she said. I'd already lived through what I considered to be a worst-case scenario, but I was looking at things through a tunnel. What Mom was telling me could have a much farther reach, especially now that Dad had declared me a member of his pack. The fragile peace, already pushed to the breaking point by my actions, could shatter with the slightest provocation. And the people of High Moon would be caught right in the middle once again.

"Tell me what you need me to do."

EPILOGUE

In the days following the near destruction of High Moon, Aunt Carly and several other relatives on Mom's side had popped by to see how I was doing. I dutifully played along, as if I didn't remember a damned thing. The deception was further helped by the fact that I was healing at a natural, infuriatingly slow, pace.

Mom had called and pulled a few strings at my school, arranging it so that I could go back early this year. We both decided it would be best if perhaps I high-tailed it out of High Moon while various mystical eyes were still focused here.

Once Riva found out, she offered to drive me. I happily accepted. It had been a long time since we'd taken a road trip and would offer us a little extra time together before she headed back to her respective campus. Left unspoken was that it would also get her out of the cleanup work still going on, so she could help her *poor convalescing friend.*

I gave Chris a hug as I waited out on the porch for my ride. "Stay out of my room and try to get a life."

"Okay. Stay out of jail and try not to get herpes." He turned and ran inside before I could deck him.

Mom watched him go, rolled her eyes, then stepped in for a hug. "I worry about that one."

"You probably should."

"I worry about you, too," she added.

"Don't," I said. "After this summer, college should be a breeze."

"So you say." Mom stepped back. "But be warned, I'll be watching your grades."

"Just as long as you're not watching my love life, too."

She smiled. "No promises."

Before I could form a proper retort, we heard the sound of an engine in the driveway. I turned, thinking it was Riva, but was surprised instead to see Dad returning home from his "business trip."

I'd been hoping to see him before I left but dreading it, too. The truth was, I wasn't sure how our little reunion would go.

Almost as if reading my mind, Mom said, "Go on. Talk to your father. He won't bite."

I glanced at her with one eyebrow raised.

"Not in broad daylight anyway."

I grabbed my bags and walked down the front steps, hearing the door close behind me as I headed toward the driveway.

"Hey," Dad called, stepping out of his minivan.

"Right back at you."

"How are you feeling?"

"Been better," I said. "But definitely have been worse. Can't say I'm too happy to be back on my meds again."

"It's..."

"Necessary," I finished for him. "I know. So ... Mom tells me you've been busy setting up shop as leader of the pack."

"That I have. Been a long couple of days." He approached, then stopped and we both stared at each other, neither of us quite sure what would happen next.

I glanced past him. "You'd think getting a promotion would entail them giving you a cooler car."

"Hell no. Minivans are cool."

"You are ... so old," I said, giving him a big smile.

The ice broken, Dad stepped forward and gave me a big hug. "I'm so sorry, sweetie."

I'll admit, I might have been a bit too choked up in that moment to say much of anything, but I finally managed to squeak out, "It's okay. Mom told me."

When he pulled back, I noticed his eyes were as glassy as mine. "You have to know, I would never do anything to hurt you."

I chuckled. "So you say now, but you definitely sold it for the crowd. I'm pretty sure a few of my teeth are still loose."

"They'll heal," he said. "Everything will. There won't even be any scars." Then he lightened up and returned my smile. "Which is a good thing, too, because you damn near broke my jaw. I didn't realize you could hit that hard."

I playfully punched him in the arm. "Just so you know, I may have been holding back ... a bit."

"I don't doubt it for a moment."

I stepped in to hug him again, wanting to make sure he knew we were all right. After several seconds, though, I again stepped away as I remembered something from the night of our fight. "Just one question. Right before you left, you told me not to look. Why? Was there some secret werewolf handshake thing going on?"

For a moment, Dad looked confused, but then he started to laugh.

"What's so funny?"

"Oh, that? When I changed back to address the pack, I was kind of ... not wearing anything. Figured you really didn't need to see that."

"Good call."

"Yeah, I thought so, too."

"I'm turning this off."

"Why?" Riva asked from the driver's seat.

"Because it sucks."

"Ballad hater."

"That's not a ballad." I switched off the radio. "It's some guy whining because he's too big a pussy to ask a girl out."

"He's pining for his lost love."

"It can't be lost if it was never there to begin with. Trust me, I know all about that."

Riva made a sound of disgust, then abruptly changed topics. "You want to grab a late breakfast?"

"I'm not really that hungry."

"Okay. I can last until lunch if you can."

Her reminder of the time jogged my memory – a memory that, not too long ago, I'd been hopeful to never jog again. I grabbed a bottle of water from the center console, then reached into my purse for my pills.

"Time to get high?"

"I wish," I replied, sounding more sullen than I meant to.

"Are you okay?"

"Me? Yeah, I'm cool. Just looking forward to putting the last week behind me."

Riva nodded. "I know what you mean. How's your family holding up?"

"They're fine."

"How about your Dad?"

"He's good. Got home right before you showed up."

"Are you and he ... cool?"

"Why wouldn't we be?"

"You mean he's not upset that you had to off his brother?"

My head spun so fast I'm surprised I didn't break my own neck. Had I a mouthful of water, I'd have certainly sprayed it out all over her dashboard. "What?!"

"Well, I mean, I didn't see it happen since you forced me to lock myself up at the Crendels' place with their creep of a son. I swear, Bent, next time werewolves attack High Moon, you'd better let me stick by your side or I'm..."

"Wait, you remember all of that?"

She glanced my way and threw me a wry grin. "Once we got out of the shelter it was pretty easy to put two and two together, especially with all the weird new people in town. Anyway, I remembered that your mom threatened to erase my brain, so every time someone came up and questioned me as to what went on, I played stupid and pretended that I'd already been wiped."

"You did?" I had to admit, that was pretty darn clever of her. "And it worked?"

"Believe me, I didn't think it would. Figured they'd scan my thoughts with magic or something, but I was all 'gee, I hope the police find the mean old baddies who did this.' I think they were so busy with the mess that they just assumed someone else got to me first."

"So you remember us going to the hollows, all of it?"

"Yeah."

A thought hit me, a weird memory from the night of the blood moon. "Does that include showing up just as Craig was about to knock my head off in front of his werewolf buddies?"

"What are you talking about?"

"You know, you sound kind of creepy when you appear out of thin air like you're possessed."

She turned and raised an eyebrow. "You sure he didn't just *try* to knock your head off?"

I'd assumed I had hallucinated that part but figured it didn't hurt to double-check. After all, High Moon had become a seriously weird place this summer. "Never mind. Just testing you."

"Trust me. It's all there. The hollows, you kicking ass, the look on my parents' faces when those wolves attacked us. Oh, and the fact that you were never sick."

It took a few moments for that last statement to register. I was just so happy to have someone to talk to again, and even better that it was her. "You can't let Mom know you remember."

"Duh! If I wanted to kill my brain cells I'd go to more parties. At least that way would be more fun."

"True."

"But back to the part about you not being sick." She gestured at the pill bottle in my hand. "Why the hell are you taking those damned things again?"

I lifted the bottle and looked at it. All at once my good mood evaporated. "It's safer this way."

"Safer?" she replied with a laugh. "This coming from the girl who insisted on joining a men's wrestling team and then kicking all their asses?"

"That's different. Nobody dies in a match."

"It's a sport. People get hurt."

"It's not the same thing as an army of werewolves invading our town."

"That wasn't your fault."

"Yes it was. I made a choice."

Riva glanced at me again, narrowing her eyes before turning back toward the road. "That's bullshit and you know it. What kind of choice was that? To marry some wart-covered dickhead and be their slave?"

"To not let people die."

"And you succeeded. You saved us and stopped that asshole." Before I could say anything in response, she continued. "It's your life, not your mom or dad's, and it certainly doesn't belong to a pack of monsters."

"But I caused it all."

"How? By being born? Excuse me, but fuck that. This is the twenty-first century. Do you really think anyone should be faulted for how they're born?"

I smiled back. She had a point and what she was saying made me feel a little better. But even so, I'd caused a lot of chaos in very little time. Outside of the circumstances around my birth, that had all been my doing. I popped the top on my meds.

"Don't do it."

"I have to."

"I mean it. You don't need those."

"I know I don't *need* them."

"Then don't take them."

"It's not for me, it's for everyone else. Like I said, it's safer this way."

I tried to shake out two pills but she slammed a fist into the horn, almost causing me to drop the whole bottle.

"Listen, you're not some nutcase on antipsychotic drugs. Swallowing those pills only makes it safer for the things that are already afraid of you. Taking them doesn't change the fact that they're still out there. And they'll eventually come up with a different excuse to kill each other. Believe me, they will. Your uncle's actions convinced me of that."

"He's dead."

"Yeah, but there's gotta be more like him on both sides, and you know it."

"Maybe..."

"No maybe about it," she said, sounding more adamant than I'd ever heard her. "You think you're dangerous and you are, but not to us, to *them*. You're unique, one of a kind. You're something that's maybe happened ... I dunno, once before in all of history."

I spun toward her. "Huh? What was that?"

"Maybe never," she clarified. "But most importantly, you're you. You deserve the chance to live your life how you want to live it, not how they want you to. And if the time does come when either side decides High Moon needs to be burnt to the ground for whatever reason, I sure as shit will feel a lot better knowing you're there as you, not as whoever they want you to be."

"I'm not sure..."

"I am. You're the only one on our side, the only one who was out there that night fighting for the town and its people. Taking that away, making yourself a prisoner in your own body again, doesn't help any of them. Any of us."

I let Riva's words sink in. This wasn't a decision to make lightly, but she made a lot of sense. These past few days, all I could see was the guilt and the fear of it happening again, but the only reason any of this happened in the first place was because of someone else's fear of me. If I lived my life the same way, would that really make anything better? And was that really someone else's choice to make, even my parents?

What Mom told me still held weight, though. Going against that was risky and not just for me. She'd said that this was the only way, but was that true or just another attempt to *protect me*? And was it really me they were protecting, so much as the status quo?

My whole life I'd gone against the grain, tried to forge my own path. Just because my parents didn't see another way didn't mean there wasn't one. Didn't I owe it to myself to try to find it? And maybe I also owed it to the people of High Moon, too. Even if they didn't realize it, they still lived on a razor's edge – entirely dependent on the good graces of two warring factions. The slightest tip in either direction and they'd be at the mercy of one or both. Could I willingly turn my back on that?

Riva held out her hand. "So, how about it? Are you sickly little Tam-Tam Bentley, or are you badass Bent?"

I pursed my lips at her use of that nickname but then realized I was lucky to have so fierce of a friend, one who wasn't beholden to either side in this bizarre supernatural cold war I'd found myself in the middle of. One who I could count on to tell me not what someone else wanted me to hear, but what I *needed* to hear.

Screw it.

I handed over the pill bottle.

"Good call." She rolled down the window and tossed them out onto the highway. "How does that feel?"

"Pretty good so far, but if last time is any indication, be ready to pull over at a moment's notice so I can puke."

"And once that's finished?"

I felt my sides, still tender from my injuries. But in a few hours, they'd be just fine. "Give me a little while, and then I think I'll be ready for whatever this weird-ass world has to throw at me."

"Now you're talking. That's the Bent I know and love."

Once back at college, I'd have time to think, time to figure out how to break it to my parents that things had changed for me this summer and that there was no going back, no matter how much they wanted it. One side in this war already knew I existed. The cat was out of the bag. It was only a matter of time before my mother's people found out, too. And when that happened, they'd discover that I was my own person, not a pawn to be used.

It was something both sides would have to learn to live with.

And if they couldn't, if either faction tried to pull some shit that endangered my friends or family, they'd find me waiting for them at the gates of High Moon, ready to kick their asses back to whence they came.

THE END

Tamara Bentley will return to High Moon in
BENT OUTTA SHAPE

BONUS CHAPTER

BENT OUTTA SHAPE

THE HYBRID OF HIGH MOON - 2

"You need to tell them, Bent."

"I know."

"You've had over four months."

"I'm well aware."

One of the *benefits* of being best friends since childhood was that Riva felt no compunction against pestering me about things I really didn't want to talk about. "You were supposed to."

"I've been busy."

Truth of the matter was, school hadn't been quite as boring as I'd hoped when I returned following this past summer. I'd assumed I could slip back into my normal life, but that hadn't worked out so well. As I was beginning to realize, the moment you stepped foot into the world of the weird, there was apparently no turning back.

I explained as much to Riva, bringing her up to speed on Jack the lizard thing and a few other tidbits. Needless to say, she was irked that I hadn't told her sooner. But it was for her own good.

I had little doubt she'd have abandoned her own studies to come and help me out. But I didn't want that. As awesome of a friend as she was, not everything was her fight. She deserved a normal life ... one I could never hope for.

"You want me to come in and help soften the blow?" Riva asked as we crossed the town line into High Moon.

I'd been lucky to finagle a ride home with her, having given my parents the run-around, claiming to want to spend some quality road trip time with my friend. That much wasn't a lie. It was more knowing that my secret would likely be out the moment they both laid eyes on me. Quite frankly, getting screamed at for the entirety of a ten hour drive didn't particularly appeal to me. However, my reprieve was rapidly coming to an end.

"You can't," I replied. "They think your mind is ... what did they call it?"

"Blanked," she said with a small trace of bitterness.

After the shit that had gone down this summer, in which my father's pack nearly tore High Moon a new asshole, Mom's people had stepped in and magically erased everyone's memory of that night ... everyone except for Riva. She knew the truth but, like me, had been forced to live a lie ever since. The thing was, the worst my parents could do was yell at me. For Riva, however, there was always the threat of making good on wiping her memory. I didn't want that. Not only was she my friend, but I needed someone in my corner back home who I could talk to without dancing around the truth.

"I appreciate the offer, but this is something I have to do myself."

"I understand," she replied.

"Although maybe you can sit in the driveway with the motor running ... just in case it goes badly."

"Wimp."

I stepped through the doorway, bags in hand, trying to look like I was struggling with them more than I actually was. Hopefully I looked convincing. Wrestling was my forte, not acting.

Before closing the door, I spared one last glance back. It was partially to give Riva a nod goodbye, but also to see if Mom's garden gnomes – standing guard in front of her now defoliated rose bushes – had moved at all.

"I've got my eye on you fuckers," I whispered to myself before finally turning around and facing the music, so to speak.

That would have to wait, though, as the only one in the living room was my skeeve of a little brother.

Chris had changed his hair. When last I'd seen him, he'd been going for skate punk. Now he seemed to be in a douchebag pop singer phase.

"Hey," I said, kicking the door shut behind me. "Nice 'do. Makes you look like a wannabe pedophile."

He opened his mouth, probably to say something rude in return, but then took a sniff of the air and covered his mouth. "Ugh. You smell like a French whore."

Sadly, I couldn't argue. Once I stepped out of Riva's car I might have spritzed on the perfume a little heavier than was called for. It was necessary, though. Werewolves like my dad had a freaky good sense of smell – something I'd inherited, sadly. Hell, even breathing through my mouth, I could barely talk without gagging.

For all my powers, there I was trying to forestall the inevitable by a few more minutes. Riva was right; I could be a wimp when I wanted to be. But I wasn't about to let Chris know that. He was unaware that his adopted family was a bunch of freaks. That, and he was a total dork. "How would you know what a French whore smells like?"

"You're right," he said, grinning the grin of a sibling who knows he's tempting a beating and wants to make sure he deserves it. "I bet French whores smell better."

I dropped my bags and headed toward him, stepping around the Christmas tree already up and decorated. "Time for your annual holiday beating, you little..."

"Tamara, is that you?" Mom's voice floated to us from upstairs.

I lowered my own and whispered at my brother, "Saved by the bell, you little shit."

He flipped me the finger, quickly covering it up as footsteps could be heard coming down the stairs.

I adopted my best innocent smile as our mother descended to join us.

"I'm glad you made it home when you did," she said conversationally. "The weather is supposed to turn nasty tomorrow. I hope you gave Riva my regar..." She trailed off, her nose twitching. "Are you wearing perfume?"

"Yeah ... it's called Aphrodite. I picked up a bottle the other week."

Her eyes narrowed suspiciously. "You do realize you're supposed to spritz it, not bathe in it."

"Riva hit a pothole while I was freshening up. It went all over the place. You should smell the inside of her car."

Her expression relaxed and she nodded. "I'm sure."

That was one hurdle crossed.

"Christopher, would you mind changing the laundry?"

Or maybe not.

Chris looked between us for a moment then grinned. "You gonna yell at her for something?"

"No, but if you bring up those towels without folding them, I might yell at *you*."

My brother gave her a disgruntled look as only a twelve year old could, the one that said the entirety of his life was so unfair, then he got up and did as he was told.

Smart boy ... although not really.

The fact that my mother folded her arms and waited until Chris's footsteps faded in the distance told me that perhaps my perfume ruse wasn't quite as clever as I'd hoped.

So much for happy holidays.

BENT OUTTA SHAPE
Available now!

AUTHOR'S NOTE

Some stories pop into my head nearly fully formed, while others take their sweet time gelling in my gray matter.

This story is one of those former, but the main character herself goes back a bit further than that. I had originally considered someone like Tamara Bentley a few years ago, while still working on The Tome of Bill series. At the time, she was marked for potential inclusion into that story, a sort of polar opposite to Bill Ryder. But then I realized I already had enough characters looking to kick his ass. There was also the problem that the background I envisioned for her didn't quite fit with the canon established for that series.

Normally when that happens, I move on, but Tamara refused to be filed away so easily. While other scrapped characters were good enough to show themselves to the door leading to the primordial stew of my subconscious, she stubbornly stuck around and made herself at home.

It wasn't long after that I realized the reason why. She was destined for her own series of stories. Once I understood that, the concept behind GET BENT! materialized soon after.

And now here we are.

It's both new territory for me, while still feeling like walking down a well-traveled road. Tamara and her family dynamic, her friend Riva, the town of High Moon itself, all of that offers exciting possibilities. At the same time, Tamara herself feels like someone I've known forever.

Of course, if I said otherwise she's liable to kick my ass when next I close my eyes. Let me tell you, being a vivid dreamer isn't always wine and roses.

My mental bruises aside, though, I hope you enjoyed meeting her and, like me, can't wait to see what she gets up to next in the fictional town of High Moon.

Rick G.

Also by Rick Gualtieri
THE HYBRID OF HIGH MOON
Get Bent!
Bent Outta Shape
Bent On Destruction

TALES OF THE CRYPTO-HUNTER
Bigfoot Hunters
Devil Hunters
Kraken Hunters

THE TOME OF BILL UNIVERSE
THE TOME OF BILL
Bill the Vampire
Scary Dead Things
The Mourning Woods
Holier Than Thou
Sunset Strip